"THE KING"
Cara

UNHOLY TRINITY BOOK IV
ADRIANA BRINNE

Copyright © 2022 ADRIANA BRINNE
CARA "THE KING" (UNHOLY TRINITY #4)
All Rights Reserved.
Cover Design by Cat at TRC Designs
Formatting by Adriana Brinne
Editing by Elsa Gomes - @bookishaurora

This book or any portion thereof may not be reproduced, distributed, or transmitted in any form or by any means, including photocopying, recording, or other electronic or mechanical methods without the express written permission of the author except for the use of brief quotations in a book review.

This is a work of fiction. Names, characters, businesses, brands, and places are fictitious in every regard. Any similarities to actual events and persons, living or dead, are purely coincidental. Any trademarks, service, marks, product names, or named features are assumed to be the property of their respective owners and are used only for reference. There is no implied endorsement of any of these terms used.

Dedication

For the ones that love hard and unconditionally.
The world needs more humans like you.

Playlist

Stream on Spotify

"Hostage" – Anaís
"Black Hole" – Griff
"Good In Bed" – Dua Lipa
"Bones" – Imagine Dragons
"House On Fire" – Mimi Webb
"Boyfriend" – Dove Cameron
"Psychofreak" – Camila Cabello
"Counting Crimes" – Nessa Barrett
"She's All I Wanna Be" – Tate Mcrae
"I Would Die 4 U" – Holly Humberstone
"Call It What You Want" – Taylor Swift
"I Burned Down LA Down" – Noah Cyrus
"It's Only Love, Nobody Dies" – Sofia Carson

Authors Note

Cara "The King" is the fourth book in the Unholy Trinity series. The story contains sensitive topics that might be triggering for some. It deals with death, foul language, sexual abuse, mention of child abuse, suicide, and torture. Please keep all of this in mind before starting the book.
I hope you enjoy Lorenzo's journey. It is a wild ride…
Trigger warning: This book contains very disturbing situations, strong language, and graphic violence.

What is the Unholy Trinity

The Unholy Trinity is the most notorious crime organization in the United States of America. The organization was once ran by three crime families who joined forces after a war over Detroit City. They each rule over their own family but only one has full control of the entire organization. Currently, the organization is fair game since the Volpe family was extinguished and the Holy Trinity was taken over by the two remaining families and the Irish (O'Sullivan Family) Now, the Nicolasi and Parisi family hold a small percentage of the city while the other half is fair game to the Irish and Russians. The Holy Trinity is not pure anymore.
It is Unholy.

The Unholy Trinity is composed of the Nicolasi, Parisi and from now on the O'Sullivan family. The Nicolasi family deals in the gun trade, the O'Sullivan family deals in the drug trade and the Parisi handles the more legitimate side of the organization including the casinos and strip clubs.

For years, the three most ruthless crime families of Detroit City ruled together in peace. The Capo fell from grace and now the others lead by greed and sin.

Who's who in the Unholy Trinity

NICOLASI FAMILY
Cassius Nicolasi (Father of Andrea and the twins)
Andrea Valentina Nicolasi
Lorenzo Antonnio Nicolasi
Valentino Alexander Nicolasi

VOLPE FAMILY (No longer part of the Holy Trinity)
Lucan Tomas Volpe (Andrea's husband, Ex Volpe Boss)
Giana Alexis Volpe
Cara Mia Volpe

PARISI FAMILY
Arianna Luna Parisi
Kadra Sofia Parisi
Mila Areya Parisi

OUTSIDERS
Fallon Alicia James
Rian O'Sullivan Madden
Vladimir Solonik
Vitali Solonik
Dion Arnault

"For never was a story of more woe than this of Juliet and her Romeo."
— The Prince of Verona

Blurb

CARA

I was always the girl that kept a smile on her face even when everything was falling apart.
I did what was asked of me,
like any good mafia princess would.
I was also the bastard child of the Volpe family.
The one they whispered about.
Until him.
Now, I am the devil's favorite plaything because
I fell in love with a nightmare.
The Nicolasi boss.
The one they call the Mad King.

LORENZO

I made a deal with the devil when I decided
to take what didn't belong to me.
The one woman everyone idolizes.
America's sweetheart.
To the world, Mia Madden.
To me, Red.
I am not the hero in her childish story.
She has no idea what loving
someone like me will do to her soul.
I want her regardless.
Because this city will be mine as
I need a kingdom for my queen.

PROLOGUE

WICKED SCARS

"She has the devil's eyes." - D

Past

There is so much blood.
So much red.
All over me.
Everywhere I look there it is.
Mocking me.
Torturing me.
Staining not only my skin but also the pristine white sheets. It is there and no number of times I close my eyes will make it disappear.
How did I end up here? One day I was madly in love waiting anxiously for the day I would bind my life to the man of my dreams and now I am here lying motionless between these godawful sheets.
Broken.
Tainted.
Soulless.
Hopeless.
My eyes are swollen, and it hurts to shed more tears, but I let them fall as it is the only time I allow myself to cry.
 I don't want them to see me break.

Shivers spread all over my weak body when I think of what is to come.

Nothing good.

Absolutely nothing good can come out of this.

Taking a deep breath, I stand tall— even when, on the inside, I am broken. I am so very weak that, at times, it's unbearable to keep my head up. I hiss when I manage to move from my position on the bed and rise to my feet.

Everything hurts.

Looking down at the burning spot between my legs, I witness a drop of blood run down my right leg until it falls to the white marble floor, taunting me with the horrific crime I was a victim of.

A painful whimper escapes when I realize what this means for me. Placing my hands on my mouth, I refrain from crying and yelling out to the heavens and asking why. Why did this happen to me?

What did I do to deserve this nightmare?

Why did the lord forsake me?

Was it because of the crimes of my father?

Am I being punished for the cruelty of this family?

Perhaps.

But in the back of my mind, I know it's all his fault.

I curse the day I ever smiled at him.

I curse him and his name.

I hate him for making me feel like it is my fault when he is the only one to blame.

He did this, not me.

I chant this as a prayer, yet it doesn't seem to sink it.

He's at fault, not me.

I know all of this, but the cruel whispers plaguing my thoughts say otherwise.

They say once the devil taints you—he claims you, and you no longer belong to yourself.

"There is no part of you that doesn't belong to me, sweet Darya…" He vowed to do it.
He has now made it happen.
He ruined me for all men.
He took what I was not willing to give him.
What I saved for another man.
A good man.
A man with honor and a kind heart.
The same man that won't look at me the same after realizing I am no longer his.
I am no longer pure.
I was touched by the sinister hands of his enemy.
This family's enemy.
My worst nightmare.

***

Nine months later

"I'll never let you go." I still feel his cruel hands holding me down as he fucks me brutally without any barrier between us to protect me. His cruelty has no bounds. The devil kept both my wrists in one of his hands while he used the other to silence my screams of agony and shame. "Stop fucking fighting me. You wanted this. You want me."
A soft kiss on my forehead brings me back to the present and rips my thoughts away from the painful memories that have been keeping me underwater for the last months. I am a shell of the free-spirited and happy girl I once was.
 Nothing makes me smile anymore.
Nothing at all.
Not even the soft whispered promises of forever and sweet kisses of the man that used to put the sun in my sky.
I feel empty.
The horrible man stole everything from me and left me with nothing but shame, trauma, a broken heart, and the product of the sins he committed against me.

A reminder of that painful night.

"It is time for her feeding, princess." My chest feels tight every time he calls me that. The man I love most in this world. The man that looked at me with pity written all over his face when once all I could see whenever he looked at me was wonder and love. So much love. But not anymore. Or maybe I'm just imagining things. Nothing is as it once was.

The scars on my heart and my body attest to that.

The crying child in his arms never lets me forget.

With her father, my nightmare began.

With her, my dreams faded into dust.

I feel Damian move behind me and extend the child toward me, but like every time since the day she was born, I shake my head and step away from them. I hear him sigh and feel him walking toward the bassinet and laying the girl in it.

The girl.

The devil's daughter.

I gave birth to his daughter.

Not Damian's.

A moment later. the door clicks softly shut, and Damian is gone, leaving me alone with my dark thoughts and the quiet whimpers of the tiny baby. Sometimes I don't know what haunts me more, the horrific memories her father left me with or her painful cries for a mother's touch. I tried to harden my heart, but with every small smile she offered me on the few times I allowed myself to hover over her crib and watch her for hours, she slipped through the cracks of my bleeding heart and made room for herself, leaving me defenseless.

How could someone so beautiful and innocent be the product of something so ugly? The seed of someone so cruel?

And although his blood runs through her veins, all I see when I look at her is myself.

The same bow-shaped lips.

The crimson red hair and even the adorable dimple on her right cheek every time she smiles. God, she's so beautiful.
I can't breathe when she's nearby.
I'm trying to climb out of this hellhole I was thrown in, but with each passing day, it seems hopeless. Not even the fact that an innocent life depends on me helps me snap out of it. Not even Damian's love has the power to heal the wounds that are slowly killing me.
The baby's cries grow louder, making it impossible for me to ignore her. I close my eyes and take a painful breath before walking toward her and picking her up. I only hold her when it's just the two of us. When no one is here to witness how my hate and love for this child intertwine until I give in to her demands.
I concentrate on my breathing but it's hard.
Even breathing hurts lately.
Rocking the baby side to side, I walk to the window and look at the city lights. She quiets the moment I hum the same lullaby mother sang to me as a child whenever I was afraid or sad.
When the night seemed scary with thunder and lightning in the sky, she would sing to me and pacify my racing heart.
God, why?
Why did it happen this way?
This is what I prayed for since the very first day I laid eyes on Damian.
I longed for a beautiful child to call my own.
Our own.
A little piece of heaven. Instead, I was given her.
Half hell.
The devil's spawn.
The product of the most heinous crime.
A living and breathing reminder of everything that was done, and although I hate what she is and whose she is…

I love her, too.
God help me. I love her just as much as I hate her.
That's why this isn't easy.
I won't ever be the mother she needs.
The mother she deserves.
It seems selfish to keep her with a mother that will never be able to look at her without breaking down or going into a fit of rage over the memories she triggers in me.
What if she grows up to be a monster like her father?
Holding her close to my chest, I press my nose to her soft cheek and inhale her sweet baby scent.
So very sweet.
"I'm so sorry, little one." I whisper to the crook of her small neck while I feel her small head moving side to side as if she's comforting me. God, this is not fair.
I whisper in my language how sorry I am.
How I wish things could be different.
How I prayed for months while she was in my belly for God to give me the strength to fully love her despite the punishing demons whispering day and night to end it all.
I couldn't end her life.
I should've.
I should've spared her of her fate.
Her father will come once he finds out.
There's no doubt about it.
Her life will be in danger the moment the evil man's family learns the truth of her bloodline. Not only them, but my family, too, if they learn that she's half our blood mixed with their enemies'.
I am a danger to her, as well.
A pang in my chest makes me stumble when I realize how this will all end.
The only way out is to end a life.
Bury the secret.

Take a lie with death.

Coming to terms with my decision, I hold the child tighter to my chest, feeling her warmth one last time. Then I walk away from the balcony and step inside the room until I reach the baby's bassinet and set her down. Once she's safely tucked, I place her stuffed bunny, the one my little nephew gifted her, and I stand tall and reach for the only thing I have left to give. Gently, unclasping the necklace my mother gave me before she passed, I place it on the baby's tummy.

Taking one last look at the child, I stare into those indigo eyes. So beautiful but so much like her father's eyes. The devil's eyes. Right there, while staring at her little cherubic face, her father's eyes look back at mine.

Taunting me.

Breaking me more than I already am.

"I hope, I-I hope with all my heart you live a good life. I pray that you find the courage I always lacked to survive in this cruel world you were born in. I hope you shine so bright that maybe your light can find me in the dark. Be strong. Be brave. Be proud. Be everything I could not be. I-I'm so sorry." I love you is on the tip of my tongue, but I am not strong enough to utter the words.

That's how I know I'm doing her a favor.

With me gone, she won't grow up and live with the burden of the truth.

A painful truth.

She is the fruit of evil.

With one last look inside the small pink basket, I turn away with a broken heart and mind. I don't have much time. Damian will be right back with the baby's formula. God, I couldn't even produce food for her.

You failed her…

I pray to the heavens for the demons to leave me alone. Leave me to this agony but my prayers always go unanswered. Our holy father forsook me the night the devil tainted my soul with evil.

I am running out of time.

I hurry to the balcony, and in a second, I find myself climbing over the ledge and looking down so many stories down. Oddly, every fear and doubt leave my body and only the blinding lights of the city and the noise of happy civilians travel through me offering some sort of comfort. I close my eyes, take a deep breath before loosening my grip on the metal. I feel at peace knowing that the truth that will bind my daughter to hell will die with me.

My death will set me free.

Set us both free.

"I love you, Vera." I whisper to the wind before I go weightless.

I'm free of this torment.

Free of this all-consuming guilt.

I'm free.

Most importantly, so is she.

My faith.

My truth.

Part One

BLEEDING HEARTS

CHAPTER ONE
STORMS

"I trusted you. Why? Why, daddy?" — C

Cara

7 Years Old

I don't like this house.
It is so big that I sometimes get lost when I wander on my own. It's also always dark, even when the lights are on. Even when it is sunny outside, this place feels haunted. The temperature is always cold, and the long hallways give me the creeps every time I walk through them on my own. There are funny-looking pictures hanging on the walls. It is not like the pretty pictures my brother paints for me. No. These are black with ugly beasts and fire on them. So much fire. I don't like them. They come alive when darkness creeps in. Growls sound in the distance every time daddy tucks me into bed.
I hear cries, too.
Women's cries.
No, I don't like this place.
It is nothing like Jonah's home. His place is filled with colors and laughter. And love. So much love.
There's not much love here.
No, that's a lie.
I love my siblings, and they love me.
I love my mommy, too.

I just don't like the men that are always around. I don't like the scary men that work for daddy. They sneer behind my daddy's back every time I walk past them. Only me. They are not mean to my big brother, Lucan, or my big sister, Gigi. Never them. Only just me.

"Didn't I tell you to stay in your room, mia principessa."

Daddy's voice is but a mere whisper behind me. I am shortly startled, and I almost lose my footing and fall down the long staircase, but before that happens, Daddy quickly sweeps me off my feet and takes me in his arms.

I love my daddy. To everyone else, he is the boss. Tommaso Volpe But to me, he is just my daddy.

He is never mean and never yells.

Every time I stare into his eyes, there is always warmth swimming in them, but tonight they look like the eyes of every other man who works for him.

The ones that are never kind and like to mock me.

I've never felt scared in his arms until this very moment.

"I'm sorry. I was looking for Giana, but I couldn't find her anywhere." I did not lie. I told him half a lie. I was looking for my sister since she promised she would play hide and seek with me today. Although, I don't believe she will since the weather is acting up tonight.

It feels like a storm is coming.

Thunder booms, and I can see a sliver of lighting come through the open shades of the hall windows.

Giana hates the rain.

She says that when it rains an angel is crying, but I do not agree.

I love the rain.

I love the smell of it, too.

However, what I enjoy most is the way the dark sky splits in two to let lighting through.

It is beautiful when it happens.

I believe storms are warnings.
Warnings of what's to come.
"Your brother and sister went to bed early, Cara." My daddy's icy tone when he speaks about my siblings confuses me. He sounds mean and uncaring. That is not like my daddy. I feel him lay a soft kiss on the left side of my temple and then put me down. "You should do the same. I'll send Muriel soon to tuck you in." *Weird.*
He always tucks me in.
No matter the business, he finds the time to kiss me goodnight and read me to sleep.
Something is wrong…
Daddy waits for me to step inside my room before he turns to leave in the direction he came from.
The left wing of the mansion.
Lucan's room is there.
Maybe he will check if he's alright like he did me before he leaves to attend to his business.
Daddy works too much.
Go to bed, Cara. I should listen to the voice inside my head that tells me I shouldn't follow daddy, but for the first time, I ignore it and defy his orders.
I wish I hadn't.
I wish I would've just gone to bed and pretended this home isn't a curse.
I could've pretended that what daddy does to my brother is a figment of my wild imagination.
But I didn't.
I can't pretend.
I witness how cruel and evil my hero is.
To everyone but me.
I always thought my big brother, Lucan, was just clumsy like I am.
That is not the case.

He's strong.
Brave.
He's also hurt.
He hurts every time daddy visits his room.
I peek through the slightly open door and watch from the outside how daddy forcefully manhandles Lucan and slaps him a couple of times. I whimper and gasp when my brother falls to the floor, and I catch a glimpse of blood on his teeth and a wide gash on his left eyebrow.
I'm afraid.
When I'm afraid, I run to him but what if I make it worse for him?
Not thinking clearly, just wanting to stop daddy from hurting my brother, I take a step forward, but the moment I do, my brother's eyes find mine.
There, I don't find love nor the tenderness that's always there when he looks at me. Instead, I find hatred and fear. Not fear for his life but… mine. I touch the door handle, but I stop dead when he shakes his head once and mouths run.
With a heavy heart, I do as my brother says.
Because as much as I love my daddy, my big brother Lucan always knows best. Unlike daddy's orders, I don't dare go against what Lucan says.
I run.
Not toward my room.
Not toward mommy.
I run toward the storm.
Once outside, I run through the garden and find myself hiding between the bushes of red roses my mommy loves so much. I fall to the ground, not caring that it is pouring or that the sky is falling. Here, I can breathe. Here in the middle of a thunderstorm, I find the comfort that is missing inside my home. Dirt covers my peach pajamas and the rain that falls from the sky mixes with the water that falls from my eyes.

Why, daddy?
Why do you hurt Lucan?
Then, I think back to all the times I have seen my brother hurt with bruises all over his skin and realize how they all lie to me.
One lies to protect me, and the other lies to give me a false sense of reality.
Yes, daddy lied.
Lucan is not clumsy.
He is…hurting.
Mommy and Gigi, too.
They are all being hurt.
By the very same man that calls me princess and hugs me when I'm afraid of the monsters hiding under my bed.
Maybe the monster was right in front of me all along. Maybe the scary paintings and the dark hallways inside our home are not the scariest things after all. My daddy is.
"Why are you crying?" I almost don't hear the softly spoken words with the thunder booming all around me. I cover my eyes from the rain and squint, trying to make out the person that's now standing in front of me. The dark silhouette is barely visible in the dark, so I squint harder, trying to catch a glimpse of his face.
A boy.
A tall boy.
It's almost impossible to see him clearly with how dark it is outside.
Lightning strikes and illuminates the half of his face not hidden by a hat.
Lorenzo?
Valentino?
Which of the twins is it?
It doesn't take me long to realize that it couldn't be Valentino. Valentino dresses funny unlike his brother.

He is dressed from head to toe in black with a red baseball cap pulled low over his eyes and a hoodie on top to cover himself from the rain.

I'm still coming to terms with the fact that I am no longer alone when I feel strong hands pulling me up from the ground. Before I know it, he takes off his cap, pulls the hoodie over his head and covers me with it, shielding me from the rain. The thing is twice my size and fits me like a dress.

Lorenzo Nicolasi.

One of my brother's friends.

Well, I wouldn't exactly call him a friend.

He's the one that never acknowledged my existence and barely speaks when talked to.

He is speaking to me now.

Lightning strikes, and I'm able to see him clearly once again. "T-thank you." I start to shiver from the cold. A second ago, the cold didn't bother me as much, but now it does. It lasts but a moment because when I look into his dark blue eyes, I find warmth there.

Strange…

I heard the whispers about him.

Cold.

Detached.

Mean.

An animal in training.

That's what daddy's men and even Lucan say about him.

He doesn't seem cold to me.

Lorenzo's blue eyes narrow, and he shakes his head. Then, rather roughly, he yanks my hand and guides me toward the garden. There, we stop when we reach the tallest tree in the area where my treehouse is. I don't have time to ask questions because, before I know it, he is hauling me onto his back and begins to climb the wooden stairs of the tree trunk until we find shelter from the rain.

Once inside the treehouse, I feel much better. This place is where I run off to when I don't feel like myself. Sometimes my mood changes, and I don't understand why. I could be happily playing with my stuffed animals, and a second later, feel a wave of melancholy hit me out of nowhere without reason. Therefore, I hide away here to just breathe.

Daddy had this tree house built for me after months of me asking for it. My brother and sister also come up and spend hours upon hours here before finally climbing down.

"Why are you crying?" He asks again, but unlike last time, I don't keep my mouth shut. I don't know why I tell him what's wrong. I don't know him.

Not really.

I play with one tendril of hair and make a face that has him sighing in exasperation.

Huh.

I remain quiet while I watch as he turns his baseball hat backward and drops to the floor next to me. Then, I hear paper wrinkling as he looks through the pocket of his hoodie that I am now wearing. He pulls something out and shoves it in my face. "I'll give you this shit if you tell me."

Moving the wet hair out of my eyes, I see that he's holding a cherry, heart-shaped lollipop.

My favorite.

What a coincidence that he carries those around. They're hard for me to get since daddy banned junk food and sweets. I quickly reach for it when my cold fingers touch his, and I feel it.

A weird tingling sensation in my belly.

It feels like small bugs acting silly there.

I watch as his blue eyes narrow and his nostrils flare. Lorenzo is looking at me like I look at Lucan when he uses big people's language I don't understand.

What did I do wrong?

Silence creeps into the small space and all around the night. It's so dark that when lightning crisscrosses through it, I watch in fascination and wait for the crack of thunder.

I don't mind the silence that lingers.

It's almost… comfortable.

I feel the brooding boy next to me still. His uncaring and unafraid attitude should make me feel uncomfortable, but it does not. He could stay up here with me if he wants. I don't mind. It feels better than down there, where there's pain, broken hearts, and so much betrayal.

"My sister, Giana, says storms are the sky's way of letting us know that an angel is sad." I break the silence first since it is clear he won't say a word unless I start the conversation, and mommy always says that is the polite thing to do when in company of other people.

The boom sounds over his exasperated sigh, "She does, huh?" He chuckles, and I begin to wonder what is so funny. Rain begins to hammer against the wooden exterior of the tree house. "Or maybe it's the sky's way of telling us an angel has fallen from grace straight into the burning pits of hell."

Huh.

What an odd thing to say.

Curiosity always gets the best of me, so I ask.

"Interesting…" I say. "So, when the sun comes out, it means that heaven is smiling even after losing an angel?"

Seconds later, the storm is now but a mere rumble fading beneath the patter of rain, "Maybe. Or maybe it's all made-up shit. Who the fuck knows, really?" He looks down at the lollipop and rips the plastic wrap before handing it to me.

"Thank you." I mumble while enjoying the cherry flavor hitting my taste buds. I do love my lollipops. I get lost in the moment when he grunts next to me, making me look up at him.

His eyes look weird again.

"Tell me why you were crying back there? I'll take the lollipop away if you don't fess up. Now, tell me." he commands darkly, sounding a lot like the storm outside.
"My daddy scared me." I confess.
"Your dad is a bitch," he snaps.
My breath hitches the moment the foul word leaves his mouth. No one dares to call daddy names. Not even the grown men that work with him.
No one.
Does he have no manners? It's not polite to call people names. At least not to their faces. That's what mommy says. I called the kids that are idiots at school names all the time. In my head, at least.
"H-he hurts my brother." I confess, not caring about him taking the lollipop away from me. Which something tells me he won't do, but I have a feeling that here inside this small space with this boy with a dark mood but warm eyes, I am safe.
Lorenzo makes a humming noise. "He does."
I look up at him, confused by his uncaring tone. He is my brother's friend. He should care a little.
He should be as upset as I am.
But he is not.
There is no concern or even pity in his gaze.
He doesn't lie to me and tell me that everything will be okay.
"Does your daddy hurt you?" I whisper, wanting to understand the why of it. Are all daddies mean to their children?
"No one does," He whispers darkly, making goosebumps rise on my cold skin. "No one ever will."
He didn't say much else, but he didn't need to.
That night I learned how he is unlike every other boy I met before.
He doesn't think the same way I do.
Like most people do.
He is not programmed that way.

The next day, I woke up alone in the treehouse, still wearing his black hoodie and with five lollipops on the floor next to me. The storm is long gone, and with it, Lorenzo Nicolasi.
The sky is no longer crying when I hear voices below. My siblings. Lucan is shouting for me to get down.
Giana whispers worriedly, "Did she spend the night up there all alone? You know she's afraid of thunderstorms."
No, I'm not. I am not afraid. I want to tell her.
Never have been, and after last night I won't ever be afraid of them. Of anything.
I was more afraid of what lurked inside our home, but not anymore. Monsters don't hide in the shadows. The monster inside our home is in plain sight.
Lucan grunts. "Go make sure no one comes back here. I'll get her down." He does just that.
A moment later, my big brother climbs up the tree and helps me down. Back down to reality. Where he gets hurt.
Where they all get hurt except for me.
Where nothing will ever be the same.
I squeeze my brother tightly when I notice the beige Band-Aid on his face and the angry-looking bruises on his right cheek. I feel him hug me tighter to him, trying to comfort himself. I want to cry but not because the tinted, rose-colored glasses were cruelly removed from my eyes. The ones that led me to believe all was alright. No. I want to cry for my brother. The one with scars in both his skin and heart.
But I don't.
My heart hurts for him. For all of them, but if I cry, it will only make him sad.
Instead, I look down at the lollipop in my hand and smile. A genuine smile.
I remember last night.
The good and the bad.
Nobody caught us.

He disappeared like a magic act. In the middle of the night and in the middle of a storm.
He was gone as if he was never here.
My smile grows wider.
Lorenzo Nicolasi.
I don't think about the repercussions of me disobeying daddy. I only focus on the thoughts about the emotionless boy with dark clothes and dark blue eyes.
That night was the first time I told Lorenzo a secret, but it wasn't the last. I told him all my secrets because he eventually became my most treasured one.
I also became obsessed with cherry heart-shaped lollipops, the color black, and the odd smell he left on his hoodie that is now mine.
No one ever found out about our meetings every time the sky cried and raged.
Every time there was a storm outside, I found him.
The most beautiful chaos.
My Enzo.

CHAPTER TWO
DEATH IS MY FRIEND

"On rainy nights I miss you the most." — C

Lorenzo

11 Years Old

"This place gives me the creeps." A cold and condescending voice says from my right while I stand in the middle of the Volpe mansion's living room. I tune out her voice and ignore her comment because what is there to say? Every place Arianna Parisi visits gives her the creeps, and how hypocritical of her since her home is the devil's playground, and yet this place with more love than ours gives her the creeps. Yeah, it reeks of tragedy, too, but there is no denying that the Volpe children have known pain just as much as they've felt love. On the other hand, the Parisi sisters and my brother and I were raised in the dark with not even a sliver of light to slip through the ugly and permanent cracks in our souls. Love.

I mentally scuff.

It's only for the weak.

I've come to find that what my grandfather, Benedetto, said is true.

Love weakens the mind and taints the soul.

You no longer have control of your emotions and actions. It suddenly all becomes about the other person, their wants, and needs, or so I've read in the silly books my twin loves so much.

Like Romeo and Juliet, for example. *It's all bullshit.*
I've never felt the need to put someone's wants before mine, except for Tino, but that shit doesn't count since sadly and very fucking unfortunately, the twin bond is something I can't seem to get rid of, but as for others? Hell no, and I don't ever plan to.
"What are you waiting for? Let's go. We're already late as it is." I sigh, trying to ignore her not-so-very pleasant presence. I'm in no mood to pretend today. Pretending has become exhausting these days. At home. At school. Everywhere.
"Why are you talking to me?" I mumble when suddenly an intense feeling of awareness crawls up my spine, spreading shivers around my body — making me turn in the direction of a huge glass door that leads to the outside area of the mansion. Without as much of an explanation, I walk away from Arianna and let my feet drag me. When I reach the door, I look up at the sky and the weird sensation I felt seconds ago lessens when I notice the sun is long gone, hidden between gray clouds, and the rain has begun to fall. I feel something else. Thrill. I feel a thrill taking over me. I recognize the feeling.I've become accustomed to it as of lately.
It grows by the second when I notice a small figure huddling over one of the rose bushes outside. Red.
Turning the knob, the loud noise outside drowns the noise inside. Most importantly, Arianna's pointless conversation. I do not intend to be her crutch today. I put up with her because she fascinated me once. Her cold exterior and how well she played everyone around her intrigued me, but like with everything else, I got bored. I got what I wanted from her. She's broken just like the others. They allowed themselves to fall victim to their parent's cruelty, and that's when she lost me. I had high expectations of her— of all of them. They want to be kings and queens, but they don't even know themselves. They are all hurting, slowly decaying on the inside.

All because of what?
Love?
Familial bonds?
All of it is useless.
Love won't get me the crown.
It will only get me into the ground.
That's what Benedetto told us the first night we learned what our futures hold.
Weak men don't eat.
That's his religion and our way.
"I wasn't talking to you, halfwit." The eldest Parisi sister snaps, making me turn in her direction once again. I take her in slowly. Arianna stands straight with her shoulders back and head held high like she's carrying an invisible crown. So proper. So clean. So boring. She wears a sparkling pink dress with a matching headband, pulling her blonde hair away from her face.
Restraints.
That's what I see every time Arianna walks into a room.
An obnoxious mess of pink.
What a distasteful color.
Red, on the other hand…
"Ooh, you wound me, ice princess." I make a point to call her the same name everyone calls her. One that's been messing with her lately. I don't see anything wrong with it, yet she flinches everytime I call her that. It is truly fascinating how one little, insignificant word can ruin someone's day. She gives them too much power.
I give her my back, not wanting to deal with her drama a moment longer. I turn to look at the wild creature now running in the rain toward the direction of the pool area instead. I frown when I notice her jumping in puddles of rain while laughing like a maniac.
What a strange individual this one is…

What could she possibly find fascinating about getting herself wet and covered in dirt?

Covered in someone's blood, I can understand.

That shit looks fun, but cold water and mud?

No.

"Well, suit yourself. It's your ass on the line and not mine." Arianna's cold remarks do nothing to persuade me. I remain in place, looking out the window, trying to figure out the youngest Volpe. Her siblings, I got them pegged, but not her. If I'm being honest, I've never paid much attention to the girl. She's not a friend nor a rival and that makes her useless in the grand scheme of things. Seconds pass, and then the soft click of a door behind me lets me know that Arianna is gone and I'm alone.

Finally.

Your ass is on the line…

Her words serve as a warning because we both know what happens when we disobey orders. It never goes well for any of us, especially when Benedetto's word is law around here.

If he orders you to jump off a cliff, you jump to your death without question.

That's how tight he has the leash wrapped around all his loyal dogs.

But even the most loyal of dogs get hungry.

Hungry for more.

More power.

More money.

More reach.

Just more.

That's what happened to Benedetto's successor, my uncle Demetrio. He wanted more, but he wasn't smart enough.

Clever enough.

He was a hungry dog like everyone else around here.

Desperate for a scrap.

They do not see the big picture.
Oh, but I do.
I don't need experience.
Age.
Wisdom.
No.
I have the burning fire that accompanies hunger.
One cannot be without the other.
I want more, yes, but all in due time.
While Benedetto is loved by many and hated by a lot more than that, he still has plenty of alliances that will take years to weaken.
Oh, how do you do that? Well, by showing the hungry dogs what they're missing.
And that's how an empire crumbles.
Disloyalty.
Envy.
Hatred.
The recipe for Benedetto's end and my beginning.
Shutting my mind off, I turn the knob and greet the cold rain as I step outside, walking in the direction the little monster ran off to.
Thunder booms.
Rain falls harder.
This is the second time I ignore the instincts that tell me not to follow the girl.
I cannot explain why I do it.
It vexes me to no end, especially knowing every time I am in her presence, I end up wet or covered in dirt. Yet, follow her anyway.

CARA

As the years passed, I learned to love the dark and all that hides in it. I found a true appreciation for the dark corners inside our home and the scary paintings decorating the walls.
The storms and the night.
The disturbing paintings don't scare me.
The men who treat me as a nuisance don't bother me.
This home doesn't trigger nightmares anymore.
Because nothing could hurt me more than the ugly truth my father tried so hard to hide.
I even started appreciating the color red.
It used to be insignificant before, but not now.
Now, it means something.
Mommy told me once that she hated the color red until the day she met me. It used to remind her of blood and pain, but now it only reminds her of me. I think she only says it so I don't feel bad, but she secret still hates it.
I don't mind.
Not really.
I love my hair.
I love the color.
Even the shade, crimson.
The one that reminds me of blood.
The same color covering the small and frail body of the bird laying in agony on the dirt.
He looks so defenseless and in so much pain.
Looking around the pool area, I notice that I am alone. Daddy's guards must be doing their rounds around the premises, and they've yet to come check on me. Good. I can play in the rain for a little while longer before they find me and tell on me.
They're always telling on me.
Huffing, my eyes find the bird again, and I watch in fascination as the neck hangs in a weird angle and blood covers his light gray feathers.

Such a pretty bird.
What a horrid fate.
Should I help him?
Daddy will be mad if I bring him inside.
He does not like animals or allows any pets inside our home.
I like animals.
I like dogs.
My friend Jonah has the cutest Greyhound named Snowball. I don't know why Jonah named him that. The puppy doesn't look like a snowball to me, but I don't understand half the things he does anyway.
The tiny bird makes a little noise laced with pain, bringing my attention back to it.
It feels cruel to leave it in the cold rain to rot.
I'll take it to Lucan.
He will know what to do.
Not thinking twice about it, I make a move to grab the bird, but before I have a chance to do so, a black boot stomps on the poor animal.
Even with the loud rain and thunder sounding all around me, I don't miss the disturbing sound of the bird being squashed to death. I sit frozen, staring down at the black boot covered in mud belonging to the person who successfully murdered the poor bird.
How heartless…
Who would do such a thin—
My stunned eyes leave the boot and look up at the person before me, and my heart goes crazy, beating in my chest. Maybe it is the adrenaline of what I just witnessed him doing, or it's just the look in his eyes.
Lorenzo.
He's back.
Since I overheard one of the house cleaners say it would rain today, I wondered if I would see him, but as the day flew

flew by, I forgot all about it. Why would he come back after leaving that morning? I'm no one special to him. I'm just his friend's little sister. Surely, he forgot all about me. Therefore, I set the hopeful thoughts aside and went on about my day, but I still hoped he would show up, and here he is.

In the middle of a storm…again.

"Don't touch," His tone is rough. My eyes stare into his darker shade of blue, and I'm taken back by the frown on his face. Why does he look constipated? He's the one that squished the poor bird to death.

"You killed him," I grimace when I realize how cold I sound. I don't mean to be insensitive, but sometimes I let it slip. There are lapses of times when I don't react as a sane person would. For instance, my sister, Giana, would've picked the injured bird the moment she saw it hurting on the ground but not me. I felt the need to sit on my hunches under the rain and in the cold mud to stare absently at the animal while it was clearly in pain and need of help. I try to suppress the weird thoughts that sometimes plague me, but I give in to them occasionally. "I set him free." Lorenzo says before moving his boot back, and without mercy or empathy, he shoves mud over the bird in a half-assed attempt to bury the animal.

"I was going to get him help!" I look up, bewildered.

"All you were going to do was get yourself in trouble for touching the filthy thing." He says absently while looking down at me with that irritating frown of his again. "Besides, there's nothing you could've done for the bird. It was as good as dead."

The bird was badly hurt, but I'm sure something could've been done for it. Maybe mommy or Lucan could've— My thoughts are interrupted when I hear him snap at me. "You got your dress dirty."

Looking down, I notice there is mud staining the pink dress daddy got for me the day he came back from his business

trip.
Pink.
I expressed once how it was not my color of choice, and he dismissed me like I was just a kid who knew nothing. I know many things. I know things I shouldn't, and I wish I could forget.
I cannot.
I cannot forget.
I can't act oblivious to what's happening around me because then I would be selfish.
So, I pretend for the sake of them.
Because when I act like the perfect child, it makes daddy happy, and if he is happy then he stays away from them.
They don't hurt.
Even if I do.
I hurt because I cannot be myself.
The rain stops falling, and suddenly the sun comes out from behind the gray clouds. I got lost in my thoughts again and completely forgot that the scary twin is speaking to me. Looking up, I smile a genuine smile because, lately, all my smiles, the real ones, are directed at the moody boy in front of me. I guess it is because with him, I don't have to pretend like all the others.
With him, I feel like I can be myself.
The Cara that no one else gets.
"I don't really like this dress anyway." I say truthfully before rubbing my hands, which are covered in both dirt and spots of blood, up and down the skirt of my dress. "I think it looks better this way, doesn't it?" I mumble, but I don't look away from the epic mess I've made of my new dress. I allow myself this one time to do something like this that might trigger my dad, knowing that he won't find out. I've gotten good and gotten away with things. When you get so good at pretending to be someone and something you are not, you go

unnoticed. No one believes you are capable of many things.
Lying.
Sneaking around.
No.
The youngest Volpe principessa would never dare.

LORENZO

"I don't really like this dress anyway." She smiles up at me as if nothing happened. I don't know if I should act disturbed or proud. What would her brother say if he was in my predicament?

He most likely would give the kid one of his hour-long, boring-as-fuck speeches on how to be a normal and sane member of society.

Sorry, kid. Can't really help there.

The storm has settled, and the sun is shining down on us. The rain has come and gone as if it wasn't here, pouring down on us at all.

Fuck, how I hate sunny days.

The birds fucking chirping happily during the day. I find that extremely annoying. I'm rather fond of the one currently buried in the dirt below my feet, though. It fascinates me.

Speaking of the sun, it is shining down hard on the girl's hair, giving the illusion that it is set aflame.

Huh.

In normal light, her hair looks on the darker side, almost like blood, but with rays of sunshine hitting it from all angles, it almost looks like a burning flame.

Which is it, pretty princess? Blood or fire?

How strange.

I never paid much attention to her until that night. From then on, my thoughts have strayed to her once or twice. Everything and everyone around us seem so bleak, boring, and fucking ordinary. They all move and talk the same way.

Not her. She's different.

There's a rarity to her.

There's a fire there. One that is not present when others are around.

But here with me.

"I like you." Softly spoken words fall out of her mouth as she looks nervously at me. I don't process her ridiculous words. Too busy staring at her pretty red hair. What would it feel like if I touched it? Not one to deny myself anything, I reach forward and twirl a small piece around my finger. I look from the red tendrils wrapped around my index finger to her pretty blue eyes. She says she likes me, but would she still feel the same after coming face to face with my true nature? Will she still look at me the same way when she realizes that I am cut from the same cloth as her father? As the same man that hurts the ones she loves? I don't believe so, but she will learn soon. They all do once they see me for me. "You don't know what you're saying, Cara Mia." I tell her, and a smile almost forms on my lips when I see her scrunch up her face in displeasure.

"Please don't call me that." She gets up from the ground and stands proudly before me. What the hell is going on? I find her amusing, and I'm not one to find anything amusing. Not really. This tiny girl with a stained dress, wet hair, and scowl on her face is the most fascinating creature I've met in a long time.

I see it in her.

The fire.

The recklessness and need to break the rules and challenge authority. I also see curiosity when she looks my way when she believes I'm not paying attention. I am always paying attention to everyone around me. That's how you survive in this ugly world. You survive it by studying others and learning their weaknesses to later, when it's beneficial, use agaisnt them. "What should I call you then?" I slip my hand inside my hoodie and pull out the candy she loves so much. Once in my palm, I remove the wrapper and offer it to her. When she reaches forward, I pull back. "I asked you a question, little monster." Her eyes grow big before she tilts her head to the side and taps her chin as if she's contemplating her answer. Right then, I learned something about the Volpe princess that maybe a lot of the people around her don't notice. Cara Mia Volpe is older than her nine years of age. She's wise beyond her years, and something dark lurks behind her pretty blue eyes. I can't put into words what it is yet, but I'll uncover it soon enough.

"Call me Cara or Mia, but not my full name at once." She frowns again and looks down at the hand that's holding the lollipop. This kid really does love this shit. It tastes like medicine. What on earth does she find tasteful about them? "I don't like my name."

Her name suits her, but I won't placate her. if she says she doesn't like it, then I'll call her by the name she prefers. Names are just names, and humans give them too much power over their personalities. Do I look like a Lorenzo or Antonnio? Yeah, no. I don't think so, but it is what it is. It is tradition to give Nicolasi kids an Italian name.

Traditions.

I don't really care much for them.

Rules, either.

"Mia it is, then." I mumble before handing over the lollipop, which she snatches from my hand in a flash while grinning up at me. Two dimples form on her cheeks. Rare, indeed. "Thanks."

I grunt but say nothing else.

I can't say the same about the kid.

She blabbers away as if we are the best of fucking friends. Could you imagine that shit?

Someone like me— who wears only black, likes dark shit and is fascinated by blood —friends with a tiny, freckle-faced kid with disheveled red hair. What a pair we must make.
"Do you like superheroes, Enzo?" She looks up at me with a small smile. Most kids don't look at me that way when I'm this close to them.
Then it sinks in.
Enzo?
Now she gave me a nickname.
Oh, that is just great.
"No," I tell her, annoyed that she shortened my name. "And the name's Lorenzo, not Enzo."
She shrugs as if she couldn't care less that I reprimanded her. "I do!" She completely ignores what I just told her. I not only find her wild nature fascinating but irritating, as well. How odd. The kid's brows furrow, and she takes a few seconds to think of what to say next. "I love Ironman. He has lots of money, cool gadgets, and he's sooooooo cute."
Cute?
"You're like four. You shouldn't think of boys as cute." I mumble, already annoyed with myself for the fact that I'm entertaining this silly conversation with this odd kid.
"Why not? I think you're cute, even when you don't smile all that much. You should try it. It won't kill you." She points a small finger upwards toward my face and gives me an annoyed look. "And I'm nine years old, silly." An amused smile almost forms on my face, but I kill that shit before it happens. It irritates me that I find her somewhat adorable instead of completely annoying.
Jesus.
I need to leave right the fuck now.
As she enjoys the lollipop, I move past her on my way back to the mansion. I've wasted enough time, and as much as I enjoy poking the ugly beast, I cannot push it all the way just yet.

Soon, but not quite yet.

"Get inside, kid." I tell her over my shoulder. Someone might come looking for her soon enough. It's strange that none of her father's men have come to get her yet. This is the second time I've found the kid on her own in the middle of a bad storm. I hear her mumble a soft okay before I feel her move in the direction of the house cleaner's quarters. "Hey, Red?"

I turn her way.

I watch her halt her steps before turning.

"Yes?"

"Why do you like that lollipop so much?" Why did I ask? I don't know. I'll blame it on my lack of sleep lately.

Smiling, she holds up the red heart-shaped lollipop to her face. "They taste like cherries. I also like the peach one." Her smile disappears, replaced by another annoying frown. My brows pull down on their own. Why do I care if she frowns? It's disturbing that I can't come up with a proper answer.

Don't ask.

Leave and go back inside.

Shit.

"Why are you frowning now?" I snap, exasperated with how invested I am in the brat.

She shrugs and pops the candy back in her mouth. "Dad banned all candies and junk food from our home." Her smile is long gone. "I-I miss how things used to be before…"

Before she witnessed her perfect world crumble with the force of her father's wrath.

The wind blows and light thunder sounds all around us. It will start to rain again…

"Get inside."

"Are we best friends now?" She smiles my way once without giving me a chance to respond to her ridiculous assumption. Friends? Best friends? "I say we are. Bye, bestie!" She waves twice with a mischievous grin on her freckled face

before skipping all the way back to the mansion's back door.
I watch her every step.
The fuck just happened?
Friends?
Best friends?
What a waste.
I don't have friends, especially nine-year-old little girls who love to talk my ears off about useless shit I'm not really interested in and run in the dirt in the middle of storms.
No, I don't have the time nor the patience for that. I have plans, and none of them involve the little monster with blood-red hair, ocean eyes, and a breakable heart.
Or so I thought.
I should've known that Cara Mia Volpe was more than what she let on. She witnessed my demons and faced them head-on, never once backing down.
She even made them her own.
I should've stopped whatever it was that started to grow between us every time a storm hit home.
I was too selfish to stop it.
Not when she made me feel things after years of thinking it was impossible.
I was immune to it all.
Until Cara Mia.
The most dangerous of storms.
She changed everything.

CHAPTER THREE
REVELATIONS

"What a shame." - L

Lorenzo

P ower.

12 years old

What is the meaning of it, really? Is it the same for everyone? Would every man and woman push themselves beyond their limits just to obtain even a small amount of it?
No, I don't believe so.
Power for noblemen means safety. It gives them the ability to survive this dog-eat-dog world. But even the most noble of men crave it and sometimes even abuse it. They're so strung up on it that their morals go out the fucking window all for the high only power can provide.
For me?
It's like a drug that feeds my very being.
It is more of a life source than even blood.
It's all I've ever known and all I've ever wanted. Not because I need safety and protection from the cruelty of this life but because it gives me the upper hand when facing an opponent. Power earns me respect.
But fear? Fear guarantees me the loyalty of the ones below me. The clock strikes midnight, and I don't wait a second before throwing back the bed covers and jumping out of bed.

At this hour, the Nicolasi mansion is eerily quiet, and the only voices that travel through the walls are the ones from the dead. Well, almost dead. Women and men both waiting for their sentence at the hands of a Nicolasi made man, or if they're unfortunate, they'll meet their end by the hands of Benedetto. Opening my bedroom door, I step outside the room and close the door quietly behind me. Valentino sleeps like the dead. I'm not worried that he'll hear me from next door, but the men that work for our family are always on my ass, making sure I stay in line.

To their dismay, I never follow their rules, and by consequence, they pay for my insubordination and disobedience. I should care that my actions affect others, but I do not, and I am done trying to figure out why I feel no remorse. No empathy toward them.

I make my way toward the back staircase, the one that leads to the underground wing of the mansion. There are three wings in the Nicolasi residence. The right one is Benedetto's, with half of the rooms being for his overnight guard dogs, and the left one was left to us. The underground area is where most businesses take place. There's a gym.

The security room, and my personal favorite, the torture chambers. Tonight is not the first night I sneak off and come down here. I've been doing it since I can remember. I don't even know how it started.

Oh yeah, I know.

I heard the loud shouts and pitiful cries of the unfortunate souls that committed the worst crime of all.

They betrayed the family and got sent down here to pay their dues to the family they swore fealty to.

Loud whimpers sound in the distance as I get closer to the torture chambers. A sleek-black wooden door is slightly open, making it easier for me to witness what is going on behind it, although I clearly know what's going on.

The second my chest touches the door, it opens without a sound. It doesn't alert the men inside of my presence. I've done this so many times before that, at this point, I walk through the dark halls and corners of this place as a ghost. Unheard and unseen.

Peeking inside, all is as it always is. The cold room has white walls, white floors, a seat in the middle of the room for Benedetto's playthings, and a black table near the far end of the room pressed against the walls where all kinds of torture equipment lay.

Every gun known to man.

Benedetto's knife collection. It goes from the most normal ones, like kitchen knives, to his favorite ones, hunting knives. There are also different types of torture gadgets that I haven't been able to figure out what they are yet, except the gags and whips. Once I get a closer look, I'm sure I'll know exactly what they are and what their use is.

With my left cheek almost touching the cold door, I watch as Benedetto steps into the frame. A six-foot-one lean man dressed in an expensive Italian suit and black leather shoes. One thing to know about men like my grandfather is that they love to dress the part.

Italian suits.

Leather shoes.

A clean-shaven face and a nice haircut.

He looks like your resident decent businessman.

We know better. He hides behind it all.

I won't ever be caught dead in one of those monkey suits. I won't ever hide or abide by the rules created by men.

Nope.

Cassius might be a waste of a human, but one thing Dad got right was his rebelliousness and his inability to fit in with everyone else in this family. He did what he wanted when he wanted, despite knowing he had a powerful and spiteful

for a father and as boss of an entire city. Yet, he stood his ground and did what was right for him.
It blew up in his face, but at least he tried, no?
Dear old Dad chose love over an empire, and that's where he went wrong.
"Please, Don Nicolasi, please." The pitiful woman cries harder, capturing my full attention.
Don Nicolasi…
A buzz runs through me the moment she whimpers in agony. I take a closer look at the woman and notice that she's bound to a chair with dirty ropes keeping her in place. My eyes take her in from the top of her platinum blond hair to her bare feet tied to the chair. Then, I take in the red welts around her neck as if she was strangled, and she most likely was.
Strangulation is one of Benedetto's favorite torture methods, alongside waterboarding.
I recognize the woman as one of the dancers from the Parisi underground clubs. Melina? Melinda? Who the fuck cares, really? She's dead anyway.
She's naked.
What makes me stare longer than I normally would is not her state of undress but the crimson red running down her skin, making her look like Carrie.
Blood.
So much blood.
In her hair.
Between her legs.
Everywhere.
God, I really am disturbed.
"Puttana," Benedetto spits at his feet before stepping closer to the woman and pulling her by the hair until she's looking upwards at him.
I see the sadistic side has come out to play with the way his

his left eye is twitching. I study people. I've learned to assimilate their actions and reactions to my convenience. I carefully study every move they make. Know your enemies and all that. The crying woman flinches when Benedetto pulls harder on her hair but doesn't dare speak another word. The look on grandfather's face says it all. These are her last minutes on earth, and no amount of begging will save her from her tragic fate. "Didn't anyone teach you to never bite the hand that feeds you?" He seethes, showing her way too much emotion. It is written all over his displeased face. He gives them too much power because, yes, their asses are as good as dead, but they go out knowing they caused damage. Knowing their betrayal affected you. And by the calm look on the woman's face, I know she just realized nothing, and no one will save her, but at least she got him good. With fear in her eyes and a trembling voice she says. "Benedetto, ple—"
Slap.
Slap.
"Shut your whore mouth." Grandfather spits.
What an idiot.
Both of them.
One for going against one of the most ruthless men in this country and the other for failing his organization. It's clear the moment your people betray you and go against your back that it is because you failed to instill fear and secure their loyalty. Soft laughter comes out of the woman's mouth, and her face contorts in rage, finally showing her true colors. They always do. This is not the first time I've seen this same scene play out. Almost every night, Benedetto has a guest down here, and after torturing them for hours upon hours, he finally has mercy and sends them straight to hell. I know by heart what happens next. They die.
With either of two ways.
A bullet to the head.

A knife to the jugular.
My favorite is the latter.
The messier, the better.
Red.
Red.
Red.
What would Valentino think of me if he saw me now? He would probably think what a nutcase I am. So fucked in the head with an obsession for blood and death.
"I'm glad you find this amusing, darling. You can laugh all the way down straight to hell." Benedetto slaps her hard twice before pulling out a knife from his breast pocket.
So, the knife it is.
"I'll see you there. You will burn." The woman, no longer crying crocodile tears, spits blood onto his brand-new and perfectly polished shoes. She did it now. "One day, everyone will know just how much of a fraud you are. The title of Don is too big for you because you are small, not even an ounce of what he is—" Without warning or thinking twice about it, Benedetto steps forward and shoves the knife into her neck. Loud gurgling sounds come out of her as fast as the river of blood that's now falling down her throat to her naked chest.
Gasping.
Shocking.
Drip.
Drip.
Drip.
Dark red meets pristine white floors.
The sound of choking and Benedetto's angry murmurs fade into the background as I stay focused on the river of blood, now staining the floor. My heart beats faster, and my hands twitch, wanting to take a closer look. Moments that seem like hours pass before I'm back, staring at the now dead woman. She's gone, and all for one idiotic mistake.

Weak.

Then my eyes turn to look at the spot where Benedetto was standing, but I find it empty. He's not standing close to the woman's dead body, but he's on his knees in front of one of his watch-dogs.

Marcelino?

Mercurio?

No, Manuello.

This moment will forever stay burned in my memory. Not because of the blood on the floor. Not the sadistic torture done to the woman.

But the image of one of the most savage men I know. A boss of an entire city. The head of an organization, and the capo of the Holy Trinity, down on his knees sucking the cock of one of his guards. A man with barely a title. Not even made yet.

I step back in disgust. Not because of the act he is performing but for the disgrace of falling on his knees for someone so beneath him, for pretending to be something he is not.

He is not a boss.

A boss kneels for no one.

Not even God.

Not the devil.

No one.

What a disgrace.

Does everyone know about Benedetto Nicolasi's late-night escapades? How he loves to get on his knees and suck another man after killing an enemy?

Does nonna know?

I don't think so.

Without a glance back, I step away from the door and walk back to my room with only a thought on my mind as I walk. If only everyone knew the man they swore loyalty to and followed blindly was not the man he portrays to the world.

He is weak.

I take the dirty little secret and stash it inside my vault and wait for the day when I can use their secrets against them all. What a fun time that will be.

The next time I slip out of my room in the middle of the night, I find myself staring at the same scene.

A traitor.

A gunshot or knife wound.

Grandfather on his knees.

CHAPTER FOUR
PINK EXPLOSION

"I told you he was insane." - C

Lorenzo

12 years old

Fucking pink.
It looks like it exploded everywhere.
It literally did.
Pink confetti is covering half the lawn and pool area, making it look like a fucking unicorn shit all over. The huge pink crown piñata that was hanging from one of the trees now lays on the ground after the birthday girl beat the absolute shit out of it just twenty minutes ago.
Shaking my head, trying to get rid of the pink confetti that fell on my head, I wonder why the hell I even came here. Oh, right. Got to keep up with appearances, but then I look all around me and deeply regret it.
Pink all over.
I honestly find the color deeply disturbing, and frankly, it offends the shit out of me.
I walk farther into the party and find that there are pink and silver balloon arches on every corner of the patio and pool area. The centerpieces on the tables are silver princess tiaras. The main table with the birthday cake sits in the far corner. A three-tier pink cake with an obnoxiously big cursive C

and a pink crown on top of it. There is also a light pink food truck serving those nasty trendy fruit bowls everyone, who thinks they're-hip lately eats. Shacai? Açaí bowls?
Some shit like that.
Pink cotton candy.
A pink piñata.
A pink and white bouncy house and even a small ass pony with its mane and tail painted pink, making it look like one of those horse toys I've seen her play with when she was younger.
My little horse, was it?
What-the-fuck-ever.
This gathering clearly shows how little they know the little monster.
They don't know her. That part is obvious.
She loves red.
Red candy.
Junk food.
Superheroes.
Bugs.
But not today. Today, she looks like a good little princess with a pink gown, her unruly red hair is tied back from her face, and a princess tiara sits on top of her head. Nothing at all like the freckle-faced, unruly monster that loves to run in the rain and play in the mud by herself.
Looking around the area, I notice every member of the three families is in attendance. Of course. The Parisi boss and two of his daughters.
The youngest one is nowhere to be seen. The asshole must've left Mila at home, too preoccupied about his reputation and not at all concerned about hurting her feelings. There's something about Benedetto's long-time consigliere that rubs me the wrong way, and it's not the fact that he breathes the same air as I do— that's part of it, yes—but there's also

the way that he thinks of himself above women.

He belittles them. I see the way he treats his wife and his daughters. It is obvious that, in his eyes, women are beneath him.

Benedetto stands on the far right, almost near the pool, with all the bosses surrounding him, all deep in conversation. His lover or hole for the night stands back as a good little dog guarding his boss.

This is not a celebration of Mia's life. Not really. This is what it always is. An opportunity to pretend. To show how superior they all are and build connections by talking amongst themselves and possible allies.

There's nothing wrong with it.

It's just the pretending part that irks me.

I do it out of necessity, because it helps me take steps in the direction of that crown that hangs tilted on Benedetto's head.

It doesn't fit.

It's too big for someone like him.

Someone that claims to be larger than life, but it's obvious how he always needs the attention on him to survive. Men like my grandfather love the notoriety of being a boss.

The title.

I, on the other hand, want it. Crave it.

Not for the popularity it might bring but because of the need to juggle someone's life in the palm of my hand.

The control.

The rush.

"You came!" A tiny hand wraps around my much larger one, snapping me out of my thoughts and making my gaze leave the men on the right and look down at the small explosion of nauseating pink. "Thank goodness you're here." Her hand leaves mine before I have the chance to chastise her for touching me without my permission, but something tells me this little monster would shrug it off and do it again the first chance she gets. She scrunches her nose and looks up at me, expecting an answer, but I give her none. Too many people around to witness it. Instead, I use both hands to fix her tilted crown that must've moved while she was jumping on the bounce house. "There. Perfect." I mutter under my breath, grateful for the loud chatter and the music all around us. She didn't hear. Good.

"Come, let's—" she's interrupted by her older sibling.

"It's time to sing happy birthday, topina. Dad is asking for you." Lucan grabs her hand and snatches her away with a warning glare my way. My hands start to itch, and my vision gets blurry. I hate sharing my toys, but most of all, I hate when I am denied.

Power will give you everything…

You won't have to share anymore.

Not their time.

Not their lives…

***

An hour goes by, and after singing happy birthday to the girl, everyone settles and resumes their conversations and whatever the hell they were doing before stepping away to cut the cake.

I stay back near the tree house when Valentino joins me with a hard look on his face and a book in his hand. My dear brother wears his emotions on his face, and that's where we differ. He doesn't fool anyone. He is and always will be himself. "What are you reading?" I mumble while I chew the nasty ass yogurt Mia's mom gave me before I decided to come hide here. I watch as my twin sits down on the ground next to me. Valentino hates crowds and would rather run off somewhere he can find silence.

I hate it.

As always, he doesn't answer. He's deep in his mind, reading about better places and times than the ones we live in.

I don't take offense to it. I wait for him to come back down and let me into his little world. Valentino changed out of nowhere. He was never a social Suzy, but he at least tried to fit in like everyone else. Now, he's harsher and even more quiet. He even skipped a grade and left me behind. Again, it shouldn't bother me, but it does not. Sometimes, I wish I could care more about him. Be everything he needs, but I simply cannot. I'm not wired the same way he is, and with every step we take in opposite directions, we come to terms with the fact that we're no longer what we used to be. "Why are you hiding here?" Tino breaks through the silence after closing the book on his lap. "You're in your element here."
"I can leave, and I'm not hiding. I'm just done with people today." I make a move to stand, but his soft whisper stops me.
"You don't have to go." He looks my way as if I'm one of the puzzles he loves to decipher so much. Sorry, big brother, this one will be a bitch to crack. Valentino takes a deep breath, making me look away from the party ahead of us and look at his face. It's odd how two people can look the same and share the same DNA, but everything else is so different. Valentino needs the shadows to stay sane, while I love the recklessness I find in the light. He enjoys reading while I enjoy drawing sick shit with black ink. He dresses like a prep boy, covering himself in black turtlenecks and sweaters that make it seem like he's a damn college boy. I, on the other hand, prefer to be comfortable. A simple hoodie and dark jeans will suffice.
It's torture enough to pretend to be a normal feeling human like everyone, but I refuse to abide by their social standings and codes.
Yeah, I'm a mess of contradictions. I did tell you I'm all kinds of fucked up.
"I mean, why are you here? You usually skip events that require you to socialize with others."
That is the honest-to-God truth.

"I needed my monthly dose of human interaction, little brother." I shrug, not wanting to give him anything else. He has secrets of his own, and I don't push him to tell me. Maybe you should… Therefore, I cut my time short every time I'm with my brother. Somehow, a little nagging voice most call conscience seems to slip through my defenses and bitch at me. "I'm older than you, dickhead." His tone is laced with boredom as per usual.
"By a minute, big deal."
"By two, actually." We have this discussion almost daily, and yet I think we both got the minutes wrong every time. Who will tell us otherwise? Our drunk father or our no-show mother?
"Who gives a fuck?" Tino snorts.
"Clearly, you do."
Before I have the chance to continue our useless banter, he says, "She's crying." He's looking in the direction of the bounce house where I last saw Mia. I turn my head and find her there with her back turned to the party and subtle movements shaking her small frame.
She's crying…
There's a pang in my chest that annoys me a little bit less than the thought of her crying. Without thinking it through, I get up from the ground and rush to her side. Why is she always crying? Why do I care?
Annoying little monster, release me from your grasp.

CHAPTER FIVE
PRETTY LITTLE MONSTER

"Sometimes, I even scare myself."
— L

Cara

10 years old

You're so weird.
That's why they call you a bastard, isn't it?
Look! She's crying.
Laughter.
I hold my head tighter, but the memory keeps assaulting me.
"Why are you crying?" A harsh voice snaps furiously from behind me.
Lorenzo.
I keep my head down and try my best to dry my tears. My scalp is still burning from Samael pulling on my hair because I told him he had shit for brains. I don't like to offend people, but he asked for it. He hurt my best friend's, Jonah, feelings. My actions are justified, or that is what my big brother says anyway. We bite back, *topina*. We bite, and we do it hard until we draw blood. That'll teach them not to fuck with us.
So that's exactly what I did.
He also says that real men don't lay their hands on women, yet Samael yanked on my hair and called me names. One I don't quite understand the meaning of, but the expression

on his face told me it was far from a compliment. He's a butthead. He really is.

I'm too stuck in my head that I forgot Lorenzo was waiting for an answer.

He sighs softly, leaves my back, and comes to stand before me. From this angle, he looks like a furious God — like the ones Lucan is always talking about and paints. Lorenzo gets on his knees and takes my chin in his cold hands. His eyes look weird again today. They always look so intense. I swear, if I look closely enough, I can see tiny flames dancing in his eyes. Fire. That's what I think of every time I stare into his eyes.

The chatter and music all around us fade into the background. "Why are you crying, Red?" I don't know why I feel safe with him, and like I could tell him anything. He's mean and scary to others, but he's always been kind to me in his own weird way.

"He called me a bastard." I whisper ashamedly. I don't know what the word means— I will look it up in my dictionary when I get home — but it couldn't be anything nice because everyone laughed while he was taunting me.

"Who did?" His dark tone makes me jump a little in my spot. So scary.

"Samael." A terrible, cruel smile appears on his face, and his blue eyes sparkle with mischief. He nods and stands up from his hunches. He says nothing else and makes a move to leave. "Wait." I don't know why, but I grab his hand. His warm hand. I shiver at the contact. He stops and stares down at our joined hands with a puzzled expression. I think he might shake me off or chastise me for touching him without his permission again, but he just holds tighter to my hand. "What is a bastard?"

Lorenzo rubs my hand with his thumb as he stares at my hair.

"That piece of shit is the bastard, little monster. Never you. You get me?" Not really, but I don't want him thinking I'm stupid, or worse, a baby. So I just nod. "Go enjoy your party, Mia." He tilts his head toward his house and lets go of my hand. I feel weird. A sense of loss runs through me the moment he turns in the direction Samael ran off to.

The bouncy castle.

Not even a minute later, kids scatter out of the bounce house, screaming and some crying in all directions, looking for their parents.

And I just know that he did something.

I shouldn't find myself smiling at others' pain.

Princesses are kind and noble.

They would never befriend the villain in the fairytales.

Superheroes and villains are not friends.

That is exactly what he is. Mean.

Scary.

Sometimes crazy.

Okay, almost all the time.

Still, I smile and dry my tears because he cares.

He cares about… me.

I stand back and wait for him to emerge from the castle.

LORENZO

Red.

It's all I saw the moment I stepped foot inside the bounce castle and saw the little shit laughing with the other kids like he did not just make the girl cry by pulling her hair and calling her ugly names.

I look down at my shaking hands and imagine all the ways I could hurt the little asshole.

I can dismember him piece by piece and let his mommy clean up after the mess I make, or I could walk to his side, wrap my hands around his neck

and squeeze. Squeeze until his eyes bulge out of his face and the air leaves his body. Yeah... that'll do. Looking away from my hands, I tilt my head and smile.
You fucked up, asshole.
I hate when people touch my toys.
I hate it even more when they make kindhearted girls cry.
How hypocritical of me to be mad about the punk hurting Mia when hurting others is what brings me the most joy.
My hands are itching with the need to hurt.
I'm not a complete psychopath. There are people I wish to cause harm to and others I want to keep from pain. I've yet to understand the why of it, but I don't feel compelled to hurt innocents. I don't hurt little girls with kind hearts and good intentions. Fuck. I really need to stay away from the brat or teach her to toughen the fuck up. Life is cruel, or so I've heard. She needs to sharpen her claws, although the little monster is almost there.
She's got potential.
I think back to the tears she spilled because of this ass-wipe. I'm getting madder just thinking about it.
As the rage grows, so does my need to cause him pain. It always happens when I'm on the verge of losing control. My heart races, my breathing becomes uneven, there's a ringing in my ears, and my palms begin to twitch.
An episode, it's what Cassius and the foolish head doctor call it.
Or, in a more professional term, intermittent explosive disorder.
Sudden outbursts? Check.
Rage? Check.
Irritability? Check.
Fighting for no reason? Nope. People piss me off. That's reason enough.
Need to pound an asshole's ugly face? Double check.

After an episode, the no-good doctor explained that I might feel a sense of relief followed by regret and embarrassment. She got the relief part right, but I've never felt regret, and I sure as hell never felt embarrassed.

"Breathe, son. Breathe through the rage and count to three. It'll pass." I can hear my father's words—on the rare occasion he's sober and present—but I don't want to count to fucking three. I want to let it take over.

I've never let the rage take full possession of my actions before.

I always manage to pull myself back before I fall completely. Today, I do.

For her, I did what I swore I would never do.

I let my true nature come out to play in front of others.

I let them all see.

One moment, I'm walking closer to Samael, and the next, everything turns black with spots of red.

"Stop! Oh my God, you little monster, what have you done?"

"Son, let go of the child."

Yelling.

Weeps.

Imploring.

Curses.

It's all around me.

Fueling me.

Urging me on.

"Samael."

"He called me a bastard."

"Mommy!"

Voices blend and play through a loop inside my head as I pound his face without the need to ever stop. My fist hits his face repeatedly, and not even his begging deters me. Not even the way he cries for his mommy makes me loosen up on the attack. It only makes me hit him harder.

Bones break.

Skin splits

"Let go of my son, you freak." I feel harsh hands pull me away from the asshole still crying on his back. My eyes try to focus, but all I see is a blur.

A beautiful mess of red.

Once my vision clears, I take deep breaths but don't count to three. I breathe in and let the memory of bones breaking and skin splitting center me. I feel a sense of peace I never felt before today.

Relief.

It feels like I've been unshackled.

Released.

You freak.

You freak.

You freak.

The woman screamed at me in fear while I assaulted her son. I'm indeed a fucking freak. Maybe now she'll teach her bitch son to never lay a hand on innocent girls and to shut his mouth about things he knows nothing about.

Once my breathing goes back to normal, I take in the scene around me. The bouncy castle was cleared out, and all the kids left. There's blood covering the inflatable pink walls.

There's blood everywhere.

My white sneakers have drops of blood on them.

My hands, too.

Looking down, I see my knuckles split open, my nails covered in blood, as well as my fingers.

I've always imagined this moment. When I would completely lose myself to my urges, but nothing that I envisioned comes close to this feeling.

I feel a buzz in my chest.

The red all around me doesn't scare me or disgust me. Not at all. It makes me feel like I belong.

It's warm, too. The blood, I mean.
It reminds me of her.
Her hair.
"Lorenzo, come out." I hear the shouts of my father from outside, but I don't hurry to him just yet.
I look around one more time and smile. A genuine smile. Those are rare for me. All I offer the world are fake ones, and I'm okay with that. They always get me what I want.
Not now, though.
What a pretty mess.
All because of the little monster.
Once I'm good, I step outside the bouncy castle and face the crowd of people standing by, most likely waiting to see the kid that beat the other boy to an inch of his life.
I do put up a good show if I must say so.
I lazily look away from my blood-covered hands and inspect the scene before me. There are all types of reactions. There are the prudish ladies clutching their pearls and looking at me like I'm the son of Satan who's come to claim their souls. Those reactions are always my favorite ones.
Then there are the curious ones. The ones that look at me with both pity and as if I'm an experiment they wish to study. A puzzle they want to solve.
Sorry, you're fucked.
And the one that I care the least about but will get me faster to my goal.
The proud smiles of the Made Men around me and my grandfather.
Feeling strong hands grip my shoulders gently, I look up to see my father, Cassius, sober for the first time in months, pulling me forward. "Let's get you cleaned up." He takes me away, but before I'm all the way gone, a shy voice stops me.
"Thank you, bestie." I turn to my left, look down, and there she is.

Trouble. With a big fat T. "Don't call me that, brat."
Mia steps forward and hands me one of her favorite lollipops before closing her small hand around my bloody one. I look down, confused as to why she's thanking me. There's also the fact that I hate how her pale hands are now covered in the idiot's blood. I notice how the tiara that was on top of her head is now down on the floor next to her feet. Why does it bother me so much? Why do I care? My head begins to pound.
This kid.
I shake her hand off and completely ignore her small smile as I continue the path to the Volpe home.
I've been doing shit I don't normally do.
Things that are not part of my plan.
And in the middle of everything, there's her.
It all comes back to her.
Once I'm far away from the celebration, the music begins to play again, and everyone goes on with their day as if I didn't just beat another human being almost to death.
And they think I'm a freak.

***

Mia's birthday celebration was almost over when I sneaked away from Cassius, not wanting to deal with any more shit. The guests are clearing out, and the only ones that remain scattered around the Volpe home are the house cleaners helping Mrs. Volpe clean the mess that was made. I ran into her when I was being led to the bathroom inside the mansion to clean off the idiot kid's blood, and Cassius and I found her trying to conceal a very fresh-looking bruise on her right cheek. We didn't stop to ask if she was okay.
I didn't care enough to do so, and Cassius was too busy hurrying me to clean the blood off my face and hands. I don't know what his hurry is. I've never looked better than I do now.
With a satisfied smile and busted-up knuckles.

I didn't lie to the girl when I told her father is a bitch. He is the biggest one I know after Benedetto, of course. He likes flaunting the hurt he causes his family to everyone that will see and listen. Natalia Volpe recovered quickly after running into us in the hallway leading up to the guest bathroom. She excused herself and acted as if nothing had happened. As if we didn't witness the scars left behind after the abuse she clearly suffered.

I might have trouble understanding human emotions and their reactions to other human beings' odd behavior at times, but something I learned from nonna and even my father is that women—good women— are meant to be treasured and not hurt. My nonna is a good one.

Something tells me Natalia Volpe is too.

She must be because her three children are the very best of the three families. They're also the weakest.

They love, and to love means to lose a part of yourself to another. That makes them weak in my and most of the members' eyes.

They're good.

Too good.

Even I know that.

Too good for this shit.

I find myself walking past the kitchen where the servers are clearing out and make my way to the main entrance. One of grandfather's lap dogs surely must be waiting to take us home. I'm ready to leave.

When I'm almost to the main doors, I stop dead when I hear the loud, distinct voice of Benedetto. "You know damn well they won't stop until they make us pay for your mistake. They are relentless." Benedetto never raises his voice and never breaks the calm and gentlemen-like persona unless he's dealing with an enemy.

A rat.

I move slowly toward the sound of his voice, trying not to get caught. Sticking my head out, I squint my eyes, trying to see who the person on the end of Benedetto's wrath is, but the hallway is too dark for me to see clearly. All I can make out is a tall figure.

That's all I can spot.

It could be anyone.

"They have no fucking proof that it was me." A whisper-shout slips past the mouth of the other man. It sounds desperate. He reeks of desperation. "S-she was the one I wanted. I fucking—" His slurs sound just like my father when he drowns his pathetic sadness in his favorite bottle.

"Listen to me, Tomas." Ah, I should've known by his trembling tone. Tommaso Volpe. The volatile one. "Your daughter's blood is filth. Now, I allowed you to keep the girl, but over my dead fucking body will she ever have a right to your title. Do you understand me? She's not fully Italian." Who is he referring to? Giana or Cara? I knew there was something different about the little brat. Something that didn't quite fit in here with us. "It's not enough that Parisi birthed a defective child, but you had to keep a child with the same blood as theirs." Benedetto seethes.

Tommaso sighs before trying to reason, "Boss, my other children don't have what it takes, but she does. She's me. I see it in her eyes every time I look at her." The idiot man pleads, damn well knowing there's no reasoning with his boss. His word is the law around here and rarely does he ever concede.

"Listen to yourself." Benedetto laughs harshly in disdain. "That child is all her. She's the whore's. You're delusional if you believe she will ever be capo material. Bastards weren't born to sit on thrones. Get that through your thick skull before I must take matters into my own hands."

I hear an intake of breath before a loud thump sounds. "Fuck." Tommaso whispers apologetically.

"Don't forget who you are, Tommaso." Benedetto spits. "You're my fucking underboss. You are beneath me, and you'll always be. Now, handle this shit before it infects my city." With that parting comment, hard steps sound, and I push back into the wall to remain unseen.

Benedetto steps out, but Tommaso remains in place.

I don't move from my position in the dark hall until he does. Until he makes a call.

I don't know who he calls, but what he says next will change the life of all the Volpe children.

The sins of the father will fall upon the daughter.

All that runs through my mind as I make my way outside to finally leave this day behind is not the celebration, Mia's crying face, or the blood on my hands, but the nasty words Benedetto and Samael spewed referring to the girl.

Filth.

That child is all her.

Whore's.

No title.

Bastard.

"Are you good?" My twin whispers as we both get inside the Bentley to take us home. Benedetto sits on the passenger seat, rubbing his temple as if he had a day from hell. My eyes trail down to his exposed neck now that he has loosened his tie, and I closely watch where his pulse is supposed to be.

One.

Two.

Three.

I take in deep breaths and practice the bullshit technique Cassius taught me that helps me fight off the urge to shove one of his favorite knives into his neck.

I smile and turn to look at my twin's face. A mirror of my own. "I'm better than ever, little bro." He narrows his eyes, but doesn't correct me like he usually does.

Bro.
What an atrocious term.
Tino must be thinking the same.
 Oh, well. I'll do whatever it takes.
I'll play the part grandfather wants until I get it all.
Until I am the last one standing.
With a title.
With everything.
With his blood on my hands and his crown sitting proudly on my head.

CHAPTER SIX
TRUTHS

"You are magic, baby girl." – N

Cara

10 years old

"Sweet girl, why are you still up?" I hear mommy's soft whisper as she quietly steps inside my room. I always notice how she looks scared all the time. Scared to talk. Scared to come closer. Sometimes I even think she's scared to hold me.
Now, I know why.
She's afraid of him.
Dad.
They're all afraid of him, and for good measure.
My heart hurts inside my chest every time I think of what they've gone through and how helpless I am. Things seemed to be going well in our household. Mommy was smiling more. Lucan was even drawing more pretty pictures and leaving them on my bottom desk drawer for me to find.
Giana came out of her room more.
And none of them seemed to have visible bruises.
Until today.
I tried my best to get daddy's attention away from them, but clearly, by the purple-ish bruise on mommy's cheek, I didn't do a great job. Frustrated tears threatened to fall, but I held them back.

If mommy sees me cry, then it'll only worry her more. I have to be strong. I have to be strong for them and not give them a reason to worry about me. My pain is nothing compared to theirs. I remind myself that every time I feel frustrated or sad.I look up at mom's face and smile my best smile. The one I practiced every day in the mirror until I fully perfected it. Until it was impossible for my loved ones to see through it.
"I was waiting for my goodnight snuggles." I whisper, finding the strength to fake it for her. "I thought you forgot about me."Mommy laughs softly and then takes a seat at the end of my bed, leaning her body toward me. "How could I ever forget you, Cara Mia? You are a part of me. The very best of me." With gentle hands, she brings my small hand toward her lips and kisses my palm twice. "Like all my babies."
I sometimes think how unreal my mommy is. She looks like a Disney princess with her unique beauty and grace. Her long honey-brown hair falls in soft waves down her delicate face and passes her shoulders. Her eyes are cat-like and a stunning green that only adds to her beauty and gentle presence. I look nothing like her, and it used to bother me until I realized that maybe I was not blessed with her stunning good looks like Giana and Lucan did, but I got her heart. The most beautiful and valuable part of my mom. We all inherited it. The subtle movement of her hand makes me look down at her lap, and there I find a small black notebook.
Pointing at it, I ask, "What's that?"
Mom looks down at the black notebook and smiles. "This was left on top of the pile of presents you were gifted." She hands it to me. "Here, take a look inside." There's a smile in her tone.
I quickly grab the notebook and open it to the first page. It doesn't say whose it is from, but at the bottom of the page, written in black ink, it says 'little monster'.
Little monster.

I find myself smiling down at the rare gift.

There's only one person that calls me that odd nickname.

I've yet to discover if it's a term of endearment or an insult. When it comes to him, maybe it's both.

I flip the pages. Images appear out of nowhere as sketches and doodles, like a film. There's a drawing of a girl with wild hair blowing softly in the wind as if it's on fire. A big bright smile on her face, and she's draped in an oversized black hoodie. She doesn't look like a girly girl but a tomboy.

Is this... me?

I keep flipping the pages, and lighting appears around the girl, followed by a drawing of a tornado, rain drops all around her and puddles of water around her small feet.

The storms?

Did he draw this?

Finally, the last pages are of the girl smiling while jumping over puddles of mud.

How?

When?

Wow.

The sketches tell the story of... me.

The day we first spoke.

Holding the notebook close to my chest, I smile brightly up at my mom. The gift brought the biggest smile to my face. To my mom's face as well.

"That's quite an impression you've made, baby girl." Her amused face lets me know she wants to know more, but I don't want to say.

At least not yet.

So, I hold her hand and scoot closer to her body, wanting to feel her warmth. "I love you, mom." Changing the subject.

"And I, you, my baby." The smile drops from her face and, for a second, I wonder if I said something wrong. "You must've been pretty scared today."

My brows furrow, not understanding what she means. "Today?"

"The disturbing scene the Nicolasi kid caused at your birthday party." Mommy sighs, and with the hand that's not holding mine, she pushes a tendril of hair that has fallen free from the messy bun on top of my head behind my ear. "There was a lot of blood. It must've been so scary for you. Is that why you were crying?"

"I was not afraid, mom." I tell her the truth, suddenly bothered by her thinking that Lorenzo scares me. He does not. "H-he was only defending me." There, I said it.

I inwardly groan because now she will ask, and I don't want to make her sad, but I couldn't let her think that it was all Lorenzo's fault. Yes, what he did was a bit much, but sometimes people only learn with violence, or so he's said.

"Defending you?" Mom's voice sounds concerned. "Defending you from whom, exactly?"

"Samael."

"Melinda's son?" Her brows furrow. Mommy sometimes has dinner with Melinda, a haughty woman that looks down at me every time she comes to visit.

"Yes."

"Did he— did he hurt you, Cara?" I've never heard mommy sound so harsh. Even the look in her eyes is one I've never witnessed before. Mommy is demure and soft in every way. I've never seen this side before.

"He just called me a name. It's stupid." I hung my head, not wanting her to see my expression. After the party was over, I searched for the word bastard.

A child whose parents are not married.

Samael is not only mean, but he is stupid, too.

My parents are married, so the hateful word doesn't apply to me. "What did he call you?"

"Bastard. He called me a bastard." I sigh.

A strange silence follows. Mommy doesn't say anything, and I look up to find her looking down at me as if she's seen a ghost. *What's wrong?*

Suddenly a loud bang sounds from downstairs, and loud footsteps sound in the distance. What is going on?

I feel gentle hands grab my face. "Listen to me closely, Cara." Mommy's words are rushed and almost… desperate, but not sad. She does not look scared at all. Only determined. "I need you to listen closely and always remember that I love you. I love you more than there are stars in the sky, scars on my skin and heart. You are a part of me just the same as my other children."

"What's going on, mommy?" The shouts in the distance become louder, making me nervous. Why is mommy talking this way? She always tells me she loves me, and when words fail her, she lets her actions speak instead.

"My beautiful heart-daughter." Mom brings my body closer to her until my chest presses against hers. "There's something I must confess. Something you need to know."

There, for the second time in my short life, my world spins on its axis and not in a good way.

Mom shares her truths, and the next day, she is gone.

Nothing was ever the same.

Nothing will ever be again.

Part of my heart left with my mom.

CHAPTER SEVEN
STORMY NIGHTS

"Where are you? I need you." - C

Cara

11 years old

A storm is fast approaching, the newscaster says as he shows a slideshow of all the areas of the city that will be impacted by it. It's been raining all week, and I haven't been outside to enjoy the rain and the spooky weather like I usually do when there's a storm outside. I shut my computer off, not wanting to listen to any more of the news. There's always something going on in the world, and lately none of it good. When the world inside these walls seems as if it's caging me in, I tune into the news or even social media now that I was gifted a computer for last Christmas.

Rising from the bed, I place the computer down on my nightstand right next to a copy of my favorite romance novel as of lately. The news and my silly books, as some of the house cleaners call them, are my escape lately.

Rain begins to pour outside, pulling my attention to the window. Is he out there? There is a storm coming, and I should feel a thrill since I love this weather, but I do not.

The storm inside my heart has numbed me to the point nothing brings me joy.

Nothing feels right anymore.

Nothing lifts my spirits lately.

The mansion is quiet, and I swear if I concentrate hard enough, I can hear the walls weeping, but it's just me.
I know I am not alone, even if that is how it feels.
My brother is here, but not really.
I can tell his mind is elsewhere.
Lucan doesn't cry.
He's just angry all the time, and he now sports more bruises than he did before.
Both of them do.
Agonizing pain takes over me every time I open my eyes in the morning and face the cruel reality that the heart of this dark home is gone.
Mommy left us.
That's what daddy said, but I know better.
She wouldn't leave willingly. A fact I told daddy, and he lashed out at me like he's never done before. I told the same thing to Lucan, and he closed up and shut me out.
No one believes me.
No one hears me.
Not even Gigi.
They don't care anymore.
How could they not care when she gave everything to us?
For us.
Her pride.
Her heart.
Her soul.
Thunder sounds in the distance at the same time as an ugly crack forms in my heart.
Walking toward the window, I move the curtain aside and stare into the dark night. The moon is very bright and full tonight, with tiny stars twinkling around it, and yet I feel nothing. Nothing good.
Not even the ugly weather and pretty moon can brighten my mood.

Here inside this room, where no one can see me, I let the tears fall. I don't have to be brave and strong. I don't have to pretend all is well. I can let it all go and cry for the woman that made my heart sing with joy every time she kissed me good night and hugged me hello. The woman who would put herself on the line of fire for us, knowing the burn would hurt like hell.

"Where are you, mommy?" I whisper into the night, but only silence greets me.

I'm sorry.

I'm so sorry.

Because of me, you are gone.

Lightning appears in the sky, followed by another thunderous sound. I now understand why Gigi said that when the sky cries, heaven loses an angel. Because that's exactly what it feels like to lose her, even though this home is no heaven.

It is barely a home now that she's gone.

Daddy has gone on with his life as if mom was never a part of it to begin with.

Heart-daughter. That's what she called me the last time I saw her when she kissed me goodnight after telling me a truth that broke my heart, and yet in this very moment, the pain I felt back then feels so insignificant now.

Barely there because the pain I feel now is too much to bear.

"Lean on your siblings, Cara. They'll need you now more than ever." Sighing, I push away from the window and head to bed.

Storms only last for so long, little love. The next day the sun will come.

I'm not so sure, mom.

How can it be when you're gone?

CHAPTER EIGHT
STOLEN KISSES

"Sweet poison that's exactly what you are." - C

Cara

14 years old

This can't be that hard.

I drop the magazine onto the floor and move around, trying to get comfortable before I start the mission.

Mission: New hairstyle to get rid of the old lady look I have at the moment.

Dad won't let me get my hair professionally done because he says I'm too young. Therefore, I'm taking matters into my own hands. I hate asking him for stuff anyway.

I remove the Red Sox cap from my head before the swooshing sound of the walkie-talkie Lucan gifted me for Christmas interrupts my concentration. Only one person could be waiting at the end of the line.

"It will rain soon. Come down." My brother's tough voice sounds extremely loud inside the small tree house. I made this little place my place away from the world, and lately, I wish I could stay here and never come down.

I press the button on the left side and say, "I will spend the night up here, Dad is away, and no one will find out." I snap. I'm tired, and I'm mad. Not mad at my brother. Never him,

but at Dad. As the years flew by, I started to see my father for who he is. A man that does the things he does to his children is not capable of love and is not worthy of it either. How could I ever love a man who hurts the two people I love the most in this world?
A father who hurt a mother until he made her disappear.
That's easy.
I can't.
They say love lives inside us forever, even when the other person disappoints us, hurt us. It is not true, love can be killed.
Selfishness.
Hatred.
Absence.
All of that can kill love, and it did.
I don't love my father anymore even when I promised Mom, I would never let my heart be corrupted by the pain he caused. I failed her.
I'm thankful for the soft-spoken words of my brother coming from the gadget. "Have it your way, topina. If the weather gets worse, I'll go grab you myself."
"Understood." I mumble.
"And Cara Mia?"
"Yes?"
"Ti amo."
And just like that, my bad mood disappears and I feel warm all over on this rainy night. My brother is not someone of many words like my sister Giana, and he doesn't express his feelings like most people do, but I know he loves me. He loves me the most.
"I love you, too, Superman."
Light chuckling sounds before he disconnects.
Smiling, I drop the gadget onto the carpeted floor and crawl around the tree house, looking for the scissors I dropped

before I answered Lucan.
Where was I?
Ah, right.
The hair.
Looking at myself in the mirror, I try to see what they — the ones who think of me as ugly— see. Pale skin and red-flaming hair, unhinged, never styled to perfection like most girls at the academy keep theirs. It's wild. It's free. It's me. There's a subtle dusting of freckles right on top of my cheeks, but barely visible unless you look closely. From afar, you can't tell I have them. My lips are not soft pink like my sister's, but a natural red, and one of the lips — the bottom one— is plumper than the top one, giving me a doll-like look. My teeth are pearly white but not perfectly straight because that is one thing I am not. Perfect.
I'm me.
Don't really know how else to describe myself.
So, I concluded that the ones that run their mouths about how ugly or lacking they find me are only projecting their own insecurities. If it makes them feel better to belittle me to raise themselves up, so be it. I know my worth.
A loud snap like a tree branch breaking snaps me out of my thoughts, making me look away from my reflection in the mirror. Instead, my eyes trail the tree house. Taking everything in, a sigh of relief leaves me.
This little treehouse has seen me grow up more than my father has. In here, I've spent countless hours that turned into days and nights away from home whenever I'm able to step away.
In here, I am not a girl without a mother and an overbearing father that loves to pretend everything is well in my world.
In here, I don't have to pretend to love him just so he keeps away from my siblings. I don't pretend that my efforts are slowly failing as the years pass and my siblings harden

their hearts to shield them from our father's cruel hands.
In here, I am not the bastard princess of the Volpe family.
I am me.
I am Cara.
The girl who loves fantasy romance and vintage comic books. The same girl who enjoys flipping through magazines and admires art and the latest fashions. The one that binge-watches 90's sitcoms because everyone knows that modern TV shows are a poor substitute for the good old days. I don't know where I got my love for comics and vintage stuff from since both my parents weren't into it, and my siblings aren't either.
But then I remember there's her.
The woman I know nothing about and the one I'm too afraid to think of.
Shaking my head, I take in the twinkling white lights hanging from one side of the treehouse to the other, giving the room a magical glow in the dark night. The posters of superheroes decorate the walls, replacing the ugly frames of unicorns and Disney princesses that were forced on me so long ago. A furry black rug lays down on the floor, right next to a large white beanbag. The same one I sit on for hours reading to make the time pass away.
The same beanbag that still smells like him.
No one comes up here anymore.
Not my siblings.
Not the house staff to clean and organize the treehouse.
No one.
Just me.
Just him.
Thunder cracks in the distance, and I wonder why he's late. The first time he was here was not the last. He came back. Sometimes, he just stares at me while I talk, and others, he watches my favorite series with me until I fall asleep,

but something never changes.
As soon as the sun rises, he's gone.
He'll be here.
He never fails.
Shaking my head, I pick up the scissors from the floor and scoot closer to the small mirror I have sitting up in a corner. I look down at the magazine with the supermodel-turned-fashion mogul, Valerie Turner. It's an old photo of hers. One from when she first started, and now Swizs Magazine is paying her an homage. She's effortlessly stunning, but what's most beautiful about her is her heart. I don't know her personally, but I read about all her good deeds, and she's remarkable. She's not just a pretty model on a cover or a genius businesswoman, but she's a humanitarian as well. I stare closely at the hairstyle she's sporting and try to give myself the same one. It can't be that hard. My hair is already styled the same way. I just need to get my bangs right.
Sticking my tongue out in concentration, I gather a chunk of my hair and slice it. The sound of the scissors slicing my hair should give me anxiety since lord knows I don't know what the hell I am doing, but hey, it's just hair. Right? It'll grow back., eventually.
"You fucked up, Red." I'm momentarily startled by his gravelly voice. I should be used to this by now, but he always manages to catch me off guard.
Looking at myself in the mirror, I see I indeed fucked up my hair. Okay, it doesn't look so bad, besides I can always cover it with a cap or push it back with a headband. Whatever.
"It's not that bad." I mumble, brushing the bangs sideways, trying to make them stick to one side.
"It looks like shit." He mutters.
"Geez, tell me how you really feel." I can always count on him to tell me the truth.
He doesn't spare feelings. Ever.

"I always do." He grunts before he climbs all the way until he's completely inside the small space. I look at his reflection in the mirror, and I take a moment to shamelessly take him all in. There's something about Lorenzo that makes you believe God carved him himself, paying extra attention to detail while creating him, but that's the irony since there isn't anything Holy about the man-boy standing at my back.

His boyish looks are gone, and now, at sixteen, he looks like a man. A man with sharp cheekbones, inky black hair, and the palest blue eyes. He always had a bad boy aura around him, with dark clothing and a permanent scowl on his face whenever I saw him, but now, he not only looks bad to his core but cruel and sometimes frightening. Now, he has dark tattoos inked on his knuckles, neck, and chest. Not long ago, I found out he did them himself. I knew he was good at sketching from the illustration he gifted me for one of my birthdays, but he is extremely talented. The tattoos on his skin seem almost real. There's this one dragon on wrapped around his left arm, from his bicep to his wrist. The dragon is breathing fire and has glowing red eyes. How does he do that. I don't know. He has his right ear pierced with three-diamond studs perfectly aligned one after the other. He has an eyebrow piercing, too. Everything about him screams danger. The kind of danger most girls would fall on their knees for, without a care of the repercussions.

He. Is. Trouble.

Always has been.

And it has nothing to do with the blood clearly visible on his hands or his split knuckles.

Yet, girls at the academy flock around him, begging for his attention, not caring how horrible he treats them. He does treat them like they are replaceable because they are. For him, they are.

Not wanting to think about him with other girls

and what that means for me, I offer him a genuine smile because even when I hurt, I smile through the pain.

"I thought you had a game tonight." I murmur as I leave my spot in front of the mirror and crawl to the beanbag before taking a seat. Sniffing the air, I smile, making grabby hands at him. Double stacked bacon cheeseburger, my favorite.

He drops fully onto the floor with his back to the wall before he reaches inside the greasy takeout bags and pulls out the food, tossing it my way. One burger for me and two for him. One thing I've noticed throughout our unusual meetups is that he eats more than a pregnant lady with quadruplets.

Two cokes.

One large and the other medium-sized.

French fries, three orders of onion rings, and five boxes of chicken tenders.

He brought enough to feed his football team.

I quickly grab the burger and wait for him to push the bacon and cheese French fries my way. My mouth is watering just by the smell alone. The onion rings won't ever be appetizing to me. I mentally gag and push them away from me. He can have them like he always does.

I have a weakness for candy, junk food, and my best-kept secret…

Lorenzo.

Ever since I was a kid and told him how candy and junk food were banned from our home, he takes it upon himself to bring me my favorite candies and foods on the rare times he comes up here. Before, he did it every time it rained, but after, he started coming around whenever he felt like it and brought me food or a comic.

Now that he's mister popular, captain of the football team, and the academy's most eligible fuck boy, his visits are rare, but I still treasure them the same.

Many things have changed between us.

For example, before, he used to spend hours without speaking a word, and he would sit as far away from me as he possibly could, but now, he touches me. My hair. My hands.
He draws fake tattoos on me whenever he doesn't feel like talking. I let him practice on me. I don't mind. Not really.
I could never mind when all of it brings a smile to my face every time.
I need more of that.
Genuine smiles.
I watch him bite into his burger and shrug. "Didn't feel like playing tonight." He says between chews and stares my way as if I just asked him a dumb question. Condescending jerk. "What? You actually miss an opportunity to cause major pain on your opponents?" I tell him dramatically, causing him to roll his eyes at me. Laughing, I eat the last bite of my burger and take a sip of his drink. He hates it. I know he does when I take his things, eat his food, or touch anything that's his. I still do it anyway because he lets me. He doesn't deny me. It bugs him that he can't deny me anything lately. I've noticed that much.
The straw drops from my lips when I hear him say, "Why was the little fucker here yesterday?"
"Who?"
"Don't act dumb." He says lazily, while shoving his leftovers inside the takeout bag. "It doesn't suit you. You're the smartest person I know."
That is not true.
He knows it, too.
There are people who are smarter than me, both book smart and street smart. For example, his own brother and my siblings. I'm not belittling myself, but I know my strengths. I have to study twice as hard as my siblings because academics don't come so easy for me.
I'm more interested in the arts.

Fashion.

Literature, and not the classics either.

Every time I mention I love to read, everyone assumes I stay home at night reading Hamlet.

Nope.

I rather stay at home and read about the bad boy billionaire who falls madly in love with the outcast girl after making her life shit.

Riveting, isn't it?

I'm pulled away from my thoughts when a cold French fry hits my forehead.

Damn bully.

Flipping him off, I grab a napkin to wipe off ketchup from my skin. He usually finds my defying him amusing, but not in this instant.

He looks frozen with his gorgeous yet infuriating gaze burning holes into my skin. *What is he going on about?*

Oh, right. Little fu— I mean Jonah. My friend. Right, right.

I clear my throat, feeling shy suddenly. "We came up here to finish our end-of-the-year science project. It's worth half our grade. We have to make a model of—"

"I don't give a fuck what you came up here to do." Blue eyes resembling a vengeful storm stare back at me, trying to intimidate me. This is something I learned recently, too. He loves to play games with me. It started as silly and innocent games of cat and mouse, hide, and seek, but through the years, it graduated to things more to his speed. He likes to make me nervous to the point I stutter my words. Sometimes, I watch him study me in silence as if he's trying to decipher what goes through my head. How my brain functions. Other times, he does creepy things like poke dead birds with a stick, or stares absently at his bloody hands after a fight to see if I run screaming, but I never do and it irritates him.

I don't cower, even if I sometimes get scared when

he pushes the limits. "Why do you ask, then?" I find my voice and meet his stare head on.

"Cut that shit out."

"And what might I ask, do I need to cut out?" I play with an invisible string on my sleeve.

"Bringing him up here."

"This is my place, and he is my friend. He will always be welcome here." I know I'm pushing it, but I do enjoy when I ruffle his not-so-delicate feathers. "No."

"You're not the boss of me, Enzo." I tell him, narrowing my eyes, not backing down.

Lorenzo steps forward, his eyes turn darker, and I swear it feels like he's draining the room of air as if I'm underwater. Without giving me time to push away from him, he comes closer, almost touching my nose with his. My breath hitches, and my stomach tightens when I realize how close I am to his mouth.

My family would skin him alive if they found us in this position. They would bury him right next to the bird if they found me in any position with Lorenzo, even the most innocent one. Then, I think about how I've never been this close to a boy before. Not even Jonah.

"What did you say to me?" His voice sends a chill down my spine, and for a second and only a second, I think about backing down and giving him what he so clearly wants. But I was never one to back down from a challenge, especially one that he started.

I push closer to his face until my nose is squished with his, and I almost blush when I feel his hot breath on my face. Don't blush, Cara. Don't give out how inexperienced you are. Hold your own against this beautiful nightmare. "I. Said. You're. Not. The. Boss. Of. Me."

A low growl escapes him before I feel him move away from me. I don't know what comes over me.

I think I've lost my mind, but the next thing I know, I'm snaking my arm behind his neck, pulling him closer until my lips are pressed against his. Oh, I did it now. His entire body goes rigid against mine for a moment, and then something I never imagined would happen does. His body goes limp and soft under my touch. Oh, my. I'm kissing him, and he's not pulling away. Why is he not pulling away? There is no tongue like I see in the movies.

It's innocent.

It's barely a kiss, but it means something.

I know it does.

Then, Lorenzo abruptly pushes himself away from me as if my kiss burned him. Maybe it did.

Reality comes crashing down, and as I stare into his startled gaze, I realize I messed up big time. What did I do?

I just kissed my best mate.

Lorenzo.

My Enzo.

I don't know what came over me. I don't even have the words to explain myself to him. I can't just say I'm sorry. So that's what I do.

"I'm—"

He angrily pushes himself off the floor and crawls like a demon on fire to the open door. Once half of his body is outside the tree house, he turns to me with an unreadable expression on his face. Not anger.

I know what his anger looks like.

This is something else, something I can't decipher.

He opens his mouth, and I'm sure he will tell me off. He will shout at me how he's done with our unusual friendship, but he does the opposite. "I better not catch the kid up here again." With that, he climbs out and leaves me there, wondering what the hell came over me and why it would matter to him if Jonah was up here with me.

Emotions.
Now, I understand why he loathes them.
I'm starting to think that maybe he has it right.
Emotions just play with our hearts.
Sighing, I shut off all the lights inside the treehouse and climbed out the same way he did.
Hopefully, this is not the last time I see him.
It wasn't.
He was always close even when I didn't see him.
It's safe to say that Jonah never visited my treehouse again.
Not because he told me to, although it might seem that way, but because something inside me told me Lorenzo felt betrayed, even if he couldn't express it to me.
This is our secret.
Our place.
Ours.
Nobody else's.

CHAPTER NINE
BEST FRIENDS

"I'm a stranger in my own skin. All thanks to her." - L

Lorenzo

16 years old

Another day, another fight.
Fight nights are every night in the Nicolasi household. We go at it between the families and some of the men that work for Benedetto. We go round after round pummeling each other until around sun-up. Fighting is in our DNA. It goes with the territory when you run the underground business of a city. We fight for money.
We fight for fun.
Sometimes some of the men do it to get rid of pent-up energy.
Not me.
I do it for fun.
Always fun.
The cash is a plus.
Nights like tonight are when we make the most of the fighting. More cash than usual comes in when then men around here get fucked up, run their mouths, and throw money around with bets they lose every year. Hell, every day. Yet they do not learn.

Tonight is All Hollow's Eve.

Some say it is a night to be feared.

When the damned come out to join us for one night a year, or so nonna says. She is fond of old folktales and repeating shit that makes no sense. The damned are already walking the earth and not hiding in dark corners waiting to snatch a soul. No. Evil is here. Evil walks among us every day. It can lurk behind a friendly smile or a kind gesture you wouldn't even know it.

Yet the naïve believe in ghosts and monsters with horns and claws come out to play on this night.

Tonight though, idiots run around the crowded street dressed as their favorite superhero, mass murderer, or Disney princess. They go around the city stirring up shit, drinking, partying, and fucking till the wee hours of the morning. This city doesn't sleep on Halloween.

It's the most wonderful time of the year.

For me, at least.

I've been on edge all week, and not even a hard fuck with one of the bitches from school has helped with my shitty mood. It'll only serve to piss me off more than I already am. Paisley, my on-call pussy is getting on my last damn nerve lately, asking for shit I never promised.

Dates.

Meeting parents.

Attending the academy's festivities as a fucking couple. Jesus, fuck. The hell's gotten into her?

I never once treated her like the girl you bring home to your mother. And me not having one is not the only reason I would never bring her around, or anyone really.

Sex.

That is what I want from her.

Her pussy.

Not her love, not her heart.

Fucking.

That's it.

A hard punch to my left cheek makes me stumble backward on the ring but helps to get me out of my head. Fuck. This motherfucker has a mean hook.

"That felt fucking good." A smug-looking Lucan says as he rounds me and then ducks once when I return the punch. I miss his face, but I crack a rib. I know by the way his left eye twitches, and his body bends forward, trying to ease the pain. Keep laughing, bitch.

"And I bet that felt even better." He wheezes in pain, and through gritted teeth, he tells me to fuck off but not once does the crazy asshole give up. He throws punch after punch, but there's not much he can do to me with a broken rib.

We go at it for two more rounds before I throw the last punch, sending him down.

Fighting the asshole is always a delight. I get to pound his pretty face and shut his mouth in the same process.

"It's always a pleasure fucking you up, love." I smile down at him while wiping the sweat and blood from my face with the back of my hand. This shit always makes me feel alive. The sick fuck that I am.

"Alright, you mouthy fuck," Lucan says, gripping the right side of his body while attempting to get up from the floor. I stick my hand out to help him up. Normally, he would rather chop his arm off instead of accepting my help, but tonight he does.

Emotions.

His are all over the place, I can tell.

It was in the way he fought recklessly and miscalculated every hit.

His head wasn't in it, and in this job, one mistake can cost you your life.

Your head should always be in the game.

I force my eyes from his hand, meeting his gaze.

He knows I know.

That everyone knows, yet he holds my stare. Never one to cower.

Lucan Volpe wears his emotions on his face, and I've yet to uncover if it's a weakness or his strength.

I'm leaning toward weakness.

His mother is one.

A weakness, I mean.

Everyone knows she left her husband and kids not long ago and never looked back. Everyone with a brain also knows shit like that never happens in our world. Both women and men are not that lucky to walk out alive. They go, but never willingly.

There are only two ways you can walk away from the families.

Number #1: You turn rat and get whacked.

Wouldn't recommend that.

Number #2: You start a war and win.

No one has the balls to stand up to the Holy Trinity of Detroit, so that is unlikely to ever happen.

We both step outside the ring, and then he's dropping cash down on the table where the men are handling the bets and splitting the earnings between them.

Sometimes, I keep the money. Others, I let the Nicolasi men split it between them. It's not like I need it, and, it also gives me points with them.

They believe I'm one of them.

In some ways, I am.

What they don't know is that I fight them not to fit in or win brownie points with them but because I genuinely enjoy beating the absolute shit out of them and spilling their blood. Some of them get to walk away with only some bruises that will fade within a week, but some aren't so lucky.

Those are the most fun.

After the incident with the little punk kid that hurt Cara, I was never the same. I always felt the sick urges boiling under the surface of who I trained myself to be so I could fit myself into the annoying little boxes Benedetto and even society laid out for me. That day, I let my true nature out to play, and I haven't stopped since.

I fight.

I taunt.

I play mind games with my prey until they meet sweet, sweet death.

At only sixteen, I've killed many men and women disguised as the dutiful soldier in line for the throne, but in reality, I do it to satiate the hunger. The need.

To kill.

I don't ever feel guilt.

Not about the killings, anyway.

A normal person would.

A sane one would be ashamed of sending another human being to hell with a smile on their face, but I don't feel it. I don't feel anything good. Normal feelings healthy humans feel. Happiness. Love. Empathy. I can't associate those types of emotions, and I'm counting on never.

One thing for sure has changed lately.

I have been paying no mind, trying to shove it back down to the obscure part of my brain where I can never think about it again, but it is futile.

I felt something.

Guilt.

Fucking guilt.

Not toward my victims.

Not my family.

But her.

Mia.

I felt guilty that night. When she leaned forward and touched her innocent lips to mine.

There was no doubt in my mind that the kid was hurting. Grieving the loss of her mother and she needed some sort of comfort.

People need that shit when they feel sad or some shit like that, and that day, she lost her goddamn mind and acted on impulse.

I watch and study her.

She fascinates me like no one has ever been able to before.

Not in a sexual way.

She's a child, for fuck's sake, and an impressionable one at that. But there's something else in her, too, that keeps me going back.

I'm not interested in her heart.

Or anyone's heart, for that matter.

Cara Mia has fire in her. One that burns so bright, it's almost impossible to put out. No matter how hard life kicks that kid down, she cries, wipes her tears, and doesn't stay down for long. She sees all the dark shit that I do and stays around.

That kid must be cut from the same cloth I am.

She's a whole lot saner.

Sometimes, I try to push her limits to see how far she'll go. If she will break and run off screaming like most do, but she never does. She sits quietly reading some days, and others, she talks my ear off. I don't know when or how, but I started getting used to her presence.

To the point that I need her around.

I need to make sure she's alright.

That she's eaten.

That no one's messed with her.

Fuck.

I lowered my walls, and without regard to her own sanity and wellbeing, she slipped past and made room for herself.

A hard clap to my back brings me back to the now. Lucan is already dressed, with his keys in hand, ready to step out. "See you later, man. Need to get my topina her costume." He grimaces clearly in pain, yet he smiles when he mentions his sister. If only he knew that his little topina sneaks off at night to see me. If he knew his baby sister kissed me, Valentino would be putting dead flowers on my grave.

I would be dead.

I could taunt him with that tidbit of information. I do enjoy riling him up to the point his head looks like it'll explode at any given moment, but damn it. Using her to hurt her brother seems wrong, and fuck me twice with a corkscrew, because I care.

I. Don't. Care.

But lately I'm losing my fight against the brat.

She's grown to be ballsy and tends to run her mouth and give me sass. If it were someone else, I would've shoved their eyeballs down their throat, but it's her.

It's Mia.

I've yet to understand why I need her around, and I'm not even sure I care to, but it is what it is.

She's here.

Inside my brain, like a vicious little tumor.

Growing every day, leaving me nothing but severe irreparable damage.

Fucking shit.

"Are you taking her to beg for candy on the streets?" I ask without looking his way. I concentrate on my bloody knuckles instead.

"Now, why do you gotta say it like that, man?" I follow him out of the underground gym in the mansion and walk toward the main gate to see him out. I find myself wanting to know more. "I'm taking both of my sisters trick or treating around the neighborhood, and Cara insists on going

as the billionaire with the hole in his chest. She's been down lately, understandably so." His tone turns dark.
Iron Man.
I should shoot myself for knowing that shit.
I grunt and watch as he steps inside his matte-black Maserati, roars the engine to life and lowers the tinted window, middle finger salutes me, and speeds the hell out of the driveway.
Prick.
The second he's gone, I spit blood on the ground and think back to what Lucan said.
She's feeling down...
Dammit.
Once I've showered and changed my clothes, I find myself heading out the door into the night.
Halloween Night.
Parties.
Hot and clueless chicks.
Mayhem.
I'm sure I'll find something to do to get out of my head.
Go fucking figure, all roads lead back to the brat.

CARA

It is a scary night tonight. The night of the haunted. Mom used to hate this night, and my big brother does, too.
 He says all the little shits go out on Halloween to cause trouble.
I get it.
A lot of kids get fucked up and do bad things on this night, but this night is like any other night. Kids do dumb stuff every night. They just get bolder on Halloween, knowing they will get away with most of the things they do tonight.
It's just another night for me.
Nothing different besides wearing a costume and knocking on doors, asking for candy.

That comes once a year, and I love when my brother spends time with me trick or treating.

Besides, I am not afraid, but I am cautious. My brother taught me to always be aware of what hides in the dark. I don't have the heart to tell him that those monsters are the ones closest to my twisted heart. Because I am not the girl, he thinks I am. I am not the kid that gravitates toward the light. Instead, I rejoice walking in the dark, holding onto the devil's hands. I've witnessed firsthand some of the twisted things my brother and Lorenzo do to the people they consider rivals or jobs, yet I care for them. Deeply.

I do.

Sighing, I reach for my back pocket, trying to reach the flashlight I always carry with me when I go out at night, but I don't feel it there. I must've left it at home when I changed into the costume Lucan got me.

Iron Man.

After years of being pretty witches, ladybugs, and princesses, this year, I opted to dress as my favorite superhero instead of what others wanted me to be for Halloween.

Being a pretty ladybug or princess always made mom smile. I agreed to wear the silly and boring costumes just for that, but she won't see me. She won't be here.

My heart clenches the moment I think of my mom.

I miss her every day.

Not a day goes by that I don't think of her.

That I don't wonder if she's okay. If she's with another man somewhere in the south of France, dipping her toes in the sand and basking in the sun, leaving behind not only her children, but the scars that cut deep from her past? Or is she dead, lying in a ditch, or buried somewhere no one will ever find her?

Debilitating guilt.

Excruciating pain.

Sometimes the feelings are so intense that I can't even find the strength to take deep breaths or keep my head above water. Somedays, I push through it, and others, I drown in the pain her absence left behind, just enough to remind myself that she was here. That she fought hard for us and loved us with the same ferocity.

Gigi might try to erase her memory to not feel the pain.

Lucan might taint his memories of her because he's hurt.

Not me, though.

I keep her memory alive, even when it cuts me deep.

I bleed for her.

When I bleed, I hurt, and when I hurt, the memory remains alive within me.

It won't ever leave me.

I won't forget.

Trying not to think of mom for too long, I concentrate on other things. For example, tonight.

After both Lucan and Gigi took me trick or treating around the neighborhood, like they always do, on the rare occasions Dad allows it, we found ourselves in the Parisi mansion. This year is their turn to host the Halloween get-together for the families.

I found it extremely odd since they rarely attend the events my family and the Nicolasi family host.

This year they did, though.

Thoughts of mom consumed my every thought while everyone else was having a good time, so I stepped out for a second to clear my head. I don't want to be sad. I don't want to be that girl. I want to be the happiness both my siblings are missing right now. If only for a little while, or for as long as they need it. Need me.

Looking to my right first and then my left, I try to find my way back to the mansion, but it is almost impossible to see clearly.

It's so dark outside that I can't seem to find my way back to the terrifying mansion. I hate it here. I always hate it when we visit the Parisi home. It's scary, even more so than ours. At least mom used to fill our home with love when Dad only screamed and hurt her and my siblings. Lucan and Giana still don't think I notice the screaming or the bruises on their skin, but I do. I've known for a while now, and I wish it were me. I wish I could take their place. I am the bastard child, after all. Not them. It is not right that they get it worse when I'm the shame of the family.

Taking a deep breath, I try to push the ugly thoughts to the back of my mind. Think positive, Cara. Don't be sad. Come on. For them. My daily self-pep-talk works enough that I manage to calm my breathing.

The night is chilly, and the sky is lit up by a full moon and stars. It is rare to be enjoying calm weather after weeks of only rain. I breathe in the night air until my lungs are full, then I release it. Here, I can breathe, while inside, I feel like I'm suffocating. There's always someone breathing down my neck in our house. If it's not Dad, then it is one of the many men and women that work for him.

"Boo!" A sinister and mocking voice sounds next to my right ear. I'm shortly startled, almost lose my footing, and fall face first down on the concrete floor. I was so lost in my head that I didn't hear him approach, but even paying the utmost attention wouldn't have made any difference. Lorenzo has the ability to appear out of nowhere without being caught. Yes, he always takes me by surprise, but I'm never afraid.

The funny thing is that it bothers him. Me not being afraid, I mean.

Oh, well.

I know who he is.

I wasn't scared of him when I was a child. I'm certainly not afraid now.

Lorenzo thinks he's so scary, but he really isn't. I find him amusing, but I don't think a lot of people share the same opinion. I find him fascinating. His beauty is scary, almost too perfect to be real. It's the kind that creeps up on you, and you don't even realize it until it's too late. Until it is too late for you to get out and save yourself the heartache. It is inevitable. He's much taller than the other boys around here and at school. He towers over me, and it's almost intimidating how small I am compared to him. He never makes me feel small, though. He makes me feel like I matter. Like I'm not the bastard most of the members in the family say I am. He has fought and bled for me. He's my accomplice. My ally. My... friend.

Nobody knows.

They can't.

Gigi once said that dating one of the other kids in the family is forbidden. Not that it matters, anyway. He made it abundantly clear that he's not interested.

My sister told me once that she heard Dad talking to Benedetto Nicolasi about potential marriages between the kids. The boss of the Nicolasi refused, saying that they don't want us to mix and pollute our blood. I think it's stupid, but nobody cares what I think. It's like my voice doesn't matter, and they try their best to silence me. I am not pureblood Italian, and to the Volpe family, that is a stain on their name. "Why are you here?" I whisper, trying my best to see him when it's this dark outside. "Why aren't you with your friends?" I know the older kids are throwing their own parties tonight. The popular kids. The ones Lorenzo loves to hang around so much lately.

I try not to be bitter about it but fail.

Silence falls upon us for a long minute before he replies. "You're here." Then he shrugs like it's nothing. Like that's reason enough. He confuses me so much.

When people are around, he never shuts up. He's the life of the party, but when it's just the two of us, he doesn't say much. Always staring off into the distance and answering my questions with grunts or one-word responses.
I won't deny that his simple response makes my heart skip a stupid beat.
"Why aren't you dressed up for the party?" Everyone has a costume, even my brother, who says Halloween is for babies. He smiles, and the only reason I know that is because the moonlight is shining down on him, and at this moment, he looks like a God. A very terrifying one. I was wrong, though. He has a costume. Black ripped pants, black shirt, and a skeleton mask with blood all over it. It looks kind of cool. So realistic. I step closer to him until my sneakers are touching his black boots. With my right hand, I reach up and touch his mask. It doesn't go unnoticed that the blood on it is warm and not gooey like fake blood should feel like.
I freeze, only for a second, before rubbing my fingers together and smearing the blood all over my fingers. Lorenzo hisses but doesn't pull away. "What have I told you about touching me, Red?"
Not wanting to give much thought to the blood, damn well knowing it is not fake. He was probably off fighting someone before he stopped by.
 "I didn't exactly touch you, did I?" I say what first comes to mind— what comes naturally when I'm with him, taunting and challenging him.
He laughs darkly.
It's kind of sick that his mocking laugh is my favorite sound.
"Are you afraid?" I feel him getting closer.
"Of you?"
 "Nothing else should scare you, Mia." He whispers harshly before taking my hand in a painful hold, but I don't show him it hurts.

Just a bit, but it hurts still. "No one will ever get close enough to hurt you."

"I'm not afraid of you." Grabbing his other hand, I tell him the truth. "You don't scare me, Lorenzo."

"You're so fucked-up, kid." He breathes out but doesn't pull away or shake my hold on him. "You should be afraid. The things I enjoy doing. The images that live in my head would scare even the bravest of men."

I think back to the time he squished the poor bird without care. I should've been afraid or at least concerned, but I wasn't. The time he came out of the bouncy castle with blood on his shirt, hands, and a satisfied grin on his handsome face. I wasn't scared then either.

"Well, I'm not." He grunts but says nothing else.

At times, I don't know which is worse. His silence or the fake persona he uses with the rest of the world. When he pretends to be someone he is not, that is the worst. Definitely. I rather have the real him. Moody. Quirky. Dark humor. Sarcastic.

That's who he is.

That's what lies beneath the boy-next-door persona he shows his peers at the academy.

But sometimes, I get irritated with him when he remains quiet. It infuriates me when he shuts me out, but I let it happen because when it comes to him — my favorite person in the world, I will always give him the space and quiet he sometimes needs. We stay silent in the dark for a couple of minutes, just holding each other's hands, when a ruffling sound in the distance spooks me. Someone is coming. Did someone hear us? Did someone see us?

"What is that?" I let go of Lorenzo's hand and started to walk in the direction the sound came from, but his strong hand on the back of my neck stopped me. Air leaves me for a moment, and I try my best to keep my composure and not show what his touch does to me.

It burns. It sends a shock of electricity through me. Always. "That is your treat." The hairs on the back of my neck stand the moment I feel his hot breath close to my ear. I shiver, not from the cold but from the contact of his hand on my skin. "My treat?"

"Trick or treat, little monster." He lets go of me, walks toward the bushes and grabs something from behind one of them. I squint, but I can't see much. Only his silhouette.

Lorenzo walks back to where I'm standing, and the moment he reaches the spot I'm standing in, I hear the cutest bark in the dark night. A dog. "You got another puppy?" I love his little beasts. They're terrifying, just like their owner. His father, Cassius, got him his first puppy, Amon, the day he got into his first fight at school. Mr. Nicolasi thought a companion would do Lorenzo some good, but that dog is as wicked as his owner. To this day, the dog refuses to learn tricks or behave in any shape or form.

"He's yours."

"Mine?" I reach for the tiny pup and instantly wish we had better lighting so I could see him better. I don't need to see him to know I will love him, though. The moment he's in my arms, I just know he's mine. "You got me a puppy?" The small puppy licks my face, making me smile aloud. Warm licks. So damn sweet. I fell in love for the second time in my short life.

"You've been bitching about getting a pup for a year now. I thought it might shut you up,"

"Cheer me up, you mean?" I sass him while trying to keep the pup from slipping through my arms. He wants down, but he's too small, plus I want him all to myself.

"Did you miss the part where I said shut you up?"

"Nope, but I think you meant to cheer me up."

"You're a brat."

"And yet you got me a puppy." I smile triumphantly, knowing he can't see me.

He says nothing to that and steps back to light a joint. I know what it is because my brother is always lighting one whenever he thinks he's alone. I see him. I see all of them, even when most people don't see me. My heart is young and might not always understand what it's feeling, but in that moment, I know that there's no one else I'd rather walk in the dark with than Lorenzo Nicolasi. I hold onto my new puppy and rise on my tippy toes so I can reach his face. I don't know what drives me to do it, but it feels right. It feels right every time I do it. I drop a soft kiss on his bloody mask.

And when I do, I feel his body begin to tense, but I remain glued to his front.

"Grim." I whisper up at him.

"W-what?" He clears his throat and pulls away. I sheepishly grin because I know I affect him just as much as he does me.

"That will be his name, Grim."

That night was one of many times Lorenzo cracked under my touch. He won't admit it, but I know it deep down in my soul. He fell for me then, without even understanding what he felt. Later, he will tell you he fell for me first.

Bullshit.

I did.

I fell for him the first time he carried me up the treehouse and gave me his hoodie to shelter me from the cold.

I fell every time he got me my favorite food and candies just to see me smile.

The time he showed me his dark urges. Whenever he lost control and hurt someone who wronged me.

I fell for a beautiful nightmare that each day, little by little, felt more like a sweet and twisted dream.

CHAPTER TEN
A WORLD OF MY OWN

"You are my Messiah." - C

Cara
14 years old

For over a year, we kept meeting in secret on nights where it was too dark and cold outside. Then he stopped coming as frequently as before.
It was gradually.
His visits at the tree house became less and less throughout the months.
It's funny how one innocent little kiss has the power to shift things. Change everything.
He never stopped being my friend, but he did try to put barriers around the friendship. I, on the other hand, always kept my walls down around him, letting him know that he was always welcome in my heart.
Inside the peaceful little world I created for myself.
Because I care about him.
I more than care, and maybe that's why his distance at times hurts so much.
Especially here.
Within the walls of his fake kingdom.
Holy Trinity Academy. The beautiful three-story

architectural masterpiece my father's father founded alongside two other families. Crime families. A lot can be said about this place— some good and some not great, but even I can appreciate how remarkable and breathtaking this place is. With its modern turrets, pinnacles, and the enormous white marble crest in the middle of the building. There are so many fascinating elements to the exclusive school.
It is a place you would find somewhere in Europe, with its old-school artistic details giving homage to the masterpieces created by the greats—Dali, Picasso, Gogh. I'm not really into art like my brother, but I do pay attention to him when he explains the kind of art he admires and the artists who inspires his vision. Although, I don't really care about it, I sit my butt down and listen to him until he is done. Every time he talks about it, his mind wanders somewhere far away, most likely to a small cottage near the ocean in Italy or maybe in France, where he can hide away and do what he enjoys. What he loves.
Pouring his heart and soul into clay.
Marble.
A white canvas.
Whatever he feels like doing that day.
The fire that our family snuffed out so long ago burns brighter when he shares his passion with me, and it is truly fascinating.
"Come on, topina, you're already late." My brother drapes his arm around both my sister Giana, who is standing to his left, and me. He hugs us close to his body as if he's shielding us from anything that could hurt us inside these walls.
Nothing can.
Not really.
Nothing would be worse than what they go through when they go home, yet they both remain strong.
They stand tall.

Me? Nothing could hurt me more than witnessing their pain while being spared the same. Mean words? Snooty classmates? Nothing fazes me.

It's child's play.

The ringing of a bell and the loud commanding voice of Principal Wallace boom through the intercom, welcoming us to another day of learning and being productive members of society.

I snort, causing both of my siblings to look down at me with amusing expressions on their faces. Giana gets out of Lucan's hold and begins to walk up the stairs to the entrance. I take my time taking her in.

I take them both in and admire their beauty, so different from mine.

Giana with her light bronze skin that glistens even when the sun is not kissing her skin. Almond-shaped green eyes that have small specks of gold in them, making her look so exotic and so different from most girls here. My sister is a nerd. In the best possible of ways. I mean, she enjoys school, and her grades will most likely get her to the college of her choosing. If she was allowed to go to one, that is.

I never understood why she worked so hard and killed herself to be the best student and have the highest qualifications when there is no way all of that will change our father's mind. He'll never allow her to not only be a beautiful woman who marries a man of his choosing for his gain and one with a brain and a future she crafts for herself. I know now that if she stops doing what she loves, if she gives up her dreams, then Dad wins. The men who believe that a woman's place in our world is to stand behind their man, with our mouths closed, and to pop out a couple of kids without being heard or seen.

Giana steps closer and drops a gentle kiss on my cheek before she turns away and leaves me standing on the stairs with Lucan looking mad as hell about something or someone inside the academy. "See you around. Don't be trouble." My brother murmurs, squeezing me tight and letting me go to head inside.

"But trouble is so much fun." I whisper.

"Say that again." An easy going and charming voice says from behind me, making me turn and find Jonah looking down at me. Jonah Shane. My best friend besides my siblings and the one who shall-not-be-named. The one acting like a tool, and frankly, I am not in the mood to acknowledge his presence, even when I can feel his eyes burning holes in the back of my head. I ignore the prickling on my skin from his stare and focus on Jonah.

Geez, my friend is handsome.

He looks like one of those Roman warriors Lucan has in his art books. He is tall, with a lean physique and curly blonde hair that falls adorably to his forehead, almost covering his eyes. Speaking of his eyes, today, they don't shine like they usually do. Every time I see him, there's mirth and a bright light in his eyes, but not today.

He looks solemn.

Lost.

My heart is hurting for him without knowing what the matter is but knowing something is wrong. I reach forward and take his hand in mine.

"What's wrong, Jo?" Before he can answer me, the loud roar of an engine appears out of nowhere. I turn and watch as Enzo's Matte-red Lamborghini Huracán EVO pulls up to the parking area, right in front of where I'm standing with Jonah. There are countless other places for him to park, but no. Of course not. He has to be the center of attention. He has to be seen. Here, he does. He's so confusing at times. I wonder if I will ever truly know all of him.

Probably not.

Everything ceases to exist the moment he steps out of his car, taking my breath and most likely everyone else's as he walks this way. Lorenzo doesn't have to command attention. It's already his. The moment he steps into a room or walks by you. It is effortless. Just like his beauty. Some might not think of him as beautiful, not like Jonah or my brother, but he is. Not classical beauty. Just the one that creeps in without you even noticing. Today, he's wearing a black hoodie on top of the uniform's dress shirt, dark jeans instead of the usual black slacks boys are required to wear, and his black boots.

No one can get away with breaking the academy's dress code, only the Nicolasi twins.

My eyes roam every inch of him discreetly. He now has even more tattoos than he did the last time we saw each other. Two full sleeves, the backs of his hands and knuckles. He added a few more tattoos on his neck. I've never seen him without a shirt, but by the look of the extensive tattoos on his chest I know there have to be more. Tattoos are, for Lorenzo, what paint and clay are for Lucan.

A part of him.

They tell stories, and if you pay close attention, you'll be able to decipher them. Well, if you get close enough to them without being stabbed or shot.

Staring at him now, there's no denying that he is a work of art. He is magnificent.

He is also a cruel, condescending, and most of the time, an unbearable asshole.

I also notice he's not alone. He got out of the car with a girl, and not with just any girl but 'the girl', Presley. They both walk past me without giving me a glance, or anyone else, for that matter. Her, with a clueless look on her face, and him with his mouth pulled up into a cruel, dismissive approximation of a smile that makes my stomach take a nosedive off a cliff.

It's a low blow.
He doesn't owe me anything, I know. Yet, watching him with her, with anyone that is not me, burns and cuts me deep. I don't let it show. God, no. I would rather stab myself in the eye twice before showing others I am hurt. That their words sometimes influence me because I'm a semi-sane human. It can be avoided. So, I smile and lift my head as if nothing touches me. Not even a little, and it annoys him.
Presley Davis is beautiful. I mean, out of a Vogue catalog and Victoria secret runway stunning. Legs for days. The boob gods blessed her, but they weren't all that kind in the back area. She's perfect to them, though. The kind of girl guys chase, and girls want to hate or kiss her ass until she does them a solid and befriends them.
She, like all the others, has always been insignificant to me. Not because I feel superior to them or find them lacking in any way, but because we just don't click. As much as I love fashion and makeup and like boys, that is not all there is to me. Sadly, that's all there is to them.
Plus, most of the girls that go here are bitches to everyone they deem unworthy.
My name might be on every corner of this building, but that doesn't stop them from snickering and whispering behind my back whenever they pass me and my brother and sister and nowhere in sight.
It is safe to assume that they find me lacking.
Unworthy of their precious time.
That's fine by me since I really don't care about them at all.
Once I graduate, they will all be an unpleasant and distant memory.
Forgotten.
Because I never look back. I just keep moving forward.
The only painful memory I carry is that of my beautiful mother.

That's it.

I avert my gaze, not wanting him to catch me ogling him, not that I'll ever admit it, and train my focus back on Jo. Focus on Jo. The rest don't matter now.

Ground yourself, Cara.

She doesn't matter.

She's just one of many.

My grip on Jo's hand tightens, and I pull him closer to my body while smiling at him.

My friend clearly needs me.

I'll deal with Enzo later.

Yeah.

I'll deal with my emotions and everything that has to do with the devil later.

Two can play games. Messing with Enzo has always been one of my favorites, if not the best.

But first comes my friend, who's not afraid. The one person that has always been the same with me aside from my siblings.

In private and around everyone else.

CHAPTER ELEVEN
SWEET ALLY

"I could never regret you." - L

Lorenzo

16 years old

"Yo, Nicolasi, heard your tapping that sweet ass, Presley." Some tool from the team shouts as he adjusts his helmet and puts his mouthpiece on. Maybe now, he can finally shut the fuck off. Mitchell Fort has been on my ass since I started giving Presley the time of day out of complete boredom. Not going to lie and say I haven't enjoyed her sweet ass fuck mouth, but after the act is over, she fades into the background with all the others. They never keep a single thought of mine hostage. No, apparently, only five-feet-two little hellions with bloody red hair have that power over me.

It infuriates me just thinking about it. She's a goddamn kid. Lucan's kid sister. Not that I really give a fuck if he doesn't approve. Not really. But that kid has gotten inside my skin just as permanently as my tattoos. Not that I would ever admit that shit aloud. So, like with every other vice I do what most men, my family included, aren't capable of doing. I try to rid myself of it. Of her. I'm trying hard, but I haven't been successful yet. Which pisses me off more since I'm great at everything I do.

At this I'm failing.

Nothing.

Absolutely nothing fazes the girl.

Not what I do.

Not the thoughts inside my head that I sometimes share with her when I'm feeling particularly cruel or chatty. Which is almost never, but you get my drift.

Yet, she just smiles up at me and carries on reading her books, and sometimes, she even grabs my hand and doesn't let go until she's had enough.

No amount of asshole behavior seems to get through to her.

But lately things have shifted between us. She looks at me differently than when she was a young and impressionable kid fascinated with the circus freak. Now, she looks at me as if I am someone. Someone important to her.

Those ocean-eyes look my way, and my skin starts to heat up. My palms itch.

My heart races, and at times, my breathing comes out uneven. I'm not an idiot.

I notice how it tends to happen when I'm eager to hurt someone. When I'm causing someone pain.

I've prided myself on not having weaknesses. Because how can you have a weakness when you don't have feelings? When don't you particularly care much about anything or anyone?

But that brat changed it.

Somehow, she got inside my skin, my head, and made me feel things I've yet to fully comprehend. I just know I don't wish her harm like I do everyone else. I find myself sitting quietly, watching her go on and on about the shit she enjoys.

I watch her.

A lot.

And ain't that just a bitch.

It's troublesome for me.

Because now I have her older sister, Giana, literally breathing down my neck, hounding me about the kid. I don't know how the fuck she found out or who the hell told her that I'm close with her little sister, but now she knows.

No one could find out. Look at you, just like the rest. Keeping her a dirty little secret. Annoyed with myself because as much as it fucking frustrates me how everyone else treats her as if she's unworthy of her name, as if she's not enough for them. I know keeping her a secret makes it seem as if I'm ashamed as well. As if I'm the same as them.
I'm not.
I couldn't give one single fuck what anyone thinks.
They're all lacking.
Not her.
She's not that innocent either. The little brat loves meeting me in the dark when the world is asleep. She enjoys the thrill of a well-kept secret.
Secrets.
Now, I have to put some distance between us, not only to get her sister off my back and stop her from asking questions, but also to think clearly. I cannot do that with the kid around. She takes my time, my thoughts, fuck, even my demons, and keeps them for herself, leaving me defenseless against her.
Rival.
So young, yet a dangerous threat.
A sweet ally, as well.
The only person I consider worthy.
I'm so fucked.
A clearing of the throat gets me out of my head. Annoyed with the fucker, Mitchell, I begin to rise from the bench after finishing strapping my gear to find him gone. I must've been so deep inside my head that I didn't even notice the idiot leave and the woman come inside the locker room.
My eyes meet hers, and I'm taken aback.
I can count the few times someone else's presence has caused me confusion.
Two times.
Mia and now this woman.

Why is she here?

I look at her wavy brown hair that falls around her round face and wonder if it's as soft as it looks. Mentally beating myself for even caring, I carry on my assessment of the stranger. Pink lips form an 'O' shape, and big brown, almost-honey eyes look at me as if she's seen a ghost. I resemble a lot of things, or so I've been told. A demon from hell— my personal favorite from the mouth of your resident dumbass, Lucan. An asshole with a death wish, another favorite from the bratty mouth of your Royal bitchiness, Arianna.

Psycho.

Freak.

Cruel.

Yeah, a lot of fucking things, but ghost ain't one of them. That's more my twin.

"Did you get lost, lady?" I snap, successfully startling the sophisticated and elegant woman standing inside the nasty-smelling locker room. She looks like a fish out of water for only a second before she fixes her composure and stands tall. Almost proud.

Ahhh, there's the woman everyone knows.

"I-I'm looking for my son." Before I can get a word out, she's interrupting me. "Number 22." She anxiously looks around the locker room, completely oblivious to the fact I can notice her anxiety coming off in waves.

Number 22.

Beauregard's number.

I don't care for any of my teammates, and I certainly don't pay attention to their shit, but I know for a fact Beauregard's mom is an older lady who has her nose stuck in every school activity and association. A meek little thing who is obsessed with school activities and clubs more than her bitch of a son is.

The lady in front of me is a liar.

The worst kind. The one that has many tells.

The way she shifts on her feet clearly indicates that she's uncomfortable. Lies. The way she looked down at her hands while telling me the number of her supposed son. Avoiding eye contact. Lies. Rapid blinking. Lies.

She's not a very good liar, and it might be safe to assume that she's not used to fibbing by the way she's handling herself. Besides all her tells, she still manages to lie through her teeth with a genuine smile on her face.

Her mouth is lying, but her eyes hold some truth.

Her son is part of the team.

I know him, in fact.

I stand on my feet and walk her way. I'm not a small guy by any means, and I happen to know that others find me intimidating, not only because of the scary tatts on my skin but also because my fuck-with-me-and-I'll-fuck-your-face attitude is not something most people find endearing.

I think it's one of my best qualities.

"As you can see, there's no one else here, lady." I state the obvious while keeping my eyes trained on her pretty-golden ones. I've never seen eyes as enchanting as hers before. They look like warm honey.

"I-I. Yes." She laughs it off and holds my stare. We both stare at each other for what feels like hours before she grows bolder and takes a step closer to me.

Several steps, in fact.

I have a mind to step back and get the fuck out of the locker room and leave this woman behind, as I should've done the first time I saw her as a young boy.

I couldn't then, and fuck me, I can't now, so I remain in place and let her get all up in my space.

The first thing I notice is the sweet, almost flowery scent of her perfume.

It suits her.

"I guess I just got lost." The woman offers me a shaky smile, but she still stays in my space, not moving, just staring at me as if she's soaking me up. I feel that way. The same sensation the little monster stirs inside of me. Air is hard to find with this woman so close to me. My heart rate spikes up, but I still don't move. I don't ever back down. Never, even when I desperately need to. Like in this very instant. "I just wanted to wish him luck and tell him how much I love h-him." Her words come out raspy as if she's holding back tears.
Fuck.
God is fucking punishing me for all the disturbing shit I've done. He has to be because why else would he send this woman, who has the power to disarm me with just one gentle smile and a kind word, my way?
Wish him luck.
I love him.
Feeling an episode start to take over my senses, I step away from the woman, but the moment I do, she comes forward.
The walls are closing in.
My vision gets blurry.
Fuck, not here.
Not with her this close.
I shouldn't care.
Let her see.
This is me.
But I care.
Fuck me, I do care.
What the fuck is wrong with me?
"Leave." I bark, startling her for a second, yet she stays in place. "He's not here, lady."
"I just want –"
"Please…I don't have much time." My ears start ringing, and I just know I'll lose this fight if I don't step away from this situation.

I beg. I fucking beg this woman to leave because I'm not as strong as I thought I was. Not when it comes to her.
I don't have much time. What the fuck does she mean?
A heavy sigh falls from her lips, "Alright. I'll go."
Closing my eyes, I count to ten because three won't work for shit right now.
One.
Two.
Then I freeze on three, not because I manage to contain myself but because of the gentle hands on my cheeks.
She's. Touching. Me.
She's fucking touching me, and she's still breathing.
My breathing goes back to normal, and the room stops spinning when I open my eyes.
All I see is her.
Watery gold eyes.
Pain.
So much fucking pain that I can almost feel it strangling me. You don't have to be an expert on feelings to understand the magnitude of regret and pain swimming in her gaze.
In this moment, I feel something I've never felt toward a woman before, not even her.
Hate.
Hate for getting under my skin.
Hate for making me feel something, anything, while she touches my skin.
"I said leave." I grit out through clenched teeth, trying really fucking hard not to snap.
"I-I will." Her hands leave my face, and I'm flooded with a sense of loss I've never felt before. This shit is all new to me. I've suppressed many things throughout my childhood, and now it's all bottling up, threatening to fucking explode all around me.
One day it will.

You can't run from it.
The woman steps back, making me look down on her. She looks through a small purse and reaches for something inside before pulling what looks like a black chain out.
"Could you—Could you maybe give this to my son?" Her voice cracks the second she says son. Liar. Beautiful liar. Go away. "It used to keep him safe, but he lost it. I found it."
She found it.
She found me.
I don't know why but I reach forward and take the black rosary from her. For a moment, I believed the holy object burned my sinner skin, but it was only the warmth of her hand.
She's warm.
Gentle.
Gold eyes.
Flowers.
Pulling my hand back, I sidestep her and make my way toward the metal doors that lead to the crowded field. Once open, the loud noise of the crowd and chants of the cheerleaders center me.
Breathing in and out, I hold the door open with my back and turn around to face her.
The braveness and courage leave her body, and her shoulders drop as if she's lost the battle. I harden my expression and lift all my walls again. For a moment there, a moment of weakness—one that makes me ashamed as fuck— I let myself feel something toward the stranger I've only seen a handful of times through a television.
A stunning and sophisticated business-woman.
A supermodel.
A mother.
My mother.
A woman who stumbled up here with her heart on her sleeve and hope shining in her eyes, wanting to see number 22.

22. Lies.

She lies just like everyone around me.

I despise liars.

Yet, I don't completely hate her, and that just complicates things more.

It would be easier if I felt nothing at all, as I do for the most part with others.

I feel, and a lot.

All at once.

For this stranger who really isn't one to me.

To my twin.

I look into her eyes and put the rosary on as she watches me with kind eyes. She looks as if she's holding her breath, waiting to see if I'll reject her further than I already have.

I don't know why I sometimes do the shit I do.

Call me insane.

Reckless.

But today, I am kind to this woman. Because with a gentle touch that lasted only seconds, she has shown me more warmth and gentleness than anyone. I grip the rosary that now hangs from my neck and shove it inside my Jersey for safekeeping, all the while never taking my eyes off her.

"Tell me your son's number, Valerie." I raise my voice so she can hear me over the roars outside. A sound resembling a wounded animal leaves her lips the moment I let her know she did not fool me. I know exactly who she is. A tear falls from her pretty eyes down to her cheek, but she doesn't wipe it away. Why doesn't she? "And don't lie to me. I hate liars more than I hate cowards. Something tells me you're a fighter, ma'am."

It visibly pains her when I address her as ma'am or lady, other than Mom. It's clear with the way she falls back on her heels that it was as if I shot her.

Maybe I did.

Others say words hurt more than any physical wound. I wouldn't know. Waiting for a response, I silently hope she lies to me. Lie to me.
Make this easier.
But nothing can ever be simple, can it?
"Twelve." Her voice is hoarse, but strong. Her eyes hold a fierceness that I didn't see before. "My baby boy's number is twelve."
My baby boy.
12.
Thump.
Thump.
Thump.
My chest feels tight.
I need to get far away from her.
"Goodbye, Mother." Even with the noise outside, I was able to hear her gasp of shock.
Pain?
Elation?
Happiness?
I'm not quite sure.
I step outside the locker room and into the field while everyone waits for me, eager for another win.
Another show.
Another useless moment.
These people love the game. The thrill of winning against a rival and rubbing it in their faces.
I don't.
I enjoy the thrill of being in the field, yes.
But for different reasons.
I get to cause others pain under the disguise of a friendly football game.
The moment my sneakers touch the fake grass, I leave the woman behind.

The woman that gave me life.

The woman with more demons in her eyes than any criminal I've met before.

If I had a heart, I would've hugged her. I would've given her that, but I didn't.

I walked away with her rosary of a Saint and left her with tears inside the locker room.

If I were someone worthy of a love so pure, I would've told her that she was in my thoughts more than I cared for, but she was there. She was everywhere.

But I didn't.

I walked away as I always do, without knowing that she risked everything to just get a few seconds with me.

She tried to hold on as long as she was able to before it all was taken away.

Until she faded into the dark and unforgiving darkness.

That was the first time in my miserable life that I let someone that close to the useless organ in my chest.

Her.

My mother.

A couple of weeks later, I had her stunning golden eyes permanently inked on my skin.

I won't realize it until it was too late, but that was the first time I fell in love.

It was too late when I figured it out.

She never knew just how much she changed me that night.

Just how far inside my rotten soul she touched with one simple loving touch.

Her body left this earth, and all I had of her were the heartbreaking letters she wrote on her deathbed.

CHAPTER TWELVE

FIRE ON FIRE

"Would you die for me?" - L

Cara

15 years old

Fifteen candles.
A monumental time for most girls my age.
That's what my sister and most of the women on our house staff have been telling me for the past few weeks leading up to this night, my birthday. All I've heard is how, by fifteen, they had started growing into their bodies.
Boys started noticing them.
Crushes.
Dating.
Heartbreaks.
All the things normal girls my age are into.
I get it.
It's an exciting time for most.
Not for me, though.
It's just another number, really.
I grew into my body at fourteen.
I was an early bloomer, just like my sister.
When the boobs came in, so did the attention.
Boys, and even weird men, started noticing me the moment

started to change.
My first crush keeps crushing me. So really, there is nothing exciting about that.
Dating? Meh.
I won't ever be allowed to date, so why even bother?
And heartbreak?
Well, I was cozy with that one from a very early age.
Still a couple of wounds and ratty bandages on my heart won't deter me from opening it for the right one.
So, fifteen candles feel all the same to me.
The same as fourteen.
Not quite like the years before.
It is a darker time now.
Maybe that's the only difference.
But that's not quite true, is it?
The baby fat is gone, and when I look at myself in the mirror, I don't see the lanky kid with freckles and crazy hair. No, I see a young woman with crimson hair that falls almost to her butt in soft curls and an hourglass figure. A young woman that is not always sunshine and wildflowers but still manages to form a smile whenever the ones she loves need one. Someone with dreams too big for the world she was born into. A sister who loves her siblings sometimes more than she even loves herself.
But that's not all.
I'm also the girl who enjoys dark things most people would consider ugly or lacking. I sometimes find myself wanting to be alone for long periods of time because I need room to breathe when inside my home it feels like I'm suffocating.
I have mood swings.
I'm complicated.
I'm growing and changing every day.
I'm evolving.
And that's okay.

I'm not the girl who I was yesterday, and tomorrow, I won't be the same as today.

That's the beauty of life.

Something that's different about this birthday? He's not with me. Since the first time he celebrated with me so long ago, we have spent all my birthdays together in our secret spot. Until this one.

He didn't show.

He broke his promise.

And as the years pass, he's pulling away from me.

I'm losing him.

He's different now.

Harsher, if that's even possible.

Darker.

Unhinged.

He fights a lot, too.

At his games.

During classes.

In the cafeteria.

Everywhere.

He doesn't even need an excuse. He just picks fights whenever he feels like it. There's anger in him that wasn't there before. He was always looking forward to when he could inflict pain, but now it is as if he wants to hurt others as much as himself.

So I came here because he won't get away with breaking promises. That's not what we do.

Who we are.

We might be unconventional, but one thing we do have in common is that we never lie to each other, even when the truth is harder to stomach than lies.

I won't allow him to push me away like I don't matter.

No.

After my siblings sang me happy birthday and gave me

my presents, everyone went their separate ways. I waited inside my room for everyone to fall asleep, and when I was sure no one would catch me, I slipped out with the help of Amara, one of the younger house cleaners. At first, I would use my cute age and charming ways to get her to cover for me when I wanted to go unnoticed, and now that I'm older, she just gives in and gives me what I ask. It's a shit move to use her emotions for my own personal gain, but there's not much I could do inside that prison. Amara dropped me off here on her way home. She works for Dad, and then, at night, she travels long hours to get to her son. Her boy is lucky to have her. She's a good woman, and by the way she talks about her son, it is clear she's a wonderful mother to him.

Not wanting to ruin my mood, I ignored the thoughts of my mother that threaten to come to the front of my mind.

Not today.

I focus on the huge and elegant mansion that looks almost identical to my own, except this one has a Gothic Style in contrast to ours, which has more of a Greek Revival style.

The Nicolasi Mansion.

It is truly, hauntingly beautiful, with balconies spanning all three floors, supported by grand columns.

Men in suits surround every inch of the mansion, both inside and outside the gates. This is reckless and maybe I've lost my mind for being here. Risking getting in trouble, but I had to see him before everything changed because it will. It started happening since his long-lost sister appeared out of nowhere.

He will change even more soon.

When he gets everything that he ever wanted.

The crown.

The title.

This city.

I pull up my hood over my head and find myself following

the path behind the mansion that leads to the garden. One good thing about not speaking much means I'm able to listen. I listen to everything and everyone around me. I found out through a conversation my brother was having with both Lorenzo and Valentino about the stone path that's never guarded by their security, and that's how they were able to go out unnoticed when they were younger. No, they don't have to hide. They go as they please, without a care in the world. No one tells them anything.

Once I find myself at the back of the mansion, I run carefully, trying not to make much noise, and make my way to the pool house.

He stays there now.

Another thing I learned from my brother.

Overheard is more like it.

He doesn't share much with me anymore.

They've all gone their separate ways. They love me. I know they do, but I'm not clueless. I see what's going on. The choosing of the Capo will be happening soon.

Then, the Omerta.

Greed has spread like a killing virus through the families, and everyone is out for blood.

They all want the crown.

Some for selfish reasons, and others out of survival.

Moving closer to the main door of the pool house, I notice only one light is on.

He's here.

My heart thumps, making me stop before I turn the knob.

What if he's not alone?

Those kinds of thoughts hurt.

More than a bullet to the heart.

Do I really want to break my own stupid heart and scar myself for life?

This is stupid.

Thinking better of it and with a heavy heart, I turn around. I should've thought of this before, but in my hurry to see him, I completely disregarded the fact that maybe he was too busy with someone else.

He's always busy lately.

Like a coward, I turn to leave, but when I take a step in the direction I came from, the crystal doors open, making me stop dead in my tracks without turning around.

Busted.

"Running again, little monster?" A low whisper filled with venom sounds from behind me. Goosebumps spread all over my body, and my neck becomes hot from the heat of his eyes on my skin. His voice is dripping with venom. With challenge, too.

I know him.

I know him even more than he knows himself at times.

Pushing my feelings aside, I put on my armor, raise my walls, and prepare myself for war. Because lately, every interaction I have with Enzo feels like a war.

Strangely, we are always on the same side, even when he tries to leave me behind.

He can't escape me.

Just like I can't escape him.

We're two bleeding hearts.

Two drops of blood from the same scar.

When I manage to control my breathing, I turn to face him, and my jaw almost hits the floor alongside my heart, which drops not far behind when I come face to face with him.

My Enzo.

***

The first thing I notice is how cold the temperature in his room is. I wonder why he decided to leave the room he had inside the mansion for the pool house. I don't have to wonder long, just looking around his space, I can imagine why.

This place is his.

He can do whatever he pleases here without worrying about the men that work for his family butting into his business. Not like he would care what anyone thinks or has to say. That's not who he is.

The second he moved aside to let me in, I had a feeling something monumental would happen. I've never been allowed inside his world. Not the one his grandfather crafted for him, but the one Enzo built for himself.

The one where he can lower his guard and stop pretending to be like everyone else. He is free to be himself here, without pretenses and the burden of being what everyone else wants you to be. One thing I've learned about Lorenzo throughout the years is that he silently plays the players, not the game. He is so good at it, too. If you don't know him, really know him, you would think he really is just like every other boy at the academy who loves to rub elbows with the elite, screw girls just for fun, and party it up like most teenagers do.

But Lorenzo is not like most people.

Every move he makes has a purpose.

It leads him to an endgame.

Taking a deep breath, I wrap my arms tighter around my body, trying to find warmth from the cold. Even with my hoodie on, it is freezing inside this place. Why is it so cold? Looking around, I take notice of everything and what a mess it is. He has dozens of sketches on his gray walls. You would think most guys his age would have semi-naked-women and cars posters all over their walls, but not him.

He has all types of sketches in black ink.

I move in circles, taking a good look at every single sketch, not wanting to miss a single one. This is him. The real him, and there's not a part of him I would ever want to miss.

Not one single part.

The ugly one, the dark one, and even his insane one.

It's all the same to me.
There are sketches of women, but I can't put a name to them.
The silhouette of a delicate face.
Big, beautiful eyes with specks of gold in them.
The drawing is beautiful yet haunting.
There's a sadness to it.
I move farther inside the room and become instantly enthralled by a huge sketch of a dragon in black ink. The stunning creature is breathing fire.
Then, I stop dead when I come face to face with the wall where the window is. There, he has sketches of naked women in all types of compromising positions, but instead of looking porno-ish, the drawings look erotic and tasteful.
Sensual.
One of the drawings catches my eyes more than the others.
A naked, delicate throat being strangled by bulging hands.
Oh, wow.
Did he do this?
What am I saying? Of course, he did.
While Lucan draws and makes beautiful art with anything he can get his hands on, Lorenzo draws.
Sketches.
Really epic ones.
I knew he was good by the drawings he made me, but I didn't know he was this good. I keep moving until I'm standing in front of his desk, where many pencils, his tattoo gun, and bottles of ink lay scattered around the table.
How different Enzo is from my brother, yet they're both incredibly talented.
He's so different from his twin, too.
Valentino is the calm, whereas his twin brother is the storm.
Wild.
Unhinged.
So beautifully reckless.

So him. "You shouldn't have come here, Cara," he replies, breaking the silence first, a slight bitterness in his tone.
Cara.
Not Mia.
Great.
I turn around and face him. "You didn't show up." I reluctantly looked into his eyes. I don't want to see the emptiness that is in them whenever he looks my way. He was never one to be all heart and flowers with me, but there was warmth every time our eyes locked.
Now, he looks at me like he looks at everyone else.
Like I mean nothing, and it feels like an arrow to the heart and not the fun kind. More like the one that splits it open until blood seeps out, leaving you empty and hopeless.
I'm losing them all.
And I don't know what else to do.
I can't be the only one willing to fight.
I'm exhausted from always being the one holding too tight to the rope while everyone just lets go as if it's so easy for them. Why is it so simple for everyone to leave me behind, but I can't find it in me to do the same?
He brushes off my comment and sighs before taking a seat on his bed. It's a huge king bed taking up half of the room, with black sheets. I gather my thoughts before saying something that might make me seem childish or something that I could never take back. I came here trying to hold onto the only real thing left in my life before everything crumbles down around me. Enzo is the only solid thing I have left besides my siblings, and that's quickly going to hell as well.
We both remain silent— him sitting on the bed with his head hanging low while looking down at his busted-up knuckles. How different he acts when it's just the two of us. Silent. Reserved, almost. Guarded. The total contrast to how he acts when others are around.

His chiseled jaw clenches and unclenches, but his lips remain pressed together.

He's shirtless, only wearing black basketball shorts. His shoulders are broad, and I admire his physique. He's even bigger than he was last time I saw him. I don't know how he does it. Oh, yeah. All the fights are a great way for him to keep in shape.

Black ink covers half of his body and the entire front of his throat. If he keeps it up, soon there won't be any skin left for him to tattoo.

The piercings are new, though.

He had one ear pierced and his eyebrow.

Now, he has his nipple pierced.

Heat spreads over my neck and cheek, and I'm thankful for the dim lighting that makes it difficult for him to see the flush on my face.

His jaw is carved from stone, and his black hair is styled differently now. He shaved his sides closer to his scalp, and the hair on top of his head was longish and brushed back.

He's incredibly handsome.

But I never know if I'm safe or in danger around him.

Both.

Definitely both.

I know I should leave. It's better for my heart if I stay away, but every time I try to stay away, it feels like invisible chains wrap around me and pull me back to him. The same feeling that tells me I'm right where I'm supposed to be.

Enzo raises his head, and blue eyes meet mine. Did he catch me ogling him? Ugh.

I bite down on my lip and lower my gaze. "You forgot." I say the first thing that comes to mind. "You forgot my birthday." Maybe it's silly to him, but to me, it hurts. He forgot, or maybe he just doesn't care anymore. But whatever the case, I need to know so I can move on.

I don't plan to stay in the dark corners of his world while he goes on to live as if I don't exist. Nope.
I'm not that girl, and I don't ever plan to be.
I fight for the ones that I love as long as they're willing to get in the ring with me. His blue eyes narrow as he regards me. Understanding seems to dawn on him, and anger twists his features up. "You're here because your silly little girl's feelings got hurt." He laughs mockingly, but there's no laughter in his eyes. So this is how he wants to play it. Okay. Let's play then. But he's not done spewing venom. "You're mad because I didn't wish you a happy birthday, Red? Is that it?"
"No. I'm mad because you broke your fucking promise."
"Watch your mouth."
"Or what?"
"Or I'll punish it." He says darkly as he stands from the bed to his full height. I'm so much smaller than him that, from this angle, he looks like an angry god. Heat creeps in when I focus on what he just said. Or I'll punish it. This is happening. He's never talked to me or acted in an inappropriate way with me. As much as I pushed him, he always kept himself in check, but not tonight.
I look at him and find his chest moving up and down in a rapid motion and his hands clenched at his side. I've never pushed him this far.
Shit.
As much as I like it when he gives me something more than the cold and aloof facade, I don't want to hurt him, and when he loses control, he ends up not only hurting others but himself as well. He might enjoy that, but I don't.
I don't want him to hurt.
So I change the topic and hope to bring him down from the high.
Instead, I ask what I wanted to ask since he gave me the cold shoulder at the academy on my first day as a freshman.

"Are you ashamed of me? Is that it?" I manage to ask through the lump in my throat. "I mean, I'm well aware of what people say about me behind my back. If you feel the same way, just tell me, and I won't bother you again." There. I don't pity myself, and I don't want anyone else to do so. I'd rather cut my losses than waste my time on someone that finds me lacking or is ashamed of who I am. What I am.

I take a step back when he says nothing and just stares at me like I've grown two heads, and when I step back, he grips my left wrist. There's an intense look in his eyes, the same as when he's causing someone else pain. A fierceness that hides behind those deep soulful blue eyes. "Don't ever fucking say that again, Mia." He whispers darkly and so intensely that I swear I feel it down to my bones. He says my name not as a prayer but as an oath.

Now, now, stupid heart, he's just being kind.
There's not a kind bone in his body, girl.

Both the devil and angel in my shoulders whisper in my ear.
"Then why? Why did you not show up at the treehouse?" I start to pull away, but he doesn't let my wrist go.

"I was busy." He says while keeping a tight hold of my wrist. I feel his thumb run circles on the inside of my wrist absently. I'm not sure he even realizes he's doing it.

"Try again." I whisper, still looking down at our hands. I don't believe that for a second.

"You know, Mia, I really hate when others question the shit I do."

"Too bad. We're friends, and friends don't bail on each other." His brows furrow as if he's genuinely confused by this notion.

"We're not friends." He says darkly while holding my wrist tighter, but not painfully. "We could never be friends."

Never.

That hurts.

Another shot through the heart. There's a faraway look on his face, and I wish I could read minds so I would know what's going through that dark space of his. Feeling bold all of a sudden, I push my body closer to his, and to my surprise, he doesn't step back or push me away. He just looks down at me with a look of complete confusion, and I swear it would be funny as hell if I didn't know how difficult it is for him to sometimes read a room. A situation. Emotions.

"Don't push me away. Not you, too." I whisper closer to his lips. Something flashes in his eyes, and his nostrils flare. "I know I'm younger. I'm not the type of girl you usually go for and I'm also a disgrace to some of the members, but I'm your friend, and you hurt my feelings when you—" I'm stunned when he cuts me off with his soft lips crashing hard on mine. He's kissing me.

All kinds of thoughts cross through my mind, but I shut everything off and just savor the moment. He initiated it this time.

He's kissing me.

It is different from the first time our lips met. That time I took the first step, and he didn't return my kiss.

This kiss is much more intimate.

And I feel it down to my bones.

Our kiss doesn't last long because just as soon as it's started, he's pulling away. Then I feel his powerful hands thread into my hair as he pulls me slightly away from him so he can look at me. His blue eyes blaze with possessiveness. "Don't ever fucking say that again." His breathing comes out uneven, and I can feel the wild beat of his heart while my hand lays on top of his chest. "You're not a disgrace, and I've never and will never be ashamed of you. Cut that shit out." When his thumb brushes across my cheek, I close my eyes and relish the tender touch. "You're everything that is good, kid," he says, his eyes dropping to my mouth. "Too good for me."

No, I am not.
You're perfect for me. I want to say.
Looking up at his mouth, I can't find the right words to say.
"You scare me, Red." He pulls away, walking toward the window. How is it possible for someone like him to be scared of me? There's no way.
"Why?" I remain in place, not wanting to spook him. Lorenzo, at times, reminds me of a small child. "I would never hurt you." He laughs bitterly but doesn't turn my way. I keep staring at his naked back while he looks out the window. "Oh, sweet little monster, but I will hurt you. It's bound to happen. It's what I do. I'm not like your brother. I'm not Superman."
I will hurt you…
It's what I do.
Yes, he can hurt me like no other, and yet he's afraid of hurting me. Someone who doesn't care wouldn't be worried about that. He can be kind and gentle, and yet he doesn't even know it. I don't understand this connection between us— foreign and strong— but it is not something I'm willing to give up. With him, I feel seen and heard. It feels as if I'm home. My mother used to say that people have two sides.
A good side and a bad side.
A past and future.
And that we must embrace both in someone we love.
I knew I was in love with Lorenzo Nicolasi long before that night.
What I didn't know was that with just one kiss, he bound my soul forever with his.
Things went back to how they were. How they were always meant to be.
Lorenzo and I in our own little world.
Nothing from the outside could touch us.
It didn't last long.
It could never be that easy with us.

CHAPTER THIRTEEN
LIES & HEARTBREAK

"Don't touch my toys." — L

Lorenzo

17 years old

"She's here," Arianna offers flatly. "Why is she here?" Lately, everyone seems to be testing my limits. Questioning the shit I do.

Pushing me to feel things I was never meant to feel.

Not me.

"She's a Nicolasi." I state the obvious. Andrea Valentina Nicolasi is one of my father's many secrets and part of his long list of fuck ups. I, of course, knew who she was before she got dragged into this world by Benedetto.

The heiress to our mother's empire.

The one she kept.

The one she didn't give up.

It's not hard to see how she was everything Cassius needed, and now that she's back, she's managed to work miracles. After years of our father going on drunken benders, he's managed to stay sober for more than a month.

He's doing it for her.

I could care less.

What I do care about is how this affects me.

She's the eldest Nicolasi grandchild.
She has the same rights to the title as Valentino and me.
I'm not worried, though.
This isn't and will never be her world.
It's obvious how she has one foot here and the other back in her city. Back where her heart and dreams are.
But what if she decides to—
A frosty voice interrupts my train of thought. "It's kind of pathetic how Lucan can't keep his eyes off her. As if he's never seen anyone quite like her before." I follow Arianna's gaze and find Lucan standing in the far-right corner, with his back to the wall, looking straight at Andrea as she speaks with her strange friend, Fallon. Benedetto gathered us here tonight to introduce Andrea to the families.
The Volpe are here.
Lucan and his sisters are standing close together as always, watching us from afar. Those three have one foot here and the other wherever their silly hearts take them.
I disregard the older Volpe children and keep my eyes trained on her, suppressing the strange feeling of genuine laughter. The little monster will never stop surprising me. Whereas every other girl in this room is dressed to impress, all except Fallon James, of course— Cara is wearing an ugly, oversized superhero shirt, with her curly red hair loose around her delicate face. She's wearing white sneakers with knee-high socks matching her shirt.
In all her strangeness, she manages to stand out.
She's beautiful…
Fuck, this kid has been fucking with my head since the first day I made the mistake of talking to her. Yes, mistake. Since that moment, she has proven to be a headache of all proportions. She won't leave my thoughts. Good or bad, whatever the hell they are— she's always a part of it.

Taking my eyes off her, I concentrate on everyone else in the room. My brother sits in the back, glaring daggers at his little obsessions' back. Meanwhile, his best mate, Kadra, sits quietly next to him, staring at the wall with a blank expression on her face. This gathering is not for pleasantries but for duty. Three of us will be chosen as the boss of our families, but only one will be crowned the capo.

***

I'm headed out after the meeting is over when a harsh voice that sounds a lot like Lucan stops me halfway out the door. "You know she's too good for this shit. You both are, Giana." He takes a deep breath before continuing. "Cara, though, her heart is too pure for the hell she was born into. She needs a good man who will cherish and honor her, and maybe she won't suffer the same fate as her mother."

"I know, but—" A soft sigh sounds in the corner of the hallway. "What do you want me to say, Lucan? He won't stand for it. You know he won't, and there's just a matter of time before we end up like Arianna. Just pretty trophies on the shelf of some sick bastard. Just like *mama*. Just like all the others." Desperation is evident in her voice.

My blood runs cold when I realize who they're referring to.

My pretty little monster.

Inching closer to where they're standing, I try not to draw attention to myself by staying away from the light. Fucking ironic that every time I eavesdrop like a creep, it's always about her.

Her.

A painful throb takes over half of my head as I think back to all the times I let her get close enough to ship away a piece of my dark soul. One thing I always prided myself on is being one-step ahead of everyone else, and to some degree, I am and most likely always will be, but so will she. She's never far behind.

In my thoughts.

My memories.

Even in my goddamn sleep.

She's there, making a home for herself.

She's even branded her taste on my lips, and no amount of mouthwash could get rid of her innocent kiss.

Other's lips will fail, as well.

She's the blood that runs through my veins, giving me life, and isn't that just fucked up.

I can't shake her, even if I wanted to.

She's in my every breath, and I didn't realize how primordial she was until this very moment.

Until her future is being decided for her as if she doesn't matter. As if her dreams and aspirations don't mean shit.

One thing I learned from Cara since the very first word she spoke to me is that her hopes and dreams make her who she is. It's what has kept her sane after everything she's witnessed from a young age.

"Hey, now. What have I told you? We don't lose hope. We don't cower. We fucking fight with everything we have, and when there's nothing left, we still get up and fight." I remain stoic, listening to their conversation. Even if I wanted to, I wouldn't be able to turn and leave. Everything that is her concerns me. "Once I become Capo, no one will challenge my position. Tommaso won't have a fucking say, and you'll both be safe and free to do as you wish with your lives. You'll get to make all your dreams come true. I fucking promise." I look their way and watch as Lucan pulls his sister closer to his chest before dropping a gentle kiss on her head. Looking at them, I realize how different my relationship with my siblings is from theirs. My relationship with Valentino is more hate than love these days since he lost what little he had of his heart left. And Andrea? Well that shit is nonexistent. They got fucked harsh in the ass the day I was drawn out

of the gene pool. I can't offer them comfort and a safe space like Lucan does to his sisters. No.
I don't know how.
It doesn't come naturally to me.
The right words.
The right things to do.
They, too, deserve better, and coming to terms with this might bring me a step closer to being a semi-decent brother to them, but I know it's not enough.
This shit is hard.
Instead of worrying about stuff that I might never understand, I decide to stop trying so hard to comprehend the shit that lives inside my head and just let myself feel whatever-the-hell it is I feel in the moment. Then, I'll decide if it's in any way useful to me or if it's just meant to be forgotten and never thought about again.
"You really are superman, big brother."
Superman.
A low chuckle leaves Lucan as he steps back and looks down at his sister with the same look my father gives Andrea when he sees her nowadays. How Cara looks at me…
Fuck.
Not wanting to deal with the repercussions of the little monsters' feelings for me, I focus on her siblings instead.
"That little brat thinks too highly of me." Then his voice turns darker. "One day soon, she won't look at me the same way. She will see him in me when I do the shit I need to do to keep you both safe."
"I promise you. You're not papa and never will be. I know this. She knows it, too." Giana says with conviction. "Cara is not a child anymore. She knows more than we give her credit for, and with blood on your hands or not, we'll love you just the same or even a little bit more because no one loves us like you do, big brother."

That's the thing about the Volpe children that differentiates them from the rest of us.

Their hearts.

Their unbreakable bond.

Love.

Even when their sick motherfucker of a father tried to ruin them, they rose above the pain and their nightmares.

Then, an idea comes to mind.

That night changes everything for me.

For her.

For all of us.

Sacrifices must be made until all falls into place.

What I didn't expect was to feel something, especially something like pain and regret.

Because for me to keep the only thing that brings me joy in complete emptiness and darkness, I must first set it free.

CHAPTER FOURTEEN
DEATH & REBIRTH

"Show me your worst and let me love you anyway." – C

Lorenzo

I 17 years old chose to leave with my sister instead of staying with our traitorous grandfather when Arianna betrayed Lucan and broke my sister's hearts by exposing Valerie Turner's cause of death to the world.

The petty bitch got a hold of the media and talked about things she knew shit about, causing my sister to leave this city in the middle of the night.

The best decision she's ever made.

Tino stayed behind. He had his reasons, but I didn't.

I left with both my father and sister.

For the first time in my life, I did something for someone else. I had to… I had to make sure she was okay.

For some unknown reason, I felt obligated to because of her.

My mother.

The woman whose memory was tarnished by the same world who kissed the ground she walked on when she was alive.

But now, I'm back.

There's unfinished business.

"Boy, how dare you come here after you left the city with your traitorous father?" Benedetto booms from his spot in the middle of the room. "The moment you left, you forfeited your right to my throne. Andrea will come back, even if I have to drag her by the hair my damn-self, and only then will we choose the Nicolasi successor." Benedetto looks wild, nothing like his usual self. He's coming undone, and it is obvious that little by little, he's losing hold of his crown.

I stand back and just stare at him, sitting like a scared little king on his throne, waiting anxiously for it all to crumble down at his feet. That is exactly what will happen if I have any say in this, which I do. Then, my stare leaves him and finds the other two men with close expiration dates. Both current bosses are sitting with murderous expressions on their hideous faces, trying hard not to lose their composure. These men's reign on this city has run its course, and they all know it.

They expected it, of course, but they never expected to be betrayed by their flesh and blood.

By their sons and daughters.

Not only will they not agree to a woman leading the Holy Trinity, but also the Parisi boss is also skeptical of a stranger running and being the face of the entire organization.

I can't stand the asshole, but I don't blame him for that.

Not really.

My sister was not born for this, nor was she born into this life. Hence, she hasn't bled for it like we have, and that, in their eyes, makes her a threat. A risk to everything their forefathers have worked hard to build and the power they maintain in this city.

Their legacy.

I believe a woman is just as capable of running a city, but not my sister, that's for sure. She knows shit about this life. Besides, she would be eaten alive, and that's a fucking fact.

She also made it clear that she wants nothing to do with Benedetto or anyone that's in this city.
There's only Tino in my way.
Not wanting to give any more thought to what will inevitably happen today, I carry on before the tiny amount of guilt I've been feeling lately makes me hesitate and ruins everything for all of us.
For Andrea.
For Tino, too, even if he does not see it yet.
"You know, grandfather, I'm really getting fucking sick and tired of your laughable and not very convincing threats." The moment I step forward toward Benedetto, his men all stand straight with firm hold on their guns, obvious to the threat to their boss. Benedetto's mouth curves into a sinister smirk or at least he tries to, but like everyone else here, he has a tell. Tino has the very same one. The eye twitch. It is subtle, but it is there if you know what to look for. "Are you threatening me, boy?" Benedetto's heavy breathing is the only sound in the room.
"I am." I smile broadly.
Shit, this will be fun.
"What are you going to do about it?" The boss raises his hand and slaps me across the face. The loud smack echoes all around us. Benedetto always hit like a girl. No, that ain't true. Kadra hits harder, and that says a lot.
Laughing, I spit blood onto his shoes.
Yeah, this is fun.
Watching Benedetto lose his temper has always been the highlight of my fucking day. "You hit like a weak bitch." I wipe my bloody mouth with the back of my hand, and then with blood on my hands, I rub it all over Benedetto's white dress shirt. "It must really hurt you, huh? That I look the most like her?" Her. Valerie Turner. My mother. Even though Valentino and I are twins, some traits are more prominent in me.

The dimple on my chin. It's hers.

The lopsided grin. Hers.

I tried to ignore it, but it is impossible to escape my mother. She is everywhere, even in death.

These days when I look at myself in the mirror, I see her staring back at me. I see her the same way she looked the first and last time I saw her alive.

The regal and larger than life woman with kind but sad eyes. Suddenly, all I see is red, and a pain in my head threatens to debilitate me. Rage.

Dear old flame.

All I feel when I think of everything that went down with our mother.

Her disease.

Her inevitable death.

The newspapers and gossip sites are writing shit to taint her memory.

Then, I see it.

Her face smiling shyly up at me the time she got the courage to find me and give me her crucifix. The same one that's burning my skin. The same one I've never taken off since that night.

The one that reminds me that she loved a monster like me even when all my brother and I brought to her life was tragedy. Our father was her downfall, and so I keep it tightly secure around my neck, choking me with the guilt and pain of her last days.

I wear the damn thing even if it burns me. I wear it to never forget.

I close my eyes for a second before her sweet face transforms into Cara's tearful one every time someone belittles her for the blood that runs through her body. Then, I hear the words they were both called.

Whore.

Bastard.

Filth.

It fuels the beast that's dying to come out and play with the man responsible for the pain of everyone that means something to me.

And I lose it.

I let my urges to cause pain and draw blood take over.

Opening my eyes, my smile fades as I look into his rage-filled eyes. "Step down."

He huffs, looking at everyone in the room, and looking back at his loyal dog. The same one that sucks his cock whenever he has a chance to get him alone. Yet, he doesn't move. Neither does Madden, his main guard dog.

No one moves, and no one dares to say a word, and that makes this all the more fun.

Oh, how lovely.

I step closer to Benedetto so only he can hear what I'm about to say. "Not even your personal cock sucker will save you now."

Benedetto's eyes grow big, like huge saucers, and he begins to shake with obvious rage. "You insolent little shit, you shut your goddamn mouth before I sew it shut my damn-self." His voice is trembling now. He knows this is it, and he is nervous. The time has finally come for me to rise to the top, and for that to happen, I have to step on the necks of everyone that stands in my way. Looking at where Valentino is standing, with his back to a wall, he shows no emotion on his face as usual.

Lately, my brother has been a walking dead man.

He doesn't laugh.

Doesn't get mad.

Nothing.

Emptiness.

He is just like Cassius.

They fell for a woman, and that led them to their ruin.
I smile when I see the subtle flutter of his left eye. His nervous tell. How sweet.
He's nervous for me because I'm running my mouth, and to him this looks like a suicide mission.
I watch as Valentino moves forward, and I know the self-righteous idiot, even when mad at me, will still find it in him to look out for me. Out of the corner of my eye, I watch my reflection on the floor-length mirror next to the private bathrooms and notice one of Benedetto's men move forward with his gun trained on the back of my head, but before he can pull the trigger, Valentino tackles him to the floor.
Not thinking about it, I act. Using the commotion to my favor, I stick my tongue out with a smile, not caring about my fucked-up mouth, and grab the tiny blade that's been sitting under my tongue this entire time, cutting me up. Before Benedetto has a chance to run, I move forward and slit his throat. I won't ever forget the sound of Benedetto's body hitting the ground with a loud thump before me and the beauty of all hell breaking loose around me.
Madden makes no move to help his boss. He just stands there smoking his cigarette and cleaning the blood that now stains his black combat boots.
The Irish fucker proved to be useful today.
The remaining bosses stare me down, but the fear behind their gazes is evident. How pathetic. Grown men afraid for their lives.
Then my eyes move to everyone else.
Every Made Man is facing each other now that their leader has fallen at my feet.
The families are no longer one.
Not in this instant, at least.
Nicolasi, Volpe, and Parisi.
They're all standing like they're in the middle of a battlefield,

and they have chosen their side.

They stand behind their family.

"Now that the useless fuck is gone, we can carry on." Spitting more blood on the ground, I scrunch down to where Benedetto lies dead. Reaching inside his suit pocket, I find the holster and grab his gun before straightening to my full height.

I look down at the gun and know that everything will change from now on, but I need something first.

I need to hear it from him even though I've always known which path he will choose.

Walking toward my twin brother, the crowd parts to let me through.

I can feel it.

A shift happened, and everyone knows not to fuck with me if they value their lives. If they don't want to end up like the great Benedetto Nicolasi.

I face my twin.

Knowing exactly what this is.

How it will be from now on.

Two brothers on opposite sides.

It was bound to happen.

We both want to be king.

"So, what will it be, little brother? Will you stand down?" I ask my brother.

"You know I can't do that." Valentino hisses.

I know he can't.

Even after all that hurt, he's still holding onto hope.

For her.

I nod once before inching closer and pressing a soft kiss on my twin brother's forehead. "Very well. May the best of us win."

It's all bullshit because the very best of us is him, and yet, I know, deep down, I'll walk out of here, and he… might not.

Giving my brother my back, I face the room. All eyes are on me now. Everyone wears all types of mixed emotions on their faces. Rage, confusion, betrayal, fear, and the most obvious of them all…pride.

The more blood you spill, the more respected you'll be in this life.

The more souls you take will secure the crown on top of your head.

Taking out a family member?

That should make you a rat, wouldn't you think?

Not in this corrupted family of ours.

No.

It makes you feared and revered.

"The Holy Trinity has always been the most feared crime organization across the country and worldwide, but somehow, we have lost the respect for most of our allies, and our enemies have found ways to penetrate our folds and infiltrate us from the inside. There are rats, and we will flush them out. There is no better choice for capo than me, and I will show you today why I was born to lead." I share with all of them the words they so desperately want to hear from me. Today, I not only betrayed my brother, but myself as well. For her. For both. "Welcome to the new dawn of the Holy Trinity." I spread my arms out and look every single one of them in the eyes. "Does anyone want to challenge me?" I direct my question to the remaining bosses, both Tommaso and Gabriele. As expected, they don't utter a word.

"I didn't think so. Let's move on with the ceremony, shall we?"

Holding onto the rosary on my neck with a death grip, I give everyone my back, ready for the fight of my life.

***

This is the end of me.

The end of everything as we knew it.

I have no problem fucking up Lucan and the Parisi sisters but my brother? I'll lose the only remaining human trait about me. Not that I have many to begin with. Tino refuses to back down, and I get it. He sees it as his only choice to protect her. He still harbors resentment toward me for what I did, but I did it to protect him. Benedetto would've never accepted the weird girl, just like he rejects Cara Mia. He was relentless in his quest to keep them apart, and I wouldn't put it past him to hurt, or even worse, kill the girl. So, I did the dirty deed and kept them both safe, but did they thank me?
Nope.
Now, here we both are, facing off against each other. Tino, for selfless reasons, and me, as always, the opposite. I want to keep them all safe, and the only way to do that is to take out my brother. I want it all. I want to be Capo of the Holy Trinity, but the other half of me is standing in my way. "Like generations before us, we must prove ourselves worthy of the capo position." I look at my brother now. "You completed your task, brother. Now, it's my turn." A look of shame and anger crosses his eyes. A word I have never uttered in my miserable life threatens to fall from my lips, but I stop myself.
Think of the endgame.
Everything will fall into place.
It has to.
"What exactly is your task, Lorenzo?" The sweet voice belonging to the redheaded little monster that haunts my dreams and reigns in my nightmares. I don't give her my attention. I can't. She makes me feel, and I need to keep my emotions in check for what I'm about to do.
But Valentino knows. I don't need to say it because he knows what needs to happen next. The Nicolasi family can only have one boss.
Me.
Tino steps forward and walks toward the fighting ring.

He climbs inside and closes the cage's door, trapping us both inside. The sound of the door closing is deafening. We won't come out of this unscathed. The one left standing will be the next Nicolasi boss. My twin brother takes off his black turtleneck and meets me in the middle of the fighting cage. I look at my brother, and besides his platinum blond hair, everything else is a mirror of myself. If I were a better brother, I would let him take the title and get the girl, but I am too selfish. I am like my late uncle, Demetrio. The one responsible for causing my parents so much pain. Valentino and Andrea are the good ones.

Not me.

I am the worst of them all. This only proves it. I can handle my own against my brother. I'm sure I can take him out, but Lucan? He's the best fighter of us all. He's been fighting to survive his entire life. I want this more, and that makes me his toughest rival. Arianna and Kadra are no match for me. The families know this, and still they gave them hope that one day they could lead the Holy Trinity.

Though shit.

They won't be leading me.

Not because I find them lacking or unfit to rule men, but because I know I was born to be the boss of the three families.

It is in my blood.

There's nothing I wouldn't do for it, even play along. Play the part of the dutiful soldier that stays in line. Shit, that's no fun. From the corner of my eye, I watch as Tommaso comes forward and faces the room.

"Today, you fight for your title. You are no longer friends or siblings. The person next to you is your enemy, and what do we do to our enemies?" Tommaso cruelly smiles before he continues. "We annihilate them until there's nothing but flesh and bones...until there's nothing but sweet, sweet chaos." How quickly this bitch forgot Benedetto's body lying dead on the floor. He was his closest friend, confidant, and the underboss of the Holy Trinity for almost thirty years. That goes to show how friendships don't last in the mafia. There are only hidden threats disguised as a trusted friend. I look down at my right arm and notice I'm still holding Benedetto's gun. Valentino is watching me like a hunter would his prey. I open the cage's door once again and throw the gun at Rian's feet. The asshole makes no move to pick it up.

Of-fucking-course. Benedetto's lap dog never does as he's told.I make my way back to where I left Tino, standing in the middle of the cage's floor. I don't even make it to where he is standing before I feel a hard blow on the side of my face. Fuck. I'm disoriented for a second, but I don't lose my footing. He caught me off guard. Val never plays dirty. He's acting reckless. I curl my hand into a fist and aim for the front of his face. My fist hits the bridge of his nose, and once the blow lands, blood splatters all over the cage's floor. Fuck, but do I love pain. Not my brother's. Never his. Every blow I land makes me die a little bit more inside. Valentino stands up from the floor and hits me again until I taste blood. He keeps hitting me, and I just take it until he tires out. I slam my hand hard into his ribs, and Valentino winces in pain. We both land hard blows that hurt like fuck, but we still won't concede.

We're Cassius's sons.

We won't ever stand down. Always stand strong.

Pain ripples across my chest when he lands a good punch to my throat. I feel it closing up, and it throws me off balance. I push through the pain and recover quickly. I throw my feet out and hit Val on the back of his knees until he falls to the ground beside me. Before he gets a chance to recover and hit me again, I straddle him and grab the sides of his collar before pulling my hands into the center and crushing his Adam's apple with the knuckles of both my middle fingers.

The move allows me to cut off his airflow and debilitate him. I stand to my full height before my brother, who is fighting for breath on the dirty and bloody cage's floor. With pain in my dead heart and shame in my dark soul, I stomp on my brother's face until I see his eyes rolling to the back of his head. The loud crack echoes in the room. The sweat and bloody smell is all around me, making me feel like the scum of the earth.

It is done.

I took my brother out.

I'm the Nicolasi boss. I won, but why does it feel like I lost more than I gained today? I have the title of boss, but I lost my brother. There's no way we are ever coming back from this. I could give a million excuses like I am the best choice or that, for selfless reasons, I want to be the boss, but I would be lying. I do want to keep Andrea safe from a tragic future and Tino safe from himself, but I also breathe for pain and chaos. This life was meant for me.

I won't give it up.

Not even for them.

Forgive me, father for I have sinned. There's nothing I wouldn't do to be king. I betrayed my brother and brought him to his knees. Now, I pray to the devil, for he is the only one I seek.

May God have mercy on my enemies because I sure as fuck won't.

A-fucking-men.

It all happens so fast. One second my brother is down on the floor, unconscious in an even worse condition than I'm sure I am right now. And the next second, I look down, and his body is gone. The only reminder that he really was there is the blood that remains on the floor.

My blood.

My brother.

I sacrificed both of us.
He won't understand.
None of them do.
But I do.
This hurts now like I never thought it would.
Fuck it, burns. But in the end, it'll save both of us.
My pulse is racing so hard that I think I'm about to have a fucking heart attack. It takes ten solid, deep breaths before my pulse slows and reaches an even rhythm.
I won the title of boss today but lost the title of Capo of the three families.
All I ever wanted was that, and yet, for her, I had to betray myself and fall in line under her brother's command.
Lucan Volpe.
The Capo.
For now.

CHAPTER FIFTEEN
GOODBYES

"You are more than what you think you are." – L

Cara
15 years old

The average human body holds approximately ten pints of blood. I know this because, from the very first moment I first saw a drop of the red substance, I was fascinated with knowing more about it.

Now? Not so much.

Because blood is all over the people I care about.

On my brother.

On Enzo.

Blood's never bothered me before but seeing it all over the ones I love? Yeah, that's a whole other thing completely. They hurt each other. A piece of them died today. I can see it.

I can see it in the way my brother let go of everything that was holding him back from becoming cruel and what kept him from becoming just like the men that work for dad.

Ruthless.

Savage.

And if I didn't know any better, almost… heartless.

But I do know better.

I know his heart, and for that, I am not afraid, nor will I ever be afraid of him.

I want to run to him and hug him until he goes back to looking the same way he did this morning.

Like my sweet brother who would do absolutely anything to shelter me from the horrors of this world.
No.
Right now, said horrors are in full display, and I wish I could say that it is what bothers me, but it is not. Not really.
I know it bothers my brother, though.
He wasn't built for such cruel violence against the people we grew up with.
Not wanting him to see the pity in my expression, which might make him feel as if I'm being judgmental or might feel different about him after what I just witnessed, I turn away until I my eyes find Lorenzo. I find him still inside the fighting ring, staring absently at the spot where he knocked his twin brother out just a couple of minutes ago.
I've seen him fight before, but nothing like today.
Kids at the academy.
Jackasses that run their mouth around him.
Even saw him fight one of his grandfather's men once.
But not his brother.
Never his twin.
Everyone else is slowly retreating until only Lucan, Enzo and I remain. Arianna was taken by a group of men resembling secret service agents or bodyguards of some sort after facing her middle sister Kadra and renouncing the Parisi name in front of everyone.
I wish I could say we all tried to stop them, but no one did.
We can't get into their family's business.
Even if all I wanted was to get in between her and those scary-looking men and save her from her fate I couldn't. That's one of the many things I hate about being a woman in this life of crime.
With our fathers in charge, we don't have a voice.
A choice.
Maybe that will change one day.

After that, Kadra stepped out without a glance back, just leaving a trail of heartbreak behind her wake. She might not see it now, but today she made the worst mistake of her life, but who am I to judge? They all suffered enough as it is.

Their sisterhood once was unbreakable, now destroyed.

They don't have anyone to rely on now.

My siblings have me.

They don't have that anymore.

What a shit show.

Turning my attention back to Lorenzo, I watch him with his head down as blood and sweat mix together, and drip down his skin, covering him in his crimes.

This couldn't have been easy for him, and he can talk all the shit he wants about not feeling anything toward anyone but himself, but it's half a lie. He does feel for his brother and a lot, but today he treated Valentino even worse than he does his enemies.

I guess that's what they all are now.

Enemies just as much as allies.

I walk closer to Enzo, knowing that we are not alone. There are eyes on us.

The moment I'm close enough so he can hear me, I whisper, "Are you alright?"

I know the moment my words resonate with him when his shoulders stop shaking, and he goes completely still. The air leaves my lungs when he raises his head and looks up at me from his position on the floor. His right eye is swollen, and I can see a blood vessel popped in his eye. Blood pours from a gash on his temple. There's also more blood running down his nose, and when he smiles like a child who got away with doing something bad, I can also see red coating his teeth.

Jesus Christ.

No.

Anti-Christ.

Yeah, that's more fitting. After too long, Enzo's nostrils flare. "I'm fucking peachy, Red. Thank you for asking," He smiles that frightening smile of his. The one he reserved for the people that tend to piss him off. Sarcasm drops from his tone like poison. "I'm sorry you had to go thr—" He rudely interrupts me mid-sentence. "Nope. Let's not do this, Cara." Cara. Of course. Not Mia. "Let's not pretend that we both don't know I enjoyed every fucking second of what happened here today. Every-fucking-second, and you know what?"

"What?" Liar. You're lying. Why are you lying?

"I don't regret it." I refuse to believe that he enjoyed what he did to his twin. No matter how messed up in the head he is at times. There's just no way that the boy I've come to care for so deeply enjoyed hurting the other half of him. There's no way. Something doesn't add up here. Enzo has been counting down the days to the ceremony. He's wanted this title more than he wants to see another day. Thinking back to his fight with Lucan, he barely fought. Yes, my brother is strong and a great fighter, but Enzo lives and breathes pain and mayhem. He is in his element, and yet he lost. What are you playing at, Lorenzo? Something deep inside tells me there's more to this than what meets the eye. "I don't believe you." I tell him what's on my mind. Well, part of what's on my mind.

Enzo stands to his full height and gets all in my space, crowding me and at the same time, trying to make me feel inferior due to our differences in size. Too bad. He doesn't intimidate me. Never has and never will.

"You don't believe me?"

"I do not." I nod once, not oblivious to the fact that my brother is right behind me, most likely ready to tear Lorenzo apart again for being this close to me and in a threatening manner. I know he won't do anything, but Lucan doesn't. I watch as Enzo drops his head lower until I can feel his breath all over my face. "I know you. I know that you would never—"

Lucan, having had enough of this, steps forward and grabs my arm, pulling me back from Enzo, successfully cutting me off. I don't miss the way Enzo's brows pull lower as he stares at my brother's hand on my arm. And I think he'll say something, anything to let me know that my friend is there underneath the cruel smirk and evil glint in his eyes, but no such luck. I watch as his smile grows wider, and his eyes turn darker with malice swimming in them. "That was your first mistake, kid. Thinking you were more than a distraction. You were but a new project to rid me of my never-ending boredom." Laughing, he spits blood onto the floor. Not caring how his words cut me deep, but even when I bleed because of him, I don't let him see. I never let them see. Not that they hurt me. No. "It was fun while it kept me entertained, darling."

Bloody idiot.

What a horrible liar he is.

But okay.

"Bullshit." I step closer, not backing down. When he pushes me, I will push him twice as hard.

"Back the fuck off, Nicolasi, before I rearrange your face again." My brother barks while pushing me backwards toward his body in a protective gesture. For the first time in my life, I wish my brother would just stay back. I can handle Lorenzo.

"What, Volpe? You're not the only one with a sister fetish." He laughs, squaring up, ready for another fight. And a fight is what he got.

One moment, I'm staring up at his blue eyes as they look at me with an expression I can't quite decipher, and the next, I'm being pushed aside, and fists are being thrown.

Grunts of pain.

Skin hitting skin.

More blood.

I stand back and watch as Lucan completely hands Lorenzo his ass with brutal force, but I see. I see what no one else does. He's taking every punch as some sort of punishment.

"Stay the fuck away from her. I won't tell you again." Lucan throws one last punch, which has Lorenzo cackling like a maniac down on the floor with a poodle of blood underneath him. Giving up, I turn and follow my brother out the door, but before I step outside the threshold, I look back at him to find him looking at me. Hands clenched at his sides. Eyes burning and nose flaring.

Chest rising and falling.

Idiot.

You wanted to push me away. Now, you get to watch me leave. I'm done fighting for people that find it so easy to discard me like I was never a part of them.

I wish I would've stayed and fought harder because then I wouldn't have lost so much time with the man that owns my soul. Next thing I know, my world fell apart for the third time, but life went on. I found the strength to carry on when I left half of my heart back in Detroit with Enzo, and the other part died with my sister.

Until one day.

Until the day I provoked the beast, and it had no choice but to break down the doors of my new world.

A world that has no color until my king comes home.

Part Two

HIDDEN TRUTHS
8 years later

CHAPTER SIXTEEN
ROMEO WITH NO JULIET

"Who the fuck asked you, anyway?" - A

Lorenzo

NOW

Dumb motherfuckers have it all wrong.
Romeo was not heroic nor was he smart.
He was naïve.
He was a dumb-fuck.
Bitches like to glamorize their story but come the fuck on, it's stupid as fuck and quite frankly it makes me want to laugh every time a bitch I fuck calls me Romeo. No, darling. My life is not a love story. It's a cautionary tale.
You're so hard up for cock that you would fall into bed with the devil himself and then call him fucking Romeo.
Pathetic.
I never quite managed to grasp the concept of love.
Never understood the appeal either.
One thing I do know, and from a very young age, is that love fucks you up.
It turns the toughest motherfucker into the biggest bitch.
I've witnessed how fucking lethal the useless feeling can be.
The pathetic emotion hurts those stupid enough to let it consume them.

Those who fall victim to it.
And that's something I am not.
A fucking victim. Of anything.
Not of my circumstances, upbringing, or unnecessary emotions.
Love.
Devotion.
Faithfulness.
To feel love is to give your power away to someone else.
Fuck, no.
Thank fuck I learned how to suppress useless emotions at an early age.
I shoveled down what little I felt until there was nothing.
Literally.
There's no love here.
At times, it all starts to slowly creep in like it did from time to time when I was younger, but I kill that shit before it consumes me like it does others.
I don't think I am capable of love.
Sure, I have my twin, and I would do anything for that bastard, mainly because we shared a womb for nine goddam months, and a twisted bond was formed. A sister I don't dislike as much as I used to and nephews and nieces that don't bother me as much as other breathing things do.
However, profound love is something I'm just not capable of.
Real love between a man and a woman.
Monogamy.
I screech into a parking space just before an old hag and flip her off when she calls me a son of a bitch. Just because the bitch is ancient doesn't give her a pass in my book. But apparently, she didn't get the memo. Respect your elders, my ass. Sliding from my cherry red Aston Martin, I slip into my jacket as I pull out a smoke, cupping it to block the wind, then lighting it.

I take a drag and blow it out as I use my ass to shut the car door.

Doctor number 15 is waiting for me.

I still have ten more minutes before our session begins, so I enjoy a smoke as I walk down the street.

And there she is.

The only monster that haunts my nightmares.

Mia.

On a big fucking billboard, taking half the building's space. Rising social media star Mia Madden. Wedding announcement.

Wedding.

Wedding.

Mia Madden.

Thump.

Thump.

Thump.

Staring up at her, my vision blurs, and my head begins to throb.

Fuck.

Now you're just playing dirty, Red.

Good for you because that's the only way I like to play.

Fucking filthy.

I stare at the digital slideshow showing photos of Cara and the man that has a motherfucking death wish. I already see it. All the ways I'll make the son of a bitch bleed and regret ever thinking he was worthy of her.

Red.

That's all I see.

She looks as beautiful as ever. She was always stunning, but something about her is different now. Even through a fucking billboard,

I can see it. She found her voice and chased her dreams even when all odds were against her.

That's who she is.
Who she's always been.
A fucking fighter.
A wildcat.
Beauty in dark places.
Cara is a tiny little thing compared to me, but despite being so small, she has curves in all the right places. Petite with delicate features and a killer smile. A killer body. Killer eyes. She's the epitome of sweet and angelic—everything I'm not.
A new message pops up, making me look down at my phone, away from Red's stunning and treacherous face. I feel the beast growling, ready to tear apart every threat lurking in the shadows of her picture-perfect world.
You are the threat…
I am.
I've always been the nightmare that has haunted her dreams.
Me.
Only fucking me.
I look at the billboard one last time before I throw what remains of my cigarette to the ground and stomp on it.
Only one thought crosses my mind while my eyes remain glued to her stunning face.
"You've given me no choice, Enzo. Don't say I didn't warn you."
Vicious little monster, you have no idea what you've done.
Cara always liked to play hide and seek when she was a little kid. Before, she used to do a shit job at hiding.
Always wanting to be found.
Now, things have changed.
She's no longer hiding.
She's all around me.
In the news.
In the papers.
Every-fucking-where.

This is no longer hide and seek.
This is my favorite kind of game.
The cat and mouse game.
I might not be able to feel deep, soul-shattering love for another human, but I sure as fuck feel obsession. The kind that holds my sanity hostage and makes me do stupid shit.
Obsessed.
Fuck me.
And fuck her, too.

***

Tick-Tock.
The needles of the clock on the left wall of the good doctor's office move at a slow ass pace.
Haunting me, almost.
Provoking me, too.
"You're late, Mr. Nicolasi." The nasally voice of my latest chess piece sounds from the far right of the small room.
I grunt as I play with the metal rings on my fingers, not looking up.
Denying her what she clearly wants today.
My attention.
Today, I'm not pretending.
I'm done pretending I function like everyone else around me.
I'm also done pretending I care what this bitch diagnoses me with.
Romina Nazario M.D.
Black straight hair that runs all the way down her back, green eyes behind black-framed glasses, and cock-sucking lips.
To the naked eye, she looks perfect.
Not a single strand out of place, and not a single wrinkle on her maroon dress.
She's a fucking knockout and very accomplished from what I read about her.
But she's like every other bitch I've come across.

They all want something from me.
They see the shiny exterior, and they want it, completely disregarding the fucked-up mess inside my head.
The tattoos and dark vibe surrounding me excites them, making them believe they can save me.
They believe they will be the one that will 'change me.'
What a joke.
The only reason I keep coming back is that she sucks cock like a pro, swallows, and helps me bind the time.
I should have bounced the moment she looked at me with stars in her eyes while on her knees after licking a drop of my cum that fell to the corner of her mouth.
Bullshit.
Still, I stayed.
Because she said something on the last session that has been fucking with my head ever since.
Alexithymia.
One in ten individuals has this shit, and she believes I happen to be one of them.
Having difficulty with feeling emotions.
"Are you listening to me, Lorenzo?" Romina's nasally voice interrupts my train of thought. I've been doing that lately.
Thinking.
That's one thing I don't do much.
I act.
I act on impulse and urges, but lately, something has been holding me back.
Well, it was until ten minutes ago.
Until I witnessed her betrayal on full display.
Taunting me.
She did always know how to push my buttons to make me react.
That's why I've been staying away all these years.

I might not understand her feelings like most men would, but one thing I do know is that she deserves better. She always did.

But something changed today.

She awoke something within me that I've been ignoring for years. Something I only felt once before.

Always with her.

The all-consuming need to own her.

Her body.

Her mind.

Her thoughts.

Her days.

Her soul.

For fuck's sake, her heart, even when I have no single fucking clue what to do with it.

It is mine regardless because it is a part of her.

And Cara Mia Volpe has and will always be mine.

"Did I give you permission to call me by my first name, Miss Nazario?" My eyes leave the rings on my busted-up fingers and find her confused stare.

She really is a stunner.

Too bad she does nothing for me.

None of them do lately.

"I ah—" She stutters, not knowing what to say. There's no excuse as to why she felt like she could address me in such a personal manner when she's been nothing to me but a means to an end and a warm hole. I come here once a week and make my family feel a fake sense of hope toward my recovery. I should feel guilty as fuck for fooling them, but I don't. I need to get my sister and father off my back if I want to be around their children. For some odd reason, the brats don't bother me as much as their parents do, so I endure this shit so I can get Andrea's paranoid ass off my back, and I'm allowed to spend time with the kids.

I enjoy spending time with the little fuckers.Romina clears her throat and interrupts my thoughts again.

It's irritating now.

"Tell me something, Romina. What would you do if I told you I am planning on doing a very bad thing?"

She smiles seductively at me. The nerves leave her body when I shoot a smile her way. One smile.

That's all it takes to fool them.

I see what she does.

A handsome fuck with lying eyes and a perfect but mocking smile. For all the diplomas and awards hanging off her office walls displaying how brilliant she is in her field, it is safe to say she's not as bright as she believes herself to be.

A common criminal without a degree, just a high school diploma can pull one on her more than once.

Emotions cloud your judgment.

"How bad?" I notice how she swallows hard and how fast her pulse is beating in her slender throat.

Excitement.

Those are it.

The basic signs.

I laugh softly before sitting up on the white leather couch and placing my elbows on my thighs. "Very fucking bad. Lock me up and throw away the key kind of bad." Her eyes grow big, but this time it is not because of excitement or basic horniness.

It is because of the tone of my voice.

There's no charm.

My true nature.

I see her subtly reach for the red button that is hiding underneath her chair.

She's afraid.

And the bitch says I can't comprehend basic human emotions.

I know she's afraid.

Her confused eyes track my every move, and there's a small amount of sweat on her temple.

Tsk, tsk. And here I thought she was different.

A coward.

Oh, how I hate them.

Having had enough of the useless session, I stand from the couch and walk her way.

Romina trembles when she sees what I've been hiding the entire time.

Shiny metal.

My knife.

The moment I'm close enough, she bolts, but she is not fast enough. Grabbing her by the hair, I placed my hand on her mouth to conceal her screams of fear.

I didn't want to do this.

I really didn't, but she asked for it.

She thought the fact that she was feeding information to the fucking Russians would go past me, and I wouldn't find out. Un-fucking-lucky for her, I did.

"Get o-off me," she mumbles and shakes in my arms.

"You really shouldn't have gone rat on me, Doc. Here I thought we were the best of friends. Since you love to choke on my cock and all. What a greedy little bitch you are, huh."

She sucked my cock, and at the same time, she gave my enemies intel.

Fake shit I fed her.

I push her down on the carpeted floor and straddle her waist. The moment my hand leaves her mouth the bitch screams like a banshee.

Ah, I do enjoy them screaming.

"Want to play a game with me, Doc?"

"Nooo! Oh, God. Wait!" She flails beneath me and tries to push my body away from hers.

That shuts her up.
She becomes eerily still, and her whimpers quiet.
Well, that's no fun.
I look into her eyes, bend over until my nose is almost touching hers, and bring the knife down from her eyes close to her mouth.
"Now scream for me, darling."
It takes only a second, and she's screaming and crying again, but this time with blood running down her chin.
Once I'm done, I get the fuck out of the building and find my way outside again. Looking up at the billboard responsible for triggering the episode, I drop the piece I kept from Romina.
One thing she'll miss dearly.
The thing that got her in this position.
Her loose tongue.
I throw it on the ground and stomp on it as I make my way toward my car. Once inside, I voice dial the one man that always has my back, even after I shoved knives on his once or twice.
"Yes?" His quiet voice sounds from the speakers of the Aston Martin.
"I need cleaning, brother, and a whole lot of it."
He sighs once and hangs up, not needing or wanting an explanation.
Not that I'll give him one.
These days I don't call my brother for this shit as much as I used to, but when I do call him, he always picks up and shows up without me having to ask twice.
That's who Valentino is.
Loyal to a fault.
He might not agree with the shit I do sometimes, but he never judges.
He enables me.

We both know it.
We're both okay with it.
That's who we are.
Who we'll always be.
Cara Mia Volpe is mine.
Always has been and always will.
God help the bastard who tries to take her from me.
Even Mia herself.
I might not have single fucking clue what to do with her heart but I'm claiming anyway.
Every single part of her.

CHAPTER SEVENTEEN

HOLLYWOOD

"I'm not just a pretty face." - C

Cara

I once read that the human mind tends to forget whatever it was that caused trauma. It does that because trauma keeps you from evolving or moving forward in life.
Time heals all wounds, they say.
It's bullshit.
It doesn't.
Yeah, the wound doesn't sting the same way, but it never really heals.
At least not in my case.
As much as I would like to tell you that I left my past back in Detroit, that would be a big fat lie. I carried it with me when my brother put me on a plane and shipped me off out of the country to my dream school when I turned eighteen to chase all the dreams that lived inside my heart.
He made all of it possible the moment he took out our father and made sure to save my sister and me from the same fate other women in that life are subjected to.
Becoming wives and mothers never to be heard and barely seen.
I could also tell you that I'm fine.
I'm not.

I have good days and bad days.

Some days I'm barely hanging on, but I try my best to move forward without the painful memories of my past drowning me every night.

The loss of my mother.

The death of my father which made me feel guilty for mourning him. I did mourn the man I believed he was. The little girl that had the rug pulled out from under her feet the night she found out the man who was supposed to keep her heart safe from harm was the one who broke it first with his lies and cruel actions toward my siblings.

My brother's sacrifices for me.

Even years later, I still carry the guilt of binding him to a life he never wanted in the first place. A life that was never meant for him. He's living the life he deserves now, yet I can't shake off the feeling of guilt even now.

Then the memory that has haunted me for years now.

What he did to his own flesh and blood.

Our sister.

My love and hate for him.

I never thought there would come a day where I would stop talking to my hero. My Superman. I did. For a year after finding out he murdered our sister, I couldn't even look him in the eye, let alone utter a word toward him, but as life changed, I had to extend an olive branch because of my nephew. And looking back now, I can't imagine a world where I wasn't part of Roman's life.

It's painful to think about.

Not being in his life would be like losing her all over again.

As crazy as it is, I see Giana every time Roman belly laughs. His laugh is as infectious as Giana's was.

God, I miss her.

I don't miss the life we had back in Detroit, but I do miss my brother and how close we used to be.

I miss what could've been.

Then, memories I tried to suppress so I could move on with my life come to the surface when I'm alone at night or when it rains. When the sky lights up in the middle of a storm.

I think of him, too.

I miss him, too.

My dark protector.

My friend.

I think about the last time we spoke to each other.

I replay the night I was attacked by two men working for my brother's enemy, the boss of Chicago, Thiago Sandoval.

That night, I learned how strong and resilient I really am.

I also realized that no matter what goes on in my life, good or bad, I always go back to him.

So many memories, dreams, and nightmares, all in one.

Just like him.

"Oh, please tell me you didn't!" Arielle's pissed off voice breaks through my thoughts, making me look at her reflection through the vanity mirror in my dressing room. Arielle Morgan has been my agent since Andrea, my brothers' wife and world-renowned badass, hooked me up with an agent and media trainer to help me navigate the intimidating yet exciting world of fashion and Hollywood.

I am very blessed, and I'm aware that I have a privilege others don't. I had the advantage of having someone as influential as her in my corner, but it hasn't been all that easy for me. I didn't want it to be easy. I wanted to earn my place. Hence why I didn't allow her to use her status to get me fashion campaigns and to open fashion shows around the world. I didn't want to start a career knowing I didn't bleed for my dream like every other girl in my shoes would.

I worked for it, and I'm still doing it to this day.

It all started with social media, and then I blew up.

I was first a social media influencer.

I posted hair tutorials and fashion hauls, grew a loyal following, and from there, it was all history. Now, I'm here.

Moments away from shooting the final scene of a horror movie directed by Albert Wyans based on a true story. The day Arielle came to me with the script so I could read it, I was hesitant. I'm a model, not an actress, although it has always been a dream of mine to graze the big screen. And here I am. It's surreal. It's also bittersweet. All my dreams are coming true, and I wish my family was here with me every step of the way, but it wasn't in the cards for us.

"Earth to Mia!" Arielle snaps her long nails in my face.

Mia. Once upon a time, only one person called me that, and now the whole world only knows me by that name.

I'm no longer Cara Mia Volpe.

I am Mia.

Mia Madden.

Madden for my mother.

I get to live the life she couldn't, and I honor her by living each day as if it were my last.

Sometimes it is hard to keep a brave face, but I do my best for her. For them.

I look down at the phone Arielle has shoved in my face and take it in my hands. Shit.

I thought I had at least a day to break the news to my family. But with my hectic schedule, I completely lost track of time, and now the truth of my decision is plastered all over city billboards, the internet, and television.

The moment my brother's name flashes across the screen of my phone, I groan, already knowing what awaits me when I answer the call. Okay, announcing my engagement to the world before my own family is not one of my finest moments, but desperate times call for desperate measures.

My friend needs me, and there's nothing I wouldn't do for the people I love.

Scrolling through Arielle's phone, I read every article I'm tagged in.

Rising social media star Mia Madden has just announced her upcoming nuptials with co-star and longtime friend Jonah Shane.

This just in! The Hollow co-stars Mia Madden and Jonah Shane are tying the knot sometime this autumn, and we're here for it!

After years of speculation as to what kind of relationship they have, supermodel-turned-actress Mia Madden and male model and lead role in the Doomed franchise, Jonah Shane, are finally coming out to the world as a couple. Do you ship them? The engagement might be true, but the rest is all speculation. We haven't decided on a date yet because we both know it won't come to that. That was never part of it.

We're buying time. I'm hoping my friend will find his way soon, but until then, I'll hold him down like he has done for me time and time again without asking anything in return.

In a business as cutthroat as this one, it's a blessing how I've managed to build healthy and genuine longtime friendships, but I have. My team is my rock, and I don't know what I would do without them.

Handing Arielle back her phone and sitting back on the makeup and hair chair, I look at myself in the mirror before speaking over the loud noise of the small flat screen TV on the wall replaying the news of my engagement with more lies and speculations. I'm used to it by now.

"Should we release a statement before it gets out of hand?" I mutter as I watch my team do my hair and makeup for the last scene of the movie. The makeup is subtler than what I usually wear.

"It's already too late for that," Arielle's green eyes narrow before going back to typing furiously on her phone, most likely doing damage control.

"You should've told me, and maybe we could've kept a hold on it before it spread. Also, I'm shocked. You two never gave me the impression you were into each other." She looks up suspiciously before going back to typing.

We didn't want to keep it private.

We need it to spread all over the news and our social circle.

This is it.

There's no turning back now.

It's already done.

Sighing, I stare at the girl staring back at me in the mirror, no longer a girl but a woman. A hard-working and independent woman with the world at her feet, and yet nothing fills me completely. I don't feel fulfilled, and maybe that makes me ungrateful, but I honestly don't care. Andrea once told me to never sacrifice my heart for this business, and I don't plan to, but with every year that passes, it feels like I'll never fill the empty space in my chest.

The lights, the cameras, and the glamor make me happy, but at the end of the day, when I wipe the makeup off my face, put my hair down and slip between the cold sheets, I'm faced with the reality of my life.

That I'm alone even in a sea of people.

Do they love me for me? Or the woman I want them to see? Would they love me the same if they knew what lives inside my soul? Looking up, I find myself surrounded by my glam team crowding me while Arielle sits next to me, now talking on the phone.

Probably with Jonah's publicist, Moira St. James.

I sit completely still as I watch Maison beat my face until I look like a million bucks, while at the same time, Trina is trying to tame my unruly curls into a high ponytail. They always come through for me, and I wouldn't trade them for anything. Maybe I'm biased, but to me, they're the best in the business.

Then, I look down at what I'm wearing and smile for the first time tonight.

I'm wearing my sister-in-law's latest collection for the last scene of filming today. The Bloody Valentine collection. A collaboration I was a part of. She gave me the opportunity to work on it with her, and of course I said yes. I've been a fan of Valentina Co. since I was young, and it's an honor that she chose me, even though I was hesitant at first. She didn't accept a no for an answer, arguing that she wanted to reach the younger crowd and my image would help her do that.

So, hell yes, I said of course.

The piece I'm wearing is a satin black tube top with a matching skin-tight skirt that hugs my body in all the right places. It also makes the tattoos on my skin stand out.

In some countries, tattoos are frowned upon in mainstream media, so my team does a great job at hiding them with body foundation, but here in the States, I don't have to hide them. Hide myself. I look down at my hands and stare at the tattoo that means the most to me. The first letter of the names of my family. L for Lucan.

G for Giana.

N for Natalia, my mother.

R for Roman.

Now that we have new members in the family, I have to schedule an appointment with my tattoo artist to add an A for both Allegra and Artemis, my nieces.

Once Maison finishes adding the last touches to my makeup, my favorite peach lip-gloss, there's a knock on the door.

"Come in." I yell over the noise inside the room, and not even a second later, someone appears at the door, completely concealed by a large bouquet.

"Miss Madden, this was delivered to you and left at the front desk." It's Julio, one of my bodyguards. He is so silent that sometimes I forget he is even around.

Julio has been with me since I first landed in Los Angeles to chase my dream all over the city, and he hasn't left my side since. I stand up from the chair and walk his way before reaching out and taking the gorgeous arrangement of flowers from him.

"Thank you, Julio." With the flowers in hand, I turn around, but his calm voice stops me.

"There's something else." I stare at him expectantly and watch as he retreats out the door and reaches for something on the floor. He returns, holding two red boxes and drops them on the makeup counter. "Happy birthday, Miss."

Happy birthday.

Ah, yes.

A day I equally love and hate.

Love because it is the one time a year I hear from him, and hate because it is the only time he allows himself to reach out.

I sit back on the chair, stare at the large arrangement of bleeding hearts, and feel my heart skip a beat like every damn year. He sends them every year on my birthday, and each year he sends more than the last.

The bleeding hearts.

In the language of flowers, a bleeding heart symbolizes passionate love and romance, but a more morbid definition would be unrequited love or a broken heart. I never understood why he chose this flower until the first arrangement he sent years ago.

White bleeding hearts.

Purity and elegance.

And the following year, pink and white blossoms were delivered at my door like clockwork.

I tried to understand how his mind works, but I always came up short. It was frustrating until I gave up trying to understand a unique mind like his.

Maybe I won't ever get to fully understand him.

Now looking at the beautiful and sometimes mocking flowers, I'm reminded of how our story goes. It bloomed, and then it bled until there was nothing but the memories of stolen kisses and sweet memories.

And heartbreak.

Because my heart did break the day I left him back in Detroit to reach for the stars, when all I wanted was to stay in the dark with the guy that made my heart smile.

Foolish.

Hopelessly in love with a boy that didn't know what love was.

I stroke the pretty flowers and smile when I find a card hidden between the petals.

Tick Tock, Red.

It reads.

Tick Tock?

I place the card down and reach for the small box, first hoping there is more to it than a cryptic message I don't quite understand. He used to never send messages with the flowers.

He only signed the cards.

Nothing else.

This year is different.

Flowers, a card, and two other gifts.

Something must have triggered him to break his routine. That something might be the news of my engagement. Oh, well. We both never played fair.

It's not our style.

Opening the lid on the box, I'm stunned to find a beautiful gold choker in the shape of a dragon and when I look at it closer, in the dragon's eye is my birthstone, the ruby.

Dragon.

He used to sketch them all the time, and even has a couple tattoos of dragons of all sizes spread throughout his body.

I grew fond of dragons after obsessing over the meaning behind them.Dragons are unpredictable, subtle, and adventurous dreamers. Lorenzo is very unpredictable but subtle he is not.I'm in awe of the expensive piece of jewelry that looks like something that once belonged to a queen. I stroke the ruby and wonder what the meaning of this gift is. This is unlike him. Looking at the choker more up close, I notice it resembles a collar.

The gigantic ass.

Yeah, I will never understand what runs through this mind and how it works, but that's the beauty of him, really. How unpredictable he is, just like the dragon. He never ceases to surprise me. Placing the choker back on the box, I open the larger one, and when I do, I find all my favorite chocolate bars, red lollipops, and burgers that are still warm.

What?

What are you playing at, Enzo?

The junk food, candy, and bleeding hearts I understand, but the jewelry and the odd message? That, I don't understand.

Arielle comes to stand next to me and looks through all the gifts with curious eyes. She doesn't know about Enzo. Nobody does.

He has always been mine.

My secret.

Never to be shared with anyone else.

Just mine.

Then the phone that's been sitting all this time on top of the vanity buzzes with a new message. I quickly grab it, unlock it, and freeze the moment I open the new message from an unknown number.

Unknown: Tick, Tock. — E

Tik,Tok.

There it goes again. Before I get a chance to reply, another message pops up, but this time it's a photo.

When I click on it, my entire world stops, and everything else fades into the background.

Unknown: Call it off, or I'll turn his entire face bloody red.

"Fuck." I whisper under my breath, not wanting anyone else to find out.

There, on the screen, is a photo of a billboard with the news of my engagement.

Enzo.

I knew he would react, but I thought his issue would stay with me and not touch my friend.

Shit.

I should have known.

I did my friend a solid and figured I could kill two little birds with one stone.

I could get him to see that I'm done waiting.

I know what I want.

Throughout the years, we've played this mouse and cat game, but he always holds himself back.

My move unleashed the beast inside.

The one I've been eager to meet again.

Your move, king.

CHAPTER EIGHTEEN

SAPPHIRE EYES

"Here we go again, lover." – C

Lorenzo

I broke my cardinal rule.
The one absolute law I have always abided by.
Never let anyone know they have affected me.
In my inebriated state, I gave into my reckless impulse to reach out and tell the little monster exactly what I would do to her little bitch if she didn't call off her engagement. When I was younger, I broke a lot of rules for her in moments of weakness, but I'm not the boy I used to be. I'm worse, and if she doesn't do as I say, she will witness firsthand why I told her to move on with her life years ago.
There's no taming the beautiful darkness that lives inside of me. The same darkness I kept her safe from all these years. She's pure and too good for the sick shit in my head, yet I can't ignore the fact that she's been there, inside my brain for longer than I care to admit. Co-existing with the darkness. Now, she knows she holds some sick hold over me, and it seems to tip the scales of inequity in her favor, but not for long. I only have one regret, one that hasn't let me have a peaceful night of sleep since it happened but lying to Mia so she could let go of whatever silly fantasy she had of us in order for her to find her place in the world is not something I'll ever regret.

But that's the thing that fucks with me the most, the fact that I don't regret anything. Anything at all. Not when it comes to her. "Huh," someone says over the boom of the club's music. "I guess she finally moved on and realized she could do better." I know exactly who he's talking about. The damn news of her little stunt has been playing on a loop all day as if it's the second coming of God or some shit that requires an unlimited amount of coverage all over the news. She'll regret that. The music grows louder when the intruder stands by the door without shutting it behind him.

Of course, not.

Fuck, I can't even hear my own thoughts with how loud everything around me is. The music, the chatter of idiots throwing their hard-earned money in my hands, and the buzzing sound of the machine gun currently piercing my skin.

I've been sitting for half an hour staring at Draego's face as he finishes the piece on my throat. I've been meaning to have it done for a while now, but shit has been busy lately with my intrusive needy sister and her three brats, and let's not forget the people I've pissed off coming for my neck. While fucking with the bosses of other territories brings me great pleasure, the impromptu family activities my sister, Andrea, hounds me into are really getting on my nerves and taking a lot of my time and effort.

Add to that a sister-in-law that has attached herself to me like a parasite and wants me around for her kid's shit, too.

"And to what do I owe this displeasure?" I ask, lifting the glass of vodka to my lips and meeting identical eyes to mine. "Didn't realize you were back, brother. You should have sent a message before popping in unannounced."

"Oh, like you do every fucking time you come around my home?" Tino says while keeping a close eye on Draego. It's safe to say both men don't get along. Hell, I can't even stand the two of them half the time.

"That's where you're wrong, little brother. I'm always summoned." I smile over the rim of the glass before setting it back down on the table where Draego dropped his ink supplies. "Just ask your wife." It's an asshole thing to imply, but I'm an asshole.

"Watch it." Valentino hisses but walks inside my office before shutting the door behind him.

I feel Draego's hand leave my neck, and a second later, he's turning off the tattoo machine, adding ointment and then the plastic wrap before turning to leave as if he was never here. Quiet as a mouse, that one.

"I don't trust him." I take a long sip of my drink, keeping my eyes on my twin.

He has trust issues and is overly dramatic.

I trust my right-hand man as much as I'm capable. Draego has proved to be not only efficient but loyal time and time again. Especially after Mathias went down singing like a canary when he was read his last rights by the boss of Chicago. The recent bane of my existence.

I swear it's as if an annoying Chihuahua and a loud as fuck harpy mated, that motherfucker would be the result.

I watch as my twin looks at me with his usual blank expression in a poor attempt at being intimidating.

How adorable.

"I don't really care what you think of my men, Valentino." I do, but I'll never voice that to him. I need him far away from my shit for his own sanity and mine, too. Lord knows I don't need his wife, Fallon, bitching to me more than usual because her husband is deep in my business.

"There's something off about him." Tino tries to reason but it falls on deaf ears. Oddly, I trust his judgment, but he has to trust mine on this issue.

Draego is not a threat.

"Shit." I laugh as I stand to my full height and face the other the other half of me. "Then what must you think of me, love?"

"You, too." His sapphire eyes narrow.

Palming my chest, "You flatter me."

He stays quiet, but I don't miss the small spark in his eyes. He looks at me the same way he looks at his kids when they do something extremely stupid or shit their pants. I should be offended he looks at me as if I'm a toddler that amuses him, but after everything he's gone through, after almost losing him twice, I would dance the fucking Macarena if it made my twin brother get out of his head and leave his torments behind.

There aren't shadows in his eyes.

No.

All he has now are beautiful memories with his wife and two kids.

I feel… happy.

That's a rarity, but I do.

Lately, I feel a lot when it comes to my family.

So for that, I tolerate the weird gnome of a woman that stole my brother's heart and made him her well-behaved and loyal bitch.

She also gave me Poe.

The little shit Vade, too.

I look at my twin and notice how different he looks now. He's put the weight he'd lost after that piece of shit attacked him back on. Six-feet-four and built as powerfully as me, whereas before he wasn't as strong. He even dyed his hair back to blue and got rid of the black buzz cut. We looked too similar for my comfort.

Glad he cut that freaky shit out.

"She misses you." Tino moves around my office before taking a seat where I was lounging a couple of minutes ago.

She.

My lovely, sweeter than sugar niece, Poe. My girl. Fuck. Me. A look from that little girl disarms me in ways I'm still not comfortable with. I don't mind my sister's children and Vade, Poe's twin, but there's just something about Poe that I can't yet explain.

Her quiet nature stirs something inside me.

Her fucking giggles make the world stop for me until all I can focus on is her smile.

It's the same feeling I had the first time I saw Mia.

The same feeling I felt when I saw my mother's sad eyes.

"So, you added another pair of eyes." Tino's voice interrupts my train of thought before I go there. To that dark place I got out of years ago, and I don't ever plan to go back to. I'm thankful for the interruption but irritated as well, knowing where he's going with his useless observation. "Their eyes look good on you, brother."

I finish my drink, my jaw tightening. "Drop it." I don't want to hear it.

He nods once, and my attention suddenly goes to the new ink on his body. His children's names around his wrist. I thought he would've tatted their names on his chest, but that spot has been taken by their mother.

The big bastard is completely gone for his witch.

He's obsessed with his children, as well.

Good for him.

"Very well." Sighing, he turns my way. "I'll get to what I came here for."

Oh, goodie.

I reach for the bottle of vodka and pour myself another glass, gesturing to my twin if he would like to join me. He refuses. I knew he would, yet I offered anyway. "Do tell."

"It's about Cassius." His tone is laced with sadness, not resentment as it used to be. How things have changed. Maybe fatherhood has softened his heart a bit toward our father.

"What about him?"

My eyes leave my twin and look toward the TV where another news segment about Mia and her dead man walking is playing. Fuck, I won't escape this shit for God knows how long. Reaching for the remote, I turn the damn thing off.

The little brat has ruined TV for me now.

"There's a target on his back." My twin's voice snaps me out of my thoughts. I focus on his face and try to make sense of what he just said.

Our father has been an alcoholic for half of his life. Hell, most of our life was barely functional until recently. What the hell did he get himself into for someone to go after him?

"How do you know this?" What I really want to ask is why didn't I know about it until now?

Then my brother proceeds to tell me what he knows before leaving me to think about everything that was just said.

And fuck, what a fucking mess.

I guess I know now where I get my penchant for trouble.

Dear ol' daddy…

Shit.

CHAPTER NINETEEN

AMERICA'S SWEETHEART

"The world hates what they don't understand." - C

Cara

The loud chants and roar of the crowd, no matter how big or small, never get old. It's always so surreal to think of how blessed I am to be here and have people who follow and support me on this journey. Strangers who don't really know me yet want to see more of me.

They ask for my autograph and want to take selfies whenever they see me. Some even take time out of their day to leave kind messages on all my social media platforms.

It's wild that this is my life now.

But there's also the ugly side of this industry, one I've been warned about repeatedly.

I was first introduced to the world as a social media influencer, then a fashion model, and now I will reintroduce myself as an actress.

It's downright scary.

I won't lie.

So damn terrifying to put myself out there with my heart and dreams on my sleeves. For others to tear me apart just because they feel ownership over me. I don't want to be another cliché, so that's why I keep my head firmly planted on the ground and reiterate to myself how lucky I am, and I shouldn't let fame get to my head.

Stay humble, Cara, and you will always shine bright... My sister-in-law's advice stays with me everywhere I go and helps me with the nerves right now.

Now, when I'm seconds away from making my first appearance on Late Night with Connor. I've been watching these shows for years, and now I get to be a guest.

Crazyyyy.

The theme music of the late-night show starts to sound all around me, mixed with the cheers of the crowd and for a second, I stop and take everything in before I step into the stage where the host, Connor Brandt, is waiting for me.

Jesus, this is real, and no, I'm not dreaming it.

I'm here.

I did it.

I take in the blinding stage lights, the big crowd clapping and smiling as they wait for me to appear from the side of the stage where I'm still standing and breathe it in.

Yes, I did it, but sudden grief hits me full force like an angry wave in the middle of a stormy day. My brother, the one who killed his own sister, sacrificed everything he ever wanted to get me here. To this moment. To the very moment all my dreams and hopes for my future came true. God, it hurts. I resent him for what he did, but I can't stop loving him. I cannot forget all he has ever done for me and isn't that fucked-up? I should hate him, but I can't. I won't be able to ever hate him.Holding my phone up, I take a quick selfie of me with the show's logo on the back and send it to Andrea so she can show my nieces and nephews. It warms my heart knowing that they're my biggest fans and I will always be their number one supporter in whatever they choose to do with their lives. A loud voice booms over every speaker in the set.

"Ladies and gentlemen, now joining us is social media sensation and one of the most well-paid models in the world, Mia Madden."

"Go! Go, go, go." Arielle takes my phone and gently ushers me forward till I'm almost on stage. I look at her over my shoulder, and instantly, I'm back to being Mia Madden, and all my media training comes to the front of my mind. Here we go. Two steps later, the crowd grows louder, and the lights dim a little, allowing me to get a better view of the steps leading up to where the host is waiting for me. Once I'm in proximity, Connor Brandt smiles his pearly white smile and reaches forward to help me with the steps. I smile and wave to the crowd, leaving all nerves behind, and then I'm sitting down.
"Oh, man. Look at that." Connor smiles and gestures to the crowd while the band stops the music and settles down. "I haven't seen a crowd act this wild since Paul Medley was here a while back." Connor says with a grin on his face, and the crowd grows louder at the mention of Paul Medley. This industry loves the man and his craft. He can do no wrong. Both men and women of all ages love him, not only for his roles in high-budget movies but also for his charismatic personality. I haven't met the man yet, but I know Andrea's best friend, Fallon, has a major crush on him. He's playing her favorite superhero in the next Batman movie.
"Thank you so much." I smile brightly at the crowd while I get comfortable in the red chair this show is best known for. The hot seat. Arielle coached me with the questions they might ask, and she also told me he might get slick and try something that wasn't approved by my team and for me to be ready. Arielle told me they tried to add a question about my engagement, but we shut it down quick. She got me off the hook by telling them I didn't wish to speak about my personal life and instead I would rather answer questions about the movie. "And thank you for having me, Connor."
He smiles back. "So is it true that this is your first late-night show appearance?"
"It is." I tell him honestly.

Connor looks at the crowd and then back at me. "That's awesome. Now, let's get to it, shall we?"

He starts asking me questions about my childhood, and of course I lie.

Well, I do not lie exactly.

I just conceal the dark part of my childhood and reveal some pretty truths.

I mention how I have a supportive brother and his wonderful family cheering me on every step of the way. They don't ask anything else after I make a point for them not to mention my parents or any more siblings. I'm not willing to share that part of myself with the world. It opens too many wounds that haven't healed yet, not fully.

But I know as I grow popular, people will feel entitled to all my truths and my past, and it will be just a matter of time before my past comes knocking on my door.

So, I smile and do my job.

Entertain.

Be myself without giving away too much.

The appearance lasts half an hour, and then I'm saying my goodbyes to the host and the crowd and walking back to the dressing room that was assigned to me, where Arielle and my glam team are waiting for me with celebratory balloons and a bottle of Dom Pérignon.

As I'm embraced by their words of encouragement and support, I don't miss the extravagant and beautiful arrangement of red roses taking up all the space in the vanity chest.

"You did awesome." Arielle offers me a warm hug before pushing something my way. "These were delivered while you were on stage."

Looking down, I grab the small, white card that came with the pretty roses, turning it over. I'm surprised to see the writing on it.

Time's up. – E

Enzo? Roses? He never sends roses. Time's up?

Chills run down my neck, spreading all over my body, causing goosebumps to rise on my skin. Shit. I've done it now.

I raise my head, pocket the card, and notice everyone has left the dressing room. Only my bodyguard remains waiting for me to follow him out of the building, and Arielle is gathering her things to head out with me as well.

"Okay, so get some beauty sleep." We both walk behind Julio as he ushers us out the back of the studio. "You have a press conference at eight in the morning, and your Vogue shoot right after that. Oh, and we need to sit down and figure out a schedule that works for us so you can fit in some press for the movie and still walk for Victoria."

I try to pay attention to what she's saying, but the message and the meaning of the roses take permanent residence in my mind. I can't shake the eerie feeling that something is wrong. I know he would never hurt me, but to make a point, he might push all my limits. Dammit.

I grab my phone and hit Jonah up. Only one ring, and he picks up. "Well, hello there, love of my life." His charming voice sounds from the other side of the line but does nothing to rid this awful feeling in my chest. It's dawning on me to know that no matter how brave I am, Lorenzo will always have the upper hand. Why? Because he has no morals. He doesn't care for others while I do. "You did so well, babe, and you looked ravishing, might I add."

I manage to laugh through the anxiety because he has the ability to do that. Jonah, I mean. He is and will always be the calm after the angry storm. "Look, Jo, I need you to get" – I don't get to finish my sentence when an incoming video call from an unknown number pops up on my screen. Normally, I would ignore it since my phone number has been leaked more than once, but something in my gut tells me not to. Crap. "Jonah, give me a second. Stay on the line."

"What's wrong?" His tone is no longer playful but worried. I ignore him, slide my thumb over the screen, and accept the video call.

Once the call connects, my heart stops in my chest.

It's a computer in a dark room while live footage of Jonah inside his Calabasas's home, looking out the window with his phone to his ear on the line with me.

He's naked with a black towel wrapped around his waist.

No, no, no.

Shit.

"I know it's you." I breathe out, fear taking root in my heart for the first time since I met him. Not once has he made me feel this way, even with the crazy things he did when we were younger. Not once did I feel like he would hurt my heart willingly. Hurting Jonah will hurt and so fucking bad, and he knows it. I did this. I thought I could bring him back to me, but now my reckless taunts have only served to make him madder than his usual self. "Please call your man off. Don't hurt him." Someone is clearly inside Jonah's home filming him as Lorenzo watches from somewhere else and tortures me with it.

"Do you love him, Red?"

My heart skips a beat, many beats. I feel it stop in my chest while I hold my breath. I take a second to gather my thoughts. One wrong word, and it might set him off. Lorenzo is smart, but he is impulsive. "I do. He's my friend. Don't do this, Enzo. Please don't. I didn't thin—"

"Huh." A dark whisper comes through the speaker of my phone.

The angle of the camera playing on Enzo's screen shows that whoever it is, is hiding in a dark corner of Jonah's living room. "You're so pretty when you beg, little monster."

Is that what he wants me to do?

Beg?

He was always cruel, but never to me but serves me right for starting a game with someone that stopped being mine long ago.

Because he was mine even when our unusual friendship never crossed the line of platonic. He was mine, and I was his.

It always felt right.

But now, I am caught between saving my friend from the man that haunts me each night when I close my eyes and not throwing a friend out to the wolves of this industry. "I will beg if you want me to, but please just don't hurt him. He hasn't done anything wrong. We don't—"

"You're mine, Mia. He doesn't get to play with you." It's sick and disturbing how that statement makes me want to hug the shit out of him and shove my red bottom heels up his butt. He won't even let me finish a damn sentence. I want to shout at him about how he doesn't get to act this way now after pushing me away. After many years passed without claiming me as his. But now that he feels like a toy is being taken away from him, he throws a tantrum. "Call that bullshit engagement off. This is my last warning. Fuck." He hisses, but it's barely a whisper. "Make it fucking stop."

Make what stop?

I underestimated what I meant to him. Does he care? Or is he only reacting because the claim he feels entitled to is being threatened?

Before I can answer him and keep trying to reason with him, he ends the call. The call with Jonah disconnects at the same time.

"Come on, Miss." I feel Julio lightly pull me over the door until we're both standing in the back alley of the studio where our SUV is waiting to take us home. I don't watch where I'm going as the cold air hits my face, and I keep trying to call Jonah, but the call won't go through.

"Shit." I try repeatedly, but nothing.

Then out of nowhere, a car honks loudly without stopping. I look up from my phone, but it's too late. It all happens so fast I can barely make sense of what's going on. One second, I'm looking over Julio's shoulder and notice a man slumped over the driver's seat of the SUV with his face pressed over the car's steering wheel. Is he dead?
Oh, my God.
"Julio," I grip his strong bicep before he falls to the floor. "Run inside, Miss. Hurry." I look down, and I'm taken back to the time when I was barely nine years old, and there was a wounded bird at my feet covered in blood. I stand there, battling with the need to do as he says and the impulse to drop to my knees and help him. "Go!" Julio manages to hiss, followed by a wheezing sound.
"He will kill me i-if s-something were to happen to you."
Who?
I decide to listen to the man that has been loyal to me since I arrived in Los Angeles years ago and turn away with a heavy heart, running toward the metal back doors of the back of the studio, but before I get close enough to bang on them for help, I feel strong arms envelop me from behind. A chill like I've never experienced before crawls up my spine and triggers this fight or flight impulse, and I do just that. I struggle with the stranger that's dragging me backward, away from safety into the dark night.
"Let me the f—" but my sentence is cut short when the stranger puts a black and what feels like satin cloth over my nose and mouth, which smells slightly sweet.
"Shhhh…" His hot breath causes goosebumps to spread on my skin. "Don't make me hurt you." A man's voice. A dark voice heavily accented.
I fight harder against the stranger, using my legs to kick him, my hands to push his from my face, but it's hopeless. He is much stronger than I am.

Oh, God.

Julio.

Did he bleed to death?

What will happen now?

Who is this man?

All that runs through my mind are the memories that keep me from giving up and letting this man take me from my world to God knows where.

My niece's giggles.

My nephew's playful grin.

My brother's hugs that would make our loud world quiet down.

Giana's soft smile.

My mom's angelic voice.

Enzo's stormy eyes staring back at me.

All I see.

All I hear.

All I feel is them as the world around me goes black.

CHAPTER TWENTY

HELLHOUND

"She loves the darkness that lives within." – L

Lorenzo

Children are innocent.

That's our rule.

The only rule I won't ever break, no matter the circumstances. Fucking ever. Just thinking about what that kid went through at the mercy of this animal makes my blood boil, and I feel an itch. The moment this filthy son of a bitch decided to hurt children and break our rules, he became number one – okay, maybe number two on my shit list. The number one spot is reserved for Hollywood's pretty boy, Jonah Shane. That motherfucker is walking on the thin thread that is my sanity. It took everything in me not to order my man to bring me back his head when he comes back into my city. But her distraught face immediately popped into my mind after the thought of that bitch. I can't do that to her. I can't take away someone she clearly cares for. Someone that's been there when I couldn't.

No matter how much the image of them together drives me mad, to the point, all I want is to beat his face to a bloody pulp. The image of his hands on her skin makes me want to chop them off so he could never touch what's mine. Because make no mistake, she is mine in every sense of the word. Yet, I always hold myself back.

From hurting her heart.

That doesn't mean I can't make her believe her lover boy's life is in danger. She knows me better than I sometimes know myself. She knows my cruelty has no bounds.

But she begged for his life today.

Begged me to call my man off.

She is lovely when she begs.

But not on behalf of another man.

Fuck that.

Cries and pleas for mercy bring me back to the beautiful scene before me. "Please, have mercy. Just please let me go or end me now," the sick fuck begs as I strap him to the surgical table, securing black leather belts around his middle and legs, giving him no choice but to stay bound and at my mercy. He can't even move a muscle, not that he hasn't stopped trying to save his life since I dragged him down here, to the hell on earth I created inside my mansion.

Hell on earth, that's exactly what it is.

For them, at least.

It looks more like heaven to me, but oh well.

It's all about perspective.

"You've heard of me?" I made a point to get rid of the men that used to follow Benedetto, the old boss before me, my grandfather, blindly. I didn't have any use for men that were weak and whose vision for the Nicolasi family didn't align with mine. The Nicolasi family is no longer pure. No longer full-blooded Italian, and neither is the Unholy Trinity organization of Detroit. Once I got rid of the old-school made men that were part of the family, I acquired new blood. Tainted, polluted, and to my image.

I found teens and men from the streets and gave them a purpose. A family.

From all kinds of backgrounds and walks of life.

Made men have codes they abide by.

Some even have morals.
My family no longer does.
They're now mercenaries.
But like every family, there's one or sometimes more than one bad apple.
This bitch is one stupid apple.
He thought he could do as he pleases, and no one would ever find out. I have eyes everywhere, and my men might be street dogs with no morals, but they all agree on the same thing.
We hate fucking dirty pedophiles.
Grown men and women who prey on the innocent.
Paolo fucked up. Not only did he double-cross me by giving information to the boss of Chicago, but he's also responsible for Mia getting hurt. And he was also involved in a sex ring. That's why he's down here with me, waiting for death after weeks and weeks of going back and forth between my men who each got their turn with him.
You can never not call me generous.
He looks and even smells like death.
How sweet.
"We're rich. Tell me what you want, and it's yours. I swear."
A chuckle slips past my lips because I should have expected something along these lines from him. Always the daddy's boy, ready to throw money at whomever to shut them up. Too bad for him it won't work this time. Goose bumps pop up on his skin as I put on the latex gloves, snapping them against my wrists. The sound echoed through the space.
"Y-yess." He wheezes out in pain. "Please, I will pay anything."
I smile down at him, catch his terrified stare, and watch as a bead of sweat falls from his hairline down to the right side of his head. Then I move my eyes to watch the blood drip from his broken nose, which has been cracked more than twice.
Shit.
I do enjoy the sound of bones breaking.

Paolo manages to talk despite the pain, trying to bargain for his life. There's nothing he can offer that even remotely interests me. There's hope swimming in his eyes as he looks up at me. Oh, how I love it when they hold on to hope. It's useless— a useless emotion in most cases, but in this instance, it gives him the determination to not give up.

Nothing will save him.

His ass will meet his maker tonight.

"I'm bored," I finally say after a couple of seconds of silence, and his eyes widen at the sound of my voice. It is no longer chirpy but emotionless. Paolo squints, fighting with the bright light that's positioned perfectly over us to allow me to see my victims better.

Also, so they can see me better.

It's flattering that I'm the last face they see before I watch the light leave their eyes and the blood run down the drain which sits below the surgical table.

"Oh, God, please, no." He cries, and in this instant, he almost resembles a little boy. Did he get off when his victims cried out for their mommies and daddies? Cried out when they were hurt by sick motherfuckers like this one.

The anger inside me grows stronger until all I see are the faceless children.

All I hear are the cries of the children that we rescued from the basement of this son of a bitch.

"Scream for me, love." He does, and a familiar thrill rushes through my body, filling my blood with euphoria at the prospect of bringing this poor excuse of a human unbearable agony. He will know no mercy.

Looking down at him, I smile when I notice there's no part of this bitch that hasn't been touched by my men. Greedy bastards.

I reach inside my back pocket and retrieve a pack of cigarettes, taking one out and lighting it.

The sweet sensation of the nicotine rushes through my body while I enjoy the scene before me. He's crying louder now, but no one will hear him, and if they do, no one will save him. This room has soundproof walls that Benedetto had installed to keep his extracurricular activities, both the killing and fucking younger men, behind my *nonna's* back.

I made sure to take that shit out. Hell, I completely renovated the Nicolasi mansion until all reminders of the past were gone. I bend over and grab the small gallon of gasoline I have under the table, opening the cap quickly as I get to work. I bathe the motherfucker in gasoline while imagining the flames taking over his skin, making him scream in agony. I'm getting hard just thinking about it.

"Do you want to hear a joke, Paolo?" he gasps, shaking his head wildly and trashing his feet on the table.

"Please, it was a mistake. I won't ever do it again." Oh, the famous line. They lie. They all lie when faced with the reality of their life's choices. The outcome. Death. Animals don't change. Once you've experienced the thrill of the chase, sunk into darkness, and wore it like your second skin, there is no going back.

"Knock, knock."

"Stop it! You sick fuck." Ahhh, there it is. He isn't so nice now. The mask has slipped.

I try again. "Knock, Knock."

"W-who's t-there?" He hiccups while struggling to breathe with the liquid spilling out of his mouth. He's coughing as well, and I think I see vomit spill out of his mouth mixed with the gasoline. Perfection.

I bet Valentino would love this scene. I should've recorded and sent it to him, but his sense of humor has always been… well, nonexistent. Plus, I don't want to give him another reason to suspect I'm not upholding part of our deal to remain in his kids' lives.

Whatever happened to loving and accepting family as they are? Yeah, I accept them as the freaks of nature my brother and his wife are. He mumbles incoherently, and I take it as a response to my attempt at a joke.

"Satan." I laugh at his confused expression. "Say hi, to Satan for me." I joke, but I fail miserably, right before I grab his micro dick and cut it off. His agonized screams fill the basement and bring me much-needed joy. He screams and screams, and then I ram his dick in his mouth that's filled with gasoline. And while he chokes on it, I take out my zippo and light that motherfucker on fire. His screams grow louder, like music to my ears. In time, his screams stop.

I take a deep breath and look around the scene, suddenly unsatisfied. The monster in me still rages because killing doesn't feel like enough. But he had to die, regardless. No one betrays me without consequences. No one gets away with it and does not suffer in the harshest ways.

Romina betrayed me like a bitch in heat typically does, and she paid for it. I got her tongue. This bitch, too.

Many others, as well.

There's more to come.

Oh, I'm sure.

***

After reaching the edge of the cliff, I throw his burned body inside a plastic bag into the river, where he lands with a loud splash, immediately going down while I grin, saluting him. Hopefully he burns in hell for all eternity. "Yeah, say hi to daddy for me," I say and go back to my car, where Draego is waiting for me.

Once I step inside the car, I'm about to order Draego to leave me back at the club and go finish delivering all the kids we saved from the sick pedo, but the look on his face tells me something is not right. Fuck. What else?

Reaching for the glove compartment, I take out a cherry

lollipop and pop it in my mouth. "What?"

"Volpe called your phone. I answered."

"And?"

"His sister is nowhere to be found." He goes on to tell me all the details, but nothing seems to be registering except for the words: Nowhere to be found.

"Here," He shoves the phone my way and hits play on the footage of Cara Mia leaving the studio with her bodyguard in tow, one I set up for her, might I add.

Something I've never felt before happens.

I can't find my next fucking breath.

Gripping the phone so tightly I might break it if I don't ease up, I zoom in with my fingers to the part where a man dressed in all black and wearing gloves puts his hands on her and drags her backward.

Black.

Gloves.

Three stars on his fucking neck.

The Russians.

"They fucking swore they would let shit be." I hissed.

Fuck.

"The jet is ready for you—I'm guessing we're changing directions?"

"You guessed fucking right." I ground out, replaying the footage. Her face as her bodyguard-turned-friend motions for her to leave him. Her small body struggling in the hands of that son of a bitch.

I memorize it as I have done with every person and moment where someone has ever done her wrong.

I've made them all pay.

The stupid kids that hurt her heart when she was younger.

Benedetto, who called her names not worth repeating because she is nothing short of perfect.

Thiago Sandoval got a taste of his own medicine when I

took his man out as retribution. Now, I'll take care of that whole city if I have to.If it comes down to it.

"Where to?" Draego murmurs as he turns on the car.

"New York City." I lean back on the passenger's seat and try to calm my breathing. This shit is not happening. Not to her. Fuck. "There's something else, boss." I turn to look at him and try my best not to murder one of my best men. Scratch that, my best man. He is something made from nightmares. Looks as if the devil and the angel Gabriel had a child of their own. Bright blonde hair that curls at the end and falls to the top of his shoulders that he sometimes puts up in a man bun whenever he's getting messy with his victims. Out of all my men, he's the one that gets the most ass thrown at him, yet I've never witnessed him give into the bitches that desperately try to jump on his dick back in my club. Staring into his big gray eyes, I think back to the first time I saw him pickpocketing a man on the streets as a scrawny teenager. Look how far he's come. He's almost as big as me. The motherfucker is scary as fuck, too. As some of the screams of his victims make me believe. He's one of the few people I tolerate being around me, mostly because he's quiet and gets shit done without pissing me off. Tonight, though, he's the bearer of shitty news."This was left back at the club with one of the bartenders." He pushes what seems like a crumpled-up news article my way while keeping hold of the steering wheel with the other. "And before you ask, I checked the cameras, nothing weird. The asshole was smart. As if he was aware of where the cameras were and was careful not to be caught on them. He approached Rocky, handed her that and said to give it to you before stepping out." I look down at the article I now hold in my hands, and the first thing I see is Mia's sweet face smiling at the camera, but looking down, I notice a big ass red X right on top of her heart. Her heart. A threat. Fuck.

Who the fuck is playing with me by using her?
The Russians have no motive to hurt her. They have no beef with her, and they goddamn well know that she's no longer part of our world, and that makes her an innocent.
This shit I hold in my hand was done with malicious intent.
Further down the article, there's a message with letter cutouts of different fonts, sizes, and colors. The person who's behind this is trying to imitate a ransom letter like the old fucking days. How fucking original.
The second I read the message, the organ inside my chest stops and every noise fades into the background until all I can focus on are the words that have a bigger impact on me than a knife to my chest.
You failed her, like your daddy did your mommy.
I failed her.
Mommy.
Cassius.
Demetrio.
We all know what that sick bastard did to her the moment he found her defenseless and vulnerable to his twisted intentions. The motherfucker behind this has no idea what he just started. I've killed men for less.
Punching the window of my car repeatedly, I'm pleased with the numbing pain spreading all over my fist and wrist because it helps me focus on the rage I feel bubbling inside, promising retribution to every single person that has fucked with me tonight.
I should have never let her ass out of my sight.
After this, there's no fucking way in hell I ever will again.

CHAPTER TWENTY-ONE

FAMILY TIES

"There's beauty in madness." - V

Cara

Men shout in a language I do not understand.
Spanish? I caught one word— carajo— one that my sister-in-law uses daily while dealing with my brother.
Yes, Spanish.
I feel pain in my stomach.
Blood spreads inside my mouth from the blow the stranger landed on my face.
There is an excruciating pain in my hand where I felt the cut of a knife.
Strange hands are gripping my arms, trying to haul me off the bed.
Grunts.
Shouts.
Blood.
More shouts.
Bang.
"Shoot first, little monster. I'll handle the rest." He promised me when he was just a kid himself.
Angry tears slide down my cheeks as I will myself to calm down and start to run in the direction where I have always felt safe.
Toward him.

***

An annoyingly consistent sound of loud honks in the distance pulls me from the recurring vivid nightmare that's haunted me since it happened. Since I pulled the trigger and ended someone's life. Haunted me not because I regretted it or feared it, but the complete opposite.

The lack thereof.

In that moment, I had a choice to make, and I chose myself over someone else's life.

There was blood all around me, and I didn't feel remorse.

Nothing but the need to get out of their clutches and find my way back to my family.

To safety.

To Lorenzo.

Not wanting to dwell on things I cannot change, I blindly reach toward the nightstand—like I do every morning to check on any missed messages or calls—but as soon as my fingers skim the table, I feel nothing.

Weird.

I shoot upright in bed, and the events that transpired last night instantly play through my mind.

The dark alley.

Julio falling on the wet concrete, pleading for me to leave him behind wounded.

To run for safety.

The dead man inside the black SUV who was supposed to take us home.

And then…

I vividly remember strange hands covering my nose and mouth with a wet cloth that smelled too sweet before I went under and became limp in the arms of a stranger.

It only takes me a second after opening my eyes to realize I'm not home.

I'm not safe yet.

Bolting out of the strange bed, the first thing I do is check for injuries or any signs that I've been abused. Running my hands up and down my body, I feel fine. No visible bruises on my exposed skin and no discomfort between my legs. My clothes are intact, yet I look around for a mirror so I can inspect myself more closely.

God, what time is it?

How long have I been asleep?

My head pounds a bit, and my body feels light as if I've been asleep for several days straight.

I notice the stream of daylight sneaking through the partially shuttered blinds and walk around until I find a floor-length mirror right beside what I presume to be the bathroom door. I cringe a bit when I see my reflection. My hair is a mess, sticking out in every direction, and my makeup is ruined, but besides that, everything seems okay.

I'm okay.

No bruises.

No cuts.

Nothing.

Looking at myself in the mirror, I take a deep breath, calming my erratic heart and pushing away the nerves that won't help me get out of this situation in any way. I'm no stranger to danger, especially since I've been warned about what might happen to me just because of my last name. My brother, Lucan, taught me the first rule of survival in our world.

Do not panic.

Breathe in and out, and then look for anything that might help me stay safe from the threat. I do just that.

My phone is not with me.

They must have it.

Shit.

Okay.

That's fine.

What else?

My surroundings.

I need to figure out where I am and who took me.

Know your opponent. The next rule.

God, how I wish he were here.

Do they know?

God, does the world know by now?

My family will for sure be looking for me right now, and I trust Arielle knows how to handle the media before things get out of hand.

Yes, they'll find me.

At least I know for sure my brother would go to the end of the world for me.

I fully believe that with all my heart.

Then a thought comes to mind.

I'm always bringing him back to this life he hates so much.

Before the bitch guilt I know all too well creeps in, I concentrate on figuring out where I am and if there's anything in here I can use as a weapon.

Stepping out of the bathroom, I move around the huge bedroom and take everything in. The room looks like something out of Dracula's castle. The room has a gothic revival style and an air of melancholy and tragedy surrounding it. The moment I woke up here, I couldn't shake the feeling of familiarity. As if I've been here before. The feeling of deja vu. It's weird since I've never been inside this place, yet the feeling is there, lingering in the forefront of my mind.

I searched the bathroom, and nothing. Next, I look inside the vanity's drawers, even under the huge bed and the furniture spread all over the room, but there's nothing here. Nothing that would serve as a weapon. Shit.

It is as if they knew the first thing I would do was search for something— anything to use against them. That means they know exactly what they're doing.

I keep looking around the room and notice how everything is intact, as if the room has been vacant for a long time. Crap, nothing that helps me. Not even to figure out where I am and whose room this is.

What I do find is an old cream-colored bassinet next to the bed with a stuffed bunny inside. I hesitantly reach inside and pick up the ratty old bunny, and the strange feeling grows stronger, almost knocking the wind out of me.

I've never felt this way before, as if I'm standing right where I'm supposed to be. Well, that's not exactly true. Every time I was with him, it felt like there was no other place for me but with him. When I feel like the walls are closing in on me, I drop the bunny back inside the bassinet and step back, trying to catch my breath. What is going on? I start to panic, and I find myself running toward the balcony. Throwing the doors open, I find myself looking over the busy streets of a city. I'm still here. I haven't left the city.

I'm still in New York and not in another country I don't know. How did I end up here?

Why am I here?

I look to my right and find rows and rows of tall buildings surrounding the one I'm in. Then I look down and instantly feel dizzy. I'm not particularly fond of heights.

God, it's so high up that the civilians down below look as tiny as ants. I highly doubt they'll hear my shouts and pleads for help from up here.

But I try, regardless.

Giving up is never an option.

Never.

Not for me.

Stepping forward, I lean over, looking down. The moment my hands touch the edge, the strong feeling of familiarity intensifies, but I ignore it and open my mouth to scream for help instead.

Before I get a chance to shout for help, the door inside the room bursts open. Startled, I look over my shoulder to find a tall-legged girl with white-blonde hair with the ends dyed soft pink. Her silky hair falls in soft waves down her shoulders and around her delicate face. She is stunning and looks like a younger Candace Swanepoel, wearing a short, low-cut, pink velvet dress with a thigh slit that reveals slightly golden, smooth skin. "I wouldn't do that if I were you." Her silky-smooth voice sounds over the noise of the busy streets below. "Besides," she shrugs nonchalantly, inspecting her manicured nails as if she's bored. "They won't help you."
Her cold tone takes me by surprise and, at the same time, reminds me of someone I knew before in my life back in Detroit. An ice princess with a mean streak and heavenly face. But there was nothing heavenly about her. The girl standing before me has an air of superiority around her. She stands tall with her head held high as if she wears an invisible crown made of diamonds. Facing away from the balcony, I step inside the room and close the doors softly. The weird feeling in the pit of my stomach I felt before eases the moment I'm away from the balcony. Weird. "Who the hell are you? Why am I here?" I shoot question after question while I get closer to her. She's way taller than me, but if I try hard enough, I might be able to take her, but I know it'll make things worse for me. There's no way I'll be able to get past the security inside this big as hell building. I'm in their territory, which means I'm at their mercy. "Reyna." She smiles icily at me, and there's something odd in the way she's looking at me. She's looking at me as if she knows me, and from whatever she knows about me, it's clear that she doesn't care for it or me. "Reyna Solonik." She can't be older than I am. She looks like a teenager with a huge ass chip on her shoulder, hiding behind expensive rags and cunning smiles.
Solonik.

The name sounds familiar, but I can't place it. Where have I heard that name before? I look at the stunning girl and let my eyes wander to her neck, where an expensive-looking delicate necklace with a solitaire diamond lays. And I think back to what Lorenzo once told me while we were sitting inside the treehouse, and I asked the best way to win a dirty fight against an opponent. *Always go for the jugular, Red. It's messy but effective.* I frown and consider my options. I could try to take her down, but her cold demeanor and Cheshire cat grin tell me she's looking for a fight. Any excuse to show me who's in control here. Her. Them. Not me.

"God, you look just like her." The girl, Reyna, furrows her brows and snarls at me. What's her issue? Who do I look like?

"No wonder dad insisted on you coming home." Dad?

Home? What the hell is going on?

My head starts to pound, but I ignore it and her weird assessment of me. I ask. "You won't help me, will you?" I'm not naive. She won't help me. If she intended to help me get out of here, she would have offered the moment she entered the room instead of speaking to me as if I were the dirt under her clear heels. She smiles sweetly at me, but there's nothing sweet about that smile or this child. A child, yes. She can't be much older than seventeen. "I can't even if I wanted to." She flips her hair and gives me her back. "Which I don't. If you want to know why you're here, follow me."

"I'm not leaving this room until you tell me what the hell is going on." Frustrated and frankly over this useless conversation that's leaving me with more questions than answers, I step forward toward her.

She shrugs me off, clearly done with me as well. "Suit yourself, Cara Mia," she says my name as if it pains her. As if it burns her mouth. "But I bet you wouldn't feel the same if you knew that the answers you've been probably longing for all your life wait for you downstairs."

Looking over my shoulder, she grins evilly at me. "Don't you want to know who your mommy is?"

As soon as the taunting words leave her mouth, my heart stops, and my eyes grow big. Satisfied with my reaction, she laughs harder and walks outside the room where I stand frozen, not understanding anything that's going on.

One thing I know for sure. These people know me. Here, a part of me lies. The part that's been missing all my life.

It's no coincidence that I've felt weird since I woke up here, and it has nothing to do with the fact that I was brought here against my will. Feeling more anxious than I felt before, I shortly close my eyes, and Lorenzo's blue ones flash across my memory. Watchful. Dangerous. Comforting. All at the same time. Suddenly, I no longer feel afraid. I feel him all over me, enveloping me in a safety net. Not thinking twice about it, I leave the room and follow the snarky blonde-haired person until she leads me to the truth.

The truth of my birth.

***

Cold.

Deadly quiet.

That's the first thing I notice about this strange place. I fall behind Reyna as she leads me through various corridors and then climb down a narrow staircase. If I were left on my own exploring this over-the-top huge penthouse would be lost for days. That's how big it is. It is the top of the building, and of course it's huge. Not only huge, but the decor is something straight out of a gothic revival edition of an in-style magazine. Very antique, though. Not modern like the Nicolasi mansion was back then. Reyna leads me to God knows where. She might be leading me to my slaughter, and here I am, following her like a lost puppy. All because I want to get out of here as soon as possible. I won't lie and say that the curiosity of figuring out who these people are and

what they have to do with me is killing me.
My origin.
My mother.
There's always a pang in my chest when I refer to anyone other than the woman who loved me as a mother.
Natalia Madden -Volpe was my mother.
The only mother I ever knew.
The one my heart chose to love, regardless of my DNA.
She never treated me any different from my siblings.
Loved me just the same.
But in the back of my mind, through the years, after finding out I was not her daughter by blood, I always wondered who my biological mother was and why she left me with my father. What happened to her? Who was she? Do I look like her? What was she like? All these questions were always present in the front of my mind, but out of respect to mom, I never thought of my biological mother for too long.
Killing the curiosity and impulse to find her before it grew stronger. Reyna opens a black-tinted glass door and steps inside without looking back at me once. I walk in behind her and look around, too stunned to come up with coherent thoughts for a moment.
God, this place.
Two crystal chandeliers hang from the ceiling above a black Victorian dining table made for more than ten guests. There's antique beauty all around me, from the luxurious black satin curtains decorating the windows to the decorative accents and art hanging on the walls. One thing I have noticed from what I've seen so far is that this place is the perfect equilibrium of the old and the new.
Stylish and modern, yet classic. It screams luxury and elegance without being corny like most celebrity styles these days.
It's also different from the room I woke up in.

That one was all white with mirrors, chairs, and a cream-colored vanity table with intricate detailing.
The room seems fitted for a princess.
It screamed pure elegance.
"Dinner is served." A warm and heavily Russian accent snaps me out of it, making me look toward the small woman wearing all black with elegant posture and a kind smile. Lost in my head, I didn't realize that Reyna had left my side and sat down at the dinner table.
She's not alone.
I was so busy studying my surroundings that I missed the two strange men sitting at both ends of the table, like kings ready to be served. That's exactly what they are, I guess. Just by the look of this place, it's not a stretch to believe they're loaded.
More than loaded.
Keeping my attention solely on them, the feeling that has been assaulting my senses since I woke up in this strange place is ten times more intense now. The men have a dark vibe surrounding them.
Both men are staring straight at me with different expressions on their faces. One of them looks almost statuesque, like a Greek god sitting on his throne casting judgment down on us mortals from above. The moment my eyes clash with his watchful and calculating gray ones, I'm taken back. There's something in his gaze that seems almost… gentle, a total contrast to his posture and the air of danger surrounding him. Why am I not terrified? I should be finding ways to get them to release me without any harm. Yet I'm standing here taking them all in as if I've known them my entire life, when in fact, I've never met these people before.
Haven't even heard of them.
But their darkness, although very intimidating, doesn't feel as dangerous to me as it should.

It's weird.
So very odd that I feel this way in the company of strangers that look the way they do and take me in the manner they did. Holding my head up high, I carefully take them both in. The one at the head of the table with dark eyes, looks older than the one sitting at the far end, but my guess is that he's not much older. One thing I can't ignore is how unbelievably handsome they both are. They both look eerily similar, and the one difference is one has stormy gray eyes with two small stars inked right below his left eye, and the other has dark as night eyes that seem as if they can penetrate my soul at any given moment with just one look. The older man is dressed in a black suit with a white shirt unbuttoned, revealing an inked neck. When my eyes travel to the hand currently holding a glass of warm-colored liquid, I notice the top of his hands and knuckles are inked, as well.
Stars.
One in each knuckle.
I look up at his face and take in his hair, with no speck of gray to be seen, just tampered locks of black. The other man, the younger one, is a carbon copy of the older man, but he has a different air around him besides the obvious dangerous vibes they both throw. The older one wears wickedness and danger as a second skin, but this one seems almost… unfeeling.
Unattached.
Cold.
Even with the casted glow of the chandelier, his skin has a natural translucent glow while every inch of his face could have been carved from stone. He looks like a Greek sculpture, plucked right out of one of my brother's galleries. He's dressed similar to the older one, but the one difference is the black gloves.
Gloves.
It triggers a recollection of last night's events.

Just before I fell unconscious, I could've sworn the man that took me had gloves similar to his. Black. Who wears black gloves to dinner? He does, and what an odd thing to do.

Looking at him now and his black leather gloves, I assume this is the man that hurt the others back in the alley where he took me from.

The one that hurt Julio.

It might be a stretch, but the chills that slowly spread up my spine make me believe I'm not that far off.

Suddenly feeling anxious, I take a step back from them and turn my head slightly to the left, trying to find a way out. God, my emotions have been all over the place since I've been here. Looking around the dining room, there's really no way out.

The only double doors have been shut.

It is obvious I'm not leaving this room until they're done with whatever this creepy as hell meeting is about.

Breathe in and out, *topina*.

Take a second and breathe.

My brother's comforting words run through my mind, grounding me. I'm okay. I'm safe.

For now, at least.

I know what a man with intentions to hurt me looks like. There's a giddiness in his eyes that is hard to miss. I don't see that in these men, well, on the one with the brown almost black eyes, I don't. The one with the personality of a rock, I'm not so sure. How can someone be so still? So quiet? Is he even breathing?

"You're safe." A baritone voice sounds with a slight hint of an accent.

Russian.

Solonik.

A Russian name.

Then a memory hits me full force.

The time Dad was having what seemed like a heated discussion with someone, mentioned the Solonik family, and spat in disgust when he called them the Russians. "Take a seat, printsessa." The soft look in his eyes is gone. A blank expression has replaced it. The same look as, who I'm assuming is his brother because of their almost identical facial features. I could deny following his order and risk getting whacked inside this dining room, or I could sit down and see how this all plays out. Choosing the latter, I push the chair that's farther from the beasts of men and closer to the least dangerous of the three, Reyna, back and take a seat. "Who are you people and why am I here?" I ask the second I am seated. Not even paying attention to the delicious-smelling food that's being served by the staff. I cough into my fist, trying hard to hide the obvious grumbling in my stomach from my hunger. Jesus, I haven't eaten since before the show last night, and I didn't even notice until now that food was on my plate. The older man grins when he catches me trying not to be so obvious. "My name is Vladimir." He says while pointing a silver knife my way, and not any regular dining knife. Not a knife one would use to cut meat, no. It looks more like the same one that was used to carve the cow. "That is Vitali, my brother," He points at the other man in the room and then proceeds to point toward the rude-as-hell brat sitting next to me. I don't miss the affection in his gaze and how his tone softens when he looks her way and says her name. "I believe you've met my Reyna. My daughter." Daughter? I wonder. He doesn't look old enough to be a father. He must've had her very young.

I turn my head in silence, and look at Reyna, completely ignoring her brown eyes shooting daggers my way. Yes, a brat or mentally disturbed. Perhaps, she's both.

My throat suddenly feels itchy, and I have half a mind to take a sip of the glass of water that was laid down in front of me, but I don't.

Eating their food and drinking from their glass is a risk I'm not willing to take until I know their intentions. Instead, I smile sweetly their way, looking each one right in their eyes. "I would say nice to meet you, but under these circumstances, we all can agree this is anything but pleasant." I don't want to be rude, okay, yes, maybe I'm being petty, but I have every right. I'm so confused, and they're giving me nothing.

The man, Vladimir, chuckles softly, looking straight into my eyes. "Not only do you look like her, inherited her blood-red locks that she loved so much, but her fire also lives inside of you." Her? My mother?

Is he referring to my biological mother? Reyna implied I looked like someone, a female, and now Vladimir is, as well. Do I look like her? That's what Vladimir is implying.

All my life, I was the odd one out because of my looks. I didn't look like anyone in my family, except for my father, and only his eyes. That's it.

But looking at these people, it seems I fit more with them than I did with my own family.

I have the same pasty white skin tone as the mummy of a man sitting at the end of the table, still looking at me as if he's trying to decipher all my secrets.

I have none, buddy. You, on the other hand, know more about me than I know of myself, apparently.

But ignoring the man, I wonder if she's here.

Is my biological mother here?

No longer feeling as brave as I felt before I stepped foot inside the room, I hope my erratic heart calms down. I always felt like a piece of me was out there, even before mom confessed I wasn't biologically hers.

Now, faced with the reality that the missing piece could be here with these strangers, I feel like the little girl again, looking out the window, waiting and pleading for her mother to come home.

To come back.
Vulnerable.
With all my walls lowered, ready for the inevitable blow that will come my way the moment these people reveal the truth of my birth.
I find myself wringing my hands behind my back like I always do when I'm nervous and faced with a situation I have no clue how to navigate. My eyes look at everyone in the room, Reyna is scrolling through her phone, but it's clear from her posture that she's alert to what's going on around her.
Vitali, on the other hand, hasn't said one word. He's staring through me while he runs one gloved finger around the rim of his wine glass.
The room is eerily quiet as I focus on the rapid typing sound coming from Reyna's phone and the clink of Vladimir's knife tapping his plate.
One heartbeat.
Two heartbeats.
Breathing in and out.
Then my entire world turns on its axis the second the beast of man finishes chewing his meat and opens his mouth. "Welcome home, Vera." Vladimir says with a wicked smile on his face before he takes a sip of his wine.
Vera.
Vera.
Vera.
My name.
My birth name.
It all makes sense now.
How dad always had a love for his favorite drink, a Russian neat. The way everyone acted skittish around me whenever the word 'Russian' was uttered anytime I was around.
How I never felt like I belonged in my own home. Not truly, even with all the love.

It all makes sense now.
Vera.
The Solonik family, my mother's family, just revealed the truth of who I really am when I was deprived of it my whole life.

CHAPTER TWENTY-TWO

THE BIG APPLE

"This city reeks of dead rats." – L

Lorenzo

I blow cigarette smoke out the window of the SUV.

"I told you I don't want you smoking anywhere near me." Lucan snaps at me from the driver's side while staring at the road ahead.

"Just because your wife made you quit doesn't mean I have to suffer because you have no balls." I retorted. "Besides, secondhand smoking won't kill you." Bullshit. It will, but I love to rope him up. Lately, he's acting all prim and fucking proper and walking on the straight and narrow. Yeah, I get it. You have to make sacrifices when you become a family man. He wants to live longer for his kids.

That's admirable.

"Secondhand smoking has taken the lives of approximately 2.5 million non-smokers since 1964. Read more." He drawls while side-eyeing me.

I take a quick drag, blow a couple of smoke rings his way, take what is left of the cigarette, and toss it out the window.

"Happy, love?"

"Fuck you, asshole." He says between coughs while I laugh. Seriously, it's too easy. "Are you sure he's going to be there? We can't waste any more time running around the city without a single fucking clue where she is.

Fucking Dion is not answering his phone either, which is fucking suspicious since he's in bed with the Russians.
"That French fuck is in bed with everyone." I state the obvious. Lucan pulls the car onto the road, merging with traffic while I type out a message to Draego.
Me: Is he anywhere in sight?
Draego: Yes. He just entered the Bleeding Rose.
Me: Good. Make sure he doesn't leave, and if he does, text me as soon as he moves.
Draego: You're in their territory now, boss.
Me: Aw, how sweet. You're concerned about me.
Draego: * middle finger emoji*
Me: "kissy face emoji*
Locking my phone, I pocket it and concentrate on the road, trying to hold in the rage I feel inside. I could fuck shit up and make these bitches regret ever taking her, but Draego is right. I'm in their territory now.
A few seconds later, Lucan stops the car right in front of the Bleeding Rose. A nightclub for the wicked and heathens of this sinful city. I heard of this place. It's where the most depraved souls come to play out their dirty fantasies and lose themselves in sex and alcohol.
Sounds like fun. "Behave. I want to get my sister alive and get home to my wife and kids." I hear as soon as I step out of Lucan's car. "When have I ever not behaved?"
"All the fucking time. So shut the fuck up and do the opposite of what that little crazy voice inside your demented head tells you to do." Grinning at him, "You say the sweetest things, love." He looks at me as we walk on the concrete that leads to the club. "I know you care about her. I might hate that you do, and trust me, it irritates the fuck out of me that you have any kind of feelings toward my baby sister, but today I need you to dig deep inside that twisted soul of yours and help me bring my girl back."

Oh, she's coming back. Just not with you. I don't tell him this. No. I hate that he knows I care for the brat, but after all that's happened, I don't give a single fuck if he knows. If anyone knows. She's mine, and she's coming back to my city. With me. Grunting, I put on my fake smile, the ones that make me less intimidating and more like the good guy he is, and step foot inside the Bleeding Rose.

One step closer to finding her.

Just a while longer, little monster.

I'm coming.

***

"He said you would come." The slightly accented voice comes from the other side of the room. A big as fuck man stands in front of a window while taking a sip of his drink.

"Good, then you know why we're here. We can skip the pleasantries and get to the part where you tell me where my sister is." Lucan steps forward, and for someone who just told me to keep my beast in check, he sure as hell is not behaving.

The man, Alexei, the Russians' right-hand man, looks at us with an empty expression. Nothing. One thing about the fucking Russians is they have no sense of humor. Ironic since the funniest person I know is half-Russian. Must be her Italian blood. A full minute passes, and the asshole remains quiet, watching us with an amused look on his face, successfully irritating me more than I already was the moment I stepped foot in Russian territory. Fucking little monster, the shit I do for you. "Where the fuck is she?" Not wanting to waste a moment longer here, I direct my question to the Russian currently stepping in my face.

"Ah, I heard of you. The mad king of Detroit city." He chuckles, and it takes a whole lot of fucking effort not to stick my knife in his eyes and give him something to cry about instead.

"It'll do you well to remember you're in D'yavol's territory now."

He says it as a warning. He then completely disregards me and turns his attention to Lucan instead. Fucker. I'll remember his half-assed attempt at a threat.

"You will find her in the Solonik's building, not far away from here. Drive straight for two blocks, and you'll see it. It's a black building as big as the Empire State." With that, he turns around and is done with us. With this conversation. If he wasn't the Russian's lap dog, I think we would actually get along. He's a sick fuck with a penchant for blood. My kind of people.

But then he opens his big mouth and reminds me why I hate other people. "You have the Pakhan's permission to remain in the city for another day. Make good use of it."

Permission.

I want to rip out the motherfucker's tongue but hold myself back. He's right. This is not my city, and I have no say here. No connections whatsoever besides the man standing next to me that's considered a rat in every state in this goddamn nation. "For your fucking sake, she better not be harmed. If so, I promise you, motherfucker, I'll start with you until I'm pissing on your Pakhan's corpse." I don't turn around to hear what he says. A whole lot of Russian and laughter.

"Let's get her and get you out of this city before they kill us both."

Chuckling, I follow him out of the Bleeding Rose. I didn't lie to the asshole when I said I would come for him and his boss if as much as a hair in her head was touched.

Nobody fucks with what's mine but me.

No one.

Not even her goddamn blood.

CHAPTER TWENTY-THREE

VERA

"The daughter of Satan." - Vlad

Vera.

The Russian word for truth.

While growing up, mom always told my siblings and me that the truth would always set us free. I used to believe in that blindly, and to some extent, I still do, but there's always that one thought in the back of my head taunting me with the what-ifs.

Yes more often than not, revealing your truth will set you free, but it might also condemn you to a reality you weren't quite ready for. As much as I yearned to find that piece of the puzzle that was always missing, now I have no clue how to react to it all. Should I cry? Crying implies that I'm hurt by the truth I am not. Should I rage in anger? I'm not angry either. Maybe later, once it all fully sinks in, I'll get mad and cry but now? I just feel a sense of peace that I've never felt before. In my head, I always felt like I didn't quite fit in with my brother and sister because even when they were touched by the hands of a cruel father, they still held their heads high and walked through life without showing the rest of the world how bad they had it at home. Just how unjust the cards they were dealt were. I, on the other hand, always felt fake. Like I was giving the performance of my life just because I carry a pang of guilt bigger than myself.

In no way am I comparing pains because they had it much worse. I know this. I still hurt for them, but somewhere along the way, when I was so little, I took the burden of hiding exactly who I was to keep my father from becoming angry.

From hurting them. And in the end, they got hurt just the same. Nothing changed. It was all for nothing. Standing here, at night with the full moon hidden behind a dark cloud, I wonder how things would've turned out if these people were a part of my life from the start? If my biological mother would've been in the picture? A tightness in my chest robs me of my next breath when I think of that scenario. My mother. My heart-mother, Natalia. I wouldn't have had her in my life, not in the way I did anyway. My brother and sister, would they have been better off without me? That thought sends a knife straight through my heart. Would Giana still be alive? God, so many what-ifs and maybes, but deep down, I know it is useless to dwell on all of that. Maybe life could've been better for them, or maybe worse. Who really knows? "Darya," Vladimir's rough voice booms in the night. God, even his voice, just as his presence is larger than life. Here, surrounded by a beautiful black, vintage style gazebo, and with flowers and twinkling lights decorating the made-up garden, it almost looks like what I would imagine heaven to look like. Peaceful and serene, even with the background noise from the busy streets and civilians going on their merry way through the city. Here, I can breathe easier than inside the building. Looking up, needing a moment to compose myself before I dive into the topic of my mother and who she was, I stare in awe at all the beauty around me. From the looks of it, this place used to be a hotel, but I haven't seen any guests, not down here in the garden or the lobby where we came through to reach this part of the building. I only see large men in all types of dark clothing standing guard all over the place.

It looks like the Solonik family acquired this property and made it home for not only themselves, but their men as well. I'm not naïve.

These men look and act the part of every made man I met back home. I grew up surrounded by men like these.

Criminals hidden in plain sight, dressed in expensive suits.

Maybe I am making assumptions based on my perception of them and my own experience back in Detroit, but something tells me I'm not wrong. Normal people wanting a family reunion would've just reached out or picked up a damn phone, not taken me in the night the way they did, hurting innocent people in the process.

Staring at Vladimir's back as I trail behind him while he's leading me through the patio area, I don't miss the way he walks as if he owns the world and everything in it. His head held high and his shoulders back as if he doesn't have a care in the world. He doesn't. It's clear to see.

Yes, this large man with his dark as night suit and powerful presence surrounding him looks like the collector of souls. Calmly waiting to possess every naive angel and make him or her fall from heaven directly into his clutches.

Over the top? Yes, I know, but there's no other way to describe a being like him. I've never met anyone that oozes the same dark energy as he does. Well, that would be a lie.

Lorenzo does. He also wears it like a second skin.

At times during dinner, I stole glances of both Solonik brothers, and some of their mannerisms reminded me of Enzo. Even when quiet, they still command a room.

Just the same as him.

My thoughts are all over the place, and I can't fully concentrate on one. I have so many questions some I am even afraid to ask. Is it a betrayal to mom? To my siblings? Would it count as a betrayal if I don't figure out who I am? If I don't do this for myself?

After a few seconds of silence and contemplation, I found my voice, "Is that her name?"

"Darya Solonik."

Vladimir says while he continues moving around the garden toward the gazebo. There, he stops next to a small door that leads inside of the beautiful garden, takes out what I presume is a cigar and lights it. The flame dancing in his eyes as he looks down at the cigar gives him a sinister look, yet I am not afraid. Maybe I should be.

I don't know them.

But they had every opportunity to hurt me, and they haven't... yet. The night is still young, I guess. Maybe that's why I was treading carefully around him.

After an extremely awkward dinner, Vladimir ordered his daughter to find me something to wear and for me to get cleaned up. The exact moment he said that Vitali grunted. Maybe he was offended by how I looked or smelled. I didn't think I smelled, but it's been a day, and I needed a few minutes to myself, so I showered and then changed into some mom jeans that were a bit tight on the waist and a loose pink graphic tee. Pink. By the looks of it, princess Reyna is very fond of the hideous color.

Getting out of my head, I ask Vladimir the one thing that's been nagging at me. "Who was she to you?" I manage to ask through the lump in my throat. God, the emotions are overwhelming. Maybe Enzo had the right idea all along. Emotions are complicated and often fuck with your head, leaving you a mess.

"Who am I to you?"

Vladimir takes another hit of his cigar while staring up at the building with a dark look in his eyes. The mood changes in this one are something.

"Darya was my father's little sister and Vitali and I's aunt. Bratva's most treasured rose."

My heart drops to the floor when it all sinks in. Bratva. A criminal organization similar to the Italian mafia. Criminals. My mother was their aunt, so that makes me their cousin. Makes us immediate family. Lastly… was.

He referred to my mother in the past tense. As if she was here, but not anymore. I shouldn't feel anything toward the woman, but I do. I feel a deep sadness that I never got the chance to know her.

"Tell me everything." I hold my breath, waiting for his answer that comes a second later. "I-I want to know everything."

"The story doesn't have a happy ending." Taking a puff of his cigar, he looks away from me."

"Real life rarely does." I mumble, knowing damn well that most men and women that live inside the world of crime rarely get to experience bliss and happiness that last forever.

Vladimir frowns but doesn't acknowledge my statement. "Like I said, Darya was my father's little sister. The heart of this family." His demeanor switches quickly, and I just know I won't like anything that comes out of his mouth next. I'm good at reading the room and people, and Vladimir's eyes, even at night, looked anything but kind. "Every time I saw her, she was laughing and offering men like us a warm smile when it was obvious none of them deserved it. Not such beauty. That's who she was. Pure, so goddamn pure." This time there's a hint of emotion there. Deep sadness.

Sadness takes hold of me, too, because the way he's speaking of her is as if she's not here. He doesn't have to say it. The despair in his voice is too loud to ignore, and I suddenly find myself soaking in every detail and memory he shares since that's most likely all I'll ever get of her.

Moving closer to where he's standing, I reach the gazebo and take a seat on the solitary swing chair, watching as my feet dangle, not touching the floor. I look down to not show him the emotions written all over my face.

Regret.
Sadness.
Confusion.

"She was not much older than you are now when she fell in love with a Frenchman. A very powerful man that later became an ally to the Solonik family, but who also treated our Darya like a queen. She was… very much in love and hopeful of the future that awaited her until he happened." The fondness in his tone when he speaks about my mother dissipates, and there's only anger and hatred.

I don't have to ask who.
I know.
It's obvious.

Shame suddenly crawls up my throat, almost strangling me, robbing me of my breath and wrapping me in guilt. This goddamn guilt that's been with me since before I truly knew what it was.

"My father." Not a question.

Vladimir spits on the floor and nods before carrying on. "There's evil, Vera, and then there's your father."

Vera.

Not once has he regarded me as Cara or uttered the Volpe name. It's as if it brings shame on them. Now, I feel like the little girl that used to hide in the dark corners of her home, trying to avoid the hurtful whispers of the men that knew exactly who I was and what I represented.

Shame.

Half Italian, half Russian.

Now, I understand why they were so cruel and disapproved of me.

In their eyes, I was not one of them, even if my father's blood ran through my veins. In their eyes, I was and will always be tainted. A reminder of their enemies.

The Russians.

Not only did I represent my father's betrayal to our mother, an Italian woman, but I also carry the blood of their enemy. Vladimir throws the cigar down on the ground and looks my way, and just by the look on his face, I know I'm in for a world of hurt. "We all might not agree on a lot, but one thing, one rule we all follow is to never hurt a child and innocents. Our Darya was both when your sick son of a bitch father laid his eyes on her and convinced himself she wanted him, too. She did not." Vladimir flashes his teeth like a feral animal ready to strike. "*Papa* made the mistake of inviting that Italian filth into our home. Our lives and territory, and your father proved to us just how wrong papa was for that."

"What happened? What did Tommaso do?" I can't call him father. Not after everything he's done. My heart is beating a mile a minute while I wait for him to finish his story and drive the last nail to this coffin.

"I was young when this all happened. Very young, but I will never forget the look on your father's face when he first saw Darya. The first time *papa* opened his doors to the Holy Trinity to discuss a treaty between the cities. Darya was engaged to be married to Damian Toussaint, the head of the French mafia. Their union was not only beneficial to us as it gave us more reach in other cities, but it was also a celebration of love." He takes a moment to gather his thoughts before continuing. "I should've known that the way he looked at her was not of a man admiring her beauty but of a sick individual who fed from the misery of others. From a man that saw beauty and purity and decided he wanted to ruin it. He got off on that. On the thought of claiming the Bratva's most treasured printsipesa and taking what was not his to take. What was never offered to him."

I feel like puking.

Taking what was never offered to him.

"W-what did he do to her?" I rasp out, trying to not

let the tears fall, but I'm slowly losing that fight. I hear the subtle sound of him taking what sounds like paper from his pocket. Then, he hands me a photo.

A photo of a woman with pale skin, blood red hair, kind eyes and a blinding smile.

My birth mother.

Darya.

Taking the photo in my shaking hand, I take her in and try to save this photo in my memory. Even though it felt wrong to acknowledge her as more than a stranger, it feels even more wrong now to ignore the fact that this beautiful woman was wronged by my father and is just a stranger.

She did give me life right after my father made a cruel mess out of hers. I don't need the words because I know. Something deep down inside my soul tells me that Tommaso Volpe, my father, committed the most heinous crime against an innocent woman.

Against my mother.

"He watched her like a predator sizing its vulnerable prey every time he came around with the pretense of business with our family," Vladimir's dark voice rises, and it's edged with hatred and disgust toward Tommaso and rightfully so. "He watched and studied her until he could get her alone with the help of a soldier of ours turned rat. Your filthy scum of a father slipped inside her room in the middle of the night and forcefully took her innocence against her will until she bled in her safe haven, her childhood bed, and then left like a thief in the night." He takes a deep breath and looks down at me. I don't meet his eyes, too embarrassed of the blood that runs in my veins. True evil's blood. It feels as if I'm always apologizing for something my father did. For his sins that I've been carrying on my shoulders since the day I was born. "Darya," Another inhale of breath. God, how heartbreaking that this happened to not only Darya but to the ones that loved her, as well. They all paid for my father's actions in some form. "She never told a soul. She kept the pain and shame she felt in her heart and body all to herself until she couldn't hide it anymore."

"She got pregnant with me." God, I am not only the product of my father's past digressions and adultery against Natalia, but I'm also the product of a rape. Suddenly not feeling as strong as I felt before, I let the tears fall and bow my head in shame. I always felt so different from everyone else, and at one point, I just blamed it on being the bastard child. I made peace with that a long time ago, but this? Being the product of the most atrocious act a person could ever commit on another human? I don't think I'll ever get past this.

"How did she die?" Not really wanting but needing to know everything because if she lived it, then I can endure this hopeless feeling in my chest and this agonizing pain because she suffered worse. Letting the tears fall for her, I look up at Vladimir, who's now towering over me like an avenging dark angel. "Did he kill her? Did my father murder my mother?"

His eyes flare before he looks up at the building, "Your mother's pain was so great that she couldn't bear it, so she jumped to her death and left you sleeping soundly in your bassinet." I've had my heart broken many times before. My father was the first one to ever land a crack on my young heart, and now years later, I'm a grown woman still feeling like that little girl whose world shattered with the truth of his evil ways. Another crack in my heart because of what he did. A sound that resembles a wounded animal escapes my throat as I hold her photo close to my chest, trying to ease the pain there, but knowing it won't help. I hold her closer as if I could also feel her pain. I wish… I wish I was never born because maybe she would've stayed and found the strength to heal from that type of hurt. The tears fall harder when I realize I'm also to blame for her death. She had me.

The daughter of the man that ruined her life, who she had to look at every day and remember him. Remember what she went through.

A rough hand lands on my shoulder, and at the same time, the wind on my face blows harder. "Keep it." I wonder how he could look at me after knowing what he does, after knowing the person who caused his family so much pain is my father. "We will never know what went through her head the moment she decided to end her pain. Every day I live with that failure deep-rooted in my chest and in my brain. I feed the hate I feel toward every Volpe bastard as a reminder of what he did."

"You must hate me as well." I gulp, still clutching my mother's photo to my chest. "Why bring me here then? Will you hurt me because of what he did? Because of what I represent to you?"

"And what's that?" Vladimir ignores my questions.

"Filthy blood. That's how the Volpe family saw me besides my siblings and mother." The hold he has on my left shoulder tightens, but not painfully. "You could never be filthy, and I could never hate you. You are a part of her. You are a part of me, regardless of what I feel toward your name. To me, you are Vera, Darya's Solonik's daughter. Our *printsipesa*."

I take in his words, taken aback for a second by the intensity, but remain quiet, not quite knowing how to respond to that, not after learning everything I have. "As to why I brought you here…" He takes a breath, and suddenly his tone is no longer gentle but harsh. "Your family failed to keep you safe, making you vulnerable to the boss of Chicago to get his hands on you, giving me no choice but to step in. I won't let the past repeat itself. We stood back and watched from afar until you got hurt. One time was enough. It won't ever happen again."

I'm choked up with emotion, and so many things are going through my mind at the moment, but I don't miss the safe feeling that washes over me with his strong hold on my shoulder and his words.

My father raped my mother, driving her to her death after giving birth to his daughter. To me.

She couldn't handle living in the same world as me.

I've only felt this type of pain twice before, when I learned of mom's disappearance and Giana's death.

With Vladimir standing next to me, still holding onto my shoulder, I silently cry for all the women in my life that left me with so much pain in their hearts.

All because of me.

All because of half my blood.

Then, as if the weather felt my pain, rain starts to fall harshly around us and thunder breaks, lighting up the dark sky and us. "Get your motherfucking hands off her before I blow your brother's brains out." The moment his voice rings in the night, my heart skips a beat.

He's here.

He came for me.

Lifting my head up, my crying eyes land on him, and all the pain I feel inside doesn't hurt as much, just like every time before. Only he, my reckless demon, has the power to do that. Outside the gazebo, he stands dripping wet from the rain, pointing a gun at the back of Vitali's head. My eyes leave his, and I see my brother fuming at his side, watching Vladimir with hateful eyes.

This is it.

These men are my family, and they all hate one another.

Volpe.

Solonik.

Half-and-half of me.

Armed men come out of the shadows where they were before and surround my brother and Enzo with their guns held high. I start to panic, knowing that if Enzo does something reckless like killing the brother of this city's boss, they won't get out of here alive.

The moment Vladimir drops his hand from my shoulders and steps back from me is a sign that all hell will break loose if I don't step in. Standing up, I take his scarred hand in mine and look up at him while he looks at both my brother and Enzo with a cruel smile on his face.

Shit.

He promised to keep me safe, but that'll be the extent of his generosity, I bet. Lorenzo and my brother are fair game.

"It took you long enough, suka."

Vladimir laughs darkly as he steps forward, away from me, and over to where my brother and Enzo are standing, surrounded by men carrying guns ready and waiting for an order from their boss. Not wanting things to escalate and having to bury more people I love, I follow Vladimir and stand as a shield between him and the men I care for most in the world. Shaking my head slowly, I try to catch Lorenzo's gaze, but it is futile. When he gets in his head and lets the reckless monster out to play, there's no getting him back until he feeds the beast inside with chaos and pain. So, I try my brother next.

"Lucan, do something. You know you won't get—" I don't get to finish because a dark and menacing voice unlike I ever heard before interrupts me, making me look in the direction where Enzo is holding a gun to the back of Vitali's head. "Did they fucking hurt you, Mia?" I notice two things. One, Enzo's eyes are no longer on Vladimir but on me, scanning my face for any sign of hurt. Is that it? He's making sure I'm okay. I've witnessed him beat a kid until the kid peed himself. I've watched as he pounded the hell out of his twin brother's face mercilessly and yet he has never looked as dangerous or unhinged as he does now. There's something in his gaze that astounds me.

His blue eyes are shifting uncontrollably, not really knowing where to focus on my face, and he's snarling like a hungry beast waiting for its next meal.

Christ.

This shouldn't make my heart stop in my chest and cause heat to spread all over my body, but it does. After taking a deep breath, I release it slowly, counting the seconds.

"You have two seconds to answer me, Red. Before I blow his brains to bits and get both me and your brother killed."

The dark voice I love so much sends a shiver down my spine, and in the best of ways, as fucked-up as that sounds. Opening my eyes, I stare straight ahead into his wild ones. Enzo was volatile, reckless, some would say, mad, but despite all of that, he's always been mine no matter how far we are from each other. It's always been us in the dark where nothing could touch us.

My eyes leave him for a moment and look at Vitali. There's no expression on his face. None. Zero. Zilch. His light eyes are looking past me as if he's somewhere faraway. As if he would rather be somewhere other than here. I look down at his right arm and watch the ratty old stuffed bunny dangling from his hand, but apart from that subtle movement, there's nothing else. Statuesque.

Cold.

Dead.

My brother's voice snatches my attention away from Vitali and straight to him. I've witnessed many sides of my brother. The protective brother. The fearless father and the ruthless criminal, but the look he is giving Vladimir sends shivers down my spine. It's the look of a brother who's not leaving here alive without his little sister. "We made a deal, Vlad. A treaty. Your men attended my wedding, for fuck's sake. You don't fuck with what's ours, and we stay out of your way." Lucan spits with a furious look shining through his eyes.

His posture is rigid, but his head is held high as always. We don't cower. We don't fold. We fight. Our mantra plays on a loop inside my head while I take in the scene before me.
"What the fuck changed?"
"Settle down, puppy dog," the boss of New York City laughs darkly, and the air around us becomes heavy. "When you fail to protect ours, that's when I step in."
Does my brother know? Has he known all this time and has been keeping this secret from me? We don't keep secrets. We tell it as it is, even if it hurts.
I catch Lorenzo shift uncomfortably from my peripheral vision but still holding the gun to Vitali's head. How odd…
"What the fuck are you talking about motherfucker? Step back from my sister, or I swear to you…"
Vladimir laughs harder now. Oh, he really knows how to push people's buttons. "What, Volpe? What will you do? Please make my night." He chuckles between puffing on his cigar. "Or how about I make yours?" He holds the lit cigar in his mouth with his teeth, grinning broadly, and takes out his phone, scrolling through it before turning it over so everyone else can see the screen. "We watched as Sandoval got his hands on both of your sisters, and you failed them both. It won't be happening again. Not with Vera."
Lucan barks, "Who the fuck is Vera?" stepping forward, but the moment he does, every man surrounding us step forward, too, and hold their guns higher in my brother's direction. I was too busy worrying about his safety that I completely dismissed what Vladimir said.
Both of your sisters.Giana.
The men that took me took Gigi, too? But how? When? She's dead, and then everything falls into place. No. He didn't. He wouldn't do that to me. To us. We don't keep secrets from each other.
But he did.

He kept this gigantic secret all these years and carried the burden of the lie, plus my resentment toward him on his back. Gasping, I step forward in his direction, not caring for the guns that are trained on him as I move. Lorenzo mutters something under his breath, but I ignore it.

"Your little sister carries my blood in her veins, and with it my protection. We weren't going to stand back and watch as another Volpe motherfucker ruins one of ours, and make no mistake, Vera, you are one of ours, and we protected you when they failed to keep you safe and out of harm's way. Vladimir's words don't resonate with me since I'm too stunned to think clearly. One night. One night has revealed so many truths and too many lies. Both have broken something inside.

Lifting my hand up, I reach for my brother's chin and make him look away from Vladimir and straight into my eyes. He's stunned speechless, too. He didn't know about my birth family. At least he didn't lie about it, too. "Tell me he's lying, superman. Tell me you would've never lied to me about that, not about her."

I can get past a lie. I can. It is not just about that he lied to me about our sister's death. It's the fact that it burns me. It hurts my heart. How he didn't trust me. He didn't trust that I could go along with it even if it killed me. It would've hurt like hell to let go of my sister, but I still would've done it if it made my sister happy. If it meant losing Giana to give her a chance at the life she wanted, the life she deserved.

Lucan looks down at me with an icy stare, one he's never directed my way. Not once.

"Tell me you didn't lie." I whisper, too weak to scream the way I want to. At him. At Giana. At the Russians. My father. I never raised my voice and did what I was told to keep the peace.

After a long minute, "She wanted it this way." There. A blow straight to my already bruised heart. She wanted it that way.

She didn't want me to know. My sister wanted to keep me in the dark. It hurts. All these years, I've lived with this guilt inside of me because of her death, and it was all a lie.

Exhaling painfully, I move back without looking at my brother and turn to meet Vladimir's eyes. "Am I free to go, or am I your prisoner?"

"You're not a prisoner in this city, *printsipesa*." He says, and I ignore my brother's growl and Enzo's curses in the background. I keep staring right ahead and my newfound cousin. "We wanted you to know we're here. You're a part of this family, and we're no longer in the shadows. We're always here, and we will be watching." He looks dangerously in my brother's direction. Then I feel a dark presence close to my left shoulder, and when I turn my head, I find myself staring up at Vitali's unfazed expression, with Lorenzo still behind him, pushing the gun forward on the back of his head. God, what a mess. Holding my breath, too afraid I'll pass out with everything that's haunting my thoughts at the moment. I watch as he hands me the stuffed bunny, and that's what does it. What breaks me after being resilient and impenetrable for many years. "Vera." Vitali says darkly, but this time there's something there. Something I can't quite decipher yet. Fierceness? Tenderness?

At least he's not as cold as I initially thought he was.

Smiling weakly up at him, I turn to look at my brother, and the smile is gone.

The tortured look on his face only makes me die a little more inside. "Why? Why didn't you both trust me to keep a secret? Don't you know that I would've done it if it meant she got to live the life she wanted? The one that made her happy?"

Lucan stares at me, and something flashes in his eyes.

"Just tell me why you would let me hate you for this long?" I croak out my tears, mixing with the raindrops and falling down my face.

I get it. I do. She wanted to start over, and the career path she chose didn't require her to be in the spotlight, so she could start over without a problem unlike me. She needed to die to live, and he made it happen, but neither of them trusted me to do right by my sister. He let me cry for her. He let me... hate him for something as noble as what he did for Giana.

"I don't regret it, Cara Mia." He whispers brokenly. Right here, he looks like the young boy who protected me even knowing I was never in any danger. The superhero. My superhero. "I'm sorry I hurt you, but I'm not sorry for what I did. I did what I had to keep you both breathing and, in this world, even if it meant you hated me. You're both alive, and that's all that matters to me." He hits his chest with a close fist. "That's all that's ever fucking mattered to me."

That's it.

No excuses.

Straight to the point.

He regrets it.

"I want to go." I whisper tirelessly. I don't know what to think, but all I know is that I can't do it while being this close to him. To the Russians. On the same fucking spot, my birth mother jumped to her death because my father tore her world apart. I can't breathe.

Lucan nods. "Let's go home."

"No. I can't." I look away from him and focus on the old bunny I'm holding in my hand. "I need time."

"Topina."

"Please." Knowing he would never deny me anything, I step away from him and walk toward the silent dark man that, oddly, is the only person that's never lied to me. I love my brother, but he lied whereas Lorenzo never has. He didn't trust me enough to keep a secret that made my sister's life happy.

Ever.

I meet Enzo's angry stare and find my way to him, with every step away from my brother, and toward him, I find my next breath.

My brother calls my name, but I ignore him, focusing on Enzo. His nostrils flare, and a deadly smile spreads on his full lips. Everything else fades. My brother's voice calling out for me, the noise of the city, all of it disappears until all there is us.

Him.

Me.

And this pull that's always been present between us.

Obsessive, somewhat possessive.

But then a shot rings out.

A man falls to the floor.

Enzo's eyes never leave mine when he pulls the trigger.

CHAPTER TWENTY-FOUR

TEARS

"Make her cry again and you'll end up dickless." - L

Lorenzo

Goddam her and those blue eyes. They haunt my dreams. Day and fucking night, even when I like to pretend she has no effect on me.

Then, I see the fucking tears.

Motherfucker.

Every time, every fucking time I witness a tear falling from her stunning eyes onto her plump rosy cheek, I get the sudden itch to pull the trigger and end whatever it was that caused those tears.

In this case, it's the two Russian bastards in front of me.

They gave their word that the truth of her birth wouldn't come from them.

Goes to show you can never trust what comes out of the asshole's mouth.

Any Russian in this city, for that matter.

So, I do.

I pull the trigger, although I don't aim to kill.

New York's underboss falls to his knees, but not once does he show emotion. He doesn't scream in pain when the bullet hits his shoulder.

Nothing.

No one moves.

The Russian men don't make a move.

Of course, they won't.

The Pakhan won't risk a fight breaking out and Mia getting hurt in his territory.

Serves him fucking right.

Not long after overhearing the conversation between Benedetto and Cara's father, I found out who her mother was. The more I kept digging, the more lies unraveled until Tommaso's crimes against an innocent woman and the Bratva were exposed to me.

Until I came to know why the men in the three families called her a bastard while she was growing up.

Half Italian, half Russian.

A sin and a crime in the eyes of the Holy Trinity of the past. Every single one of the bosses back then were hypocrites since the Nicolasi heirs, my sister, twin, and I aren't full-blooded Italian. Our mother was Puerto Rican, which made us half-and-half.

The same as her.

They only cared about the narrative that best benefited them. That's why two of them are a five-course meal to worms, and the third will be meeting his end soon enough.

Their old way of thinking died with them.

Every single movement I've made since that day has led me to this moment. I might not have wanted her to find out this way, but she had to come face to face with who she is at some point.

Vera was the name her mother chose for her.

Vera, the truth of her birth.

A beautiful name.

A powerful name fit for a princess.

A Russian princess.

Also, a damn irony since she's been lied to by everyone she loved this entire time. Some lied with malicious intent, others to keep the innocence they believed she still possessed.
I, like always, did what was best for me, and I'm not even mad about it. She wasn't ready. Back then, she was not strong enough to handle the shit storm this revelation would throw her way. She lost her mother.
Her sister.
And in some way, the only world she ever knew.
But she spread her wings, found her voice and the place she was always meant to have in this world.
At the top.
Never hidden in the shadows, trying to make herself disappear to please others. Fuck, no. She was always meant to shine so very fucking bright.
A successful woman who made every single dream of hers come true. Who knows what would've happened if she had learned all this shit back then? Would the outcome still be the same?
Would she have drowned in an ocean of self-pity and regret for the shit she had no control over? Would she disregard all her dreams and ambitions? That's one risk I was never willing to take. Ever.
Not with her.
Now, looking down at her, I feel both a pang in my chest and pride. Mia holds her chin high, desperately trying to be strong, to give the appearance that she's not hurting by all that has been revealed to her today.
Now, I wonder…did they tell her everything? How she came to be part of the Volpe family? Removing the gun from the back of Vladimir's trained-dog-slash-brother, I watch as he looks at me with a bored expression before walking toward his boss and standing by his side.
I'm all kinds of fucked up.

That's been proven not only by my long-ass track record of killings but by more than fifteen certified psychiatrists. But that fuck Vitali is way off in the head. Nothing gets a reaction out of him.
Absolutely-fucking-nothing.
Weird as fuck, but oh well, who am I to judge?
Ignoring both assholes, I concentrate solely on her. One thing about Mia is that she hates to be lied to by the people she believes are hers. Her people. Her family and friends. Her brother lied to her. It was an honorable lie, in my never wrong opinion.
She's disappointed in him, and it makes me wonder how she will react when she finds out I also knew the truth.
All of it and more.
I've never lied to her before. I give it to her straight, even when I know I cause her pain, but I refuse to be like everyone else and shelter her from the truth, but some things are only meant for me to say.
Not my truth to share.
It will bite me in the ass soon enough if I don't get a hold of the situation before it's too late. Fuck, but the idea of losing her, whether it's because of a lie or because some bitch dared to take her from me, hurts like a motherfucker.
Little monster keeps messing with my head every chance she gets. Always.
"You have a death wish, don't you?" Mia whispers and manages a soft laugh, but I call bullshit. Fake. Unlike everything that is her. Staring at her face, I notice she looks like a wreck. As if the world fell on her, and in some form, it did.
The tears.
Goddammit.
The fucking Russians had to break their word and all because that fucker Sandoval had to intervene in his pathetic attempts of revenge.

She most certainly had the right to learn about her mother, but not this way. Not by snatching her, hurting her friend, who's her guard too, and dropping bomb after bomb without giving her the chance to catch her next breath.
Now, my girl has tears in her eyes and probably many scars on her soft heart.
Shit.
She's here with them, and she's fucking crying.
All these bitches made her cry, including her goddam brother. The superhero to my villain, as most believe.
My eyes don't leave her beautiful face, and I'm taken aback by the overwhelming sense of fear that leaves my body when her warm and soft hand grips mine.
I've almost lost her twice before I really had her. Before I learn what being loved by her feels like. I hold her hand tighter and bring her closer to my body, not caring about the three motherfuckers that might be contemplating every way to kill me at this precise moment, witnessing how I hold their precious girl. Mine, the beast inside me growls.
She was mine the first time I saw her crying in the rain, and she's still mine, here, in the same fucking scenario all these years later.
I need to do something about this shit. She's always crying, and if I have to annihilate everyone and everything that hurts her, I will. I will do it gladly, with a smile on my fucking face every time. "What do you want, Mia?"
Fuck what her brother and newfound cousins want. It does not matter to me. Nothing matters but her. I'm done staying back, trying to be the noble hero in her story, doing what's right for her. I'll never be the hero. Being a hero never got me anything or anywhere. Now, being the gigantic asshole that I am has always gotten me ahead, and that's where I've always belonged.
Ahead and on top of everyone else.

There's only one change to my plans now. She will be right there with me every step of the way because I'm not burying her. I'm not losing her. She's mine, and we both know it. We've always known. Now, the world will know, too.

"Haven't you heard? It's Vera." She tries to make a joke out of her situation but fails miserably, but fuck me, if she isn't the most adorable creature I've ever known. She's right up there with my beasts and my Poe.

Coincidentally, my sibling's children, Mia, and my dogs are the only breathing things that don't annoy the fuck out of me.

Gripping the back of her head with my hand, I pull her closer until our noses are touching. "Listen to me, monster." Our breath mixes together, and it almost feels like we're breathing life back into each other. Fuck, I'm a fucking romantic now. Who would've thought I had it in me? "You'll always be Mia to me." She won't ever know this because I still have my pride and dignity to maintain, but I once told her I liked Mia best because everyone else called her Cara, but that's not the truth, not really. Mia means mine in Spanish and Italian. Mine.

She was mine from that moment on and hasn't stopped being mine since. Even now that she's engaged to that annoying fuck. Which reminds me, I need to remedy that as soon as I get her somewhere safe. Over my dead body, will she stay engaged to another man that is not me.

"Take me somewhere away from everything." she whispers so only I can hear, and if I had a heart, it would've broken right there for her. She sounds small and defeated, only infuriating me further. These bitches made her cry. Pulling her closer to my body, I look the three men in the eyes.

Her brother looks at me as if he wants to murder me. Nothing new there.

"Get your hands off her, Nicolasi, before you lose them."

"Hush, love. Leave the dirty talk for when we're alone." Grinning his way, I pull his little sister closer to my side and put my gun inside my back pocket. "Here's what will happen. She's leaving with me, and you will go back to your wife and hellions, and you two fuckers," I look at the Russians now. "You'll call your bitches off and make them lower their guns and stop pointing it her way before I get really fucking mad, and I promise you, you really don't want that to happen." No longer joking, I threaten the boss of this city that is not mine. Good times. Good fucking times.

I feel Mia's body stiffen against me, but I ignore it. The Russians won't do shit. Not as long as she's in the line of fire, which she is at this moment. "She's half ours, and that makes her a target if my enemies find out about her connection to the Bratva." Vladimir says between puffs of his cigar. At least the bitch is not stopping me from taking her, not that he ever could. Not even in his goddamn territory. The Russian steps forward, still smoking his cigar. A darkness I only see when I look in the mirror radiates off him now. "You do know, the next time I see you alone, you'll pay for hurting my brother." I do love when they threaten me.

It not only makes me twitchy, but it gets me hard as fuck too. "It's a date, then." I blow him a quick kiss, angering him further."You're one disturbed individual, Nicolasi."

"Thank you. Now make sure the people you pissed off don't find out about her." Narrowing my eyes, the threat is there for him to catch. The boss of New York grins evilly at me but does nothing but amuse me.

"There is no scenario in which you'll take her from me, Lorenzo. Get. Your. Hands. Off. Her. Now." Lucan growls, stepping forward, but before he reaches her, I'm pulling her behind me as I come face to face with her very angry-looking brother.

"Move."

Oh, this fucker. I should've left his ass behind.
"You need to step aside and let me handle shit from now on. You had one job. One fucking job, and that was to keep her safe, and you did your best, love. I'll give you that, but that's not enough. Not when shit is going down, and she's the target. You have a family. My family, as well, so you better get your head out of your ass and come to terms with the fact that I'm the best bet right now. Unless you want whatever threat is lurking in the shadows to hit your picture-perfect home." Satisfied with the fact that I didn't lose my shit when he got in my face, I say for his ears only. Not wanting his sister to learn of this now that she's vulnerable. I need her to be strong. "Someone is out for her, and they're not playing games. Go home, keep my sister and those babies of yours safe, and as long as she's away from you, your family will be safe." That's a shit thing to say, but by the look on his face, I know it was effective. Truth always is, even when it comes from a selfish place. "She's my family, too." There it is. His vulnerable side. The side that makes him the wrong choice to handle this shit now. Lucan has always been lethal, but at times, his feelings cloud his judgment.

"And I'll take care of her. All you got to do is take care of mine." Make no mistake. Andrea and those three monsters are mine. My family. I didn't lie when I told him Cara being in their lives this time will only bring tragedy to their door. As much as it pains him, he knows it, too. That's why he steps back and looks at his sister with a resigned expression.

"I love you, *topina*." He whispers her way. I listen to Mia's breath hitch as she pays attention to what her brother is saying. "If you know nothing else, know that. All I ever wanted was what's best for you."

Stepping aside, I release her so her brother can take her into his arms. Cara has always seen him as her hero, and that won't ever change.

No matter what he does, she'll always think the best of him because he has always been the one to kiss her scars when she bled. The one who picked her up when she fell and the one that took their father's wrath just so it would never touch them. I stand back and watch as Cara holds him tight like she never wants to let go. Lucan kisses the top of her head, reluctantly steps back, and looks over his shoulder at me.

"You take her, and you keep her safe, Lorenzo." He says through gritted teeth, clearly annoyed that he lost this round to me, and I won't deny that it doesn't bring me great pleasure. "Don't touch her."

Don't touch her.

We both know what he means.

She's not yours to take.

Ah, sweet naive Lucan.

I don't need to touch her to know she's mine.

I will, though.

I plan to touch, kiss, and mark every part of her body, soul, and fucking heart.

Grinning, I hold my tattooed hand to my heart. "Scout's honor." Blue eyes, almost the same shade as his sister's, narrow, but he doesn't say shit else.

I won this one.

And I will win the next.

I will win everything when it comes to her.

Neither him, the Russians, nor the cowardly bastard sending threats through newspaper clippings will take her from me. Not even God himself. I dare the fucker to even try.

They will. Oh, that's for sure, but they'll all fail.

"Know this," I look the three of them in the eyes again. Blue, black, and a freakish gray resembling white stare back at me with fury, amusement, and boredom in each individual expression. "I'll kill anyone, you fuckers included, if you take her from me again."

Jokes are over.
This is life right now.
My life.
Hers.
Nobody will get in the way of what was always meant to be.
Us.
Come hell or high water, Cara Mia Volpe is mine. It's painfully obvious the little monster has taken ownership of my every thought.
My soul.
Even when she was away, she was with me in the back of my mind with the only pleasant memories I tried so hard to suppress. She owns me, and I now realize that human emotions don't make me weak.
They make me fucking lethal because I would crucify God himself again just to spare Red from any pain.

CHAPTER TWENTY-FIVE

MY GIRL

"There is no king without his queen." - L

"**Lorenzo**, get to the fucking point." I light up a cigarette and then offer one to him. Of course, he refuses. The asshole doesn't indulge in good things anymore, now that he's a family man. Lame as fuck, but understandable for a husband and a father of three. "What's going on with my sister?"

I take a puff of my smoke and look at all three of them, watching me intently and waiting for me to tell them who the fuck is after their girl. My girl. Shit. I can't give them what they want because I have no single fucking clue who the dead man walking, targeting her is.

All I have are newspaper clippings that keep appearing every-fucking-where my men or I am.

Every time it is the same.

A newspaper or magazine article that features Cara Mia, a big red X over her heart, and a threatening message. Draego texted a picture of another threat sent to the bar, and yet no one can catch the asshole. Not wanting to prolong this, I make sure Mia is far away enough not to hear what I have to say. Looking over my shoulder, I catch sight of her next to one of the Russian men standing too close to her for my liking. A primal, angry, jealous thing grows inside me.

The need to go over there, throw her over my shoulder and hide her from their lecherous gazes is all-consuming. Look at her tits again, and I'll break your fucking neck, I want to say, but it gets swallowed down with the bitter taste of I'm so fucked. So fucked in the head for her that it's not even funny. Narrowing my eyes, I notice her posture is stiff, and her eyes look out of focus, even all the way from here.

I need to get her out of here before she goes deep inside her head and blames herself for shit that's out of her control. But then she does something that makes me chuckle softly under my breath. She lifts up her hand between her and the jackass as if saying don't get any closer to me because I'm not interested. Good girl. Good fucking girl. Just when I start to worry, she shows exactly who she is. Who she'll always be.

A fighter.

Plus, her candor will never not be amusing to me. Knowing she can handle herself with a bunch of Russians, I reach my back pocket and retrieve my phone, unlocking it and scrolling until I find the photo of the threat and turn the phone over so the Russian brothers and Lucan can see.

A growl comes out of Vladimir first, and at the same time, Lucan starts cursing under his breath, trying to hide it from his sister. "Fuck." Lucan snatches the phone out of my hand and expands the image to see it clearer.

"Fuck, indeed, love." Mumbling, I drop the smoke to the floor and stump on it when an icy as fuck voice speaks up after being dead silent during our time here.

"Nobody knows about her ties to us and what she means to the Bratva. I highly doubt it is one of our enemies." He looks at me once before looking down at his black gloves without giving a single fuck about the wound on his shoulder. This freak reminds me of Kadra. I swear they were cut from the same cloth. It's like looking at the male version of the Parisi boss.

"Sandoval threatened her to hurt you, not us." He says matter of fact, with no emotion whatsoever in his tone. This asshole cares for no one.

"Vi is right. Sandoval wouldn't dare to cross me and our treaty." Vladimir's voice trails off. "The threat must come from your end. As always, your people are rotten." He snarls, looking our way with disgust written all over his ugly ass face.

"Well, pot meet fucking kettle." Lucan claps back. "Cara's blood is the same as mine. You think she's rotten, too?"

I look at Vladimir, waiting for him to disrespect her, but the insult never comes. It won't come. The Russians might be rotten pieces of shit like every single one of us in this life, but they're a loyal bunch. They live and die for their family. Full-blooded or not.

"Vera is…." Vladimir doesn't get to finish his sentence because his brother finishes it for him.

Vitali.

"Ours." One word. One fucking word makes me want to gauge his freaky eyes out because she's mine, and I've never learned to share well with others.

The reality is that she's theirs just as much as she's Lucan's. They all care for her in their own way.

Lucan moves closer to the Pakhan, and the air crackles with an energy that makes my dick hard.

"Cara Mia is mine." He enunciates her names, making sure the boss of New York understands that Vera is not who she is. He's wrong, though. Vera and Cara are the same. That's her given name. The name she would've had if her mother would've still been alive and had raised her as she should've.

"You don't fuck with what's mine. If I find out, you have anything to do with the thr—"

Vladimir laughs as if Lucan made a funny joke. "What, Volpe? You'll paint me a pretty picture? You really do like throwing empty threats around, don't you?"

269

"Enough." I'm already bored of this shit. I'm over the conversation and the pathetic threats being thrown around by dumb bitch #1 and dumb bitch #2. "We might never see eye to eye on a lot of things, but this issue? We can all agree that it matters. She matters, and all I need from you is to stay vigilant and annihilate any threat that comes my way when it comes to her. I'll handle the rest. I'll handle my city." Looking at the Russians now, "I can't stand you assholes, and I don't usually work well with others, but in this situation, there's no choice, is there? Cara has a good heart and after the shock of it all settles down, I know she'll want to be a part of your lives. That's who she is and who she's always been. She's a Volpe, too. That means you'll have to play nice with us boys." Grinning, I leave it at that. They can do with it as they wish. What I didn't say is that I'm a part of her life and always will be, and if they want to be in hers, then they'll have to behave. There's no way I'm letting them, her brother or anyone else become a problem for her.
Or get in my way.
With that said, I turn my back to them and stare at the girl that has had me wrapped around her little finger since the first time I laid eyes on her. With the wind blowing her wild red hair in all directions and her rosy cheeks and puffy eyes, she's never looked more beautiful and real. So mine. Looking over my shoulder at her brother, I make sure he knows I'll keep her safe. "Handle your family. I got her. She'll be safe with me."
And because I'm an asshole, I add. "Cross my heart." I grin widely when he starts hurling insults my way and I walk away from them toward the little monster staring back at us with a worried look on her face. Once I'm standing right in front of her, I ignore the glares on my back and the looks of appreciation I'm receiving from a mess of pink with blonde hair that's standing next to Cara Mia.

Stepping closer to Mia, I catch her subtle inhale of air when I wrap my arms around her tiny frame and pull her closer to my body. I wasn't kidding when I said I'm done staying away. I've never denied myself anything in life, only her. I'm done. I want her.

All of her.

The good girl that drives me insane with only one flirty smile. The bad girl that loves to push my buttons and test my limits. The monster that hides beneath all that sweet exterior.

Her ugly has always called out to my depraved soul.

"You've managed to piss off two powerful men and one angry brother in a matter of minutes." She looks up at me with a serious look on her face and a frown. She's worried about me. Adorable. "What do we do now?" I feel her hold on me tighten, and I swear I suppress the groan that almost slips from my lips at the contact.

Dropping my head, I inhale her sweet scent—peaches. Yeah, so fucking sweet— and press my lips to the top of her head. "Now, we go home, Red."

A shocked gasp leaves her mouth, followed by a few curses in Russian and another low growl.

And all I do is laugh all the way out of their territory, with their world holding onto my hand like she was always meant to.

Part Three

KING OF HEARTS

CHAPTER TWENTY-SIX
HIS WORLD

"And here I thought you didn't have a romantic bone in your body." - C

Cara

"Wow." I breathe in, stunned by the dark but beautiful mansion before me. I quickly get out of the car and walk closer to the huge mansion that almost resembles a celebrity house, hidden away on a hill somewhere in California that they feature in Architectural Digest. This is not the Nicolasi mansion. He took me somewhere else. I did ask him to take me somewhere no one would find me, and where I could be away from all the noise. Somewhere safe.

He brought me here.

Where is here exactly?

You would think the color black for a home's exterior would make it look gloomy, but it does the opposite. It makes it look modern and sophisticated. Boujee as hell, too. Two things the man currently getting out of the passenger side of the SUV is. Lorenzo has always had a love for the expensive things in life. Back in school, he drove the latest car in the market and dressed in expensive brands, although not as much as his twin brother. They each had different styles but were always expensive as hell.

"Where are we?" I can't seem to stop staring at the gigantic mansion, not because of how big it is, but because it fits… him. This is who he is, and his home reflects that. The house is all floor-to-ceiling windows, and even from out here, I can see inside. There's no privacy whatsoever. The house's exterior has a minimalistic vibe, and I wonder how the inside looks. Is it empty? Is it cold and detached? Or is it filled with things that make him… him?

From the corner of my eye, I watch him come over to my side and look down at me, so I pry my eyes away from the house and stare into those hypnotizing blues of his. I'm still shocked that he's here with me and that he actually listened to what I wanted and took me away from everything else. Looking at him now, after I was asleep for two and half hours from the flight, I can take a moment and appreciate how much has changed and what little remains the same.

God, a lot has changed.

He's so much bigger than the last time I saw him, if that's even possible. There's muscle on top of muscle stretching his black tee. My eyes trail every inch of him, taking him in as if I've been starving for years, and maybe I have. I went so long without him, and now I need my fix. He has added more tattoos, and there's barely any skin left from what's visible. Damn, his tattoos really do it for me. There's just something about Enzo with his pretty-boy-face, tattoos and piercings that's a walking contradiction. He has grown out his hair and now wears it slicked back, away from his face. This man… this man was made by the devil himself to tempt even the purest of souls to sin. Lorenzo was made for sin, not sainthood. He didn't have a hand in making any part of him except for maybe those mesmerizing eyes that make me think I'm looking into the deep blue sea every time I look into them. Sometimes when I allow myself to think about him, I wonder how it would feel to have those beautiful eyes look down at me while he's in— A low chuckle snaps me out of my daydream, and I can't control the heat that rushes from

from my neck to my cheeks. Great. That's just what he needs, for me to feed his gigantic ego. He knows he's gorgeous, and he uses it to his advantage, too.

Clearing my throat, I look up at him to catch him smiling down at me with an amused expression on his face. Yeah, he knows how hot he is, and he knows I know it, too.

"We're back in Detroit." I notice there aren't many men standing guard and securing the premises for their boss like most crime bosses would have. Huh.

"I gathered, but what is this place? Why here and not the Nicolasi mansion?" I believe he brought me back to his city because where else would he take me if not the city he rules over? The city where he has the most protection.

"This is my home now." That's all he says before I hear Draego, his right-hand man, shut the car door behind me and come our way.

A mess of black appears in my peripheral vision at the same time Enzo's man murmurs "incoming" in a loud hiss. Draego makes a move to stand in front of me, but Enzo lifts a hand in his direction, stopping him mid-step. "Let them be."

Before I know it and have time to prepare myself for the fury attack, I'm pushed down to the ground by two gigantic beasts and three small French bulldogs. Mine and Enzo's babies, in his case, his scary beasts of dogs.

Grimmy.

Saitan.

Abbadon.

Amon.

Hades.

I start laughing when my dogs start to wag their tails excitedly and lick every inch of my skin like they usually do when I get home and when I'm gone for long periods of time. It's been only a day and a half since I last saw them, and yet it felt like more.

I didn't worry about them while I was taken to New York because they stay with my sister-in-law and brother whenever I have a job, and I guess Enzo had them brought here. How… kind. Kind and Enzo are not words I use in the same sentence often, but when it happens, it's perfect. "Huh."
"What?"
"They're not so kind to strangers." Enzo looks down at the dogs and then at me with an unreadable expression. "They seem to like you."
"I'm very easy to like." I joke while scrunching my face up at him while Grim licks my cheek. Sweet, so very sweet. My Grimmy. The second gift Enzo has ever given me after the drawings. "It appears that you are, monster." He grumbles before shooing the dogs away.
"Hey, I wasn't done saying hi to them."
"They won't go anywhere." He looks away as if lost in thought, and I wonder what has changed since moments ago when he had a playful grin on his face. Enzo looks at Draego and tells him to show me inside and help me get situated. They won't go anywhere as if they're here to stay.
"What? You're leaving?" I ask.
"I'll be right back. I need to take care of some business." Dragon throws keys his way, and Enzo catches them effortlessly. "In the meantime, go inside with Draego until I get back." Oh, okay.
Suddenly, Draego's voice booms with a command, and my dogs scatter. I watch all the dogs retrieve to the back of the house and wonder how and when my crazy dogs were trained. I spoil them rotten to the point they misbehave all the time. Not that I care all that much. I just wanted them to feel safe, loved, and at home with me. I smile when Grimmy falls back and sniffs one of the other dog's butts. Laughing, I watch them go. Oh, yes. That's my naughty boy, too cool to be trained all the way.

I feel his firm hand come up to the back of my neck and pull me close to his face, and for the third time since he reappeared in my life, out of nowhere, he astounds me and catches me off guard. Without my defenses in place to protect me from any attack. Every sense of mine comes alive when he's this close to me, and I don't even try to hide the heat that slowly rises to my neck from his touch. "Behave, Red." He stares into my eyes for a moment as if he's taking me all in before he pulls back, and this sudden feeling of loss takes over me. Only him. I've only felt this vulnerable, yet simultaneously so strong, with him.

"Something happens to her while I'm gone, it's your head, D." He snaps at his man without even looking back as he strolls in the direction of his car. I watch as he leisurely climbs inside a Matte black Buggati La Voiture Nore.

Yes, I know my cars, especially the latest in the market. That machine is one of the most expensive cars out there, and there are only a few in the States.

Of course, Enzo got his hands on one. He does love his toys.

"When have I ever not behaved?" Only when I'm with him. The mirth in his eyes tells me he thought the same, too. I have always been a good girl. A rule follower for the sake of others well-being and happiness, but on the rare times I act out or break any rules, it's always with him or because of him. Never regretted it once.

I watch him smirk before turning the engine on and bringing that sexy as hell machine to life. Then, I think back to the question I've wanted to ask him since we departed from New York.

"Did you know?"

"Know what?"

"Did you know she was alive all this time?"

"I did."

He knew and didn't tell me.

"Get rid of that frown, Red. It doesn't suit you." Then, having enough of the questions, he slowly starts to raise the windshield, but before it completely obscures him from my vision, he says. "Wasn't my secret to tell."

I guess he's right.

We've always had our secrets, and he's always told me the truth. Always. However, it wasn't his secret to tell. It was hers. My sister's.

I always wondered if Enzo's psychologist misdiagnosed him because it's difficult for me to believe he doesn't understand his own emotions. They're always so obvious to me but so hard for him to comprehend.

"Let's go." I forgot Draego was behind me all this time, quiet as a mouse. I've never seen this one around the Nicolasi family. He must be new.

Taking a deep breath, I follow him inside Lorenzo's kingdom, and I do it with a small smile on my face and an excited pep in my step. All my troubles and sadness fade when I enter his home.

Just like always…

He's my safe place.

Nothing seems to touch me when he's around.

When I'm part of his world.

CHAPTER TWENTY-SEVEN

FOND MEMORIES

"My heart wants what it wants." - C

Cara

"Through here," Draego pushes the first door open, a huge double black door with intricate designs, and gestures for me to follow him. I do. I trail behind him and let him guide me. Now that Enzo has left me alone, I can take my time studying the man with a permanent frown on his face. When Enzo is around, he steals all the attention for himself without even trying and realizing he's doing it. That's the beauty of him. Most people would die to have the presence Lorenzo exudes just by breathing or standing tall and strong with an air of superiority around him. He's almost godly, that man, and it's mind-boggling how he doesn't even have to try. Nope. Not him. Other people fight their entire lives to be seen, but not Lorenzo Nicolasi.

I can see the same when I look at the man in front of me. Draego, that's his name. He acts the same way as his boss. There's one small difference, though. Whereas Lorenzo is loud and charismatic when he wants to confuse people, Draego is silent and broody. He's also quite young, from what I can tell. Younger than Lorenzo, that's for sure. Maybe in his early twenties? Draego is tall, ridiculously so. He's a couple inches taller than his boss, but Enzo has a few pounds on him. His skin is not tan like Enzo's and most Italian men. It resembles my own. Pale.

That's not strange since, from what I've heard, Lorenzo recruited men from all backgrounds and walks of life.

Looking at the man, I take in his dark brown hair that's cut short on the sides and longish on top. He is wearing dark jeans, a black tee, and black biker boots. Very casual instead of formal like most made men style themselves, with expensive suits and leather Italian dress shoes.

Enzo has always rebelled against traditions, even when he was a young boy. So did his father. I never saw Cassius wearing a suit, but he has his own reason for sticking it to his family any way he could.

That's one of the many things Cassius and Lorenzo share, even if Lorenzo is oblivious to all the ways he resembles his dad.

I still remember all the times we had to attend formal dinners with all three families in attendance and meetings, where every male dressed up, Enzo dressed down. Black was his color, and he only wore hoodies and sometimes tees.

Then as he got older, he started adding tattoos and piercing his left ear and nose.

Instead of looking like a white-collar criminal like most men in the three families, he stood out and was proud.

A thug.

A criminal.

Nothing tame about him.

Thinking back now, I've never seen Enzo in a suit, not even a dressed shirt. Not once, and maybe I never will. It's not who he is, and in some way, I believe it is his way of giving the middle finger to every made man that came before him.

Now, I wonder if Enzo is leading the Nicolasi men differently than his grandfather.

I follow Draego through a long and narrow hallway.

The double doors outside led to this hallway that I assume leads us inside the mansion. This place is so grand that you need to walk through a hallway resembling a tunnel to get to the inside of his home.
How strange but also unique.
Just like its owner.
I keep walking behind Draego, but I've had enough of the silence. That's one thing I've noticed since stepping foot out of the car.
Calm.
Peaceful.
Silence.
Just like the Lorenzo I know that most don't.
The real him enjoys being away from the world and the noise.
"How long have you worked for Enzo?" I try to make conversation as I trail behind Draego.
The man grunts but says nothing. Oh, awesome, he's not a chatterbox. Too bad for him, I can't stand silence for too long.
"How old are you? You don't seem older than twenty-two." I try to guess his age as he continues to ignore me, and that just makes me want to keep talking. I broke down his boss, and I'll get to him, too.
Because he'll be seeing a lot of me from now on.
Enzo brought me back to his kingdom, and I don't plan on ever leaving.
Because no matter the obstacles we face, time or miles apart, Lorenzo Nicolasi has always been and will always be… mine.
Draego opens yet another door, this one a double glass one, and finally reveals the inside of Enzo's home. I'm suddenly taken aback, not prepared for what I see. Every time I envisioned Enzo's home, I imagined minimalist decor or lots of black and white furniture. Simple, clean, and okay, a little bit of a mess, just like his childhood room.
This is nothing like what I thought.

This is him.

This is his safe place.

The first thing I notice is how high the ceiling is from the floor, making the mansion look even more gigantic and spacious. I bet if I yell, I'll be able to hear the echo all around me. That's how huge this place is.

The décor is nothing like the Nicolasi mansion. Hell, nothing is the same, and I'm glad because even if it's hard to believe, this place feels homier than all of our homes while we were growing up. Yeah, it's cold and dark, but it still feels… right. As if I'm right where I'm supposed to be. Draego closes the double doors behind me, but I completely ignore his presence as I take in everything, not wanting to miss a thing.

Black.

The decor, the walls, even the floor.

Black and… red.

My heart skips a bit when I walk further inside the living area and see the stunning silver chandelier taking up half the space of the ceiling. The lighting is at a low level, making the room dimly lit. God, how pretty. In fact, it's the only decorative item in the room because everything is gothic chic.

"You can safely explore the premises. No one will bother you and if they do, just holler." Draego whispers ever so softly, and it touches something deep inside me. How sweet and gentle his tone is in contrast to his rough exterior. Huh. "The boss forgot to give you this." Looking down at his palm, I see my phone. I haven't even thought about it once. I quickly snatched it from his hand, needing to make some calls, but later.

"Thank you, Draego." I offer him a small smile and watch him retrieve into a dark hallway.

He gave me more than one-word responses, progress.

I find myself alone. I don't wait a second before I move around, looking at everything from up close.

I start with the black walls. Black walls.
Most people would go with white paint for the walls because it brightens up a room, but not him. He's unlike everyone I ever met, and the evidence is all around me.
I can't stop the big smile that takes over my face when I see exactly what decorates this room. Not vintage and classic art from another time, no. My brother's art.
Pieces from his Greek god's collection he did in collaboration with his wife. Three years ago, Andrea had the brilliant idea to combine her fashion with Lucan's art for charity to help the children's hospitals all around the country and back in Italy. Andrea designed a unisex line in theme with Greek gods and goddesses, and Lucan painted all her marketing packages while creating masterpieces inspired by ancient Rome using glass and pieces of clothing from the Valentina Co. collection. A bit weird, yes, but it sold out in less than an hour.
Now, looking at the face of a furious-looking Zeus made of black glass and peach-colored fabrics, I can't help the rapid beat of my heart. Zeus. How fitting. The god of thunder.
For someone who claims to dislike my brother so much, he sure doesn't act like it sometimes. He cares. He cares so hard, and if every single part of me didn't belong to him already, I would've lost it all in this instant.
Moving further, my fingers touch his furniture, and I wonder if he spends time here, surrounded by the works of art made by the people that care for him the most.
Then, I see it.
Fallon James's work.
Black and white portraits of Valentino and his children decorate the walls. How can something so simple as a black and white photo invoke so many feelings? Looking at Valentino's face, I don't see the demons that used to dance in his eyes when I last saw him and when he was a teenager. No. His handsome face, identical to Enzo's , lights up

as he looks at what I assume is the person who took the picture.
His wife.
Right next to him are his children.
Poe and Vade.
Twin babies just like his father and my Enzo.
The kids wear different expressions on their faces.
Vade is grinning mischievously and looks just like his uncle when he does something bad. Happy and proud of the chaos he causes. Fallon will have her hands full with that one. Then, I look at little Poe, and my heart melts with how sweet and tender she looks. Her smile is small. You can barely see it, only for the tiny lift of her right cheek and the dimple that formed. Unlike her brother, there's nothing chaotic about Poe. She's the perfect mix of her parents, but in my opinion, she takes more after her mom in the looks department, but her quiet nature?
That's all her daddy.
Next, I see photos of Andrea sitting in what looks like a gazebo smiling up at the sun while my nephew Roman stands behind her, squeezing her neck and making her laugh. Allegra is posing for the camera dressed head to toe in pink, ignoring her little sister, Artemis, who's looking off into the distance with a scowl on her gorgeous face.
God, I love them.
And I especially love that Enzo keeps these in his home.
Shaking my head lightly while my smile grows wider, thinking about how someone that looks as if the devil and Lilith had a son has the biggest heart.
I'm not naïve either.
I know he only cares for his blood and maybe his men. The verdict is still out on that one.
Everyone else… he could care less about.
I also know that he's no saint.

So far from it.

Then, I spot a modern fireplace and next to it, there's an antique black wood shelf holding various books. Curious, I walk toward it and pick up one of the books. It is a hardback titled Dangerous Liaisons by A. A Turner.

Enzo was never one for reading.

This must all be his twin Valentino's work.

Yeah, that heart of his is so full and so damn big.

He keeps it all to himself, but now that I've had a peek of what's inside of it…

I want it.

I want him.

Dark, angry, scary, and all.

I want to be inside every corner of his complicated heart.

Everywhere.

CHAPTER TWENTY-EIGHT

FATHER & SON

"Can't even trust the
people inside your own home." - Cass

Lorenzo

Pulling my matte black Bugatti onto the side of the street, I position myself to watch my father's house. Reaching inside the car's glove compartment, I retrieve a box of Marlboros. Lighting a cigarette as I flip the lighter open and closed, open and closed, watching the house from the car.
Patience has never been one of my virtues.
I cannot stay put for long periods of time.
I get twitchy.
Flicking the lighter closed, I wait for it.
Just like clockwork, the boring-looking woman, with short strawberry blonde hair and a soft smile, steps outside Cassius's door, gets in her plain blue Honda Civic, and leaves.
I've never met the woman, and I don't wish to. Not because I have anything against her, which I don't, but because she's temporary. Nothing with Cassius ever lasts. Women like her don't hold his attention for too long. I don't have a single fucking clue why he's even entertaining the idea of settling down with her. I didn't need to have a close relationship with my father to learn his habits and patterns. I studied him like I did everyone else around me. Turning the engine off, I climb out of the car and make my way inside his door.

He gave me a set of keys the day he purchased this place, and I've not used them before now. My relationship with my father is complicated. I don't hate him. I don't hold any grudges against him.

I just don't feel anything toward him but contempt.

I'm good with how things are between us.

I was never the kid that dwelled on the things he didn't have. I focused on the things I wanted. What I craved most. I wanted my grandfather out of the picture, crownless, and swimming in the Detroit River.

I made it happen.

Grandpa did always enjoy his fish. In the end, he got to swim with them before the little fuckers ate his flesh.

I hope.

I made peace a long time ago with the man I grew up to be. I'm not like my father or my brother. Hell, I have nothing of my sister in me either. I'm… me. Through the years, I learned that, unfortunately, I do have feelings as much as it pains the ever-living fuck out of me. I care for the brats my sister and sister-in-law birthed. I care for my brother.

I care for Mia.

I feel toward the people I build some kind of bond with, hence why I don't share the same feelings toward my own father.

We weren't that close, and now that he's sober and trying, it's no use to me. I'm grown now and well-established in my fucked-up ways.

Ping.

I look down at my phone at the same time as I walk toward the creepy-looking black townhouse. A message pops up. One from Lucan, which I ignore. He's been texting incessantly since I left with his little sister. Sending me threats if I don't reply.

Fun times.

Another text from Valentino, that one I don't ignore because it's a mess of letters. It's most likely Poe who got a hold of his phone and sent it. Smiling, I think of how smart that baby is. That kid is gifted. I just know it. She got it from her father, for sure. I do what I always do when I receive a message from my Poe. She doesn't know how to read yet, so I send her a bunch of her favorite emojis. The one that makes her giggle every time she sees it. The ugly shit emoji.

The moment I hit send, another notification pops up, but this time it is a news article from some gossip site. The headline reads Mia Madden and her breakout role in some fuckface's movie. I skim through the article before pocketing the phone and unlocking the door to Cassius's home.

Before I twist the knob, the door is pulled open, and there he stands, looking irritated.

"Well, hello there, daddy." I chuckle when his frown deepens. Stepping aside, he lets me inside his place. Looking around, I notice of how different this place looks since he bought it. Before, it was hollow and cold. Now, it has pictures of everyone he cares about. His children and his grandkids. I ignore the frame on the right side of the coffee table where her face burns me if I stare at it for too long.

Some memories trigger the fuck out of me, to the point I can't get them out of my head. I haven't had one of those moments since I was a teenager when I found out what caring for someone unavailable really does to your soul.

And that she was.

So far, out of my reach, I couldn't deal with it.

I couldn't handle what caring for her meant for me, so I did the selfish thing. I compartmentalized all those feelings deep inside of myself and never thought of it until it was too late for her.

Quickly dismissing the depressing thoughts, I focus on Cassius instead.

Him, I can handle. Her? Not so much.

"What's wrong?" he barks before turning around and walking toward his kitchen.

How is this his life now? It's been years since he decided to get his shit together, and every time I see him, there's something different about him, and the asshole looks even younger than he did the last time.

Maybe I will stop with the alcohol if being off it will work wonders in my old age.

"Can't a son drop by and visit his father?"

"Valentino, yes. You? No." Cassius murmurs while focusing on the food he is preparing. I look around his kitchen, taking it all in. How odd.... I could've sworn he detested grape jelly, and yet, there's an open jar next to the coffee maker. He must've gotten it for the kids when they stay over when Valentino wants alone time with his woman.

Cassius's comment about Tino dropping by but not me is fair. I stop by, and check that everything is in order but I never make my presence known. He doesn't need to know.

I sit down on a bar stool and watch him cook breakfast. Yeah, I'll never get used to this side of him. This is the man my nieces and nephews call pops, a total contrast to what Tino and I had.

There's no bitterness in that thought. The kids deserve good people around them. A good life. I'm glad they have a sober and caring grandfather.

Even though the man looks like he could be our older brother.

The fuck.

"Is that a new tat?" I point toward the sick as fuck looking wolf on his naked back. The tattoo covers his entire back, and if you look close enough, the eyes of the beast give the illusion as if it's looking right through you.

Cassius is one odd motherfucker.

My father turns around but doesn't look at me as he cracks two eggs and drops them on the sizzling pan. "I would've come to you for it, but I thought you—" he stops mid-sentence and looks up from the eggs.

He thought I would turn him away. Shit. Why is it that every damn member of my family is so emotional? "Next time, come to me." I say, shrugging it off.

My father just nods. That's it. We don't need to hug it out or express our emotions. I can be myself with him and oddly, he never judges me. He never makes me feel like I'm a freak. Even when he got me help when I was a kid or the times he witnessed how fucked up I am. He still looked at me as if I wasn't a monster, just his son. Even when he was drunk out of his mind, he never saw me with different eyes.

Maybe that's why I don't hold any resentment toward him.

Who the fucks know how I would've turned out if I had a present and loving father? Maybe I would've turned out like every idiot I used to bully in school. No, thanks. I like myself. Bloodthirsty habits and all.

When he's done with the eggs, he drops them on a white ceramic plate and moves to sit down next to me on the kitchen island. "You hungry?" It smells really good, but the last thing on my mind right now is food.

"No." Reaching inside my left pocket, I pull out a cherry-flavored lollipop, tear the paper off, and pop it inside my mouth. Mmm, cherry explodes all over my taste buds. Then I reach for my phone, open the gallery, and push the phone toward him.

Twisting in my seat, I turn around and face Cassius. I watch as he frowns, looking down at the phone and looking back up again.

"Who have you pissed that now feels bold enough to come after me and mine?" The easy-going attitude leaves my body. This is no joke.

I would still be pissed as fuck that someone I don't know is coming after my neck but knowing they're coming after the one person that matters above all else is making me livid. No one fucks with her. Just look what fucking with my girl got the boss of Chicago.

One man short.

A low sigh slips free of my father's mouth, and I watch as he drops the phone back down onto the kitchen island and pushes his plate of food away from him, no longer hungry. He sighs, and his entire body shakes, but he takes a second to gather his thoughts.

What the fuck did you do, man?

As he gets lost in thought, I take a second to look at him. Really stop and look at the man he is now. His usual longish blonde hair is cut short on the sides and a little longer at the top. He even has a short beard now, whereas before, he didn't. He doesn't have as many tattoos as Valentino and me. From what I can see now that he's shirtless, I can only spot the one at his back and messy writing on his left pectoral.

He's huge now, too.

Huge and healthy.

He doesn't look a day over thirty-five.

Cassius had Andrea when he was a kid himself, so that doesn't really surprise me. He's not old, and now that he's off the coke and brown liquor he looks… alive.

There's something that wasn't there a couple of months back. There's darkness under his eyes as if he's not sleeping well. Shit, with the number of ghosts this man has…what moral man would get a good night's sleep?

Cassius has his own shit to take care of.

For one, the crazy harpy who's after his ass, and the kind woman with hearts in her eyes. I get it. Sweet women don't do it for him.

At least not anymore.

Maybe that's where I got it from. I like them a little crazy with a sweet side, and Tino does, too.

We got it from our daddy, I see.

"I've made a lot of mistakes when I was in a really dark place. I couldn't see past my own pity and self-regret. I didn't consider, or maybe I didn't really care, that my actions had repercussions and I hurt people." I get out of my head and listen intently to what he has to say. I need to neutralize this threat before it gets close to the people that mean something to me, and the only way I can do that is if I dig deep inside my father's past. I'm certain that the person gunning for me and Cara, has issues with this family and Cassius.

"Is it her?" I ask him, knowing damn well he gets whom I'm referring to. "Is it that little shit with a hard-on for your blood?"

He frowns and rubs his short beard before answering. "No."

"How're you so sure?"

"It's not her style." He points to my phone. "The messages and going after someone that has nothing to do with me."

"Don't be naïve, Cassius. I'm your son, and Mia—" I stop myself before I let it slip.

"Means something to you, I know." He doesn't ask. Doesn't ask me for answers. "Trust me. It's not her."

"Then who?" I bark, losing my patience. This threat has taken me by surprise.

I will give her, or him that, but I'll get to the bottom of this, even if I have to turn this city upside down to do it. "Think, man. Who did you wrong so fucking badly that they're out for blood all these years later?"

My father remains silent for a couple of seconds before looking me straight in the eyes. "You know. We always worried about you. For a time there, I worried that you had a lot of him in you. That it would be impossible to pull you back from the edge, but like always, you prove me wrong.

She used to call you her crazy baby and would laugh at your antics. You were clingy as fuck, too. For someone who doesn't understand emotions like the rest of us, you sure as hell wanted to feel us every chance you got. Maybe you wanted to feel something at that young age, or you were just a clingy little brat." I groan inside when he laughs while reminiscing. Shit. Not this. "Then, you would hold my hand, and I swear I felt like the biggest piece of shit because you were holding onto the hand of a drunk who couldn't get out of his head to be there for you. But there you were, giving me comfort even when you most likely didn't understand it yourself." He takes a deep breath while I hold mine. I wring my hands under the table and count to five. I still do what he taught me as an impulsive kid when I felt like the walls were closing in on me or I needed to go off on someone. I still don't know which it is now. "But you have nothing of him. Yeah, you're impulsive as hell and a little crazy. Okay, a lot crazy, but you care, and you care deeply, and you got that from your mom. That is all her, and fuck, I'm so thankful for that because as long as you care for something or someone other than yourself, than you will never be him. You're better. Stronger. You're meant for great things, kid. You're far better than all of us that came before you."

"That's… sweet." I try my best to smile for his benefit, but all I can manage is what I bet looks like a demon smiling back at you. I can smile a fake one, but a real one is hard as fuck to pull off.

He grunts, "I'm sorry I couldn't be much help. Your uncle and I, hell, your grandfather as well. We did shit I'm not proud of, and it was bound to fall on your doorstep for being Nicolasi blood." He stands up from his seat, moves to the kitchen sink, and drops his untouched plate of food in. Cassius looks at me while I'm still reeling from everything he just laid out for me. "Is there anything I could do?"

Rising from the seat, "Stay with Tino and his family. I don't know if this piece of shit has it in for just me or if he will go after him, too. I'll send some of my men to his cabin and some to New York with Andrea."

Cassius nods, and that's it for father-son time. I start to head out when his voice stops me, and I wish, for once, he would've just kept quiet.

Fuck.

"Read them, son. She loved you so goddamn much. Maybe it—"

"See you around, Cassius."

The sore spot of my mother will never not bother me. I fucked up when it comes to her, and I know she's my ghost, too.

And every time I try to open one of the letters she left for me, I think better of it. I want to keep the memory I have of her when she was brave enough to come for me all those years ago and not taint it with the image of her fading away, losing the war to a bitch sickness.

If I open those damn letters, I will feel all of it.

Her love.

Her pain.

Her sadness.

All I will see is her pretty face turning into something ugly.

Into the woman dementia made of her.

No.

I rather be a selfish son of a bitch and let the past be just that.

The past.

CHAPTER TWENTY-NINE

ONE DREAM

"My heart wants what it wants." - C

Cara

After I was done looking around the living room area of the mansion, I wandered off to the kitchen to serve myself something to drink and what I found surprised me even more than Fallon and Lucan's work around his home.

The moment I opened the refrigerator, I found fruits, beers, and a whole lot of frozen junk food. Which doesn't surprise me since, by the looks of it, Enzo was never one to eat healthy. Plus, he's a man. The beers are a must.

Then, I moved to the kitchen cabinets and found all types of candies. From cherry bombs to cherry heart-shaped lollipops and all my favorite ones. Did he plan for me to come here after flying to New York to get me? Or has he had all of this for a long time?

My heart beats wildly in my chest, knowing this man is a complicated box of surprises, and with every new side to him I discover, I fall even harder for him. One thing is certain I've been with him all this time just as he's been with me, in my thoughts and in my heart, while I traveled the world and the years flew by.

I was here.

In every inch of this home that he decorated in red.

In the candies and in my favorite foods.
In the peaches in his fridge.
In the cute and kid-friendly tree house sitting in his backyard.
A treehouse.
He doesn't have kids. I would know if he had them any, so why did he purchase a home with a tree house? That's if the home came with it. Maybe he had it installed.
I always knew there was a lot more deep down in that obscure soul of his. I knew it when I was just a mere child who found comfort in a dark and brooding kid who found joy in inflicting pain on others and was more comfortable in violence than in peace. I knew he was the only one for me when he showed me how far he was willing to go to accomplish all he ever wanted and, in the process, gave me my dreams. Some of them, at least.
He's the one dream I'm still reaching for.
And I'm not one to give up.
That's why I'm here.
In his city and in his home.
Because I know, deep down, he would let me go if I truly wanted out.
But he knows, just as I know, that this is it for me.
For us.
I just need him to get his head out of his ass and see we're magic together.
With his evil tendencies and my wicked heart and desires… black magic maybe.
It's still magic, though.
Now, all I need to do is get all my ducks in a row back in my world so I can stay forever in his.
Leaning back on the huge white cotton sofa, I get comfortable while scrolling through my contacts until I find Arielle's number.

The news plays in the background on the huge screen.
A home theater.
He has a home theater, and it gives out the vibe that you're at the movies without having to go out.
It's so neat.
There's Paris Barker, the host of Gossip Nights in Paris, with another co-host in the panel, speculating on my relationship with Jonah. There are many tragic things happening in the world right now and much more important matters to report on, but that is what they choose to talk about.
I get it, gossip sells, but for once, I wish it weren't this way.
I wish he didn't have to go through this just to survive in that world where appearances matter much more than authenticity. It does not bother me, but I know it bothers my friend. At least he's at his happy place back in his hometown, visiting his parents before he has to go back to filming and on the press tour for the movie. I stalked him on his social media and saw all the stories he posted of his time there.
I'm also relieved he's out of the media's eyes and Enzo's reach just in case he gets any idea of using Jonah to get me to behave.
My thumb is hovering over Arielle's name before an incoming call comes through.
It's her.
I hit accept, and the call connects.
"Hey," I answered.
"I could kill you!" Arielle's shout almost busts my eardrum. Not risking it, I put the phone on speaker. Arielle takes a deep breath as she always does to calm herself. "Are you okay? Do I need to call the police? Your brother contacted me, but he was pretty vague, and if I'm honest, I didn't believe a word that fell out of his gorgeous mouth." Rolling my eyes, I laugh out loud. She has the biggest crush on my brother. Sometimes the shit she says is kind of gross.

"I'm alright, and no, no need for the police." Arielle has always looked out for me, and I feel somewhat bad that I didn't get in touch with her sooner, but I had a lot to process. I'm glad my brother contacted her for me without being asked. That's who he is, and suddenly, a rush of sadness overcomes me thinking about him. I really do love my brother, and there's no doubt in my mind that he loves me, too. I never doubted it. He orchestrated our sister's death just to give her a new life and had to carry the burden of me seeing him in a different light after learning what he supposedly did. Lucan's love for us knows no bounds, just like our mom's. He reminds me so much of my mom. All the times I feel down missing her, I look at him, and in him, I see her.

"What the hell happened? I left you with Julio like I do every time, then I came to find out you left the city without telling anyone, and Julio is nowhere to be found." Arielle's high-pitched voice means she's nervous. Crap.

Then I think of what she said. Julio is nowhere to be found. Did something else happen? Did Vladimir and Vitali do something to him? I need to ask Enzo about it as soon as he gets back.

"I promise I'm okay. I just…" I take a deep breath and quickly try to come up with a lie to make her stop worrying without having to reveal all my truths. "I just received bad news from family members, and I needed time to digest it away from the limelight." There. It wasn't a total lie. It's not the whole truth either, but it'll do.

Arielle sighs, "Something tells me there's more to it, girl. But I'll respect your silence. Just know I'm here if you need anything. I got you." Arielle has been a godsend, and I don't know what I would've done without her all these years.

After that, she goes into work mode and starts bringing me up to speed with what's going on with the film and with the media's speculation about me and Jonah.

"The media frenzy is crazy lately. They want to know all about you and Jonah and why they haven't seen you out lately. I'm releasing a statement soon about your time away. I just need you to look it over and approve it, and then I'll post it on your social media first thing in the morning."

I appreciate my followers. I honestly do. If it weren't for them following me when I was a nobody and then rooting for me every step of the way, I wouldn't be living my dream and doing what makes me genuinely happy.

They deserve the truth, and one day, it will come out, but until then, that statement will have to do.

"One last thing, the red carpet and first screening for The Hollow will be in two weeks. Will you be okay to attend by then?" Oh, there's no way I'm missing that. I worked too hard. Everyone did. From the actors down to the amazing staff who worked day and night to get the set, the movie, and us, ready for the fans. "I thought about getting you out of it, but the contract you signed specifies that you have to do press for it, and that includes red carpets and interviews. If you fail to uphold your end of the deal, then they'll take legal matters, plus it'll leave a big stain on your professional reputation in Hollywood."

I know.

There's no way I'm missing it. I've waited so long for that moment, and it's almost here.

I still have two weeks before the premiere. All I need to do is tell Enzo. I'm sure he won't have a problem with it. I can fly by a plane, and after it's all done, I'll fly back.

Two weeks is more than enough for me to get my head straight and come to terms with all I learned about myself before I have to face the world again. Even when I'm trying to push through it, I know deep down inside I feel confused.

Who am I?

Cara Mia?

Vera? Am I both of them? Who is Vera, exactly?

I know it might seem silly, but I can't ignore the part of me that's a stranger to myself. I'm half Russian. I have cousins who are not only Russian but also leaders of one of the States and Russia's most notorious crime organizations.

I had a mother named Darya.

I was born from a rape and violent act.

It's a lot, and I know if I had gone back to my life as if nothing happened, I would've gone down a dark hole. I would've had to act as if were okay. I don't want to plaster on a fake smile. I'm done with that. I'm not that little girl that needed to pretend to please everyone else and keep the peace. I want to stand on that red carpet happy and proud of what I've accomplished. I just need time.

Before I know it, Arielle is saying goodbye and hanging up on me. The second the call disconnects, I open my messages and type a quick text.

Me: I still love you. I'll always love you no matter what. I just needed space to breathe and think after everything that was said. I don't know who I am. I do, but I don't. It's hard to explain.

A moment later, a reply comes through.

Superman: You are who you've always been. Cara Mia Volpe. My sister. Nothing changes.

I smile, because it's just like him to put it so simply. He's partially right. I'm her, and I'm his sister, but there's more to me now, too.

Me: Just tell me one thing.

Superman: Anything.

Me: Is she happy?

I don't have to say her name. He knows whom I'm referring to.

Superman: She is now. Her smile lights up her entire face, just like yours when you do what you love.

It's bittersweet knowing she's thriving when she had to leave us to find her happiness. Me: What does she do?
Superman: What makes her heart happy.
That's a vague answer. I get it. He can't say a lot without compromising her safety and whereabouts. I think of something else to ask, but another message comes through.
Superman: You have to know that it killed her to leave you behind, topina. She almost didn't go through with it. You have to understand that you chose a career that puts you in the spotlight and it makes it hard for our family's enemies to get to you without it becoming a media circus. She was always going to be easy prey. She made the right decision for herself. If she did not get out and found herself, who the fucks know what she would've done. She was drowning.
I read his message twice with blurry eyes. Only Lucan understands all that Gigi went through in that house. So, as much as it hurts that she's lost to me, I smile, knowing she's no longer drowning. Me: I understand. If you ever see her again, tell her I get it, and I'll love her always.
Superman: Will do. Get some rest.
Me: Goodnight. *Orange heart emoji*
Superman: That fucker better keep you safe.
Me: He will.
That's it.
One-step closer to finding myself.
I feel like an enormous weight has been lifted off my shoulders.
Yawning, I put my phone back on the big sofa and turn the volume of the giant screen up.
There's a rerun of my favorite TV show playing. I lean back on the sofa and wait for him to come home.
Home.
Huh.
I really like the sound of that.

CHAPTER THIRTY
DEATHLY TIES

"You should've kept your mouth shut.
Now, you got no tongue." – L

Lorenzo

"What is she up to?" I put my phone on speaker and put it back down onto the wood table next to my Bowie knife. The knife I use to carve the lucky bastards that end up here at the Nicolasi residence's torture room. I keep my shit separate from the secluded home I purchased. Not wanting to mix my business with pleasure, although my business is always a pleasure if I'm being truly honest. Mia is aware of the shit I do, yet I don't want to bring this filth to the home I have her in now. Anywhere near her.

Such ugliness shouldn't be that close to heaven.

And although I do questionable shit, I still pride myself on having morals. The men and women that end up here are the scum on the earth who don't deserve mercy for the sins they've committed. Draego's voice fills the room along with the muffled cries of the sick bastard currently slumped over the surgical table behind me.

I do love it when they cry.

When they urinate and shit, too.

It means they're scared… truly scared.

After talking with my father, I was feeling the beast roaring for blood. Screaming for chaos, so here I am.

Feeding it.

This asshole has had a hit on his head for a while now, and lucky me, I got to him first. We have been hunting him for a year. Not only us but every capo in the States and a crooked politician, as well.

Bastian Kenton offered a large sum for me to deliver this cunt to him, but his money is no good here.

I wanted the honors.

This motherfucker right here is the reason why I hate politicians and men of God. They hide behind the idea that they're serving not only God but a country, but they abuse their position of power, knowing they'll have easy access to the most innocent.

Their believer.

The naive.

Women.

Fucking children.

Babies.

Donnie Bourke.

The senator of Detroit.

Known as a leader by the citizens of this city.

I know the real him.

A greedy sick bitch who preys on children.

The leader of the sex trafficking ring we dismantled not long ago.

I was offered good money to find this pedophile and deliver him to Washington untouched. Nah, I hunted him, and now he's my prey. I get the pleasure of making him feel and go through the same things those kids went through. He will bleed just as they bled. He will cry just as their families did when they realized their babies were lost to them and most likely suffering at the mercy of monsters.

Yeah, I'll have my fun with him first.

Draego's voice interrupts my daydreaming of blood. "She took a look around the premises and now she is in the

theater room making some calls. She hasn't moved since."
Good.
Hopefully, she figured out her shit with her team.
Donnie shouts louder, growing desperate now, and I listen to the sweet sound of skin hitting metal. I don't have to turn around to know he's trying to get himself free. He's not going anywhere.
Not yet.
"Did anyone get close to her?" Draego knows how it goes. I trust the men I handpicked to join my family. I trust their judgment, and I trust they understood my warning that I will bleed any of them dry if they look at her the wrong way.
"No, boss. The guys stayed outside on duty."
"Good." I open the left drawer and grab the first item I see. Ah, perfect. A big, rubber black dick.
Since this asshole loves them so much, it seems fitting. "I won't be long."
"There's something else, boss."
"What?"
"One kid was not claimed by anyone, so I dug further, and it turns out the birth mom is a crackhead who willingly gave up her kid to Bourke for money. The bitch's dead."
Shit.
"What's his condition?"
"It's bad. He has scars on his body, and I can see bones."
Motherfucker.
I'll make Bourke regret ever hurting those kids.
"How old?" I don't know why it matters, but I ask anyway.
"A couple of months old, I'm guessing."
A baby.
Oh, this bitch will bleed.
Oh, yes.
"Get the doctor to look after him while I figure out what to do." With that, I end the call and grab the butcher knife

with my free hand.
No gloves.
No masks.
No apron.
Just my toys.
"Oh, God. No. Think about what you're—" Turning around, I look at the man. They're all the same. First, they beg for their life and try to bargain with me, and when they realize there is no getting out of here alive, they become angry.
I like it when they beg, but oh boy, do I love it when they show their true colors.
When the mask slips and they let their ugly shine through.
And Donnie is one ugly motherfucker.
Several bruises cover his face and neck. His white shirt looks pink with all the blood on it, and his pants are soaking wet from urine and hanging down his knees. The bastard is on all fours, bound to the table, completely at the mercy of my cruelty.
 "I've been dying to meet you, Donnie."
"What? Man, look—"
"I wanted to see for myself if your blood is as black as your soul." I laugh aloud when his eyes bulge out of his sockets.
I think of all the kids.
The parents.
That little baby.
All hurt by the greedy actions of sick men.
I walk to the end of the table and put the knife down.
When I'm positioned right in front of his ass, I spread his ass, and without warning, I shove the dildo into his ass and watch in fascination as blood pours out of his asshole all over the rubber toy.
 Screams fill the room.
 Music to my ears. I continue the brutal assault on his ass and make him experience the pain and make him experience

the pain and shame his victims experienced. When I have had enough with the toy, I leave it inside his ass and pick up the knife as Donnie starts to curse my name, cry, and shout.
"Please! Just shoot me." Donnie pleads.
"But what fun would that be?" I chuckle when his body starts to shake. The pain wore off, and the fear crept in. Here we go.
"You're sick!"
"I am." With that, I reach under to grip his tiny cock in hand, and in one quick swift, I chop it off. He screams like a pig who has been slaughtered. Wanting to be done with this fucker, I take the dick, slap him on the face twice with it just for fun, and then shove it inside his mouth, quieting his pointless pleas. Walking over to the wooden table where I left my phone, I pick it up, open the camera app and snap a few pictures and send them to the two men that made it clear they wanted this cunt's head on a silver platter. Too bad I got to him first. Placing the phone back down on the table, I then drop down to Donnie's level so he can see my face clearer.
"Look at me." Humor leaves the room, and all that's left is rage. The need to inflict pain on this waste of space. Black watery eyes meet mine. I'm the last person he'll ever see. "I should let you suffer longer, but you don't deserve to breathe the same air as those kids, and it's a fucking pleasure to know that I put the monster who hurt them to rest."
The asshole spits his dick out of his mouth and tries to form words, but he's losing too much blood to form a coherent thought.
With a big fucking smile on my face, I bring my knife up and slice his neck from his left ear to his right. Blood splatters all over my clothes and face.
Ahhh, that's it.
The monster in me has been fed, and the kids who suffered because of this motherfucker will be able to breathe a little easier now that I've sent him straight to hell.

CHAPTER THIRTY-ONE

SPOILED

"Your dark soul matches my own."
– L

Cara

The vibrating buzz of my phone on my left rib wakes me up from a deep sleep. I gently open my eyes, realizing I fell asleep in the theater room waiting for Enzo to come home and find me. He didn't.

What time is it?

I pick up my phone, squinting, shielding my eyes from the bright screen and notice an email pop up. Ignoring it, I see the time. It's a quarter after midnight. Is he back yet? I guess it's still early for him. Who knows what he is up to? At this hour, most likely nothing good. Sighing, I rise from the sofa and stretch my arms over my head, and when I do, I can't ignore the funky smell coming from my armpits. Gross, I need a shower. I haven't taken one since New York. It's been a lot to take in, and in my defense, my mind has been elsewhere. But I need one pronto…

Before excusing himself for tonight, Draego told me that my room would be the first one on the left as soon as I climb the stairs, so that's where I head. I take the stairs two at a time, anxious to see the upstairs of this place. It's so quiet and cold inside these walls. The temperature drops out of nowhere, and I find myself wrapping my arms around my midsection to protect me from the cold.

I don't mind the cold as much as I do the horrible heat of the summers. Giana and Lucan love warm and sunny days while I find comfort in cloudy days. Mom loved sunny days, too. One more thing I don't have in common with them. I always thought that it was just who we were, you know? Different from each other like most families, but it was so much more than that. Not wanting to ruin my mood with thoughts that do nothing but keep me down, I concentrate on the path before me. I stop on the last step of the stairs, holding onto the rails, careful not to trip and fall. From up here, I can see the inside of the mansion from a better angle.

"Wow..." This must be what a queen feels like looking down at her kingdom.

That's exactly how I feel at this moment.

Does he feel the same way I do when he looks down these stairs? When he admires everything he has accomplished at such a young age? I wonder.

You know those moments in life where you feel peace, a peace so calming that it steals your breath from your lungs and makes you feel as if your feet leave the ground. It feels as if you're in the right place at the right time.

That's how I know I'm living this moment right now.

In this dark and cold mansion, with its only colors being red and black, and an owner who sets my soul aflame even when he's not in the room.

He's not even here, yet I feel surrounded by everything that is him.

I quickly find my room on my left. I find a sleek black door with a gold doorknob. Turning it, I open the door and step inside, and I can't hold back the laughter. Joy spreads all over my body when I look all around the room. The first thing I notice is how huge the room is and the black furniture spread out around the room.

Enzo clearly has an aesthetic.

Black, red, and pretty-fucking expensive decor.
Walking farther inside the room, I open the door next to the nightstand and find a bathroom just like you would find at the Ritz. Closing the door, I turn and notice a black wood piece of furniture with vanity lights on the sides and with all my favorite records and a red Victrola Vintage record player. No way...
Oh, yes, this man was so expecting me.
There's no doubt about it.
He's not a fan of vintage items, classic bands, or comics. Yet, the room has all of that. Smiling, I turn and instantly notice a control switch on one of the dark walls. What does it do exactly? It doesn't seem like a light switch, but not one to stay in doubt, I walk over and press it, and the moment I do, my jaw hits the floor.
Holy fuck.
The walls, that are not exactly walls, disappear, and reveal a walking closet designed for a princess. No, no, for a queen.
I walk in and turn in circles, taking everything in, from the massive wall vanity mirror to the makeup area with all kinds of brands. There's a white rug on the floor, and the decor of this hidden room is totally different from the rest of the house. This is every girl's dream.
Fancy, all over.
With every step I take inside, the lights turn on automatically. Yeah, a dream.
I almost fall backward when I turn to my right and come face to face with rows upon rows of expensive designer shoes and bags. From Hermes, Chanel, Fendi, Givenchy, and more.
Those bags could pay someone's rent for years. This crazy man...
I try not to splurge with my money, and if I'm honest, most of the expensive items in my closet back at home are gifts from the designers I worked for or promoted.

There are racks of designer clothing, as well. Dresses, skirts, blouses, tank tops, everything. Even the graphic tees and mom jeans I enjoy wearing when I want to lay low with a messy bun and face rid of makeup.

He did all of this.

For me.

But this… all this makes my heart warm knowing he knows me.

He knows my love for fashion and my tomboy and geeky soul.

He knows all of me, even when we didn't get that much time to learn about each other when we were kids, but somehow it wasn't needed. Him and I? It always felt like we met each other in every lifetime.

Suddenly feeling energized and not at all sleepy, I decide to take a shower and wait for him to arrive.

I'm not wasting anymore time.

I know what I want.

I've always known.

CHAPTER THIRTY-TWO
DEVIOUS MONSTER

*"He's a dream and nightmare all in one,
and I wouldn't have it any other way."*
– C

Cara

Feeling fresh and smelling like vanilla, I finished tying the black silk rope that was left for me in the bathroom around my body. My hair falls down my back, dripping wet, and my face is bare of any makeup.

This is when I feel the most confident.

I love being all glammed up, don't get me wrong, but there's something almost freeing in feeling secure in your own skin, imperfections and all.

We all got them, so why not embrace them?

Closing the door quietly behind me, not wanting to make a noise, I step into the dark hallway. The cool air hits me, causing goosebumps to rise on my skin. There are five doors in this wing of the mansion. I should practice the manners my mother taught me as a child, but I don't. I notice a neon red light reflecting on the floor through the small opening. The door is already open, so it only takes a tiny push to find out what's behind it.

I should respect his privacy, but I won't since he enjoys being all up in my business which I don't mind. Not really.

I hold my breath the moment I take a step inside and realize this is it. This is who my Enzo truly is underneath the sarcastic remarks, evil glint, and devious intentions.

A red light illuminates the room. The same photographer would use when developing their film, and a black leather tattoo chair sits in the far corner. There's a table with a tattoo machine and all the materials one would need to tattoo. He used to have a room like this one when he was a teenager, but there's one slight difference. This one feels more intimate. It feels like I'm standing in the middle of his twisted heart.

There are also more sketches on the walls, but this time around, they're all framed and hung like in an art exhibit. He made them all.

I recognize his art.

Women's eyes.

Some are sad.

Some are excited.

Others are angry.

The dragon sketches he used to drawn are few and overshadowed by sketches of women's bodies in all kids of sexual positions, and suddenly, I'm fuming.

I know he's not a monk, and I shouldn't expect anything from him, especially since I'm not virgin Mary and currently engaged to my childhood friend. But I can't help but feel like slamming my favorite Gucci shoes on each of the drawings and ruining them.

Jealousy.

One feeling I never felt with anyone else but him.

His body has never been mine, but dammit, everything else sure as fuck is.

His soul.

His mind.

And the heart, beating strongly inside his chest.

I move closer, looking at all the sketches up close.

Blonde and brunette women spread out, looking up at the artist with fuck me eyes. No redheads. I feel an overwhelming feeling of satisfaction when none of the women have my hair color. The jealousy subsides, but not completely.

Someone clears their throat behind me, startling the hell out of me. "You shouldn't be here." Draego murmurs from behind me. I don't know if it's the green monster talking or what, but I snap. "Draego…" I take a deep breath, composing myself, not wanting to sound like a bitch. "I go where I damn well please. I'm sure your boss won't mind, and if he does, then let him be the one who says something to me." Yeah, I think I failed at not sounding like a bitch. Hey, at least I didn't curse, so there's that. There's a moment of silence, and I turn to look at the man standing like an angry statue beside the open door, but he's not angry. Something a lot like amusement crosses over his light gray eyes. Huh. I expect him to say something else, but he doesn't. He nods once and quietly leaves, closing the door behind him.

Alone again, I run my hand through all the sketches of naked bodies and faces of women lost in ecstasy. Completely lost in soul-crushing and body-consuming lust and passion. What would it feel like to be owned by him? I've never even felt close to the amount of pleasure these strangers portray in the drawings.

I've had sex, yes, I'm not Mother-freaking-Teresa, you know. But nothing I've ever experienced with other men could come close to the passion of these drawings.

Fuck, me.

I'm pissed again.

I did once dream of Lorenzo claiming all my firsts, but they were only the dreams of a little girl. That little girl grew into a woman who knows what she wants and goes after it.

At least he had my first kiss.

At least we shared that.

Moving to the far end of the room, where there's a king-size bed with unmade black silk sheets, a thought occurs to me. Did he use this bed to draw the women? Does he fuck them here? Dammit.
Mood completely ruined.
But then…
Then, I see it.
Right above the bed frame, there are countless sketches of a girl. A girl I know all too well. Sketches of smiling indigo eyes. A young girl dancing in the rain as lightning crosses the sky. Of a slender neck with a gold choker, resembling the one he gifted me for my birthday not even three days ago.
A sketch of red hair bursting into flames.
One of cherry-red lips sucking on a heart-shaped lollipop.
Countless drawings of a red-haired girl. A red-haired girl that looks just like me.
Thump.
Thump.
Thump.
Thump.
Rapid beating and short breaths.
Suddenly, all thoughts of other women and the jealousy I felt fade away, and all I can think about is him, sitting in this room drawing me while I'm miles away in another world.
Then I look to the other corner of the room, where there's a mini fridge. An open box of smokes sits on top with an ashtray right next to it and I see fashion magazines. Not only those but gossip magazines and newspapers where I'm on the cover.
Picking one up, I noticed the Vogue October edition of last year. My first ever cover.
He bought these.
He kept them here, where he spends his days sketching what is in his heart and mind.

He has my accomplishments inside his home just as he does of everyone else he cares for. Lost in thought, I barely notice the sound of the door opening and loud precise footsteps. This again. "Okay, I'm leaving you don't have to tell me ag—" I don't finish the sentence because the moment I turn and see who just entered the room, I lose my train of thought. I'm flabbergasted when I come face to face with my favorite nightmare, standing with a small smile, emotionless eyes, and covered in blood on the other side of the room.

So much blood on his face, neck, white shirt, and every visible part of him.

"So nosy, Red." I watch him in fascination like I did that bleeding bird all those years ago as Enzo steps inside and closes the door behind him, trapping us inside.

I quickly snap out of it and ignore how deliciously dangerous he looks. God, this is not sane. Thinking this way, but I honestly don't care. "The door was open," I clear my throat and shrug, causing the robe to fall, exposing my right shoulder.

His eyes move to my exposed skin, and I swear I can feel my skin burning from his gaze. He's never looked at me this way before. He's staring at me as if he's hungry and I'm his favorite meal. Enzo steps closer, not caring that he's getting blood all over the white tiles.

He moves until he's a breath away from me. I get a better view of him now, and instead of being scared, I feel hot all over.

Someone better call the insane asylum because the way my heart beats faster when a man currently resembling an American psycho is this close to me is not in any way normal. It only drives me wilder for him.

"So, you have a habit of walking into someone else's private space just because the doors aren't locked?"

Raising my chin and leaving my robe as is, I look back at his handsome face.

There's even blood on his eyebrows. What did he do? Bathe in someone's blood? I wouldn't put it past him and to enjoy it, too. "Again, if you didn't want anyone stumbling inside this room, then you should've locked it to keep me out." I smile when his nose flares, a clear sign that he's affected by my closeness. His eyes don't strain from my naked skin, and I know I got him. Lorenzo is a strong man, but a man can only take so much before he breaks. He must know where this is going. Where I want to take it.

"You're playing games you won't win, little monster." Little monster. I didn't realize how much I missed the way he said it until he used it back in Vladimir's home.

"Ahh, but I've already won." It's true. I did win because all I've seen today proves to me that I'm in his head and in his veins just like he's in mine. I rise to my tippy toes and bring my mouth closer to his, hoping he doesn't pull away, and just like when I was a kid trying to kiss the boy who consumed all my thoughts, he doesn't pull away. "Do you dream of me, baby? Because I dream of you. I dream of you doing to me the kind of filthy things you're doing to the women in your drawings." I inject a bite to my tone on that last part, still bitter than he hangs other women in his room. But I tell him the truth because the only way I will be leaving this mansion, this city, is if I get to leave with his heart, too. No more games. No more dreams of what could be.

This might be the only time I'll ever get to be this close to him. The instant my lips almost touch his, he brings his tattooed hand up and wraps his hand around my throat, causing a subtle moan to slip free from my mouth. Enzo pushes me back until I hit the wall, and I have to admit it's the sexiest thing ever. His bloody hand on my throat is not painful but more like a warning. He's showing me exactly who he is. Doesn't he know that I've never wanted anything more? Crazy shit and all.

"I do dream of you, Mia." Enzo's voice drops to almost a whisper causing the hair on the back of my neck to rise. His warm breath hits my face, and I inhale his intoxicating scent. Smoke, vodka, and candy. "I dream of you covered in red." Blood. He means covered in blood. "In my bed writhing with pleasure, watching your veins bulge while I fuck you mercilessly, with my hand wrapped around your pretty and delicate neck." His hooded eyes look at my neck, almost in a trance. He was always out of this world good-looking, but now, as a man, he's even more gorgeous. If that's even possible. In his arms, I feel safe because I know he would never hurt me unless I ask him to, and sometimes, I dream about that, too. Of him choking me while he thrusts in and out of my body. I imagine him tying me up in bed, pushing my face between the pillows to muffle my screams as he fucks me on all fours. I also fantasize about him taking me in all ways. Fucking me with abandon until I lose myself completely in him. I cross my legs, trying to ease the ache between them. He has me on a chokehold with every dirty word he whispers. "Does that scare you?" He looks down at me, and I instantly realize something. He's holding his breath, waiting for my answer. Does he expect me to say that I am? It's kind of cute that he thinks I am or will ever be afraid of him. Never. My gigantic, sweet devil.

With his hand still holding my neck, I rise again until my nose is touching his. I breathe him in, already hooked on everything that is Lorenzo Nicolasi. "No, baby. The blood and the choking only make me horny." Enzo's breath hitches a second before I'm taking his lips in mine in a hard kiss.

He certainly didn't expect that.

I was an odd child, yes, but now I am a woman who wants a man.

This man with blood on his hands and mayhem in his wicked little heart.

Yes, I'm not holding back.

One kiss. That's all it takes for my entire body to go putty in his hands. Unlike last time, he does respond to my kiss. The hold he has on my neck tightens, making me open my mouth wider, and the moment I do, his hot tongue slips inside, twirling with mine.

The ache between my legs grows stronger when I feel the bulge in his pants and his groans of pleasure, as if he's never tasted anything sweeter. I know the feeling because I, too, never tasted anything as deliciously addictive as his kiss.

But it didn't last as long as I hoped. One second we're both devouring each other's mouths, and the next, he's pulling back from my body, keeping a hold on my neck. I try to calm the rapid rise and fall of my chest when I slowly open my eyes and find him staring down at me, and I just know what he sees. The blood.

The blood of his kill stains my lips and cheeks.

"I'm not fucking you." His voice comes out hoarse. I did that. My kiss did that. He looks wild and hungry for more. So why is he denying us both?

"Why not?" I whisper back. "Show me your worst." I'll love every part of you. Rising on my tippy toes, I take his lips in a quick kiss before nibbling on them.

Then he removes his hand from my throat and slowly grabs my face, squeezing my cheeks and lips together and pulling me back from his face. My heart skips many beats when I see his blinding smile. The one that's not fake or mocking. The one that makes the butterflies raise hell inside my belly.

"We are doing things right." That's all he says before his hand leaves my neck and he steps back from my body. We are doing this right, he said. Before I have the chance to ask him what he means, he shows me exactly what he means by sucking my bottom lip and biting it gently before releasing my face. "Tell me something."

"Anything."
"Does he make you happy? Do you love him?" My eyes find his, and there, I see fury. Shit. How can I tell him the truth without betraying the one friend that has stuck by me all these years?

Him.

Jonah.

My fake fiancé.

"Not in the way you think, no." I do love him, but I'm not in love with him. I was never able to give my heart to another man because it hasn't belonged to me since I was a little girl. Before, I didn't even realize Enzo stole it. I share another truth. "And he doesn't love me in that way either. Can you trust that?"

Enzo's eyes narrow as he picks my left hand up playing with my ring finger, and I can't help the shiver that runs through my body when he touches me. "You have two days to deal with your shit before I step in."

"Don't you dare!" I snap right back because as much as a jealous Lorenzo is hot as hell, I don't want him hurting my friend in any way. "Just… trust me."

I hold my breath because maybe I'm asking him for too much. To trust me to do the right thing for all of us. "Are you in trouble?"

Without hesitating, I tell him the honest to God truth. "No."

"Is he in trouble?"

Sighing, I give him something. "Yes." Because he is. Jonah's life used to be the dream life any kid with a shitty home life would hope for. I certainly envied the family and love he had, but things turned ugly the moment he lost the one person who protected him and loved him. Later, I learned that his picture-perfect home was not at all what it seemed.

Strong hands grab my chin, bringing me back to the now. "I don't like that the world believes you're his."

"We've always known the truth." Because we do. No matter who came before him, I'm his just as he is mine. We can dance around this all we want, but I know this is it for me.
He doesn't say anything. I think he'll pull away, but instead, he bows his head and drops a soft kiss on top of my head.
And just like that, I might be able to reach the dream that once seemed so far. I feel him start to turn in the direction of the door, but I don't want this moment to end. I wish I could freeze us in time and never leave this room. Looking at the images on the walls, an idea comes to me at the same time as I hold on to his bloodstained hand and pull him back to me, stopping him from leaving. He might want to do things his own way and at his own pace, but so do I, and if I don't get his body tonight, then I'll get the next best thing aside from his heart. His mind.
Stepping back, my eyes don't leave his blue ones as I slowly untie my robe and let it fall down my arms, exposing my naked body to his eyes only.
The cool air of the AC causes my nipples to harden, and I don't miss the not-so-subtle way Enzo takes me in slowly. I know it might seem impossible, but I swear I can hear every loud beat of my heart as his burning gaze travels from my face to my naked breasts, further down until he's staring at the valley between my thighs.
Can he see how wet I already am just by having his eyes on me?
"Draw me," I whisper to him. A broad smile takes over my face when I notice how he's looking at me. There's a fire in his eyes. Desire and unadulterated lust, too. Something else happens. He puts his hand on my waist and pushes my naked body to his, knocking the wind out of me. Holding my breath, I meet his heavenly blue eyes. Triumph overwhelms me when he's staring at me like I'm the only thing he sees. As if, I am all he ever wants to see.

He looks at me like my brother stares at his art pieces once he's spent countless hours and days perfecting them. Just like the way he looks at his wife. "Draw me as you see me, king." Because crown or not, Lorenzo has always been my king.
King of my thoughts.
Reality and dreams.

CHAPTER THIRTY-THREE
ONLY ONE

"I do love your body but what
really does it for me is your fight." - L

Lorenzo

When I was a kid, the dark ink that decorated the skin of the men that worked for Benedetto fascinated me. Back then, I used to call them markings, not knowing what they were called. I just knew that the colors, patterns, and stories each tattoo held used to grab my attention. Every man had a story behind every piece of art they tatted on their skin. Some tatted the names and faces of the ones they loved. Others tatted significant moments and dates in their lives.
And others, just inked dumb shit when they were drunk that had no meaning whatsoever.
I became fascinated with ink and couldn't wait till I was old enough to get my first one. I didn't like to color in books like Lucan did or write down my thoughts and feelings in a journal, like my twin used to do. Hell, I didn't understand my emotions back then, so for me, hobbies and passions were useless and a waste of time. I would rather fight and put my energy into something that would get me all I ever wanted. That fucking crown that used to sit on my grandfather's unworthy head. But then, I studied the men that were tatted up from their head to their toes, and I learned what tattoos meant for men in this life, so I picked up a black marker and started drawing on my skin.
I found out that I wasn't half bad.

I could draw.
I did it on my skin until I started sketching on paper to save the ideas I wanted to ink on my body once I was old enough. I drew all kinds of dark shit.
Until that one drawing of honey, gold eyes staring sadly back at me.
That was the first sketch I had tattooed on my skin.
My very first tattoo.
After that, and as the years passed, I found myself sketching the little monster who plagued my thoughts. Somehow, the more I drew her, the less it burned to have her away. It made missing her bearable because at least I had that.
Sketches of her face.
Her eyes.
Her pretty mouth.
Now, here she is, looking up at me with trust, fire, and lust in her captivating eyes that have held me hostage more than fucking once. She's standing proud and fully naked, and I have the sudden urge to shove her against the wall again and ram my dick so hard inside her that there won't be any choice but to become one.
Draw me.
Draw me as you see me, king.
Nothing.
No photo or drawing will ever do the real thing justice.
Fuck, she's so beautiful.
Her pale white skin looks flushed and the same rosy pink as her nipples. My mouth waters when I let myself look down at her perky tits standing up for me, waiting for me to take them in my mouth to suck and bite them.
Oh, I'll do that soon.
Biting my lips, I look down her taut belly, my eyes traveling down until I stare at the place I would murder my own father to be inside.

Her pretty pussy, shaved bare, and fuck, I could cum in my fucking pants like a teenage boy just thinking of how it will strangle my dick.

I meant it when I told her I wanted to do things right, but she's provoking the beast inside me. The one that wants to eat her whole and never let her go.

Before I say fuck to taking things slow, I pull away from her and turn around to gather what I need. I grab my sketchbook from the bed and my drawing pencils that I left scattered all around the desk. I listen to her loud breathing as I finish gathering all the materials.

Oh, pretty little monster… you've done it now.

"Do you trust me, Red?" I take a seat next to the bed and splay my things wide, adjusting the massive boner she provoked. I look up from my lap and meet her curious eyes.

She's not nervous or shy.

Nahh… not my Red.

I smile when she starts wringing her hands, obviously impatient. Her wild red hair, wet from a recent shower, falls down her back, covering her full tits, and thank fuck for that. Her rapid breathing causes her breasts to rise and fall in sync with her breath.

Fuck, she was made for me.

God or the devil –because my Red has a little bit of both in her – took their sweet time creating her. There's nothing I would change about the woman, and that only helped feed my obsession with her until it was no longer healthy.

Fuck it, nothing about me has ever been healthy.

Perfection.

There's no doubt about that after she kissed my face, not caring that it was covered in someone else's blood. Pretty, little monster… you're just as sick as me.

"With my life, king." Her voice comes out breathless but excited and… proud.

Fuck, yes.

"Then get that pretty ass on the bed." I grin, knowing that there's no going back.

Mia gives me her back, and I have to suppress the moan that tries to slip free when I stare at her perfect peach-shaped ass. The organ that has been dead ever since she left the city years ago starts to revive one beat at a time, in sync with every step she takes toward my bed.

She lies back on the bed, and I stare at how her bloody red hair looks in contrast with the black sheets. She looks like what I would think the queen of hell would look like if she existed, or if I believed in that. At this moment, with her made-for-sin body splayed out in my bed and red hair resembling blood, I might start believing.

"Is this okay?" She looks up at me while moving around the sheets trying to get comfortable.

"Don't move." I stare into her eyes and tell her the honest-to-Satan truth. "You're perfect."

Her breath hitches, and mine stops the second she smiles brightly at me.

I wonder… if whoever the hell made me decided to send me the piece of heaven that is this girl to make me a little less hell bound and more human.

Opening the sketchbook, I begin to bring the stunning creature in my bed to life on the white paper.

I sketch her torso, rib cage, and abdomen first, focusing on her general shape and form first. Once I've done that, I move on to her hips and curves. I look up from the paper and take a few glances, memorizing the curve of her body. Fuck, this is the hottest shit I've ever experienced. The little vixen has my cock rock hard to the point it's almost painful.

She's driving me wild by just breathing, and one thing I'm sure is that I won't ever forget this moment with her.

It'll be engraved in my fucked-up brain.

I wink at her when her mouth forms a lively 'O' shape after I rearrange myself yet again because this shit is painful. I go back to sketching. After finishing the body. I draw her facial features next. Her blue eyes crinkled at the side because of her small smile. I draw that, too. Her full lips lifted on one side, smiling at me.

I lose myself like I always do when I sketch, trying to fill the blank spaces with charcoal. I lose track of time and don't even realize when I take my shirt off because it is fucking hot in here, or maybe it's just the effects this woman has on me. Lifting my head up, I catch the little monster's eyes, excited and in pain, too. I bet she's burning. I watch in fascination as her hand moves down her belly and slips between her legs with every intention to touch what's mine.

My pretty pussy. "Behave," I tell her, but she and I both know I never want her to behave. I like her reckless, wild, and unhinged for me. It's what caught my attention in the first place. She's different. She's… devious and mine.

All mine, like her pretty-pink pussy.

"Oh, but you don't want me to behave, do you, Enzo?" The little brat laughs and carries on her path to playing with my pussy.

That does it.

I throw the sketch to the floor and rise to my full height, and instead of cowering like most men and women do, my girl bites her lip in an invitation.

Fuck it, I'm starving.

CARA

On fire.

My entire body feels like I am burning alive, and I can't take it. I really tried to be a good girl and lay naked for him as he sketched me, but the way he looks right now and the way he's looking at me is making me ache.

Enzo is sitting back in the black leather chair next to the bed with his legs spread out, and the bulge in his pants lets me know he likes what he sees. So do I.

I'm enthralled in the way he's concentrating, looking down at the sketchbook while biting his plump-red bottom lip and brows furrowing. This is the hottest moment I have ever experienced in my life. Mind you, I've done sex scenes with some of Hollywood's heartthrobs, but nothing compares to having Lorenzo Nicolasi's eyes on me as he draws me naked. Nothing. Sometime while he was drawing me, he took off his bloody shirt, displaying his strong physique, hot as hell tattoos and nipple piercings. He was not stripping for me. He felt hot and took off his shirt, making me even wetter than I already am. I keep my eyes on his naked chest and lose myself staring at the ink perfectly placed on his rib. A dragon.

A red ink dragon.

But not really one but two dragons. There's a red one and a white ink dragon enveloping each other in a lover's position, giving the illusion that they're one. Wow.

And that's when it clicks.

The dragon necklace he gifted me for my birthday.

The red ruby stone.

The ink on his rib.

Heart beating faster, I look at him and wonder how I got so lucky when that thunderstorm brought him to me all those years ago.

I watch him light up a cigarette and sit back with his legs spread, as if he's a king on his throne, driving me even wilder. I can't stand the ache between my legs, so if he won't make it better, then I will.

Sitting back with my head on the satin pillow, I run my hands slowly down the left side of my body, keeping my eyes on him.

"Behave," he says, but he knows I usually don't.

Behave, I mean.

No, when it comes to him, I break all the rules.

"Oh, but you don't want me to behave, do you, Enzo?" Laughing softly, I carry on touching my body, staring at the way his cigarette hangs from his slightly open mouth while his tongue sucks on it absently and his strong tattooed fingers, covered in charcoal grip the pencil tight.

Jesus, this obsession I have for every little thing he does will be my ruin one day, and sadly, I don't even care.

He's so damn beautiful in a way that creeps in without you noticing. He doesn't have to dress up in expensive clothes or change his hair color like his twin and almost every man I know. Enzo is effortlessly flawless, and most women might only see his rough, bad boy exterior, and I don't blame them, but if you look beyond that, you'll see it.

His cleft chin makes him seem, at times less scary than he really is. His right cheek dimple that reveals itself every time he smiles. I don't see it often, but when I do, my entire body warms at the sight.

There's no doubt about it…he's stunning.

The most beautiful man I ever laid my eyes on.

The moment I watch Enzo take a quick drag of his cigarette while still drawing me without missing a beat, I give up and break my pose, trying to get comfortable while skimming my fingers down my hips.

What would it feel like to have those rough and bloody palms gripping my skin as he takes me in every way imaginable? Every scene I can imagine plays in my head like a dirty movie, and I get so lost in my thoughts of him that I don't notice he's moved from his spot on the chair. The bed dips, snapping me out of my wet dreams. The main attraction of my dirty fantasies is crawling toward me, bare-chested while his cigarette still hangs from his mouth with his midnight black hair untamed and falling to his forehead, making him look like an unhinged predator sizing his next meal.

Me. "You always were a bad girl for me, little monster, weren't you? Only for me. You behaved for everyone else like a good little princess, but never with me." My breath hitches when he climbs between my naked legs and hovers over me with a mischievous grin. One hand grips my right thigh while the other comes to the back of my head, gripping my hair and neck, pulling me closer to his face.

I love every side of him, but this one? The beast? It's my favorite side while I'm his plaything.

Sticking my chest out, he catches the movement, and I take the opportunity to snatch the cigarette from his mouth and bring it to my lips. Only when his blue eyes find mine do I blow the smoke in his face, and that does it.

Enzo loses his shit, unchains the beast and is ready to play. He takes his smoke from my mouth, puts it out on his jeans. Holy fuck.

"You know…I've been wondering if your cunt tastes as sweet as your cherry-lips." He tells me while pulling on my already dried hair harshly. I feel the burn on the back of my head, but nothing too painful. Our lips are almost touching, and our breathing is synchronized. The room temperature gets hotter. I swear I feel a drop of sweat fall down my back. I'm losing my mind.

"Eat me and fi—" I don't get to finish my sentence because he silences me with a rough kiss. He swallows my moans and moves his tongue expertly inside my mouth. Not waiting any longer, I put my hands on him. One arm snakes around his neck, pulling his face closer to mine, if that's even possible, and the other is at his back, trying to pull his body down onto my naked one.

Then, he takes me by surprise when he breaks the kiss. We're both panting, looking into each other's eyes.

He grins evilly at me, making my already erratic heart beat faster in my chest.

He lifts me up as if I weigh nothing, lays down on the bed on his back, and slides his palm from my hip to my lower back, positioning me right where he wants me. He drops me down on his face until he is eye level with my pussy. Small sparks of electricity follow in his touch's wake. I don't hold back the moan of pleasure when Enzo lifts his head and breathes in my scent. Oh, fuck, my entire body quivers at the erotic sight. "Fucking peaches," his voice is laced with pleasure and wonder. "Let's see if your pretty pussy tastes the same." He rubs his rough palms up my thighs, making me tremble in excitement. I've never wanted anything more than his face pressed between my thighs, eating me out. I've imagined it. Of course I have. On nights where I missed him and wondered what life would be like with him. Now, it's happening, and reality is better than what I imagined. "I tried to be a gentleman and take this slow because you deserve more than a quick fuck. You deserve a good man that courts you, gives you flowers when trying to romance you, and all that shit." That sounds… boring, but I can't form words to tell him. That's sweet and all, but all I need is him as he comes, but his warm breath on my pussy is making me incoherent. I moan his name instead when he leans forward and licks my clit lightly. I don't bite down on my lips to stifle the sounds of pleasure, no. I'm not quiet because I want him to hear. Hear what he does to my body and how much I like it. How right this feels because it is right. It has always been, and now he won't escape it. Us.
Me. Lorenzo dives in with fast, expert licks, slurping my juices and making grotesque sounds that some women might find too much, but it only makes me wetter. That's exactly what happens next, a flood of my juices is his reward. Lorenzo is not a gentle lover by any means. He eats me out like a starving savage while his rough hands grip my ass cheeks painfully, spreading me wide while he shoves his face deeper into my pussy.

"Oh, fuck, baby." I scream when he flattens his tongue and licks me from my asshole to my pussy, torturing me. I'm close. So close to breaking in his hands. My clit throbs every time his tongue delves between my lips. He's tasting every part of me, and by his sexy-as-hell groans, I can tell he's enjoying it, too. "Right there," I whisper. The moment I do, he slaps one ass cheek hard, making me moan louder.

He wants me to scream for him.

So dirty…

His teeth graze my clit before he bites down on it, and I jerk in place, a loud moan slipping out. I look down and almost cum at the sight of him bare-chested under me, lifting his hands to cup my full achy breasts with his large hands, pinching my nipples with the same rhythm he licks my pussy. I place my hands on his, holding onto him as I ride his face gently, trying hard not to suffocate him. I start to rock against his face almost desperately when he buries himself in my pussy, lapping at me and sucking hard on my clit, while at the same time he begins to slap my breasts.

I lose the fight when my body tenses over him, and my lips part in pure shock and ecstasy. I ride out the mind-blowing, earth-shattering orgasm while Enzo licks me gently and slow. My body spazzes with shocks. I don't close my eyes, not even for a second. Not while I come on his face, and not when he removes himself from between my legs and lifts his body to look at me. I wonder if he sees right through me while I'm coming down from the high of what he just did to my body.

I fall down on the bed, too exhausted to hold myself up, and watch as he slowly hovers over me with a wicked smile on his face. My eyes drink in the expression on his face, the wild abandon of passion on his perfect features, and I smile right back.

He's never looked more… mine.

Then, he drops down, takes my mouth in his and lets me taste myself on his lips.
I've never tasted myself, and if I'm honest, no one has ever gone down on me. It always felt too intimate, and I didn't give much thought to it unless I was fantasizing about him. I taste… musk and sweetness.
Huh.
Not bad.
I taste good on him.
Enzo releases my lips and looks down at me with fire in those blue eyes of his. The same fire that most likely is looking back at him in mine. "You're dirty," I whisper between breaths. And that's how I like him best. Dirty. Wild. Untamed. Perfectly imperfect. Him.
He laughs darkly, drops down next to me, and I turn to look at him grab another cigarette and lighting it. I stare at him with a broad smile on my face as he smokes his cigarette while bringing my body closer to his.
We lie there, him smoking, and me listening to the beat of his heart with no words between us. They're not necessary. They never have been when it comes to us. His actions tell me more secrets than his mouth ever will.
And that's how I fall under, with his arm around me, his heart singing me to sleep and the comforting smell of his cigar enveloping me in the same way his arms do.

CHAPTER THIRTY-FOUR

LEGACY

"The ones who occupy his heart." – V

Cara

I woke up at six o' clock on the dot like I do every morning as part of my normal routine. I woke up in bed, alone, and for a second, I thought I dreamt what happened between Enzo and me last night, but my naked body, the cigarettes on the ashtray and the sketchbook on the floor are proof that it was not a dream. It happened, and for the first time in a while, I woke up with an honest smile, and not the one I've been perfecting since I was child. I feel complete. Not because I need a man to feel complete, but because I finally feel like I'm living the reality I wanted for forever.

The successful modeling and acting career I dreamed of since I was a little girl looking at pretty women in magazines, hoping one day that would be.

That day is today, and that pretty woman on covers and runways is me.

Now, I also feel like I'm so much closer to getting the guy, and make no mistake, the battle for Enzo's heart is not one I ever plan to lose.

After I left Enzo's red room, I headed back to mine, took a shower, and got ready for the day, choosing a black nirvana t-shirt and loose mom jeans. With a fresh face, hair up in a messy bun, and I'm walking around barefoot.

I don't know if Enzo stayed or slipped out in the middle of the night. All I know is that it's seven am, and he's nowhere to be seen. I spotted Draego feeding the dogs. I offered to help, but he dismissed me. I went ahead, played, and fed my babies anyways. Now, I'm in the kitchen pouring myself a glass of OJ. Now that I'm alone again and my head is clearer after the best sleep I've had in years, I'm trying to come up with a game plan. Enzo gave me mere days to deal with my fake engagement before he goes ahead and does something crazy, like threaten my best friend again or worse.

I tried calling Jonah as soon as I woke up, but the call went straight to voicemail. It is not like him to not call me back, but I guess he's dealing with his own stuff back home.

Then, my thoughts go to my siblings and my newfound family back in New York, and I try to focus on the positive.

I had a mom who raised me and loved me as her own, and that is one blessing I will always be grateful for. No matter the ugly parts in my life, I got her, and she gave me my siblings. I could never regret her or them.

Finding out about the tragic life of my birth mother because of my father's evil actions broke something in me, and I think that's something I won't ever get over. But again, I make sure to think about the bonus family I got from her.

The Soloniks.

Good and bad, the story of my life.

"Vade, don't press too hard!" A gentle shout snaps me out of my thoughts, and I realize I'm no longer alone. Settling the glass down, I look to my right and find Lorenzo's twin, Valentino, trailing behind a small child.

My heart stops when I take in the little boy that looks just like his father and uncle.

"Dats okay, daddy. Austy don't mind…" The little boy, Vade, laughs sheepishly at his father while petting the baby white snake that he has wrapped around his little neck.

Oh my God. I do love some animals, but I can't deal with snakes, although that beautiful baby boy makes them look not that scary. Valentino sighs and ruffles the boy's blonde hair lovingly. I never thought I would see the day when Valentino smiled again. He didn't use to before, and now I know why. He was missing half of his soul.
Fallon James.
Speaking of, she walks in dressed almost the same as me, but instead of mom jeans, she has a long black skirt with a slit with a superhero crop top and some black platform boots. Fallon really is gorgeous.
Effortlessly beautiful, and the little baby girl that's hiding between her legs is just as stunning as her mommy.
Poe.
Black hair up in pigtails, a white shirt under a black dress, matching her mommy.
How sweet.
"Oh, hi." Fallon's eyes find me, and soon after, her entire family is looking my way. Valentino has no expression on his face. The little boy looks at me with a grin on his face and mischief in his eyes… Oh boy, this one's trouble. And the little girl stares at me curiously, studying me like her father is doing. "I had no idea you were in town. You didn't say anything!" Fallon looks at me as if I've betrayed her. The times that I come to the city are few since my brother doesn't like when I come here without him. Plus, my work doesn't give me much room to travel for pleasure. But when I get the chance to escape and come back to Detroit, I always make sure to link up with Fallon.
Stepping down from the still, I walk toward the living room where they are. "Hi, babe." I give her a kiss on the cheek and wink at Poe when she looks up at me. "I would've called, but me being here was not planned, and I—"
"You people again. Weren't you just here?" A rough voice

interrupts me. Enzo. He comes out of the corner wearing only gray sweatpants, and his chest is all sweaty, making my mouth water just at the sight of him. Damn, he looks so hot. By the look of his wet hair and chest, he must've just finished working out. Therefore, that is where he ran off to. The gym. "Your niece and nephew wanted to show you our new family member. Go ahead, baby." Fallon grins evilly at her toddler, and the little boy walks closer to his uncle and lifts his pet snake so Enzo can see. "Fuck, gross." Enzo shakes his body in disgust as he stares at the reptile wrapped around the little boy's tiny arm. "Meet Austy, uncle! So pwetty, wight?" The little boy looks at his uncle proudly but with the same evil smile as his mother. They know Lorenzo's aversion to snakes. "Austen Lorenzo Nicolasi is the full name," Valentino chimes in, holding back a grin.

Lorenzo.

I hold back a snort at Enzo's indignant expression, but if you look closer, you will catch a glimpse of amusement, too.

"You let your brats name their snake after me?" Enzo grumbles, looking down at the baby snake with absolute disgust.

His twin nods, clearly not one to deny his kids anything. "Poe wants a hamster, and she already picked its name, right, baby?"

All our eyes turn to look at the baby girl hiding her face in the crook of her father's neck. Her small head nods two times, and Valentino rewards her with two kisses on the side of her head. God, that kid is the cutest.

"And what might that be?" Enzo looks at the baby girl, all annoyance gone. He's so whipped for her, it's not good for my ovaries.

"Uncle..." she whispers so softly I almost miss it.

Both Fallon and Valentino chuckle at the look on Enzo's face, knowing that he won't protest because that's his girl. "Baby girl, I'm wounded."

Enzo sighs dramatically at his baby niece, which causes her to blush adorably and make grabby hands at him, which he obeys in a heartbeat.

Settle down, ovaries. No babies yet.

A hissing sound draws all our attention down to the hellion of a child currently hissing and shoving the snake into his uncle's hands. Enzo towers over the little boy, looking amused but still low-key repulsed, and I find myself laughing at how uncomfortable Enzo looks by the tiny snake. When I do, his eyes find mine, and I can't help but notice the desire in them, but something else, too… his evil glint.

Oh no, he wouldn't. He knows I hate them.

"Brat, go show Mia your new friend," Enzo tells his baby nephew, pointing toward me with a grin on his face. "She loves animals."

That fucker… just dogs.

The little boy walks to me and lifts the snake for me to see. I try with all my might to hide my fear and disgust toward the animal. I drop to my knees so I can be at eye-level with Vade. "That's a pretty snake, sweetie." I smile, lying through my teeth, and he laughs softly. There's just something about children's laughter that warms me down to my soul.

"My daddy got it for us because we good. Right, daddy?" Vade tilts his small head, looking up at his daddy, waiting for a response, but before his father can get a word out, Fallon interrupts.

"Val got it for them because someone"—she shakes her head lightly while looking down at her son with adoring eyes—"was acting up because he didn't get the motorbike he wanted, so daddy agreed to get him a pet snake. Because daddy can't say no to his kids…"

"Daddy loves us." A sweet voice whispers from behind her mother, melting my heart. Valentino steps closer to Poe and picks her up, lightly kissing her nose.

"I do. Very much, little witch," Valentino winks at his daughter with adoration. Fuck, my ovaries.

I think Enzo notices my reaction because, before I know it, he's ushering Valentino and the kids out the door to the patio area, leaving me alone with a laughing Fallon. "Oh, boy. I know that face."

"What face?"

"The face of a man that just saw his future, and he knows he can't escape it." She laughs softly and sits down on the white sofa. Following her, I drop down next to her, find the TV remote, and turn it on. I scroll through some channels until I find the morning news. "Trust me, I saw the same face staring back at me even when he hated me. There's no escaping destiny."

Destiny.

I turn my body away from the TV so I can be face to face with her. "You won't give me a lecture on why we're all wrong for each other?"

That's all I got from my brother's wife, Andrea, and my brother, too. Enzo is a menace, his sister says.

He's no good for you. My brother told me once. I love my brother dearly, but he's wrong. So wrong about Lorenzo.

"Nope," Fallon looks me in the eye when she says it. "Huh." I thought she would have something to say about it. I guessed wrong.

"There's no one better for that crazy man." Fallon smiles softly before looking down at the enormous diamond ring that her husband gave her. It's stunning and not the traditional diamond most men get their girls for an engagement, but what catches my attention is not the engagement or wedding rings but the ink underneath them.

The tattoo reads Alexander.

They got each other's names tattooed, and I can only imagine the level of compromise.

The love between two people that were written in the stars because, as silly as it sounds to most people, I believe we find the love of our lives in every lifetime. I refuse to believe that, in another life or world, I fell in love with someone that wasn't him. And yes, I do love him.

I've loved him even before I knew what love really meant.

True love between a man and a woman.

At first, when I left the city, I thought my silly crush would be forgotten as soon as I experienced another world, but how wrong I was. Everything I did, I wondered if he would be proud. Everyone I met, I wished it was him instead.

He was always at the forefront of my mind, never far behind. That's when I knew I could either spend my life being miserable, thinking about what could've been, or I could draw the beast out and play with him for the rest of my life, and nothing sounded better than that. Nothing.

"Can I ask you something?" I tune out the news playing in the background.

Fallon sobers up, and the smile falls from her face. "Sure. Anything."

"How did you know that Valentino was the one?"

"One day, I woke up and imagined a life where Valentino was missing from me, and it hurt. The life I envisioned without him had no color. No meaning and that's how I knew."

My heart slows as I take in what she said. I feel the same way. Whenever I picture my life and what I want for my future, he's always right there, and the times I imagined a world where he wasn't in it, I just felt hollow and empty. I don't want to walk through life half alive.

I feel warm and gentle hands grab my chin, bringing me back to the now. My blue eyes clash with Fallon's green ones. "The Nicolasi men are stubborn and Neanderthals. You must never bow down because they need a challenge so give him as good as he gives, babe.

He'll drive you nuts at times but don't back down. I can't tell you how it will all turn out, but what I can tell is that when a Nicolasi man falls, they fall hard, and baby, he's been falling for a long time. He's just too much of an ass to let everyone see it. He worries too much about his street credit and ego." Fallon rolls her eyes and laughs.

I process all she's saying, knowing it's true. Lorenzo has always chased challenges and got bored with what he perceives as 'weak.'

Both Fallon and I turn when we hear loud screeching giggles right outside on the patio.

Fallon gets up from the sofa and heads out to the patio where her family is, and I follow her, too enthralled in the sight of Enzo shirtless with one baby hanging on to his neck for dear life while he holds another by the feet, flipped upside down.

We spend all morning talking and watching the kids go crazy for their uncle Lorenzo.

Huh.

Children are the purest souls in this world, and these two right here are enamored with a man that has blood on his face and hands.

They don't see that part of him, though.

They just see the moody uncle who gives in to their every whim.

Just what I see.

CHAPTER THIRTY-FIVE

DEADMAN

"You adapted to the darkness, while I was born in it." - D

Lorenzo

"**M**otherfucker," pulling up at the old Nicolasi residence, I take in the scene before me.

Fuck!

There first thing I notice is blood splatter everywhere, looking straight out of a murder film.

Even from outside, I can see there's blood on the ground, spilling out of some of my men and running down the pathway like a river of blood.

Carnage.

Death.

All around me.

These scenes would typically excite the fuck out of me, but not when it is my territory that's being targeted.

Pissed as fuck, I climb out of my Aston Martin Vantage and walk towards the mansion, looking at the mess a sick fuck left behind, with Shawn and Gio, two of my men that cover security at the clubs spread around Detroit, trailing behind me. Tuning them out as they curse looking at the damage before us, I put all my focus into memorizing the chaos around me, so I can pay it back to the bitch who did this twice as gruesome.

Fallen men.

Young kids who wanted an out from their shitty lives, and I gave that to them. Yes, they knew the risks of working for me. Death comes knocking at every corner the moment you take a step outside.

Blood stains the marble fountain my nonna had installed years ago when she was alive, with the water turning red because of the blood of one of my men inside of it. The fountain's water runs through the marble statues of angels inside it on a normal day, but not today. Today, the angels have blood coming out of their mouth, making it seem like a sacrilege.

I take in the walls outside of the mansion, painted with black graffiti. The place has been trashed. I could care less about the Nicolasi mansion. I should have burned it down the day I sent Benedetto to hell.

My men, though, that stings. They were good men. Loyal. Brave. They came from nothing, and this was not the way for them to die.

Not like this.

Fuck.

I can't wait to get my hands on the cunt who did this.

"Boss," I snap out of my murderous thoughts. "Follow me. You have to see this shit. The motherfucker is sick, and that's rich coming from me." Phoenix, one of the boys I picked out off the streets at the same time as Draego, motions for me to follow him. He's a lanky white boy with a dark past who needed direction and this family gave it to him. He had a lot of anger in him, and at the time, he didn't know how to channel or control it. He's still a kid, but the fucker had a mean streak and is blood-thirsty, which makes him perfect for the family. He doesn't mind getting dirty and is one loyal pup. He has that Hollywood heartthrob look, hiding a lot of darkness that no one sees coming until it's too late.

"How the fuck did this son of a bitch get through security and around most of the men without getting caught?" I snap, fucking irritated that this bitch has one-upped me yet again and has disappeared like a fucking ghost.

"He came out of nowhere like some V for vendetta shit, man. It's like he knew this place as if it's his own place."

So, it's a he.

A dead he, nonetheless.

The cunt that keeps sending threatening notes has to be the same one that did this. I have a gut feeling, and it never stirs me wrong.

I've pissed off plenty of people throughout my teenage years and while being boss of this family, so the list of who could be behind this is long as fuck. While I follow Phoenix through the path that leads to the mansion's garden, I pull out my phone and type a quick message to Draego, ordering him not to leave Mia's side. He has instructions to be her shadow every second I'm away from her.

After my twin and his family left, I received a call from Phoenix, alerting me of what happened. I had no choice but to leave her behind to deal with this shit. At least, in my home, she's safe.

There's no fucking way that motherfucker will get through my beasts of dogs and the men that guard the place. Draego is a fucking tank. She's safe with him, and that's the only reason I left her behind with him.

Looking around the backyard of the mansion, I take in the damage. The fucker who did this wanted to send me a message. Wanted to let me know that he's close and he's watching.

"Ain't this some sick as fuck Ted Bundy shit?" Phoenix stops next to the rose bushes and points to the grass. I follow his gaze, and for a second, my heart stops in my chest, and my world fades to black.

Motherfucker.

A naked woman lies on the grass, naked, and beaten black and blue. The son of a bitch who did this put her in a position as if she's been sacrificed on a cross. Arms and legs spread wide.
Pale skin.
Bloody red hair.
Just like Mia.
My blood starts to boil when I push the woman's hair back, and I see what the fucker did. The woman's throat has been slashed, and Cara Mia's face, or a shot of her face to be precise, has been taped to the stranger's face.
Then, all I see is fucking red.
Red.
Red on the ground.
Red spilling out in gruesome ways out of the dead bodies of my men.
The dead bitch's body was covered in red just like her bloody red hair.
Red all around me.
It takes over my senses, making me lose my shit on whatever is nearby.
Punch after fucking punch, I ruin everything that's on my path until it hurts.
Until the pain on my knuckles is all I can focus on. Hitting and breaking shit has always helped me expel the feelings of helplessness in these situations when I'm caught off guard. When I can't make the one responsible hurt with my fists and my knives, I break shit until I'm grounded.
Pain grounds me.
Heart racing and breathing rapidly, I turn to face Phoenix, who is standing next to the dead woman. The fog in my brain clears a bit, just enough so I can form a proper thought. Still, it's almost impossible with such anger taking over my head, driving me nuts.

I feel helpless, and I fucking hate it. "Triple the security at the clubs, gather some of the men and send them over to my place. This piece of shit just declared war, and it's just a matter of time before he attacks again." I'm at a fucking disadvantage since the cunt knows me, yet I know jack-shit about him. I can't anticipate his next move unless I know his motives, and I have shit. Fuck.

"Do you need me there or at the clubs?" Phoenix crosses his arms, and the movement draws my attention to the tattoo on his arm. One way out. Our motto.One way out.

Death, or in some cases, turning rat. Disgraced. Fallen.

"I need you to take care of the girls at the clubs and make sure what happened to that woman" — I point toward the dead chick and look back at Phoenix— "doesn't happen to any of our girls."

Phoenix nods once, understanding.

"And burn this place down. This was Benedetto's kingdom. I should've let it burn a long time ago when I put him down. Do it."

I don't have time to keep old traditions and ghosts alive. In this mansion, there are plenty.

"Will do, boss."

"Watch your back and stay vigilant." The cunt is sparing no one. I have to come to terms with the fact that they probably won't find out this fucker's motives, or who he is until he wants them to. And until then, I'm at a disadvantage and at his mercy, and that only infuriates me further.

With one nod to my man, I walk away toward my car while lighting up a cigarette.

Not even the sweet rush of nicotine helps calm the rapid anger burning deep inside me, screaming to rain hell on the cunt that is out for my blood.

For my heart.

Fuck.

Climbing inside the car, I turn it on, rev the engine, and with one last glance to the chaos left behind, I speed the hell out of there toward the eye of the storm. The only one that can calm the beast inside.
Red.

***

CARA

After Fallon, Valentino, and the kids left, I went to the theater room and haven't left since. Enzo stepped out soon after, leaving me alone with Draego, who kept me company while I enjoyed some time with my fur babies. Enzo's beasts included, and it's official, Lorenzo's beasts like me enough to let me drop down to the floor and pet them for hours if I wanted, but that was a no-brainer since their owner's inner beast is obsessed with me, too, in my non very humble opinion. After that, I took a shower and got back to the theater room, needing to attend some zoom meetings and return some calls. Arielle tried to get me out of them, but I didn't want to. I enjoy what I do. Then, after I'm done with the meetings, I get on my phone and post the selfie of me and the dogs I took while I was outside playing with them and post it on all my social media with a cute caption and a dog and peach emoji. I scroll through my friend's pages and write comments under their latest posts. Arielle suggested I keep up with my regular routine, and I agreed.

I love social media. Yeah, it has its downsides, like the trolls that have nothing better to do than to shit on everyone's parade, but there's also the side where I get to communicate with my followers and share my life with them, to some extent.

I keep a lot of things private, but lately, with my rise to fame, there's not much I can keep private from the public. It's a miracle that news hasn't broken out about what happened outside the studio.

I promised myself if I ever made it big, I would not sell my soul to the media. I don't want to be known for drama, either. That's not who I ever was, and money and fame won't change that.

"Trouble in short-lived paradise?" a nasal voice snaps me out of my thoughts, making me look at the big screen in front of me. A feeling of dread spreads through my body as I watch the talk show host smile sweetly before spewing her venom to the world. "A set of candid photos of movie star Jonah Shane are surfing the web where he's seen holding hands with a mysterious man, and in others, Mia Madden's co-star and fiancé is clearly kissing the strange man. Is this why Mia Madden has decided to take a few weeks away from the public eye? Has she found out about her fiancé's betrayal? Or has she known all along about his extracurricular activities with other men?" The gossip woman smiles triumphantly through the pictures of Jonah with the man.

Panic rises, and I will my mind to shut down and focus on only one thought. So many things are going through my head, and none of it is about me. Oh, God. Someone just outed Jonah in front of the world. Who-the-hell would take pictures of him and sell them to the media without any shame? Picking up my phone, I try dialing his number two times, but it keeps ringing until I'm sent straight to voicemail. I tried changing the channel, but everyone was talking about it.

About Jonah and his lover.

Talking about how sad I must feel.

Shit.

I try calling one last time, and on the third ring, he picks up.

"Well, hello there, beauty." Jonah's upbeat tone catches me off guard. Doesn't he know? His worst nightmare is playing for the whole world to see.

"Finally! Where have you been? I've been trying to reach you since last night. Are you okay? Have you seen the—"

"The pictures of me with Payne? I have, yes." Paying close attention to his tone, it not only sounds suspiciously happy, but he sounds…raspy.
"Payne?"
"My cock of the month, yes." He says seriously, but I can tell he's lying.
I try to suppress my laugh, knowing that he usually makes jokes when he's hurt. It's been his way of coping with things since he was a kid. He used to do it a lot back then. Cock of the month, he said, but I saw the way he looked at the man with adoration in his eyes, and that's no way to stare at a fling. That's how someone in love looks at their entire world. I would know… that's how my brother looks at his wife and how Fallon looks at her little family. No way that's just a hook-up for Jonah. I'm not buying it, but I don't tell him that. Instead, I focus on the news leak. "Why are you not freaking out about this? Someone betrayed your trust and exposed your personal life to the world."
"I did it."
"Um, excuse you? I think I heard you say you did it, but that cannot be right since you're not that reckless."
"I am not. That is true. But I decided to take control of my own narrative and live in my truth." All jokes and the humorous tone fade. Sighing, Jonah continues. "I'm sorry I didn't tell you." He takes a deep breath before he continues. "But this is my way of freeing both of us. I cannot keep living a lie because I'm too much of a coward to tell the world who I really am and afraid of them shunning me for being myself. I'm done living for other people and thinking I'll lose all I worked for just because of who sleeps in my bed, and dammit, you deserve better than a fake fiancé who can't stand the idea of coming face to face with your cooch."
"Jeez, thanks."
Jonah laughs so jovially that it takes me back to the times

when he used to laugh because something was funny or because he was happy. I haven't heard that laugh in a while. "No offense, beauty. I love all other parts of you."
"None taken."
An older lady's voice shouts Jonah's name in the background. "You are free to do as you please without the burden of this fake relationship, babe. I gotta deal with a few things here, but I'll see you at the premiere, yes?"
"Yes…"
"Good, Good." He sounds distracted by something on his end. What is going on?
"I would've done it for as long as you needed me to, you know." I tell him the truth, suddenly feeling guilty that I let him use me as a crutch, but you do whatever it takes for friends sometimes. I don't regret lying to the world for him, but I'm also relieved that he stood up for himself and for what he believes in. I'm also glad that I didn't have to bury him after Enzo makes him dog chow for not ending our fake relationship sooner.
"I know." A long pause is followed by a soft sigh. "And I love you for loving me enough to lie about us just to help me. I would help you bury a body if you needed me to."
I laugh softly, knowing deep down he would so totally do that if I ever needed help burying someone's corpse. "Call me if you need me, yes?"
"Same, babe."
We hang up, and I find myself feeling ten times lighter than I did before all these truths were revealed. That's one less thing I need to worry about. I don't need to worry about my friend drowning in his web of lies. He's free now, and so am I. I'm free from that lie and free from the doubts I had since I was a little girl of my roots.
"Huh, so he likes cock." His rough and dark voice sends shivers down my spine. Turning, I find Enzo looking up

at the screen with a frown on his face. Oh, please don't say something cruel. Please don't be one of those people...
"He does." I hold my breath, knowing his heart. Although it's very dangerous and dark, Enzo doesn't give s shit about people's preferences or how they choose to live their lives.
"Perfect." His eyes leave the big screen and find me before a Cheshire Cat smile spreads over his handsome face. "I don't have to chop off his dick before fucking him to death with it, then." A slow relieved sigh escapes me, soon after a laugh breaks free. When I think I know what goes through his mind, he surprises me every time.
Putting my phone down, I watch as Enzo drops down next to me without a care in the world that he might stain the pristine white couch with all the blood he has on his clothing, face, and hands. And something must be seriously wrong with me because every time he comes back with blood on his hands, I feel the same thing— my heart races, and my pussy throbs, and I have to press my legs together to find some sort of relief. No, it's not normal at all to be this attracted to mayhem and bloodshed. Lorenzo is both and more. "Hungry?" He raises three brown fast-food bags toward me. I haven't eaten all day, and if I'm being honest, I'm not all that hungry. Not for food at least, but I nod my head because this moment right here feels like those times when he used to sneak inside my treehouse to bring me sugary treats and junk food when we were younger.
My heart warms when I think of how he remembers my favorite foods, music, books, and every little detail I told him so long ago. We're both adults who live different lives, yet here, in this moment, it feels like we've never spent a day apart. Opening the bag of food, I find the same order I always asked for and my favorite food from back then, too. Double cheeseburger, nuggets, and a vanilla ice cream to dip my fries in.

He remembers it all… I dip a fry into the ice cream and then bring it up to my mouth, savoring the delicious mix of salt and sugar. "I need to tell you something." I mumble between chews. He doesn't say anything. Only a grunt spills from his lips, making me look his way and find him looking down at my lips. "Next week, I have the premiere for the movie I'm starring in, and I can't miss it. It's in my contract, and I—"

"You don't want to attend? If you don't, I'll work around the contract bullshit, but if you want to go…" I hold my breath, mesmerized by the way he cannot seem to look away from my lips. Do I have something stuck between my teeth? On my face? Enzo scoots close, until I feel his breath mixing with mine. "we'll go."

He said we.

"We?" I pop another fry into my mouth, thinking how it would look if I walked down that red carpet with Lorenzo holding my hand, and suddenly, I feel my heartbeat faster at the possibility. All I ever wanted in life was a career and him, but his duty to this city always made it seem like an impossible dream, but he's opening the door to that dream now.

He nods while setting his food down on the carpeted floor without looking away from my mouth. Seriously, what is he looking at? Bringing my hand to my lips, I try to wipe my face when his strong fingers wrap around my delicate ones, stopping me from doing so and in the process, warming my whole body with just one touch. "If you want to go, you'll go. My men and I will make sure no threats come your way while you're walking the carpet. I can't trust anyone to protect you, little monster." He uses a joking tone, but I also detect a hint of…worry? I'm just being overly paranoid, that's all. The Russians won't hurt me. At least, I don't think that's their intention.

"You won't walk the carpet with me?" I ask, knowing the answer already but still wanting to hear it from him.

"That's not my world, Mia." He wipes the residue of ice cream from the corner of my lips and brings it to his mouth. My eyes trail his every movement, heat spreading all over my body.

I want to tell him so many things because my world might not be one he's accustomed to, but there will always be room for him because my world is wherever he is. But I understand not wanting to be caught in the public eye, especially since he's not America's most outstanding civilian, but still… I'd hoped.

Sighing, I put the ice cream and fries down and stare at him with a smile. Not wanting him to realize how it pains me not to have him there with me. I wanted to show the world who lives in my heart and to whom I belong, but I respect his decision. I think about some of the most influential people in the business right now. How some keep their romantic life separate from their Hollywood life.

We can still make it work. I can keep my life with him away from the gossip and drama. It's for the best, really.

I feel his rough hands on my chin, gently tilting my head to the side so I can look into his eyes. Those ocean eyes have the power to disarm me and calm my raging heart. "Don't do that shit with me." He snaps, looking furious.

Confused, I frown at his harsh tone, yet his touch is still gentle. "What shit?" I whisper close to his mouth. Enzo… was unpredictable. Cruel. Fierce. And many more things but never to me, and I always wondered why he treated me differently than the other girls that were around him at that time. I used to believe it was because I was just Cara Mia Volpe, weird, solitary, but then I realized that he saw in me someone that wasn't scared of him. Someone that took his bloody hand in hers and never let go, even as the years passed.

We're one and the same, he and I.

We balance each other out.

He makes me a bit more reckless, and I make him a little less hellish.

"That fake shit you do when you're around people who don't know you the way I do. That won't fly with me. If you feel sad, let me know. If you're happy, you fucking give me that smile. No games. That's not how we're doing things."

That's not how we're doing things.

I think that's the most romantic thing Enzo has ever said to me, in his own Neanderthal way.

It's…sweet. Okay.

I tell him then. I get up from the sofa and drop myself onto his lap without warning. My arms wrap around his neck, bringing his face closer to mine as our noses touch. "My world is wherever you are, king. There's no 'my world' and 'your world' between us. That's not how it goes with us." I feel his arms snake around my back, pulling my body closer to his, and I instantly feel hot all over like I always do when I'm this close to him. I love how right it feels in his arms as if it's where I was always supposed to be, and I don't ever want to leave. Hell, I hope I never do. Playing with the soft hair that touches his neck, I watch his reaction to my words. Something that looks a lot like possessiveness crosses over his face. Then, I feel his hands lowering until he's grabbing my ass in both palms and squeezing while making my front rub against his crotch. I follow his lead, rubbing on him softly while I wait for him to process what I just laid out for him. But he doesn't say anything. Instead, he roughly spreads my ass cheeks open through my pants and takes my mouth in his, stealing the breath out my lungs and keeping it for himself.

This is more than a kiss between a man and a woman that have danced around their feelings for far too long.

It's something more.

More than love.

More than devotion.
Something darker.
It is possession.
Obsession.
And he shows me with his kiss what he can't with his words. He shows me exactly how my truth makes him feel and what he feels for me, as well.
With the sound of my favorite sitcom playing in the background, we spend the rest of the night eating and sucking each other's faces. With one hand on my ass and the other possessively gripping my neck, he shows me to whom I belonged.
I am his.
Always have been, and I know I always will.

CHAPTER THIRTY-SIX

THE JOKER AND THE QUEEN

"I'm inked on his heart, not just his skin." – C

Cara

The buzzing of a tattoo gun sounds in the distance as I near the end of the long hallway that leads to the living room. It's been a couple of days since that night when Enzo kissed me as if were the only woman in his world. I'm still walking on cloud nine after I told him exactly how I felt about him being part of my world. The next few days passed in a blissful blur. I lose all concept of time when I'm around him, in his habitat.

Every morning, when I wake up, he's gone, leaving me on my own, but he always comes back to me at night with blood splattered all over his clothes, hands, and face. Like every time before, I crave his touch regardless of the state he comes to me in and return each kiss without concern for the blood he wears on his skin like a trophy for all his kills.

He doesn't tell me what he does, and I don't ask. I know he would tell me and give me the gritty details if I asked, but I know him, and I know what he does. Yet, I can't find it in me to deem it as wrong. A sane woman would question why he comes home with blood on his hands and the biggest smile on his face, like a kid who has spent the entire day in his favorite toy store. A sane woman would run from someone who enjoys the terror he spreads.

A sane woman would question why he comes home with blood on his hands and the biggest smile on his face, like a kid who has spent the entire day in his favorite toy store. A sane woman would run from someone who enjoys the terror he spreads. A sane woman, I am not. I crave his chaos.
Every dark part of him.
It calls out to me in the same way stormy nights do.
He hasn't fucked me yet, and the anticipation is killing both of us. I know it by the way he swallows me whole with just one sensual kiss and the way he so gently touches my skin, trying to control the same beast that lives inside of me, trying to crawl out, and take what it wants.
So yes, by day, he's the boss of this city, running around taking care of his business, terrorizing his enemies, and raising hell to every man or woman that crosses him. But at night, he slips under my sheets and tortures me by not taking it as far as we both want it to go.
Sometimes, we watch my favorite series in silence, while other times, he comes home and kisses me senseless before falling to his knees and getting close and personal with my vagina. He's been drawing me, too. Naked. With clothes.
While I play with the dogs. Almost every day.
Something has shifted in our relationship.
Unspoken words. We both know what this is. The start of what should have been so long ago. No lines were drawn, everything is fair game with us, and I think he's slowly coming to terms with what I've known since we were both kids.
There's no one else for him other than me, and vice versa.
When I reach the end of the hallway, I turn right and find Enzo lying down on the black sofa shirtless and wearing black sweatpants, typing furiously on his phone with one hand while Draego tattoos him. I've also come to learn that he expresses himself through the art on his body, but he also enjoys the pain they provide.

The ink coming down on his skin. The man is covered head to toe in tattoos. One day, he will run out of places to ink. Fuck me, but he's a supernova. A celestial being, even with the ink and piercings that sometimes make him look like a demon from hell, but when he's laid back with a relaxed expression on his face, he looks almost heavenly.

I stand back, and from here, I drink him in.

His black hair is wet as if he just got out of the shower. When wet, his hair looks as black as a starless night, a total contrast to his light blue eyes. My eyes trail down to his chest, where he's having his man work on what I think is another dragon. This one looks different from all the others.

This one has no red or white like the other ones on his skin. It's just shades of black.

It's the most terrifying-looking one. The upper half of its body looks like it's slithering around Enzo's neck, opening its mouth to make it seem as if it's breathing fire into the eyes of the woman Enzo got tattooed when he was a kid.

The golden eyes of his mother. The dragon looks as if it's breathing life into them through his fire. It's insane, and maybe I'm a lunatic trying to decipher the meaning of each tattoo he has, but it is obvious they all have a meaning behind them. Enzo is impulsive, yes, but very thoughtful, too.

"The shadows and dark corners are not for you, little monster. Let me see you." Enzo's sensual and dark voice snaps me out of my head, making me look into his eyes, and even from here, I can feel them burning my skin. Enzo's eyes flash, and he raises one eyebrow. "Come here," he says in a low tone.

Not thinking of it, I slowly move toward him, without breaking eye contact. Draego and the sound of the machine fade into the background, and all I can focus on is him. On the way he beckons me like he's the king of the underworld, and I'm his loyal servant. On how his eyes sparkle and his nostrils flare with every step I take.

As if he's been waiting for me all along, and now he's finally getting what he wants.

When I make it all the way to where he is sitting, I move to stand behind Draego and watch as he brings the gun down on Enzo's skin, filling in the dragon's scales, making the skin around it red with tiny prickles of blood. I stand back in silence and stare in fascination because I've always been fascinated by blood. Maybe it's the color, or maybe because it's the substance of life, but red on Enzo has always looked beautiful.

"May I?" I don't know what drives me to extend my hand out toward Draego and motion for him to give me the tattoo gun, it's an impulse, and I forget all logic and act on impulse every time I'm around Enzo.

Following my heart and ignoring whatever my mind is telling me to do.

Draego stops working on the dragon and looks at his boss for permission, I follow his gaze, holding my breath as we both wait for him to speak. "Take the night off, D," Enzo tells his man without taking his eyes off me.

The next thing I know, Draego has left the room, and I'm holding the gun in my hands. I'm standing in the same spot Draego was occupying before.

"Do you trust me, king?" I position myself between Enzo's spread legs and look down at him as I wait for his answer. I only trust two men with my life. My brother and this man, who manages to stop my beating heart with just one look.

Without missing a beat, he responds. "With my life, Red." He doesn't allow me time to process what he just told me before he's grabbing my hips and pulling me down onto his lap. Pressing my right hand to his chest, I'm careful not to touch the fresh ink.

With my life, Red.

Right back atcha, baby.

"Why dragons?" I run my fingers over his skin where the dragons are, and I don't miss the way his breath hitches. Feeling triumphant over his reaction to my touch, I skim the tip of my fingers lightly on the freshly-inked skin. Leave it to Enzo to get off on his own pain, as well. Heart racing, breath quickening, I lean back so I can see his eyes better while I grind my ass deeper into his groin.

He's hard.

So very hard.

For me.

Enzo regards me for a moment, and I can't read his expression, which makes me a bit anxious. Then he speaks. "The dragon is a symbol of evil in both the chivalric and Christian traditions. They are the embodiment of chaos and untamed nature." My body shivers when I feel Enzo's fingers drawing small circles on the smooth skin of my thigh. I've become addicted to his touch. Once he starts touching my skin, I don't want him to ever stop. Still, I concentrate on what he's saying, somehow feeling like he's letting me inside the complex chaos that is his mind. "When I was younger, and Benedetto would make us attend Sunday mass, the reverend would always use the dragon as an example for the sinning man. The idea that a mortal man who succumbed to this world's temptations somehow resembled a monstrous beast was hilarious to me. One would think the father would've used the serpent as the example for sin and not a mythical creature, but the old bastard was off his rocker." He laughs darkly, eyes trained on me, but not really. It seems as if he's looking right through me and remembering the times he's speaking of. "Then, I started sketching and tattooing the ugly beasts on my skin as a way to mock the church and everything the old Nicolasi family believed in. It used to piss my grandfather off because he knew I was mocking him and his misguided beliefs."

A low growl escapes Enzo's mouth when I move,

trying to get comfortable in his lap. His hands tighten on my thighs, keeping me in place. "And here I thought you were a holy man." Enzo's hand leaves my thigh and comes up to my neck, grabbing it roughly before pulling my face closer to his. "A holy man, I am not."

Of course, he's not.

He's so much more.

I think about Enzo as a god-fearing man, and it makes me want to laugh. Men who follow God and his words should fear everything Lorenzo represents because he is the dragon. He represents what the evil moral men are capable of in order to take care of their own and obtain everything they need and crave on earth. Power, money, lust… love. There's no doubt in my mind that there's no line Enzo wouldn't cross to achieve it all.

Looking at him now, with a darkness that is anything but holy swimming in his eyes, I try to suppress the laugh that bubbles in my chest, not wanting God to strike me down. I might not believe in an angelic being sitting on a throne in the heavens judging us, but I do believe there's a force surrounding all of us. You have to believe in something, I guess. The hand around my throat tightens, cutting my air supply, catching me off guard. Somehow, I don't feel afraid but excited. My body buzzes with electricity and untamed lust for this man. Reaching closer and fighting his hold on my throat, I take his full bottom lip in mine and bite down hard, so much so that I can taste the sweet metallic taste of blood. His blood. Enzo loosens his hold, and I'm able to find my next breath. "Oh, but you are." Enzo's eyes flash with desire but also confusion at my words. "Holy, I mean. To me." He is. I might not believe in God, but I do believe in him. Call me naive or crazy, maybe I'm both when it comes to him, but there's no one I trust more, besides my brother, than Lorenzo Nicolasi.

That's the honest-to-God truth.

I put all my faith and trust in the man who, as a boy, annihilated anyone that put tears in my eyes. The man he grew up to be that would cross to enemy territory to find me. The very same one that showed another boss and his men what happens when they touch me.

The one this city calls mad king.

I never expect much from Enzo when I give him my truths. I sometimes worry that my feelings make him uncomfortable, since he has trouble deciphering most of them half the time, but every time he looks at me as he is now, with possession and wickedness in his eyes, I know that it's alright. I know I don't need words. Just his blue eyes staring right through my soul, letting me inside his crazy mind.

Without so much as a thought, the grip he has on my neck tightens, and he's crashing his mouth down on me, stealing my breath, my heart and everything else that's mine and keeping it for himself.

Our tongues clash for dominance while my body rocks against him, trying to find a friction that soothes the ache between my legs his kiss caused.

A second later, we're both pulling back, breathless, and I find myself enthralled by the blinding smile that's on his face. Enzo's smiles are rare, and they blow me away every time because when he truly smiles and doesn't fake it, it means something.

I mean something.

"What do you want, Red?"

Taking a deep breath, I tell him exactly what is on my mind. "You."

Enzo's face is void of emotion, but his eyes tell another story. "You have me." All of you, I want to say. Your mind. Your soul. Your heart, but something stops me. Knowing Lorenzo is allergic to hearts and flowers.

That's not the man he is. The smoke is still plastered over his handsome face, making my heart beat faster in my chest, and when I rest my free palm in his, I feel the quick beat of his heart breathing life into me. "And you have me." I whisper, still looking down at his chest, getting comfortable with the feeling of his warm skin on mine. Gentle fingers lift my face until I'm staring right into his eyes. "I know." The way he says it, so sure, so cocky, should irritate me, but it only makes me wilder for him. "So cocky." I tsk while softly playing with the cross that sits on top of his heart, hanging from his black rosary. How haven't I noticed this before? "I thought you didn't believe in God."

"I don't."

I lift the tiny cross and stare at it. It's a beautiful black rosary. Yeah, I guess some people wear rosaries as fashion statements, but that's not him, so it has to mean something to him. Knowing that if I push him on it, he'll retreat and ruin the moment, I opt to ask about it later, when I don't have his covered cock grinding on my pussy.

I want to do many things to his body, but if he wants to wait, then I guess I'll have to make him lose all control for that to happen. The idea from before pops back into my mind. "Can I ask you for something?"

"You can ask me for anything."

"Will you tattoo me?" I've always thought the act of tattooing someone was an intimate act. You trust someone with a needle to draw something permanently on your skin.

He thinks about it for a second before he's lifting me off his body with a hard expression on his face and puts me down on my feet. Then, he rises from his spot on the sofa and stands tall, offering me his back where there is another tattoo, this one taking over the entire half of his body and turning toward the kitchen counter where he picks up a medium-sized white bottle and plastic saran wrap.

He says nothing, and I'm thinking he might tell me no. I can't imagine why he might deny me, but I do remember his odd fascination with my pale skin, and maybe he doesn't want to ruin it, but it's been tatted before.

My skin is no longer virgin, and he damn well knows it.

"Get your ass on the sofa, Red." His dark voice breaks through my thoughts, making me do exactly as he says. I fall down on the sofa and watch with thrilling excitement as he walks toward me with a glint of wickedness in his eyes and his famous scary, and at times, creepy smile.

***

Shit, this is torture.

Having this man's hands on me, not doing filthy things to my body should be a crime. After he told me to get my ass on the sofa, he put some cream on his fresh tattoo and covered it before he returned to where he left me. Then, he pulled out a sheet of paper and drew a quick sketch of a design of his choosing. Yes, I told him he could ink whatever he wanted, and if I end up with a big cock with his name on it, inked on the left side of my body, I'm the only one to blame. "You better not be tattooing a mega ding dong on me, or you'll be sorry." I try to muster the most serious look to show him I will cause him a world of hurt if he inks stupid shit on me.

Enzo laughs, and the sound of it shoots straight to my heart. I want to do that more often.

Make him laugh.

Now, two hours has gone by, and I'm dying here, and not from the pain of the needle on my skin but the pain in my crotch for having his hot breath so close to me and his hands touching me so intimately, but not the way I want. While he concentrates on what he's doing, I imagine all the ways we can both rock each other's worlds. I think of his mouth, fingers, and cock and all the filthy things they can do to my body.

"There. Done." Enzo positions a hand mirror so I can see what he tattooed on my body and when I see the unfinished outline of what he chose to ink on my skin, I'm left speechless. It is not finished, and I will need another session to finished it but what he chose to tattooed on my skin is perfect. It has meaning. A dragon.

A dragon that looks almost identical to his, except it's in red ink and not black. Red. The mythical creature gives the illusion that it's dancing around the left side of my body while pretty petals of bleeding hearts fall around it.

Heart beating abnormally fast, I place the mirror on the sofa and carefully lift myself into a sitting position, not taking my eyes off Enzo's face. For the first time in all the time I've known him, he actually looks self-conscious, and it only makes me melt. Red tints his sharp cheeks, but other than that, his eyes look emotionless. He chose this design.

It means something to him, and in some way, I will carry him forever inked on my skin. I'm also not oblivious to the fact that he chose my left rib to tattoo. The same placement of one of his many dragons.

"It's perfect." We're perfect. I don't need to say it. He knows it. That's what two opposite dragons on each other's ribs look like. They mirror one another. One black and the other red, the only difference are the flowers dancing around mine.

Perfect. He takes the gloves off and throws them down on the coffee table next to him. He takes his time applying ointment to my skin and then covers the tattoo with a wrap. I lay there quietly while he does his thing.

The silence that lies between us would make most people uncomfortable, but not us. When Enzo is done, he gives me his eyes and grins mischievously, and the next thing I know, he's grabbing my waist, carrying me to the kitchen island, and hoisting me up. I'm only wearing an oversized Beatles shirt, giving him quick access.

One second, he's hovering over me, giving me a quick peck on the lips, and the next, he's pushing my legs apart and ripping my tiny thong from my body, diving between my legs.

I fall back on the kitchen island and spread my legs wider, feeling like a five-course meal. Fuck, I've never felt this way before. Every touch feels like the very first time.

My eyes roll to the back of my head when I feel his hot breath close to my pussy lips. I get desperate for more and grab a chunk of his hair, pulling him closer to my pussy.

Then he licks me from my ass crack to my swollen clit, tasting my arousal. I'm so wet I can hear him lapping up my juices while he hums in appreciation. Most men don't like to eat pussy, but Lorenzo eats me like he's eating his favorite meal, and it drives me insane with need watching him look at me through hooded eyes while he swipes his tongue up and down my lower lips.

The things this man can do with his tongue would drive a devoted nun to sin. Fuck, I yank on his hair harder when I feel his tongue penetrate me. In and out. Crying out, I'm close to coming.

Enzo keeps thrusting his tongue into my pussy and then begins to fuck me with it faster.

"Fuck me, baby, I can't get enough of this pretty cunt." He mumbles between licks and then proceeds to spit on it. So dirty, fuck.

Out of my mind with lust, I clutch the edge of the table while moaning so loud I bet his men can hear me from all the way outside.

"You're way too good at this," A thought comes to mind of him doing this to other women, and I subconsciously yank on his hair harder and grind my pussy into his face, not caring if I suffocate him with it. I do not think he minds all that much with the way he's sucking my labia into his mouth and smirking against my dripping flesh.

"Jealous, baby?"

Yes, very much so. I don't tell him that. No. "You're the jealous one out of the two of us." I grin, poking the beast.

Growling, he releases my labia with a loud pop and gives my wet pussy a hard slap that has me twitching on top of the table and moaning loud.

Enzo looks down at his wet hand with my juices and draws a deep breath before licking it. That's it. That does it. I woke up the pretty beast. The dirtier, the better, and that's my favorite side of him.

His unhinged side.

"Make me come," I plead while holding onto his wide shoulders, feeling his hot skin.

"Admit you're jealous." His lips hover over my pussy, denying me pleasure. Asshole.

"Pretty-fucking-please." I ground out, holding to the last thread of sanity I have.

Enzo plunges his tongue deeper into my pussy, giving me what I want. He's always doing that, even when he likes to pretend he has full control. He can't deny me anything, and it only makes me fall harder into his lovely and addictive darkness.

Crying out, I part my legs wider, and my toes curl with pleasure. Enzo fucks me with his hot tongue as his hands hold tightly to my ass cheeks while pushing my pussy deeper into his mouth.

Then, I feel it.

This overwhelming feeling is taking root in my heart.

Possessiveness.

Mine.

With every touch he claims me as his, and I do the same to him.

He buries the tip of his thumb into my tight ass. I might not be a virgin, and he didn't get to claim that part of me, but

I've never had my pussy licked before him.
My ass has never been fucked, and oddly, I don't mind it as much if he's the one fucking it. I've heard from other women that they don't like it, but it's hard for me to believe that I won't like something this man does to my body.
I highly doubt it.
"Did another man get to fuck this ass, baby?" I cry out when he fucks my ass gently with his thumb while lapping at my pussy. My ass muscles fight the intrusion, but my pussy begs for more. I look down at him, admiring his flushed face and his usually immaculate hair all over the place, falling over his eyes, making him look wild and feral.
Shaking my head 'no', I am not able to speak because of the insatiable need to come that's taking over my every thought, making it difficult for me to form a proper sentence.
"Good girl," he murmurs against my pussy, smirking at the same time.
Good girl.
Then he closes his lips around my swollen nub and sucks.
Fireworks explode when I close my eyes, and I give into the sensation.
Fire spreads over my body, and I almost leap off the table.
I feel my pussy pulse against his expert mouth as I come harder than I ever have before.
I rock and moan as I push against his shoulders when he continues to lick my sensitive folds.
When my body comes down from the high of the release, I open my eyes to find Enzo grinning down at me like a wolf while his chest rises and falls rapidly. "Such a good fucking girl for me, yeah?" The smile falls, and he looks darkly down at me. Possessive.
"I'm fucking keeping you."
Good.
Because I didn't plan to leave anyway.

"I want to taste you, too."

"Not tonight."

"Why the hell not?" Frustrated, I huff out almost childishly, causing him to chuckle softly.

See? He can be the biggest asshole at times.

I wouldn't have it any other way, but still, I hate when he can touch me, but I can't return the favor.

Suddenly, he grabs me by the neck and takes my lips in his.

He has a thing for neck grabbing, I see.

Not that I mind.

He pulls back, yet he doesn't let go of my neck.

Grinning evilly down at me, he whispers in a dark tone. "I'll fuck that bratty mouth soon enough." With that, he yanks me closer to him and kisses me once more.

Fuck, we're explosive.

CHAPTER THIRTY-SEVEN

THUNDERSTORMS

"He would bend the knee, only for me." – C

Cara

I'm brought to consciousness when I feel warm licks tickling my face. Slowly opening my eyes, I come face to face with a tiny fur baby. "Oh, sweet baby!" I rise into a sitting position, grabbing the tiny pup and bringing it closer to my face so I can see clearer.

A black and white Cavalier King Charles Spaniel with light brown spots above its right eye. The tiny pink collar with a crown pendant lets me know it's a girl. Reading the name engraved in her collar, I find her name to be Pipi.

Pipi.

I don't hold back the full belly laugh when I remember where I've heard the name before. Allegra.

My baby niece is learning Spanish from her mother and one of her favorite words is pipi, which in Spanish means penis. I also recall my brother telling me they added another puppy to their family since Allegra has been hounding him for one since she learned her brother, Roman, has his own dog.

That girl… she named her girl dog after a boy's genitalia.

Why is she here, though? Keeping a tight hold on Pipi I grab my phone from the bedside table and notice a brand-new text message from my brother, Lucan. Opening it up, I laugh aloud when I see the photo, he sent me early in the morning.

It's an image of Enzo looking pissed as fuck while holding the dog. The message reads, Fun times with Pipi.

Not so fun for Enzo, I think to myself.

"Oh, this is priceless," I send a dozen laughing emojis to my brother and then saved the photo as my new screensaver. He looks like the devil himself with a brooding expression and his tatted-up body holding a tiny and innocent baby in its arm.

A loud noise outside my window catches my attention. Getting out of bed, I hold the puppy in one arm as I near the window.

What the actual hell…

Outside, in the middle of Enzo's driveway, there's a black helicopter almost ready for takeoff while Draego and Enzo stand back, watching a tall man with as many tattoos as them move around, checking every part of the helicopter.

What is he doing?

Is he leaving?

As if sensing me, Enzo turns around with a menacing grin on his face and lifts two fingers up, motioning for me to come down.

I put Pipi down on the bed while positioning pillows around her so she doesn't fall to the floor. Then, I grab a quick shower and dress in an oversized white graphic t-shirt that I pair with some brand-new white sneakers. I don't do much to my face but add a bit of cherry-flavored gloss to make them a bit plumper and a bit of mascara to wake me up a little.

Then, my hair…

I haven't straightened it since I arrived here, and it's been in its natural state. Wild and curly. So that's how I leave it, knowing that's how he likes me best.

How I like myself best.

Once I'm done, I pick up Pipi and head out the door, anxious to find out what Enzo has up his sleeves.

***

"You aren't serious…" I look dumbfounded at him as he moves forward, takes Pipi out of my arms, and transfers her to Draego, who doesn't look happy at all to have to deal with the dog.

"I see you met the hellion," Enzo rolls his eyes when the little pup barks at him, totally offended by his not-so-nice comment. "And yes, I'm serious. Get your ass inside." He offers me his hand, and I unwillingly take it while silently praying to all that is holy to not let me die today.

Doing the father, son, and Holy Spirit gesture, I bless the chopper before stepping a foot inside. I might not believe in all that, but when death is close, you bet your ass I pray to something. "You better not crash this chopper, Enzo, or I'll come back from the dead and shove my nine-inch heels up your ass every night." Oh, lord. I'm adventurous, but going on a helicopter ride while it's about to rain and the pilot is a reckless maniac at times? That's not fun to me. Not fun at all.

"Ouch. What the hell?" Turning around, I growl at Enzo for pinching my ass cheek. "Shut the fuck up, and let me take you closer to heaven, baby." He replies sarcastically, drops me down on the passenger's seat, and buckles me up, securing me tightly. "Although, I did take you there last night when I ate your cunt until you screamed my name like a prayer."

I double-check the seat belt, "You're so goddamn cocky."

He winks before shutting my door and turning to jog to the pilot's side. He enters the helicopter's cabin and buckles himself in before touching a whole bunch of buttons, making me nervous to the point I believe I'll puke my guts at any given moment.

Oh, please God. I know you might not be very fond of the beast beside me and some of my not so wise moments, but don't let me die today. I don't notice I said it out loud until Enzo turned to look at me with a soft look on his face.

"Stop praying to him, little monster. He forsook you the moment I put my tongue inside of that tight cunt of yours."
Enzo laughs when I blush from my cheeks to my toes, and then I feel it.
We're up in the air.
Okay, Cara, you can do this.
Nothing will happen.
You're safe.
He won't let anything happen to you.
After a few seconds of trying to convince myself that all will be fine, I take a deep breath and open my eyes. From up here, the city looks breathtaking even with the stormy weather. The view makes me forget for a little while that we could crash at any given moment.
"God, this view is stunning, isn't it?" I turn to look at Enzo and catch him looking down while keeping a straight hold on the wheel.
"The morning?" I ask, turning to look around us while nervously holding tightly to my seat.
I feel Enzo's eyes burning the left side of my face. "Your city," he whispers, and I turn to look at his face, catching my breath when his pearly white teeth are on display with that big ass smile of his that takes my breath away.
My city.
I let those two words sink while trying to calm my racing heart. The nerves leave my body when the damn butterflies attack my stomach.
"So, we're really doing this?" I whisper.
Enzo nods without looking my way and staring straight ahead. "Keep up, Red. I don't do this shit for just anyone."
This shit.
Dates.
Semi-romantic words.
Then, I think about the others that came before me, but

I push the thought back, not wanting to ruin the moment.
"I don't share." My brother taught me to share with the less fortunate, that sharing is caring, but sharing him is something I won't ever do. He's mine. "Neither do I."
"I won't share you. This is it. You and me." I clarify.
"Neither will I, and I'm glad you're finally catching up, Red." He laughs seductively, glancing my way.
"So, you'll behave?" I'm just being an ass now, but I love it when he laughs. This giant man, covered from head to toe in tattoos, looks like a boy when he laughs from the heart.
Then he gives me an 'are-you-fucking-serious' look that has me wanting to bust out laughing.
"Promise me you won't break my heart."
He heaves a sigh. "Your heart has always been safe with me, Mia."
Always been.
Yeah, because I gave it to him before I even knew what falling was. I gave my heart to a dark boy in the middle of the night when I was just a kid.
It's been his every day since.
Who would've thought that the man who has most likely taken more lives than the reaper could be so romantic? I should've seen it coming. The man beat someone almost to a bloody pulp for making me cry, for fuck's sake.
I replay the words in my mind and think about what this means. I'm his, he is mine, and now how do I make my two worlds collide?
The red carpet.
In a couple of days, I'll be back in my world, and he'll see firsthand what it all means to me, and I'll get to prove to him that he fits everywhere I'm at.
My mind.
My soul.
My heart.

In every corner of my world. Until then, I'll savor every second with him. We enjoy the ride for a couple of minutes with the city below us and silence between us. This city really is beautiful, even on stormy days.

Tired of the silence, I try to lighten the mood.

"Hey, Enzo." A thought comes to mind. One that has my entire body burning up just by the idea of it happening. The waiting is a rush, I'm not going to lie, but one can only take so much, right?

"Mmm?"

"Are you a member of the mile high club?"

"Do you really want to know, Red?"

"I asked, didn't I?" I reply snarky, irritated with myself for having asked. What the hell did I think he would say? The man is sex on legs. Of course, he's done kinky shit up in the air.

"Watch that mouth, brat." He looks at me once while grinning, then continues looking ahead.

I asked the question, and it's very hypocritical of me to get jealous when he's being honest. Still, it drives me crazy to think that I'll never get any of his firsts. "Or what?" I know I shouldn't be provoking him while he has control of the helicopter, but all rational thinking goes to hell when the green monster creeps in.

"I'll put it to good fucking use, that's what."

"Promises, promises."

All anxiousness from before leaves me when I unbuckle my seatbelt and fall to my knees between both our seats. It's not that comfortable of a position, but I'm too hot to care right now. Fumbling with Enzo's zipper, I manage to undo it, and then I pull his dick out. A harsh hiss leaves his mouth the moment my hand wraps around his length.

Thick.

Long.

Veiny, with a slight tilt to the left.
It's so big that, for a second, I worry if it'll fit inside any part of me. I force myself to look away from his dick and take mental pictures of Enzo, so I won't forget this moment. The way he's alternating from looking up ahead and down at me with so many emotions in his eyes that he probably doesn't understand yet. With me. He feels them all with me.
I try to stop time in my head—click! —and try to remember the frame for a while. He's being a good boy and not telling me what to do for once.
But I spoke too soon.
"You want my cock." He grabs my face with one hand while the other stays steering the chopper. He tips my chin up with a gentle thumb and looks into my eyes. Blue eyes sparkle with mischief and lust, so much lust. I could fall into them and stay there forever.
"We're doing this my way." I do my best 'I-mean-business' face. Enzo swipes a hand across his smile. "Have at it then."
My breathing comes out haggard. "And I really do." I smile up at him before dropping a soft kiss on the tip of his cock, which makes it twitch. I notice something while I'm this close to his length. Enzo not only has pierced one nipple but his fat dick, too.
A king's crown.
Of course, he would choose that one.
Biting my lips, I take in the piercing through the ridge at the base of his head. Why is everything this man does so goddamn hot? His breathing even makes me wet.
I have the same effect on him because the moment my skin made contact with his, his dick grew thick and rock hard in my palm.
He gets off on seeing me on my knees for him.
Since he has fallen on his knees for me twice now. It's high time I return the favor.

Enzo chuckles darkly down at me. "Show me how much, Red. Take me into that bratty mouth of yours."
And I do.
With the flat part of my tongue, I tease his tip. Then, I run my tongue leisurely over the thick veins on the base of his cock.
I feel him stop breathing. It only urges me to push him to his limits. My red lips stretch around his thickness as I slowly draw him in, deeper, harder, opening my airway until his length hits the back of my throat.
Looking up at his face, I watch him lean back on the seat and drop his head back while releasing an animalistic groan of pleasure.
While I suck his dick, I run his base up and down, keeping a rhythm that drives him insane with need. I know I'm doing a good job when I feel his rough hand grip my hair while he fucks my mouth mercilessly.
I fight through the gag reflex and enjoy the way he fucks my mouth at the same time he's flying the helicopter.
All rational thought leaves me while his fat cock is brutalizing my mouth. I watch as he looks down at me. His lids half-mast and lips parted, breathless. Christ, that look on his gorgeous face, the sheer intensity in his eyes awakens my pulse and makes me hornier for him, if that's possible.
And what was supposed to be a romantic helicopter ride turned out to be an out of this world hot porn session. After I swallowed his cum which didn't taste all that bad, he ordered me to sit on his lap to teach me how to fly the chopper.
All of this while he shoved his thick fingers inside me, returning the favor.
The fear of flying the helicopter, mixed with the pleasure he was giving me, made the moment even hotter.
And that's what a date with Lorenzo Nicolasi looks like. Reckless.

Defying death.
Hot as hell.
Just like him.
Thankfully, we didn't crash and die. Although, I almost saw God the moment he shoved three fingers inside me while whispering all the dirty things he'll do to my body when we land.
I can't wait.

CHAPTER THIRTY-EIGHT

ROMANCE & SHIT

"It's a whole new fucking world." – L

Cara

After we landed, the rain started falling hard, soaking us both from head to toe. Enzo dismissed all his men for the night, allowing us to be left alone. There's a buzz running through my body, thinking about all the dirty little things he whispered in my ear that await me inside.

When we stepped inside the living area, a dozen lit candles were spread all over, giving the room a dim light. In the middle of the room, instead of the usual the furniture, there's a small table for two with a white cloth, silverware, and two stainless-steel cloches. I look at everything. So simple, yet it means everything because he put thought into it. He could've taken me to the most expensive and exclusive restaurant in this city. He owns half of them, but he chose an intimate candlelight dinner instead. I like this so much more.

"Go change out of those clothes before you catch a cold." Enzo tells me before turning towards the kitchen, muttering under his breath all the way. I can't help the soft laugh that escapes my lips at his moody behavior. "Romance and shit."

"Hey! Most women like to be wined and dined, you know. You're doing amazing, sweetie." I joke with pride, but he doesn't get it. Yeah, I've been watching way to much reality TV lately.

"Upstairs."

"I'm going, I'm going." Taking one stair at a time, I make it to my room and take a quick shower, brushing my teeth and opting to wear something more casual since we're dining inside. Inside the walk-in closet, I find a see-through red nightgown that leaves nothing to the imagination and throw it on without underwear. Let's see how far he's willing to take it tonight. Leaving the room, I walk back downstairs and find Enzo shirtless, sitting comfortably on the table while on the phone with a furious look on his face. The moment he notices me, he hangs up and throws the phone toward the sofa without a single care that it might fall and break.

Walking toward the table, I take a seat opposite to him, and the smell of meat hits me. It smells familiar.

"I didn't know you cooked."

"I don't." He grins before lifting the lid and revealing our food. "Tino got the poetic soul and the Betty Crocker gene." He's so handsome. At times, I have trouble believing he's real. His black hair is wet and slicked back as if he ran his fingers through it to keep it from falling over his eyes. His tan skin glimmers in the candlelight, wet and so irresistible.

We're total opposites in that department.

He's a giant, and next to him, I look like his child.

His skin almost glows while mine is translucent, almost like the mythical creatures Fallon loves so much.

Somehow, we fit perfectly together.

That's all that matters to me.

Looking down at my plate, I find my favorite chicken tenders with ranch sauce and spicy French fries. He ordered from my favorite chicken place.

I would laugh, but I find it too damn sweet. He doesn't change who he is, not even to impress me, because he knows he doesn't need to be anyone but himself.

He has me.

Just like I don't need to be anyone else to maintain his attention. I'm complicated. I'm sweet, but I also have a temper from hell. I have mood swings that might scare another type of man. I laugh at things that shouldn't be funny.
Children cursing. Old people falling. Death jokes.
I get hot when Enzo comes home with blood on his skin.
It's insane, but it's me.
He gets me.
Maybe we're both crazy.
Thunder breaks, lightning strikes, and the power goes out, one after the other. The rain falls harsher against the windows, and it's just us.
It's perfect.
"Thank you for this." I bite into the chicken tender after dipping it in the sauce. Mouth full, "For this date, I mean."
Enzo frowns, annoyed with my use of the word, and I love it. He looks frighteningly adorable.
Like a baby serial killer.
I watch him pour himself a glass of scotch and me a glass of Domaine Leroy. One thing about Lorenzo is that he has good taste and buys the best of the best.
"Well…" Grinning over the brim of his glass. "It's the gentlemanly thing to do, wine and dine, before tapping that ass."
Oh, God. He did not.
Snorting, I feel wine coming out of my nose.
A twenty grand bottle of wine.
"You're a weirdo, Enzo, do you know that?"
Taking another sip of his drink, he sobers up. "I do."
That's all he says.
He knows.
I'm a weirdo, as well, since I find his strange and sometimes manic behavior endearing.
We eat our food in silence, and after, he gets up and brings dessert.

Devil's food cake. Oh, the irony.

Taking a bite of the moist, rich chocolate-layered cake, I moan loud when the delicious goodness hits my taste buds. Between chewing, I ask. "This has got to be the most delicious devil's cake. I'm guessing you didn't bake this."

"You guessed right." He mumbles while chewing with his mouth open. "Tino can throw down in the kitchen." There's not one ounce of sarcasm in his tone. I've noticed that when he talks about his twin, it's almost as if he respects him, which is funny since there are very few people on this earth that Enzo respects.

Not the Pope. Let alone the church.

Not politicians nor the law.

Not my brother.

Hell, not even his own father.

No one.

It's one of the things I love most about him. He might be the biggest ass to everyone and their mother, but family is everything to him, even when he never got to experience a conventional home.

A healthy home.

"Can I ask you a question?"

"You can ask me anything." Anything. I can ask anything.

"Do you regret it? Pushing me away back then, and the damage you did to your twin?" I have to know. Now that we're here and I have him all to myself, I sure as hell will be asking all I've been wondering for years. It doesn't guarantee that he'll answer, but I will still try, because to know Enzo, you need to dig deep beneath the hard exterior.

When I was a kid, I learned that there are two types of evil in this world. There is the type that dwells deep within human souls and rots them from the inside out. The kind that makes them do unspeakable things in the name of greed and malice.

Just because they can. However, evil can be subjective.

The day I met Enzo, I realized just how true that statement was. Not all men who battle with demons inside their heads unleash them into the world as retaliation.

Some men, like the one before me, only draw them when needed. When they feel like they're being threatened. There's always a balance in this world, and most people choose to turn a blind eye.

Good men do bad shit, just like bad men are capable of doing great things.

Good and bad, I believe Enzo is both. I don't justify the things he does and says at times, but to categorize him as a cruel bastard who has no redeeming qualities is not fair.

He's capable of good but prefers to be bad.

I like him either way.

But I have to admit that although good Enzo makes my heart stutter… bad Enzo makes other parts of me come alive.

Enzo clears his throat and drops his spoon before wiping his mouth with the napkin. "Want the truth, or would you like me to lie?"

"Truth. Always." Even when it makes me uncomfortable or hurts. I need his truth.

"I don't regret it. Never have and never will."

Some truths hurt more than lies.

"I see." I gently put down the spoon without making eye contact with him. When I'm hurt, I hide. It's always been that way, even now that I'm older. The little girl who used to suppress her feelings so she wasn't a burden still lives inside of me.

"I'm not finished."

What else is there to say? He doesn't regret pushing me away. "Did it kill something inside of me?" I find his eyes and search for the lies. None. I can always count on that. "Yes."

"Then why?"

"Some of us don't have a choice, Mia. We don't get to run away and chase our dreams and aspirations in life. The life we were born into binds us more than any shackles would. You had a privilege your brother, my brother, and even the Parisis' didn't. Years of traditions and the burden of the families didn't fall on your shoulders. You get to dream and chase all your dreams and aspirations in life, and dammit, you should. Because you're good. From the moment, I first saw you, I witnessed a fire that burned so bright, and it grew stronger every time you talked about all the things you would do once you were old enough. If I would've entertained the idea of us back, then you would've stayed, and you wouldn't have seen the world outside the cage you were born into. So I lied, and I pushed you away, even when it pained me to do it, so you could be everything you wanted to be. Hoping that maybe one day, we would find each other back here." My heart rate drops as I stare at his blue eyes burning with the same intensity he describes. "As for Tino…" he lifts his glass and downs it before dropping the glass loudly on the table. "He wanted to be the boss of our family to keep his girl safe at the time, but I bled for this family. I was reborn every single time I took a life and blessed with the blood of our enemies. I'm not a good man, Cara Mia. I enjoy the shit I do, and when I go home at night and lie in my bed, I sleep like a motherfucking baby, counting down the hours so I can do it all over again the next day. I did what was best for us at the time. I got the title of boss and freed my brother from the burden of a crown he didn't honestly want." After he's done, a long silence follows, with the sky splitting in two in the background.
"Thank you."
Enzo frowns. "You're thanking me?" I see it then. His mind is working, trying to decipher what I mean. While most people can deduce what another person is feeling and

thinking without so much trouble, Enzo has to take his time studying others to conclude.

"I am." I take a sip of my wine. "For sharing your truth with me." I notice that his hand, the one that's holding onto the glass on the table, starts twitching. Uh, oh. Pretty beast, come out to play. "One last question."

"You're extra fucking chatty today, Red."

"You wouldn't like me any other way." I grin while twirling my index finger around the brim of the glass seductively.

He grunts and then says. "Ask your question then."

"When were you planning to tell me about the threatening notes you've been getting about me?"

Enzo's entire demeanor changes, and his nostrils flare. "How did you find out? Who told you?" He frowns but at least doesn't deny it, not that I think he would.

"I found one of the paper clippings inside your red room." I shrug as if it's not a big deal.

"You've been going through my stuff?"

"Of course." I smile when a half smile forms on his face before he reminds himself that he's annoyed with me. "Plus, my brother told me."

"Your brother is a gossipy bitch."

"We're working on communicating more and building back trust." I state in fact. Plus, once I found the note inside Enzo's tattooing equipment cabinet, I called Lucan and threatened to go on a brother strike if he didn't fess up. Lucan is not one to give in so easily, but I played his love for me against him, and I don't regret it one bit. I wouldn't go through it anyway. My siblings mean the world to me, and so do my nephew and nieces.

"A sappy bitch, then."

Rolling my eyes, I suppress the laugh. "We don't lie, so why did you keep that to yourself?"

"Because, Red, it's nothing." He takes a breath and pins me

with his gaze. "I won't let anything happen to you. I'll find the cunt and bleed him dry before I let anything touch you." He fills his glass to the brim without breaking eye contact, as if waiting for me to say otherwise.

"I know." I trust him. Always have. Always will. I also know that he can't be with me every hour of every day, and eventually his world could indeed get to me. I'm fully aware that no one is completely safe in this crime world, and eventually something will happen. Look at Andrea, my nephew and Fallon, for example. The three of them had some of the strongest men I know looking out for them, and yet they were taken.

I'm not untouchable, but I refuse to tell him that and make him even crazier than he must be feeling right now, knowing that I know.

Something that looks a lot like pride crosses his eyes. "Then you see why it was useless to alarm you for nothing."

"I don't care. You tell me anyway."

A second passes before he nods. "You trust me, then? To keep you safe." Without a thought, I answer. "I put all my faith in you, king." Hunger.

Passion.

Pride.

Need.

So many emotions swirl in his deep blue eyes before he stands, comes to my side, picks me up into his arms, smacks everything on top of the table out of the way, and throws me down on top of it. "I like this side of you."

"What?" Enzo spreads my knees wide and climbs on top of me. I don't know if the table is strong enough to hold us both, but we shall see. "The horny-out-of-my-mind side?"

I breathe into his mouth. "The wild animal that plays with me and doesn't treat me like a breakable doll like most people do." The air between us grows thick.

"You like it rough and filthy, don't you, baby?" He whispers, hovering over my lips. "You like it when I make it hurt."
I do.
My mouth grows dry.
I can't say the same for my pussy.
Before I know it, a growl erupts from deep within his throat, a sound that makes my entire body hum with awareness. He slowly runs his fingers up the path of my thighs, bringing my body to life with each touch and causing goosebumps to spread all over my skin. Running my fingers through his soft, black tendrils, I pull on them, just enough to make Enzo groan in pleasure. Music to my ears.
Without notice, he grabs two fistfuls of my nightgown and tears it open. How did he manage to rip the thick material? I don't know, but what I do know is that it was the hottest thing I've ever seen. "That was expensive," I point out as my breathing races when I find him looking down at my naked body as if he just saw heaven. He's good for my ego because every time he looks at me, he makes me feel as if I'm not only the most beautiful woman in the room but also in the world. With my career as a model, I have my moments of self-consciousness, yet I always remember the way he used to look at me back when we were kids, and it passes.
He still looks at me that way now.
My cheeks grow hot as I sit back and watch Enzo rake his gaze over my exposed breasts and hardened nipples. I feel my pussy grow wetter at his inspection. "I'll buy you fifty more just so I can rip them off your body every time I fuck you," he says. "They look stunning on you, Red, but that shit gets in my way." Enzo lifts his eyes from my naked breasts, and our gazes lock.
Deep, soulful blue eyes stare at me with so much heat and passion that it is almost impossible to find my next breath. His naked chest rises and falls with the intensity

of this feeling between us.

Pushing back his hair from his face, I rose from the table just enough to whisper against his plump lips. "Fuck me, king."

Enzo's eyes harden, and then, as if time stops, an evil smile breaks out.

One breath.

Two breaths.

Then, all hell breaks loose when the beast is unleashed.

Enzo's mouth comes crashing down hard over mine, flooding the air around us with pure unadulterated lust. I moan into his wild kiss as our tongues collide and tangle, and I've never tasted anything better than him. Vodka. Nicotine. Him.

I fist a handful of his hair and tug him closer to my body, wanting to feel him all over me. Yet, it feels as if we're not close enough.

Enzo reaches around my back and lifts my hips so that my core is flush against his hard length under his jeans. I rotate my hips, enjoying the friction of his heat through the fabric against my naked pussy.

"Fuck." He grabs the underside of one of my thighs, kneading it with his hands before forcing my legs around his waist. I'm so wet just from his intimate touch. No one on this earth has ever made me feel alive the way he does.

Desperate for more, I reach between our bodies and unbutton his jeans. He helps me out by pulling back just enough so I can shove his pants and black boxers down over the tight globes of his ass to the floor, next to my ruined nightgown.

Lightning strikes again, and the rain falls harder outside, while inside, we're both covered in sweat and the heat of this passion.

Enzo kicks the jeans off his feet and is right back on me where we'd left off.

His rough hands knead my flesh.

His tongue inside my mouth, battling for control.

His hard, tattooed chest pressed against my naked and sweaty one.

He positions his cock against my opening with nothing separating us. Nothing. Just skin on skin.

Enzo releases my mouth to suck one of my hardened nipples into his mouth, biting lightly while roughly pulling my hair. I writhe against him, feeling like I might combust at any second, just from the sensation of his hard cock against my pussy. "Fuck, I need you, Red. I need you now," Enzo demands. His voice is deep and hoarse. He doesn't bother getting protection. There is no time for that. We are frantic with need. "I'm clean, baby. Haven't been with anyone since before I took you from New York." Shit.

"I'm clean, too." I breathe heavily against his mouth, "It's been a while." It's been a long while since I've been intimate with someone. I could blame my work schedule, but I also know that lately, I've had no interest in relationships. It all seemed fake and forced. I couldn't deal with it anymore, so I took time for myself, and then the whole charade with Jonah started, and well… let's just say my vagina might have a cow web or two. "Give me that mouth, Red."

He growls before his teeth catch my lip, biting wildly and drawing blood. I wince from the sharp pain, but he makes it all go away when he sucks my lips between his and by lining up the massive head of his cock with my pussy.

I hiss between kisses when he slaps my wet folds with his hard cock. Once. Twice. Four more times, rapidly, enjoying the sound our wet skin makes.

I'm driven mad with lust from the feeling of the hot silky skin of his cock running up and down my pussy lips. I shiver. "Oh, fuck, yes, baby. I need you in me, now!" I said while grabbing his ass and bringing him closer to me.

"You want my cock inside that tight, pretty pussy?"

Enzo pulls back and fists his cock, pulling on it and using my juices as lube.

"Get inside me, Lorenzo. Now." I say through gritted teeth, causing him to laugh darkly down at me while teasing me further.

In this moment, with his golden skin glistening in the dark with the help of the candles all around us, his wild eyes looking at me as if I'm the most precious thing in his world, his cruel smile promising dirty things for my pussy, he looks like a God. A malicious one, but still a God. A dark king.

"Scream for me, little monster." He moves so quickly that by the time he is surging forward, his tongue is already seeking mine, and his dick was filling me, inch by inch, while I meet his every thrust, trying to accommodate more of his monster cock inside of me.

Each punishing thrust elicits another spark of heart-stopping need.

Him inside of me feels right.

Feels like a missing part of me has fallen into place.

The way Enzo fucks me is the same way he cares for people.

The same way he loves.

Pleasure and pain.

A beautiful kind of pain I never want to stop feeling.

"Fuck," Enzo groans, pulling his lips from mine to look down where his dick is pounding my pussy. He pulls out slightly, and we both stare at his angry cock bathed in my juices, then he surges back in.

Faster.

Harder.

Deeper.

Until I feel him in every part of me.

"You're strangling my cock, Red." He pulls back again, spits on my pussy lips, and pushes his hips forward, swearing, until he's fully seated himself inside me again.

The way he hits all the right spots, stretching me wide open, causes my inner walls to tighten around him.

I gasp while he swears under his breath at the sensation.

His angry thrusts become even more powerful. More demanding. "You fit me perfectly, little monster. You were made for me. Mine. Say it. Say you're fucking mine," Enzo grinds out. I can't form a proper sentence since I'm literally being fucked senseless.

I begin to see sparks behind my eyelids every time the pleasure is too much to bear, and I close my eyes.

He might not say the words 'I love you', but the way he fucks me shows me all I need to know.

He fucks me as if I'm all his dark heart desires.

As if he's erasing every man that came before him.

We're both a mess of tangled hearts and wicked desires.

Rough.

Frenzied.

Desperate.

Perfect.

We are all of that and more.

So much more.

My moans grow wilder, louder as Enzo grabs hold of my neck and brutally assaults my pussy, pounding it with his monster cock.

In and out.

Over and over.

Keeping me on the brink of ecstasy. I barely register the sound of wood breaking before we both fall to the floor with our bodies still connected. Pain shoots through me when my back lands on the hard floor and Enzo's heavy weight falls on me, but he doesn't stop pounding the fuck out of me, and I don't stop meeting his every thrust. Nothing can stop years of pent-up frustration and this insatiable need we have for each other.

His hold on my neck tightens and loosens as he fucks me. Making it impossible for me to find my next breath, and in the next moment, I'm gasping for air. Pain and pleasure. Fuck. I've never experienced anything like this. I scream his name when it becomes too much, but I don't want him to stop. "Enzo. Oh, Oh. Enzo!" I scream his name louder, urging him to fuck me harder. The sounds that come out of his mouth are driving me insane. His grunts and hisses are the sexiest things I have ever heard. "I'm yours, baby. You are mine, too. Only ever mine." I whisper harshly in his ear.
"Look at me, Red, watch as I come undone for you. Let me see your eyes as you come for me." My eyes close when the pleasure seems too much, but I hold his gaze, not wanting to miss a thing. God, he is perfect. There is a beauty in the way his teeth gnash together as he thrusts feverishly, making him look like a wild animal. My animal.
Enzo's cock throbs inside me, and I moan long and loud as he strokes the sensitive spot on the front side of my inner walls repeatedly. His eyes harden at the same time that his lips part, and the muscles in his shoulders and biceps strain, making it look like his tattoos, the dragons, are dancing every time he thrusts forward. Beautiful.
His hair is sticking in all directions and sweat beads on his forehead, running from his temple down to the black tattoos adorning his neck and chest. He isn't breathing, his mouth hanging open, his eyes wide, and looking down at me as he groans my name with every thrust. I feel it, then.
The need to come before I lose my mind. Arching my back on the floor and digging my nails into Enzo's perfect ass, I run my pussy shamelessly against him, riding out the sweetest release.
He soon follows, his muscles going taut. His spine arches and he roars louder than the thunder outside, thrusting feverishly, erratically.

Then, he pulls out of my body and jets a torrent of hot liquid on my pussy, belly, and breasts. "The best I've ever had." Enzo's breathing sinks with mine as we both try our best to catch our breaths. I close my eyes and let this moment sink in. The best he ever had, that's right. The last one, too. I open my eyes and notice Enzo looking down at me with an intense look on his face. I take his mouth in mine, kissing him senseless while my hands run through his wet hair down the side of his face. His arms around my waist pull me closer. Breaking the kiss, I grab his face in my hands. "Lorenzo Antonnio Nicolasi, you're fucked. There's no way you're ever leaving my body." I whisper, my voice as shaky as my limbs. "I think I'm obsessed." Enzo closes his eyes and drops his forehead until it's touching mine. Nose to nose.

A lazy, satisfied smile appears on his handsome face. "Obsession doesn't even begin to cover it, little monster," Enzo says, followed by a kiss on my nose.

The best I ever had.

My heart swells in my chest.

I smile dreamily and continue to run my hands through Enzo's hair until the need rises again, and I find myself pressed against the window with his hard dick thrusting savagely inside of me. Fucking me into oblivion and into all hours of the night. Death by dick.

That's about right.

***

LORENZO

We're both a sweaty mess on the floor. After I fucked her once on the table until it broke and we ended up fucking on the floor, I fucked her two more times pressed against the window, watching the rain fall and lightning crisscross across the sky.

Poetic fucking, if you ask me.

Can't get any better than that.

"Lucan told me the capo was chosen weeks before I arrived here. Are you the—"

"It is what it is." Pulling her closer to my body, we both watch as the rain hits the windows from our spot on the floor. We haven't moved since, and my dick is still inside her. I wonder if it's scientifically possible to walk through life still connected like this. If it were, you bet your ass I would.

Mia gently draws circles on my chest, and I realize how peaceful her touch is. "You've been waiting for that moment since you held your first gun." It was before then, but I don't tell her that. "We did what we had to do, Red. It happened, and now it's over." I don't want to talk about that fucking night now. It has no room here between us, but I've never been one to shelter her from my crimes, my successes, or my failures. I tell her exactly what happened back in the Nicolasi mansion's underground a couple of weeks back. I don't tell her who was chosen, though.

Then, she passes out in my arms.

All I wanted since I was a punk kid was to be the one calling the shots. The one who decided the fate of everyone that wronged my family, the three families and me. It was not enough to just be the head of the family I was born into. I wanted more.

Then, she came along, and my obsession with the title of capo took a back seat, but it still lingered in every dark corner of my brain. Gently untangling her small arms from my body, I rise from the floor, bringing her with me. I place her down on the sofa and cover her with the blanket I use for Tino's hellions when they sleep over. Then, I pick up my phone from the floor and dial the one person that I trust aside from Red. "It's late as fuck. Cleaning can wait till morning." My twin's voice, rough from sleep, sounds from the other end of the line. Skipping the pleasantries. "How did you know?" Silence passes, and then he asks.

"Be specific, brother. We've talked about this."

Rolling my eyes, I walk naked as the day I was born toward the floor-length windows, watch the rainfall and listen to the thunder boom. "How'd you know you loved her?"

"Huh."

I suppress the urge to curse the condescending motherfucker out."

"Do you feel like you can't breathe when she's not next to you?"

I'm not answering that bullshit even though I feel a lot of shit when she's near me, and I feel particularly murder-y when she's away from me.

"Do you feel as if you've come home when she touches you?"

I feel a lot of things when she puts her hands on me, especially on my dick.

I don't answer him, but he knows I'm listening and keeps going.

"If so, then you're fucked, but we both know you've been fucked since the first day you saw her all those years ago at the Volpe mansion."

"How the fuck do you know about that day?" I never told anyone about that day.

"Volpe told me back in high school. Warned me about you sniffing around his baby sister."

Huh.

At times, I did shit to provoke the asshole. I still never let on that I had any kind of feelings toward his kid sister.

"Why didn't you say something before now?"

"I know you." Tino's tone changes, no longer condescending. "She looked at you as if the world started and ended with you, and you, well…"

"What?"

"You looked at her as if nothing else mattered." My twin says, laughing softly. Not mocking, but in… joy?

"As if nobody else existed but the little redhead you couldn't stop looking away from."

Phone in hand, I turn away from the window and look down at the sleeping beauty on my couch with her skin still red from the abuse of my touch, her blood-red hair in disarray, and her mouth slightly open while she snores like a fifty-year-old man.

Fucking adorable.

Tino is right.

I'm so fucked.

The little monster has my balls in the palms of her hands.

"Tino?" I whisper, not wanting to wake her up.

"Yes?"

"What does this overwhelming feeling in the pit of my stomach that leaves me breathless when I look at her mean?"

No jokes.

No insults.

Just brother to brother.

"You are no longer yours but hers. Every broken and fucked-up piece no longer belongs to you but her."

After that, I hang up on my brother and drop down next to her on the couch, guarding her sleep, all the while thinking of the threat that lingers outside these walls and that soon enough will come knocking on my door.

Fuck.

CHAPTER THIRTY-NINE

SUPERNOVA

"He's perfect and all mine." - C

Cara

Enzo is sitting next to me on the moving SUV on our way to The Hollow's premiere, typing furiously on his phone. After a blissful time back in Detroit, we're now back in my world, facing my reality. We landed last night here in Los Angeles. Enzo, Draego, and I.

Me: I'm fifteen minutes away. Is the team already there?

The red carpet is being hosted at the Grand Muller Theater, and we're running behind.

Arielle: Everyone is here. Once you arrive, call me, and I'll have security escort you in. The gown is exquisite, BTW. She sends the emoji with a mind-blown expression.

Me: I can't wait to see what she came up with.

Of course, I'll be wearing a Valentina exclusive for my first premiere. My sister-in-law spoils me to no end, and I'm so grateful. I'm more than proud to wear her creations.

Another text pops up. This time from my group chat with Fallon and Andrea.

Andrea: I hope you love it, and it does you proud, baby girl. We're so proud of you!! The kids send you all their love!

Fallon: So proud!!! The fam and I will be rooting for you from our couch! Valentino made the kids popcorn and got us snacks to watch it from here.

He's asking how his devil twin is holding up in LA lol.
Fallon attaches a photo of herself and her family sitting on the sofa, smiling up at the camera. All except Valentino, who's gazing down at his family lovingly.
Andrea: Wait, hold up. Is my brother with you? That jackass texted me that he could not babysit the kids because he was on a spiritual retreat. I called BS, of course, but I never thought he would accompany you. He has made it abundantly clear that he hates Hollywood, and I quote, 'F grade actors.
I laugh at that.
I know Enzo hates Hollywood.
It was clear by his sourpuss' face the entire way here.
I snap a photo of his face, frowning down at his phone, and send it to her.
Me: Nonsense! He's overjoyed to be here with me. *Laughing emoji*
"Stop that shit, Red." He mutters but doesn't look up from his phone. I take photo after photo until he's had enough and flips me the bird.
I snap that one, too.
Pocketing my phone, I turn in my seat and stare at him. It's crazy how things happen. One day, I was back in this city on my own, living the life I thought fulfilled me to my core, and now, I'm back with the person that makes me feel the most alive.
Looking at him, casually dressed in black jeans, black combat boots, and a ripped graphic T-shirt, I can't help the shit-eating-grin that takes over my entire face. "Thank you for being here."
"You really need to stop thanking me, Red." He pockets his phone and turns my way with a small smile on his face. That's one thing he does a lot. Smiling with his eyes and mouth.
Nothing fake about it.
Genuine.

At least with me.

He gave the driver a look that said keep your eyes to yourself, or I'll rip them out of your sockets.

It was as sweet as it was intimidating.

"I'll thank you every time you do something sweet and nice for me."

"I'm not sweet."

Snorting, I say. "You're the sweetest, baby. Get over it."

Rough hands take hold of my nape and push my hair until it's all the way back, and his face closes in on mine. Enzo's lips hover over mine, "Are you happy?" His blue eyes search mine. "The happiest I've ever been." I tell him the truth.

His lips touch mine lightly, teasing me further. "Good."

"You'll be watching from the sidelines, right?" He doesn't miss the touch of sadness in my tone. I would love to walk hand in hand with him down the red carpet, but it's not him, and I don't ever want him to do or act as something he's not. Someone he's not comfortable being.

"Do your thing, baby. I'll be there watching over you." I notice his eyes aren't just blue but have rivulets of gold shooting out from the center, which makes them that much more interesting, especially in the early-morning light. I shiver from his touch, and my eyes slide closed when he leans in and presses a kiss to my forehead.

CHAPTER FORTY
FLASHING LIGHTS

"The corny shit I do for her." - L

Lorenzo

"Well, you clean up nice." Draego's dry tone is drowned by the mob of people surrounding us, screaming, throwing orders around. Nonstop chatter. Fuck, the shit I do for this woman. Even the clothes I am wearing feel like they are choking me.

I owe it all to that asshole Volpe, who like the gossipy bitch he is, blabbed about my whereabouts to my sister, who then proceeded to send me a fucking outfit to the hotel we are staying at.

As much as I hate this environment, where most humans are braindead and shallow, I still went ahead and put the clothes on for her.

The suit and tie look is not for me, and my sister damn well knows that, and yet went ahead and sent me some shit her ball-less husband, and probably my twin, would wear.

Not me.

Fuck, no.

The suit is fitted to my body, cut to my precise build, and made of some sleek and stretchy material. I ditched the white dress shirt and tight tie and tried my best to make myself look less like a pretentious asshole and more myself.

Still an asshole, but at least I don't look like a pretty boy.

I came here to watch out for her and make sure no one gets close enough to hurt her, but the moment she looked at me with those puppy eyes of hers, I couldn't stand it.

I gave in.

Fuck me.

I would do anything to wipe that frown from Mia's face when I told her, twice now, that her world was not one I wanted to be a part of.

I hadn't regretted much in life, if anything at all, until that moment. Until her pretty face turned sad, even when she tried her best to hide it. Selfless. Kind. Everything I lack.

She is everything I am not, yet I want her regardless.

She's part of this world, but she belongs to me. Therefore, I have to play nice for her. I hesitated over the idea, but deep down, I knew if it made her happy, I would do it. Consequences be damned.

"Hey, D." Adjusting my cufflinks, I regard Draego.

"Yes, boss."

"Do you value your life?"

"Very much, sir."

"Then shut the fuck up and do your job." I then turn my back and walk toward the narrow hallway that leads to the room where the red carpet is being hosted. It's almost time. She will be walking any moment now. "Stay alert and make sure no one gets near her. Holler if you need me." With that, I step through the corridor and find myself outside, where the chaos is.

Famous people are all around me.

Walking and posing for that perfect shot that'll give them more exposure.

Photographers yell out orders for the celebrities to follow when they're posing for them.

My skin starts to crawl when I take everything in. This shit's not me. Why the fuck did I think this was a good idea?

Then, it happens.
God's favorite angel and the Devil's favorite plaything walks down the long red stairs, a vision in black. She's wearing a long sheer gown molded to her curves and allowing tantalizing glimpses of her milky skin. The dress looks almost painted on.
I know jack-shit about fashion, but there's no doubt in my mind that she'll be one of the best, if not the best, dressed of the night.
Fucking beautiful.
Regal.
Breathtaking.
A supernova.
The most elegant queen.
Mine.
I know now this might not be the world I wish to be part of, but there's no doubt in my mind that I belong wherever she is.
My chest tightens when I look at her smiling brightly while posing for the cameras, and waving to the gathered crowd of her fans, who are yelling out her name in hysteria.
I'm left speechless and breathless, something I've never experienced in my entire goddamn life. Damn you, Red.
Counting down to three, I swallow hard, lift my chin, and repeatedly recite why I'm putting myself through this shit.
For her.
The weird feeling in my chest grows more intense with each step I take toward her.
One beat.
Two beats.
I get close enough to her that everyone else notices. Everyone except her. The crowd of photographers turns their cameras my way, screaming nonsense I don't care for, and the asshole who's interviewing Mia while ogling her tits turns his head

and catches my death glare.

Yeah, motherfucker, look at her tits one more time. One more fucking time, and I'll give these people something to scream about.

"Enzo…"

Her shocked whisper snaps me out of my murdering thoughts, making me focus solely on her.

Her smiling eyes.

Her soft smile.

It makes everything else fade into the background until it's only us in the middle of the Hollywood chaos and its flashing lights.

CHAPTER FORTY-ONE

A GOD AMONGST MEN

"She's my heartbeat." - L

Cara

Breathe, Cara.
You got this.
Click.
Click.
Click.
Flashes blind me while the noise of men and women screaming my name makes me put aside the nerves that have been with me since I came out of the dressing room straight to the red carpet. Posing for the camera is easy.
Walking down the red carpet is a piece of cake.
The interviews are what always get me. As much coaching as I get, I still feel like a nervous wreck whenever I have to do impromptu one-on-ones with reporters.
Late-night talk shows are another thing entirely because the hosts always make their guests comfortable. And their producers send me the questions beforehand so I can approve them, and I get to think about my answers before they ask them in front of thousands or even millions of watchers.
Nevertheless, sometimes they try to sneak questions that they know we don't want to answer, and it always makes me anxious trying to answer in a politically correct way. I overthink things, and it causes me to feel more anxious.

"Mia!" One paparazzi shouts from my right. "Over here." Click. Click. The flashes go off, and I pose, smile, and repeat, trying to give them the best shots of the stunning gown Andrea designed for me. A floor-length, black see-through dress with an intricate web design that shows a lot of skin, but in a tasteful way. I feel like a queen in this, and that was her intention. For women, and also men, to feel confident and their best in the clothes she designs. I'm more honored knowing that this is a custom-made dress she did for my very first red carpet. She had it delivered to my hotel room with a dozen bouquets of pink roses from her and my brother. It was so sweet and so them.

My stylist paired the dress with black suede and, open-toe Manolo high heels, and my hairstylist straightened my hair to perfection and added extensions so that the tip of my hair runs down my back below my butt.

Flipping my hair back, I smile and wave to the hundreds of fans standing at the sides, screaming and chanting our names. This is my life.

I did it.

I made it.

"Mia, this way!" Other paparazzi shout from my left, and I turn, giving them a new angle. The dress is modest in the chest area, but it has a long slit and is backless.

The event organizer motions for me to move over, and I move to stand in front of a background that has the movie poster on it. Wow. I pose for more photos until my smile begins to hurt.

Thankfully, an older woman wielding a cell phone like a handheld recorder leans closer to me with a kind smile. "Mia! This is your first movie premiere! How does it feel, honey?" These questions are easy, and suddenly the nerves subside but still there. Looking over the sea of people, I try to find Enzo, but he's nowhere to be seen.

Where did he go? He left with Draego and gave me privacy to get dressed and ready for the event, and I haven't seen him since.

"Mia?" The reporter calls out my name.

"It's surreal! I still can't believe this is happening." I say, laughing. The reporter grins. "Believe it, honey. You have thousands of people screaming your name. Does it ever feel overwhelming? Does it ever feel too much?"

I think about it for a second before answering.

The question might be innocent, but if I say the wrong thing, they'll change the narrative until I sound ungrateful instead of human.

I'm grateful for all the support, but at times it does get to be too much. When that happens, I take a breather and remind myself why I do this.

It sets my heart aflame.

The same way I feel when Enzo is next to me. I feel like I'm living instead of going through the motions and existing.

"I'm honored and so grateful. I used to dream of this day, and I couldn't have done it without them." It's true. They're the ones that got me noticed. They followed and supported me until my social media numbers skyrocketed, and I blew up.

I answer a couple more questions from her and other reporters, savoring the moment until it happens.

There's always that one reporter that can't help but ask the juicy questions.

"Mia! How do you feel after your fiancé cheated on you and with another man!?"

Breathe, Cara.

Think before you speak.

I have half a mind to snap back at him for his uncalled question. I knew it was coming, but to throw in the fact that Jonah was seen with a man like it is worse than with a woman. As if it's something wrong that he kissed a man.

Yeah, I get that the media and the public believe he was with me, but this dude knows what he's doing. He's throwing shade at the fact that Jonah was outed. Fuck him.

Calming the anger, I smile through it and politely answer with my head held high, and with all the love and pride I feel for my friend, who will most likely face the same attack and worst when he steps down the red carpet.

"Jonah and I are on good terms. He's part of my heart, and I wish him the best. I'm so damn proud of him." There. Suck it, asshole. Smiling, I turn away, and the moment I do, the paparazzi go crazy, shouting and taking picture after picture.

What's going on?

Is it Jonah?

Then I feel him before I see him.

The crowd of other actors, staff members, and reporters surrounding me part as he walks between them with his head held high like a god amongst men.

My heart stops in my chest as I watch him slowly make his way toward me with a dark air surrounding him like a second skin. Taking my breath away, one step at a time.

So dangerous.

So perfect.

God, so mine.

Lorenzo Nicolasi

The same man that can't stand humanity, except for a lucky few. The same man that told me my world was not his. The one that swore to never be caught in a suit.

He's here.

Wearing a sleek black suit with nothing under the jacket, his tattoos on full display, a total contrast to the other men in attendance. He's here.

For me.

And wearing a suit, when normally he wouldn't be caught dead in one.

My eyes roam lower to his neck and find something gold that catches my attention.
A gold chain with a dragon enveloping a broken cross.
Without taking my eyes off him, my hands go up to my neck, and I touch the gold choker he gifted me.
A perfect match.
God, I love him.
I love him so much. It is painful at times.
It's painful when he's not near.
Holding my breath, I wait for him to reach my side, clutching the necklace in my hand.
His eyes roam down to where my hand is touching the necklace, and he grins.
Evil yet, at the same time, sweet.
The most lethal combination.
That's him.
My light and my dark.
"Who is that?" Whispers behind me grow louder.
"Mia!" One paparazzi shouts. "Is that your rebound?"
"Yes, what about Jonah?!"
What the hell?
Tuning them out, I focus only on him.
In my world, walking proudly toward me, dressed in all black and so damn irresistible. I don't blame the crowd of women and some men going wild for him all around us.
Gasps.
Shouts.
Yet, nothing fazes him.
His eyes are holding mine, keeping me in his trance, unable to look at anything or anyone else.
The madness stops, and then it's just… us.
He loves me.
There is no doubt about it.
And how beautiful it is to be loved by him.

A man who doesn't know the right words yet does all the right things. Grinning, I think to myself how whipped he is for me. Then, I feel his strong arms around my waist, holding me possessively to his body. The paparazzi continue to go wild with shots and questions, but we don't pay them any mind. Looking up at him, I take him in, memorizing how he looks right now, so I can keep it with me forever. Wild, reckless, and so very handsome. So different from the rest. So uniquely him. So damn hot.

His black hair is slicked back, without a strand out of place, and he is still wearing his piercings. I'm glad he didn't change anything. I like him just as he is.

"Why?" I rise on my tiptoes, not caring that we're exposed for the whole world to see. I nibble lightly on his chin, then whisper loudly so he can hear me above the noise. "What changed your mind?"

His dark gaze falls on me. There, I can see the possessiveness I also feel when I look at him, "I was wrong." Enzo's face shows no emotion, but he doesn't need to. What he says next sets my entire soul on fire. "My world is wherever you're at."

My world is wherever you're at.

Thump.

Thump.

Thump.

Heart beating faster, I'm left speechless once again.

I'm dead, and I've gone to heaven because there is no way he just said the right thing at the right time in a grand romantic gesture. I'm never going to let him live this down.

I take this moment in and save it in my heart forever.

Just like every second I've ever spent with him.

Enzo whispers in my ear. "You take my breath away, Red." Before gently biting my ear. I do a shit job hiding how his words and his erotic touch are making me feel right now in front of so many, but then he has to open his big and horny

mouth. "I can't wait to get my dick inside of you."
Blushing from my neck to my cheeks, I laugh it off, already counting down the seconds to get him alone. "And I thought romance was dead."
"I got more where that came from." He winks playfully. I will never get used to this playful side of him that not everyone gets. I am addicted to it, just as much as his dark side.
"I bet you do."
Someone shouts from the side, bringing my attention to them. "Sir, sir. Are you her new man?"
"Over here, sir. Anything you would like to say?"
"Mia, smile for the camera!"
I grab his hand and interlock our fingers. "You don't have to say anything." Turning to the paparazzi and reporters, I smile one last time before I move to leave, pulling Enzo with me when he stops, hauls me into his arms, and kisses me in front of everyone. One second passes.
Then three.
Until he pulls away and we're both left breathless.
I never believed in magic and fairy tales.
Until this moment.
Until I fell for the villainous kind and not the charming prince."Is he your new boo, Mia?" A woman shouts over the noise.
"Sir, sir! Who is she to you?"
They are relentless.
Needing to get tomorrow's news story.
Without looking at the crowd around us, yelling and in a frenzy, he looks down at me and says loud enough for them to hear. "She's mine." He grins at me without looking their way and steals me away.
I'm his.
He's mine.
That's right.

CHAPTER FORTY-TWO

VOYEURISM & FETISHES

"You like a little pain with your fucking, Red?" - L

Cara

After Enzo whisked me away from the red carpet, we skipped the premiere and went straight to the after gala at the Kenton Hotel.

Everyone that's anyone in Hollywood is here. The elite of Hollywood, which gave Arielle the idea of making me rub elbows with well-known producers and big-time movie executives. For future projects Cara, she said.

I get it.

To make a name for yourself in this day and age, talent is no longer the main requirement. You have to put yourself out there and make connections. Basically kiss a lot of ass until you land a gig that makes you a breakout star. Putting the glass of champagne down on a tray, I shake hands with the Golden Cage CEO and excuse myself from the group, walking towards Draego, who's been standing like a renaissance statue in the far corner, watching out for any threats. The way he is dressed helps him blend in with the security here. I get why Enzo felt the need to bring Draego as backup, but I don't think the person who's out to hurt Enzo through me will make a move here with so many eyes around.

They would be an idiot to do it here. Looking around, I notice Enzo has left his spot on the other side of the huge room. Where did he run off to, I wonder. Once I'm close to Draego, I ask him where his boss is. We've only been here for half an hour, and I was itching to get away from the snooty people that were crowding me and celebrate this night with him.

Draego nods to the elevator. "He needed to make some calls. I presume he's in your suite."

I go in search of him with Draego at my back, taking the elevator until we reach our floor. Once I'm in front of room 666B, I look over my shoulder, not surprised at finding Draego already standing back with his hands behind his back where his gun is. He nods at me once, letting me know that no one will get through him. I believe him. He's young, but he's a tank. Turning the knob, I step inside the breathtaking suite. The Kenton Hotel is one of the most luxurious and expensive chains of hotels in not just the country but the world. The owners are a legacy of politicians who run not only the government but also dip their hands in all kinds of business. Legitimate and dirty. My brother says the Kenton family is just as crooked as any other mafia family. They just hide it better, using empty promises of a stronger country, better economy, and their good looks. Bastian Kenton is the current owner after his father passed away when he was just a young man. It made front-page news all over the country at the time, so I was told. Once inside the suite, I close the door softly behind me, leaving Draego outside guarding the door. Keeping us safe. I know Enzo doesn't need security, and the only reason why he brought Draego with us was as an extra precaution to keep me safe.

Looking around the room now that I'm not so busy with all the chaos and stress of glam and hair and all that goes with the red carpet prep, I can appreciate the room we're staying in.

This hotel is truly magnificent. It not only has a sophisticated and elegant vibe, but the decor is almost like we're staying at a palace.
Royalty is what comes to mind first.
The distinct sound of traffic and the smell of smoke give me a hint of where he is, and as soon as I turn left and find the balcony doors wide open.
There he is.
Leaning against the railing, smoking a cigarette while looking into the night. I make no noise and stand back, appreciating the most perfect view, and I don't mean the city before us.
Him.
"Get a good look, Red?" A hint of humor coats his tone.
Stepping outside, I join him on the balcony, suddenly nervous that we're so high up. Christ, I get dizzy just by leaning forward and looking down. Turning toward Enzo, anxiety leaves me. "You look so handsome tonight." I tell him now that we're alone. I didn't have the chance to tell him before. "Thank y—"
Cigarette between his lips, he pulls me closer to his body, by the back of the neck. The scent of his cologne and cigarette hits me, making me weak in the knees. "You're happy?"
It's twice now that he's asked me that.
The answer will be the same as long as he's with me. Where he's supposed to be. Leaning into him, "I'm always the happiest when I'm with you." Gently nibbling on his bottom lip, I whisper, not caring that I sound vulnerable. Enzo has never made me feel stupid or less for expressing my feelings, not even when we were younger, and he didn't know exactly what to do with them. "You just claimed me in front of the world, you know." I joke. Still in awe of him. Of what he did. A boss. A criminal, to some. A ruthless bastard in his circle, but outside of Detroit he's going to be known as mine.

"You're so whipped for me."
"Shut the fuck up and kiss me." His eyes flash with hunger and madness."Gladly."
Rising on my tippy toes, I grab his face in both my hands and take his soft lips in mine.
What starts as a sensual kiss becomes a clash of power where we both fight for control.
He kisses me deeply, possessively, tightening his hand around my neck. Breaking the kiss, he keeps a hold of my neck as he says. "I've been thinking about this fucking dress all night," His eyes dip down over my body slowly before going back to my face. "The assholes around you couldn't look away from your body, little monster, and it drives me mad that they'll go back to their wives tonight, and while their cocks sink inside them, they'll be imagining it is you they're fucking."
"They can imagine all they want, king." Cupping his strong jaw, holding his gaze. "I'm only yours."
"Fuck, yeah, you are." With that, he turns me around until my belly is pressed against the railing, and he presses his front to my back, allowing me to feel the ridge of his cock through his suit pants while at the same time, keeping a safe hold on me, so that I don't feel nervous being this close to the edge.
Not when I have him at my back.
Just like every time we touch, everything else ceases to exist. I feel Enzo's strong hands unzip the back of my dress until it falls like a black blanket down my legs, leaving me in only a tiny thong. Thank God we are concealed by darkness.
"Show me how to love, Red." He whispers in my ears while pressing himself deeper into me. The cold air hits my face, but I don't even feel it because of the heat of his touch and the warmth of his soft whispered words.
My heart stops at the same moment his hands freeze at my back. I don't think he realized he just said that. The magnitude of what he just said to me.

Love.
Show me how to love.
Silly man, you already do.
I try to turn around to face him, but he keeps me in place with one hand on my naked waist while the other snakes around my torso, grabbing hold of my gold necklace, pulling on it gently until our bodies are so close that I don't even know where I end and he begins.
This close, I can actually feel the beat of his heart racing a mile a minute.
"Enzo." I whisper into the cold night.
"Mmm?" I shiver, not from the cold, but from the feel of his light stubble tickling the side of my neck as he slowly trails soft kisses on my skin before biting down hard, right where my pulse is, then gently lapping at the spot he just brutalized with his teeth.
Hissing in both pleasure and pain, "Fuck me." My hands leave the railing, and I rub his hard length through his pants, making him hiss in pleasure as well. Christ, the sounds he makes drive me wild. "Get inside me and show me exactly how you love. Wild. Feral. Without limits."
"You want my cock in your pussy, baby? Right here, where the civilians below us might hear you scream as I pound that tight little hole?"
"Yes. God, yes."
Feeling the hand that was playing with my necklace slowly moves down my front until he touches me where I want him—no, need him— the most. Enzo gives me no room to catch my breath and roughly pulls my panties aside so hard that he rips the thin material.
He groans when his fingers touch my wet pussy lips and then laughs darkly, sending sparks through my body. "That turns you on, little monster? The idea that someone might hear how good I fuck this pretty little pussy?"

He slaps me between the legs, and the sound of his palm hitting my wetness only makes him hit me harder there.
Oh, fuck.
A thousand nights would never be enough for Enzo to show me every delicious thing he can do to my body and my soul. I crave forever with him.
I just hope he wants that, too.
Arching my back, I push my ass closer to his groin, causing another groan of pleasure to escape those perfect lips of his. At the same time, he shoves two fingers inside me, making me whimper his name for only his ears.
"Good girl, such a good fucking girl for me, yeah?" I nod while biting down so hard on my lower lip that I can taste blood. My breath quickens, at the same speed as his fingers fuck me. A swell of heat spreads inside me, blooming into a raging fire so intense it makes my pulse flutter.
How ironic that, once, Enzo's skin felt so cold, and now, all I feel when I'm with him is an untamable fire that makes my skin heat with buzzing energy.
Explosive.
Intense.
Wild.
Raw.
Him and I.
Are addictive.
An addiction I cannot and will not ever control.
It is also obsessive and maddening.
He quickens his pace as he finger-fucks me. "Oh, God."
"I like that, Red."
"What?" The pleasure is so intense that I barely register what he says. Holding onto him tighter, I cannot control the need to come apart in his arms. His expert fingers touch the right spot inside me. The spot that weakens my knees and makes my pussy ache for a release.

"You, referring to me as God." He laughs softly when my pussy tightens around his thick fingers, and when I feel the sting of his teeth sinking into the delicate skin of my neck, I cum, cursing and moaning out his name for everyone who is near to hear.
I do it without shame, too.
With reckless abandon.
God.
King.
He is all of that and more.
So much more.

CHAPTER FORTY-THREE

BURNING DESIRE

"Her pussy is the happiest place on Earth." - L

Fuck. *Lorenzo*

I've never seen something more beautiful than Mia's pale, naked skin on full display for any sick motherfucker who might be creeping in the shadows to see.

I've fucked a lot of women.

In all kinds of places in all their holes, but this.

This, right here.

Feels, in some sick as fuck way, intimate.

Real.

"You damn well know there's nothing holy about you." Her voice drips with sarcasm and desire, her raspy tone making me want to shove my cock so far down her throat that she'll feel me there for days to come.

I don't need to see her face to witness the warmth of her smile.

That laugh.

That fucking laugh covers me in fucking sunshine in the middle of a cold night.

That's the little monster's effect on me.

That's what she's always done for me.

When things get really fucking dark, my thoughts wander to her, and I no longer feel so damn cold. The nights didn't feel so lonely because at least I had that. Her laugh tortured my thoughts and, at the same time, gave me comfort when I missed her the most.

On those nights, she was more of the world and not mine.

"I should punish that bratty mouth of yours." I nip her neck right where her pulse is, then I lick her, savoring the taste of her.

Sweet all over, my Red.

"You love my mouth, don't deny it." She whispers breathlessly. I do love her bratty mouth.

I'm obsessed with the way Mia never backs down and how she challenges me. Everyone before her is nothing but a blur. A lapse in time. Not worth remembering, and it's all because they didn't stand up for themselves. They pleased me but never took what they wanted.

What they craved deep down was just to keep me happy.

Mia gives as good as she takes.

And she's right.

I'm obsessed with that mouth.

I like tasting it.

Kissing it.

Punishing it, preferably with it wrapped around my dick, as I savagely fuck it.

Yeah, I'm in awe of those cherry lips.

Just like the ones between her creamy thighs.

I'm especially fond of those.

I show her just how much I like her pussy lips when I slap them hard, and she throws her head back and laughs harder, the musical sound alive with relief and breathy with need.

The best sound in this entire goddamn world.

Her laugh.

I've never believed in love at first sight. And hell, I still think it's bullshit, but something I do know is that the night I stepped foot in her family's garden and saw her pretty face bloated from crying and all that wet red hair resembling blood, I knew.

Something changed inside.

The fact that I wasn't able to understand feelings didn't mean I didn't feel them.

I did.

I felt for the first time in all my life.

That night I first saw her.

Sometimes, when I think about when I started living and not just existing, I know the truth.

It all started with a red-haired monster, and it also ends with her. Gripping her hair, I pull her head all the way back until it is resting on my shoulder. "So fucking beautiful, Red. So mine."

She was perfect. So painfully insanely gorgeous.

I gently bend her over the railing until her plump ass is perfectly aligned with my hard cock. The moment she's completely bent at my mercy, she cries out my name. What a needy little bitch my Mia is.

Such a good girl.

Such a dirty slut for me.

I quickly zip down my pants and take my dick out. The throbbing stiffness demanded he do dirty, dirty things to her body. "Hold your ass cheeks open for me." Poised between her thighs, hard and thick and pulsing with eagerness, I watch as she does what she's told, and then I line myself up and drop down enough to spit on her tight little holes.

Both of them.

Her tight little asshole and her pretty pink cunt.

I've never felt this out of control.

This famished.

I tease her clit with the head of my cock. The sound of her begging is fucking music to my ears. I rub her clit back and forth, the wetness coating my dick. "How badly do you want this cock, baby?" She purrs like a kitten every time the head of my cock slaps her clit hard.

Then, I go lower, teasing the warmth of her pussy, the wetness even thicker down there. I give her just the tip, inserting the blunt head into that tight dripping cunt. Fuuuck.

Heaven. This might be the only time I ever experience heaven. There's no way the pearly gates will ever open for me, but at least I have this.

Because every time Red opens her legs and lets me in, I see heaven and all the holy religious shit cunts preach about.

"How badly?" I freeze, denying her pleasure until I get my answer.

Her nails stab the back of my thighs.

I'm so worked up that my cock is fucking throbbing for her pussy.

"I need you."

And that's all it takes for me to give into her.

Without giving her time to adjust to my size, I push, sinking inside her body, stroking my tongue into her wet mouth, and burying my cock to the hilt.

Pulling her hair and gripping her hip so tightly that there's no doubt that tomorrow there'll be a bruise I fuck her so hard that I already feel the need to burst inside her cunt creeping in.

"Enzo! Oh, fuck! Yes!"

I fuck her ruthlessly, without mercy, as I pull her hair hard. Instead of hissing in pain, she moans loud in pleasure. Pain. She gets off on it. "I want you to scream as you come." I never look away from her ass as I stretch her and fill her so full and deep that she has no time to brace herself when her first orgasm hits. I watch her mesmerize as she explodes around my cock, screaming my name so goddamn loud and pushing me to join her.

Over the next couple of hours, I take my time with her, exploring her body, worshiping her curves, and pumping my seed in all her holes.

I taker her like I own her, and with every kiss, she freely gives into me.

So fucking sweet, my Red, even when she's horny for my cock. After fucking her every hole, I find my release in her ass, my cock buried deep. My eyes jam shut against the violent spurts of my climax. Seconds later, she joins me, moaning through yet another orgasm.

 I lost count of how many she's had.

I lift her body all the way up so that we are both facing the same way, looking straight ahead. Her, with her wild hair blowing in the cold air, with my arms covering her nakedness, breathing heavily and trying to catch her breath.

This high up with the girl who made my dead heart her home, I feel on top of the world.

The view is breathtaking.

Not the city lights.

Her.

Red.

"Enzo?"

Lowering my face against the top of her head, I inhale her scent. "What?"

"No one has ever done it like you…" she whispers as we both look around the dark night.

Somehow, I don't need to ask her what she means by 'done it'. My early words come back to me. Show me how to love, I asked her. Fuck if I know where that came from, but I don't take it back.

I won't ever take back my word or any promise.

No one has ever done it like you.

Love her.

My twin's words hit me full force.

Every broken and ugly part of me is hers.

Without saying anything, I pick her up and carry her inside, suddenly needing to be inside her heat again.

***

Hours later, I lay in bed, staring into Mia's sleepy blue eyes, fighting sleep. Such an exquisite creature. Rebellious. Fearless. Sensual.

A beauty quite like no other, who radiates warmth like I've never known before.

Ghosting my tattooed index finger along the outer curve of her breast, savoring the purring noises each caress draws from her red lips. Every touch makes me feel like I don't ever want to part from her body. From any part of her.

I want to infiltrate her brilliant mind. Her sweetheart and her dark soul. I never want to leave.

After I took her on the balcony, I took her against the cold shower wall while I washed our bodies and two more times on this bed. Every single time, unprotected.

I've never fucked a bitch without protection.

Never wanted to.

Still, I couldn't stop making contact with her.

Still, I didn't cover my dick for her.

I savored every second of spilling my cum on her belly, pussy lips, and perfect tits.

Fuck, she even swallowed.

She's different.

She's the one.

Maybe that's why a future with her doesn't seem so bleak.

Mundane.

Because she's anything but.

She is a dream.

I never had much of those growing up.

Now I do, and in every single one, she's the main attraction. She spent the last couple of hours talking my ear off just like she did when she was a child and we would hide away in her tree house. She asked me about the crimes I have committed and I told her, not holding anything back.

She listened without judgment and even asked me to describe some of my kills in graphic detail.

I always knew there was something off about Cara Mia Volpe. Something dark lurking in all that warm beauty.

Most would think it was passed down to her by her cunt of a father, but I don't believe that. Her darkness is morbid curiosity, not the darkness that craves blood and mayhem.

She was bound to be a little fucked up.

She's both Italian and Russian.

Her cousins are some of the most bloodthirsty motherfuckers I've ever met.

It runs in her veins, and yet she's never hurt a soul.

She might be a little bit off her rocker sometimes, but she's also pure in my eyes.

I've placed her on an untouchable pedestal since the first time I heard her speak, and there's nothing she can do that will knock her down from that high place.

My phone beeps from the nightstand where it has laid all night. Untangling my left arm from Mia's body without waking her up, I grab it and unlock it. My blood pressure rises the moment I see a text from an unknown number.

Someone captured us while we were outside on the balcony. The picture is blurry, hinting at someone taking it from a distance, and the faces are unrecognizable thanks to the darkness surrounding us.

Three dots appear as the person types a message.

Holding the rage, I wait for it to arrive.

Unknown: She looks so pretty when she comes undone.

Unknown: Makes you wonder if she will look the same when she cries…

Motherfucker.

I've never felt this helpless. Being threatened by a ghost is not something I ever faced before.

It's a cowardly move.

Throwing the phone down on the pillow, I get out of bed so fast that I startle Mia awake. Her confused eyes find mine in the dark as I hurry to get dressed.

I'm done playing this cowardly bitch's game.

I'm not waiting for him to attack me while I'm outside of my territory, unprotected. I gave into Mia's wish to have this night, but now we're going home.

"Get dressed. We're going home."

She doesn't ask.

The tone of my voice lets her know something is going down.

Twenty minutes later, the three of us are checking out of the Kenton hotel and ready to go back to Detroit.

If the motherfucker wants to attack me, then he'll have to do it in my home base.

CHAPTER FORTY-FOUR

DOWNFALL

"The shadows made me." - Da

Lorenzo

I need to get the hell out of this city.

Every second I spend outside of my Detroit, she's vulnerable. After checking in with my brother, and Cassius, they both reassured me that everything was fine on their end, but there's this annoying knot on my stomach that tells me something is going down.

The worst part of having a ghost as an enemy is you can't anticipate their next move since you have no fucking clue the game they're playing.

By the threatening notes, it's clear the motherfucker enjoys mind games. I love those two. In fact, they're my favorite, which tells me the asshole has done his homework. He knew which button to push to make me lose it.

Mia.

For years, I've been careful to not let it show how she's my one and only weakness. I've watched her from afar and limited my contact with her, but somehow the fucker put two and two together and pieced my puzzle.

I've thought myself invisible for years, or tried to convince myself, but the truth is she's the one thing that hurts.

It's a hard pill to swallow that I'm just like any other mortal man. A woman is my Achilles' heel.

I made it possible for her to celebrate her success without the threat getting to her, but now it's time to go back.
Back to my city.
My family.
Where my word is law.
I have zero connections here in Los Angeles except the French fuck, and there's no chance in hell I'll ever ask him for anything after I threatened the bitch if I ever saw him back in Detroit. Volpe might love his rendezvous with Dionysius Arnault, but I don't. Not after learning he's been in bed with not only the Russians but the boss of Chicago for years. One thing I learned is that you can never trust community pussy, and that's exactly what Arnault is.
"I'm fine. Yes. We're on our way back to Detroit." Mia whispers from her seat next to me in the car while Draego is behind the wheel.
Her delicate fingers interlocked with mine, trying to provide me with comfort. Bless her too-nice-for-this-shitty-world heart.
"We're on our way to the jet." I typed a quick message to my brother and hit send. Nothing. He hasn't answered a single phone call or text since I called to warn him about the asshole who's after us. He's my twin, after all, my blood, and that makes him and Andrea a target, as well.
Fuck.
Mia pulls me out of my thoughts by shoving her phone in my face. "My brother wants to talk to you." She smiles softly, not a single worry in her mind. It's both the biggest compliment and burden to have her full faith in me. Taking her phone, I hit the end button, dismissing her brother. I don't have the mind or the patience to deal with his empty threats.
"Hey! That's rude."
"I think we've established I don't really care for manners, Red."

She rolls her eyes and laughs at the same time as the car stops in the middle of a private hangar, where our family's private jet is waiting for us to board. The growing knot in my stomach gets worse the moment Draego turns off the engine and steps outside the vehicle.

Shaking it off, I turn to Mia and hold her small face in mine. "You're mine."

"I know." She nods, her intoxicating scent all over me.

"You're mine." I tell her again, this time placing a quick kiss on her lips. "And I protect what's mine."

"I trust you."

Not even that makes the eerie feeling go away. Shit.

Looking over my shoulder out the car window, I watch as Draego hands our bags to the jet's staff. My phone rings, and the screen says my brother is calling. Finally.

"Where the fuck have you been? I've been trying to reach—" Tino cuts me off, and what he says next makes my blood boil and fear take root in my soul. "Some fuck tried to snatch my girl. For a fucking hour, I couldn't reach my wife and my daughter." Tino seethes through the phone, but I don't hear anything after 'I couldn't reach my wife and daughter'.

Poe.

Fallon.

My family.

"Are they okay?"

I try to keep my head straight.

"They are now. They weren't hurt. The sick son of a bitch wanted to send a message, and he did."

"Get to the mansion. You'll be safe there. Don't fucking move. I'll be there soon." I hung up on him, pocketing my phone.

"What's wrong?" The nerves are evident in her tone.

"Let's get out of here." I release Mia's hand and step outside the car, hurrying to her, opening the door, and helping her out. The moment she's in my arms, all hell breaks loose.

Rounds of bullets shoot out, hitting the van. I tackle Mia to the ground and cover her with my body as we both hear the loud noise of semi automatics going off all around us.
Mia screams when a bullet hits the car just above where we're cowering.
Using my body as a shield to protect her, I look around and spot a tinted-glass van parked twenty feet away from ours and three men wearing black stepping out of it, on their way to us.
Motherfucker.
Then, I look under the van and catch the precise moment a bullet hits Draego, knocking him to the floor before he has the chance to get his gun out. Blood stains his light gray shirt.
This is all my fucking fault.
I shouldn't have been so reckless and brought more men with me.
I should've left the kid at home.
He's my best man and a good… friend.
Guilt overtakes me, and fuck, do I hate it.
Knowing what I have to do, I tear my gaze away from Draego and look at Mia's terrified blue gaze. "Listen to me baby. When I count to three, I'll lift you, and I need you to get in the driver's side and get the fuck out of here. You keep driving and don't you dare stop, you hear me? You drive until you're far away from here, and from the van's phone, I need you to call your brother, yes?"
"I'm not leaving you."
"Oh, yes, the fuck you are."
"No. This is not how we're doing things, remember?"
Tears are running down her beautiful face now, and for the first time in my life, I feel my heart breaking. She sounds so sad and so damn scared for me.
I make her look at me in the middle of this chaos and do what I never thought I would.

I make her a promise.

"I'll find you. I'll always find you, but I need you to get out of here." Pulling her face closer to mine, I whisper while inhaling the sweet scent of her hair. "I need you to trust me."

Two more rounds of fire are heard, and then the jet bursts into flames.

"You come back to me." Her trembling hands pull on my shirt, while she takes my lips in hers. I savor her kiss, knowing it won't be the last.

But we're wasting too much fucking time.

I break the kiss and count to three.

"One."

"Two."

"Three."

I rise from the ground with her in my arms and stumble when the burning sting of a bullet cuts through my skin. Gritting my teeth, I suck in the pain and don't let it show. The moment she knows I'm hurt, she'll stay, and I need her gone. I need her safe.

More bullets pass us while I'm exposed. I realize the gunmen are not aiming to kill. Not us, at least.

It's an intimidation tactic, one that is seriously pissing me off. I pull the passenger door open and drop Mia inside, shutting the door in her face, still covering her from the line of fire.

Another bullet grazes my thigh from the back, making me stumble a little, yet I don't fall. She can't see. I move to the driver's side and grab my gun from beneath the seat where I hid it after we left the hotel.

Turning around, I shoot at the bastards trying to hold them off. I keep shooting while turning my head her way. "Now. Leave!" I shout, making sure she understands what I'm saying through the closed window. Her teary eyes blink rapidly, and it's a picture I don't ever want to see again. Her tears have always bothered me, but it cuts me even deeper now.

Her tears hurt more than the bullets on my skin.
A second later, she's turning the engine on and driving away from the men shooting at her while trailing behind her in their van. Goddammit. They'll reach her.
I look at Draego, unresponsive on the floor, and make a choice.
Raising my gun, I empty it toward the bastard's van. I aim for their tires, trying to slow them down so Mia can get away.
Several bullets come my way, and I dodge most of them, but some of them hit me, making me fall to the ground in pain. Fuuuck.
They're not aiming to kill me, which is off, but they're trying to stop me from keeping her safe. I try to get up from my knees, but I fail. The pain is too great, but I still don't give up. I get up, hissing in pain, trying to walk in the direction the bastards are driving away until my knees give out, and I fall with a hard thump.
I watch with my heart in my throat as the fucker drives his van straight to her, impacting her.
"Nooooo!" I grind out while I desperately crawl their way, knowing it's useless. "Mia!" I shout, but she can't hear me. Both vans are too far away. "Mia." I whisper again, already dizzy from the blood loss.
Goddammit.
This is my failure.
The image of her being grabbed from the van by the gunman, kicking and screaming my name, will haunt me for the rest of my life.
I never had dreams until her.
I also never had nightmares.
This moment right here is the worst of them all.
"Get up! Oh, God. Please! Let me go!" I hear from a distance, and then nothing.
She's gone.

She's fucking gone.

The fucker shoves her inside his van and drives off to God-knows-where with my heart in his passenger seat.

Breathing through the pain on my side and left thigh, I turn onto my back and try to keep my eyes open.

Get up motherfucker, get up.

A buzzing sound from my pocket. My phone. I have it on me. Shoving my hand inside my pocket, I retrieve it and quickly answer the phone, not looking at the caller ID.

Once the call connects, the mocking laugh of a man rings out.

"Well, well, how the mighty Don of the three famiglia of Detroit has fallen, and how beautifully he bleeds…"

Don.

Not even the title of Don could keep this from happening.

"I want her back, motherfucker. I want her back in one piece, and I swear if you dare to even lay a hand on her, I'll—"

"Oh, please, do tell." The bastard sounds young, and his voice triggers a memory deep inside me, but I can't place it. It's like I know the bitch, but I can't figure out how. This is a game to him. Coughing up blood, I say, "I'll skin you alive."

"That sounds…fun." The man on the other side of the line chuckles. "But you'll have to find me first. Now, be a good boy and don't die. I'm not done playing yet. Come and get her before I see for myself if she bleeds as beautifully as you."

"You listen to me, you sick fuck."

"Tsk, tsk. Time's a-wastin.'" He laughs some more before his tone turns deadly." Hard. Cruel. Empty. "Lorenzo Nicolasi."

The line goes dead, and a second later, so do I.

CHAPTER FORTY-FIVE

FALLEN PRINCE

"You are my heartbeat." - L

Cara

Shots flying everywhere.
The aircraft caught fire.
A loud grunt of pain before Draego fell to the ground with a bullet to his neck.
The image of Enzo asking me to run and leave him behind flashes through my mind.
Me behind the wheel, trying to get to safety so I can get help and come back for him. A black van came towards me and hit me until I crashed. Fighting, screaming, and then a gun to the back of the head, and everything went black. A car door closes, startling me awake. A seed of pain sits on the side of my head but quickly blooms, spreading, and searing across my skull as I grunt. I try to open my eyes and notice my surroundings. Everything is a bit blurry as I fight nausea and manage to get a better view. "What the hell?" I blink a couple of times, putting my hand to the sore spot above my temple and hissing when I notice the blood, "Ahhh. Shit."
"Get the fuck out, princess." The gunman who took me stands outside the passenger door, hauling me out of the car so harshly that I stumble, not able to catch my balance, and fall to the hard ground.

Asshole. I think to myself, not wanting to piss him off more than I already did by scratching his face off.
"Where am I?"
"Hell on earth, sweetheart." His mocking tone irks me, making me wish I had my stiletto shoes so I could shove the sharp heel up his pompous ass. I didn't have time to put my shoes back on when Enzo hauled me out of the van to get to the jet. I'm barefoot and defenseless. "Have fun." The gunman dressed in all black and with his face covered says before climbing inside the van and leaving me to my fate.
For the first time in a long time, I'm scared out of my mind, even if, on the outside, I don't show it. My sister used to tell me to never let an enemy see me scared because they'll know they won.
Flashes of Enzo getting shot repeatedly flood my mind as a painful reminder that he's not here. I don't feel as brave, knowing that he could be bleeding out without anyone to offer him help.
I cry out when I think about a world where he's not in it. The pain is greater than my fear. Pushing through it, I get up from the floor and take in my surroundings. I need to get back to him, or at least make it through whatever awaits me here until he can find me.
"I'll find you, Red."
I know.
He fought the pain of the bullets and got up every time he was shot and fell. The bullets couldn't keep him down for long until his knees gave out, and his beautiful face twisted in pain.
Focus, Cara.
The first thing I notice is the sunset.
Night will be falling soon.
Then, I see the shipment boats and the sparkly water under the dock.

The jackass left me stranded on what appears to be an abandoned port. "I'm glad you could join me." I hear the emotionless tone from behind me, and I jerk around.

A tall man stands on the other side of the dock with a poker face, his broad arms crossed over his chest, and his dark eyes fixed on me. He's dressed in black pants, and a black button-down is loosely tucked in and open at the collar, revealing a silver chain around his neck. Where have I seen that before? Not being able to recall where I've seen the chain before, I move on to his hair. It's light brown, so light that it might look blond if the sun hits it.

His eyes, light gray like an angry storm, zoned in on me, alert and curious. His face is what keeps me looking more than once. I know that face. I see pieces of him in the man I love most. The strong jaw and straight nose. Full bottom lip, and that dimple on just one cheek.

He looks eerily similar to Lorenzo, Valentino, and of course, the man who sired them… Cassius.

I'm taken back by the realization that what he's wearing on his neck is the Nicolasi chain. The one handed down generations from fathers to their sons once they become made.

My brother used to wear the one our father gave him once he was old enough to become made. After Lucan murdered our father, he stopped wearing it and even went as far as to make one of his own with a new symbolism that he handed down to his first-born son.

"Who are you?" I nervously step forward, wanting to get a better view of the man. At first glance, you would be blinded by his rugged, good looks and sculpted face. You wouldn't believe him to be dangerous until you look straight into those stormy eyes. A million emotions swirl in them, none of them good. My eyes trail down to his hands and notice there's no gun or knife in them. I look around to notice there aren't any gunmen creeping in the shadows, ready to attack.

It's just us.

"Who am I?" his eyes leave me and find the water. A faraway look crosses his eyes. Who is this person, and why the hell did he bring me here? "Do you know who you are, Cara Volpe?" The way he says my name feels off.

I don't cower, no. I face him head-on.

"I do."

"And who are you? Please, enlighten me." There's no hint of mockery or sarcasm in his tone, just genuine curiosity. This feels weird. I don't want to entertain this stranger and his delusion, but I also don't want to set him off. He doesn't look all that stable. Not even thinking, I answer.

I've been struggling with my identity my entire life, lately more so after finding out where I came from.

In finding out where I came from, I discovered where I'm going. I don't regret a single second of my life. Not one single instant because it all led me to this moment in time where my siblings are living their own lives without the chains of a crime family holding them back, and I get to live my dreams and love who I want. No arranged marriages. No relationships of convenience to strengthen the Volpe name.

No.

Okay, maybe not this moment in time since right now Enzo is God-knows-where and hurt, and I'm here alone at the mercy of this strange man.

"I'm just me. I'm a sister, an aunt, and a woman who loves deeply and is loved the same way." I look at his profile while he stares absently at the water ahead. "My accomplishments and dreams mean a lot to me, but they're not who I am. I am the moments I spend on this earth with the ones I care for the most."

I think of my mother, Natalia, and how she loved so deeply that it cost her… her life.

I think of Darya Solonik, my biological mother,

and how she couldn't live the life she dreamed of because of my father's selfish vile acts.

I think of every moment that means something to me and keep them close to my heart. I am those moments. I am just me.

"How does that feel?"

"What?" I ask, confused.

"How does it feel to be loved?" The man asks while looking my way, the faraway look is gone, and in its place, there's a darkness I've never seen before. Not even in the darkest man I know. Enzo.

Managing to not stumble on my words, I reply. "It feels like coming home."

"Huh." The soft whispers are long gone, and his tone becomes harsher, dark. "You look just like her," he says in an eerily calm tone. It's not a compliment since he frowns when he says it, and his eyes flash with anger. I could go as far as saying it looks more like hatred than anger.

The man walks closer to me, and it takes everything for me not to take two steps back. I hold my ground. His mood swings are giving me whiplash, and the reality of my predicament slowly starts to sink in. Enzo might not find me for a while, and I don't know this man's intentions. I can't read him like I do everyone else.

So, I stall because it has worked for me before. Although I might not get out of this one unscathed, I can still prolong the outcome.

"Who's her?" Twice I've been told that I look like someone else. First Darya, and now whoever the woman is that put demons in this man's eyes.

There's an air of tragedy surrounding this man. Just as intense as the darkness that covers him like a cloak.

"Do you like fairy tales, Cara?" Again, the way he says my name as if he can't stand it causes a shiver to run through me.

A warning.

Without looking away from those intense gray eyes, I answer. "No, not really. I'm more of a comic type of girl."

"I can see why he's so fond of you." He murmurs dryly while tucking both hands inside his pants pockets. "Which comes as a surprise since men like us don't tend to get nice things in life."

Men like them?

"You know nothing about him."

"Oh, but that's where you're wrong, sweetheart." The man takes a step closer. "I know everything about the almighty capo of Detroit city." He laughs for the first time since he appeared, but it doesn't reach his eyes. It's automatic. Laughing.

Capo.

He said Capo.

So Enzo was chosen.

Then, I think back to the stormy night back at his mansion, where he confessed that he got what he wanted.

Happiness takes over me. He did it. He's the boss of Detroit city. He beat out his opponents, like I knew he would. There was never a doubt in my mind that he wouldn't accomplish it. No one loves mayhem more than he does. Everyone else needed that title for survival.

Enzo wanted it because it's in his blood.

At the top is where he was meant to be since the day he was born. Everyone that comes across him sees it.

He's not ordinary.

He was meant for greatness.

And he did it.

My heart aches, though.

For the Parisi sisters.

Lorenzo might've wanted it more, but Kadra needed it.

"I never did believe in fairytales." He laughs softly, still looking down at the water as if I'm not here.

I look around, and there's nothing but silence. Only the wind blowing and the soft movement of the water below. No one is here to save me but myself. Where are you, king? "I never got the chance to believe in anything but in myself. I learned how it felt to hurt before anything else. I was in pain every hour of every day until I was strong enough to stop it, but by then, it was too late. Now, I feel nothing." I watch as he lifts his left hand and gently touches his chest right where his heart beats. "Nothing here."

Heartless.

I don't say anything because what is there to say? It's more than obvious he could care less what I have to say.

"Do you enjoy the sun?"

What an odd thing to ask in this situation.

He's not okay.

Not crazy like Enzo, but much worse.

He's… broken.

"I like it as much as any other person, I guess."

"The first time I ever saw the sun, daylight, I was ten years old. I basked in it, feeling it warm my bones and frail body as I played with the decapitated head of the ones I loved most."

My breath hitches, and I freeze, staring straight at him. The empty look on his face is gone, and now there's a giddiness there. How can I feel afraid of and sad for this man at the same time?

The man turns my way with a small smile on his face. God, there's nothing there now. How is he able to switch emotions so fast and then completely close himself up?

"Ask me again."

A chill runs down my neck. "What?"

"Ask me who I am again."

Boom.

Boom.

I'm startled by the loud blasts going off around me.

Not the man, no.

He stays perfectly in place, smiling as we both watch explosion after explosion go off. All around us, there's only fire.

"W-who are you?" I ask, not wanting to trigger him. He's already lost it, though.

"Darius. My name is Darius, and this darling." He spreads his arms wide while looking at the inferno surrounding us. "It's what love feels like to me. Hell." He grins evilly at me, and I'm unable to catch my breath.

CHAPTER FORTY-SIX

HALF DEAD

"There's mothing I wouldn't do for him." - C

Lorenzo

"Aghhh." I'm brought to consciousness by someone picking and prodding at my wounds." When I grab the wrist of the fucker who's hovering over me blindly, they slap my hand away.

"Hold still or I'll leave you to die." When I open my eyes, I find a man I haven't had the displeasure of knowing personally, but I've heard of him. Everyone's heard of the cop-turned-murderer who served half his sentence, was miraculously pardoned, and now works for no other than the French fuck Arnault.

Arson West.

Nightshade.

If he's here with me, then that means his Fixer knows.

Oh, fucking great.

Arnault is going to use this favor against me until the day sweet death comes for me.

"Motherfucker." I grit out, looking down at his hands working to stitch me up. He's butchering me with a smug grin on his face. Asshole.

"I'm no doctor." He says in a giddy voice.

"No shit."

He purposely stabs me with the needle, causing me to jerk.

"Say thank you."
"Drop dead."
"Tsk. Tsk. So ungrateful. If it weren't for me, you and the kid would be roadkill by now." Arson mumbles while he finishes stitching me up and then moves on to bandage my left shoulder. Roadkill.
What went down today hits me full force.
The ambush.
Draego falling to the ground by a shot to the neck.
Mia's crying face when I told her to leave me behind.
The gunman manhandling her and then driving off with her.
I see red.
I push Arson's hands away, sit up in the cheap motel bed and look to the next bed, where I find a ghostly-looking Draego, looking my way, holding his phone toward me.
"Glad you're not dead, boss." Draego attempts to laugh, but it comes out as a wheezing, painful sound. "The asshole who took her sent directions while you were out of it."
I suppress the urge to break everything that's near me in an attempt to let out this debilitating rage. This feeling of dread that's taking over me every second Mia is away from me and at the mercy of some sick son of a bitch I don't know.
"Mia," I murmur to myself. "Fuck, please be alright." I rise from the bed, the adrenaline replacing the fear, allowing me to numb myself so I can get shit done.
I need to bottle down the feelings of fear and hopelessness because it's no good in this situation. So, I push the man who loves her to the background and allow the blood-thirsty beast to take charge.
I look Draego all over and make sure he's alright, but he's clearly in a lot of pain. A butch job from Arson won't do it. Turning to the ex-cop, "Take him to the nearest hospital and get him help."
"You don't give me orders, Nicolasi," Arson bites back.

I try again. "I'll owe you." Fuck me, but that was like swallowing gasoline. Love. This shit is love, undoubtedly. I'm willing to accept help from people I detest for her.

Dammit. "Boss, that won't be necessary." Draego wheezes in pain. "You need backup. I'll be f—."

"You're half dead, D. What use would you be to me? I need to get her out alive, and I won't be able to do that if I have to carry your dead weight." Draego doesn't take offense because he knows I'm right.

"He wants you to come alone."

"Of course, he does." I rise from the bed and turn to them. Draego is lying down on the bed with blood covering his neck and sweat dripping down his forehead while he shakes in place. The wound is infected.

That's obvious.

I give Arson a look that says to hurry the fuck up before Draego gets worse. I'll deal with this shit show after I get my woman. I find the bloody t-shirt I was wearing before and throw it over my head.

I'm wasting too much time.

"Here. He'll expect you to carry one with you, but just to be safe, take it." Turning, I find Arson standing tall and offering me his gun. Taking it off his hands, I nod and shove it under my shirt. Then he throws something my way, and I catch it, hissing out loud when I make a wrong movement. "You treat my baby right, and I better not find one single scratch on her."

Pocketing my phone, I look down at the keys in my hand and then at him as if he's lost his goddamn mind.

"My bike, fucker."

This keeps getting better and better.

I'll be indebted to these assholes for a long fucking time.

With a nod toward both of them, I turn and walk outside, kissing my mother's rosary as I go.

I'm not a man who prays.
But today, I do send a quick prayer, but not to God.
To her.
To my ma.
I kiss the rosary she gifted me and ask her to keep my girl safe until I get there.
Mounting the glossy black Aprilia RS 660, I start the engine and speed out of the motel's parking lot like a bat out of hell.
Not feeling the pain of my fresh gun wounds.
Not the fear of losing her.
Only the insatiable need to bleed the son of a bitch that was bold enough to come for my girl dry.
"Hold on, Red."

CHAPTER FORTY-SEVEN

MAD KING

"My soul was rotten long before I found you." – Da

D *Lorenzo*

oesn't take me long to find the location.

It's some sort of abandoned port where shipment boats are kept, from what I can tell. Turning the engine off, I climb off the bike and look around.

It's nighttime, and I'm unable to see clearly. The message said to come alone. I did.

I was not going to jeopardize Mia's life, so here I am.

I don't blink, forcing myself to go slowly, even though every muscle in my body wants to charge ahead, looking for her.

A Glock is tucked into my black pants, loaded with ten rounds, but I keet it hidden under my T-shirt. Chances are they'll see me before I see them, and I want to have the element of surprise.

Treading lightly and keeping my eyes open, I creep across the long stone pathway that leads into the dock. Something tells me she's being kept there.

A boom sounds from my left, soon followed by another loud noise coming from ahead. In an instant, the entire place is set on fire. Shit.

Hurrying my pace, I run directly to the dock. It's just a matter of time before firemen reach the scene.

Motherfucker.

He knows what he's doing.

I stop dead in my tracks when I reach the end of the long dock and find my heart in the arms of the one responsible for all this shit.

I pay him no mind at first. My eyes find her, making sure she's okay. The first thing I notice is that she's barefoot and bleeding from what I think is a head wound. There's dried blood on the side of her head.

I see blood.

On her.

"Here I thought you wouldn't make it." The dry voice comes from the dead man holding her by the throat.

"You wanted me. I came. Now, let her go."

"You. You. You." Cara whimpers when the son of a bitch yanks her hair roughly, keeping her in place. "The great Capo of Detroit city. Lorenzo Nicolasi, the spoiled little prince of Benedetto Nicolasi." He laughs harder. Before, there was no emotion in his face or in his tone, but now there's something there.

Resentment?

"You got a hard-on for me, is that it, pretty boy?" I shouldn't provoke him when he has her in his arms, but something tells me this bitch's emotions are where I need to hit him to make it hurt. Getting a better view of him now, I'm taken back when I see my father's face staring back at me.

What the fuck?

He must read the expression on my face because he smiles broadly, although it looks eerily familiar, and the smile doesn't reach his eyes.

Light brown, almost blonde hair.

The same shade as Cassius.

The same prominent bone structure.

Then something clicks.

"Who are you?"

"Oh, I'm so glad you asked. You know, I've been counting down the days so I can finally put a face to your name. The name that's been engraved in my brain since my-whore-of-a-mother first told me about the infamous Nicolasi family." His tone drips with hatred and sarcasm.

My guess was right, then.

This freak-show has a connection with my family.

Fucking Cassius and his demented offspring.

I step forward in their direction, but he takes another step back, pulling Mia with him. I catch her worried eyes looking down at the water below.

Then a thought occurs to me.

The water.

Good girl.

I look at the son of a bitch and change my tone from pissed to worried. I bet that's what he wants. To see me beg.

"Don't hurt her. She's never done anything to you. She doesn't know how to swim." I lie, hoping he buys this shit, but it's obvious he has been planning this for a while.

"No. She certainly has not, but she's the embodiment of everything I hate, and what a shame it would be if she were to slip and fall under." He smiles down at Mia while caressing her face.

Motherfucker.

I give in to what he clearly wants, instead of following my instinct and grabbing my girl before pulling my gun on him. I don't know if he's carrying, and from down here, it's not clear if he is or not.

Ignoring Mia, I focus on him instead. "Do I know you?"

"You don't."

"Then what's your beef with me? Did I fuck your bitch?"

Mia cringes, and her eyes narrow.

I ignore it, trying to make it out of this alive before we both die either by the fire or by this creep's hands.

"You did not." The asshole smiles as if I'm a child that amuses him.

Oh, what a pleasure it will be to wipe that grin off your face, bitch.

"Did I kill someone you cared about?"

His dead eyes tell me no.

"Then why do all this? Why not go after Cassius if you hate him so much? You thought going after me would hurt him? Hate to break it to you, love, but daddy and I aren't that close."

There.

A flash of something in his eyes.

So, Cassius it is.

"You know…" He clicks his tongue and continues. "For someone as lethal as people claim you to be, you're not very bright."

Now, the fucker is trying to get under my skin.

How cute.

He can insult me all he wants but never has a word done damage. They run through me because I never give them the power to hurt me in any way. This is child's play.

I look at him again and take him in. He's not as big as Cassius, even though he looks like a young replica of him.

Then, it clicks.

"Demetrio."

"Ding, ding, ding. It took you a moment to get there, but you did. Way-to-fucking-go." The asshole smiles. "You're not brain dead after all, cousin."

Cousin.

Demetrio's kid.

Bastard kid.

No one knew of this bastard, and if they did, no one talked about him. Never in all my years in the Nicolasi household was it mentioned that Uncle Demetrio had a son. Not like my sister.

Everyone knew about Andrea's existence.

Now it all makes sense.

The hatred in his eyes.

The envy in his tone.

A fallen prince.

A forgotten one, at that.

I was right when I thought the sick fuck had a hard-on, but not for me. Nah, for the Nicolasi name? The power it holds and the millions it comes with it.

Looking at Cara so calm without a trace of fear on her stunning face. I see it then. Her complete trust in me. She's not afraid because she knows there's no fucking way I'll let him hurt her in any way, not before dying first.

She walks out of here alive, even if it kills me.

I've never been afraid to die, but now standing here, looking at her so beautiful and so goddamn brave, I know the only fear I'll ever feel is of losing her.

Her indigo eyes find mine, and I tell her a million things with one look. Her eyes follow mine at the same time as I look down at the water.

I hope to fucking God she gets what I'm trying to tell her.

I need her in the water, so I can get her away from him.

I hold my rage and focus on taunting him.

"What is it then? You want a family reunion, cuz, or is this just a tantrum for not getting everything that in your head is your birthright? Huh?" I step farther into the dock and notice how his jaw ticks. Yeah, I hit a nerve. From the corner of my eye, I see the flames spreading faster all around us, trapping us. Shit. I slowly reach behind me for the gun, but as expected, the asshole notices.

I hoped he would.

"You really are a dumb fuck." The asshole laughs darkly, and yet he's never tried to hurt Mia. Not once. What the fuck is his angle?

"Put the gun down because there's no way you'll be able to shoot me without hurting her." I know that.

The moment I found her in his arms, I knew the gun I had brought with me was useless unless I got her away from him. I pull the gun from my back and place it down on the ground slowly. Mia trails my every move.

"Why are you doing this, Darius? For money, is that it?" Mia asks him without taking her eyes off me.

So, the asshole has a name. Darius.

Darius, the bastard son of Demetrio.

How…tragic for him.

Darius laughs without feeling. "That's what it all comes down to with you people, isn't it? Money. Power. How very… mundane. And no, sweetheart, I bled for everything I have. I don't need his money or his filthy name."

"Why do all this shit then?"

Darius smiles but it doesn't reach his eyes. "I wanted you to see."

"See what?"

"How easy it would be for me to take everything from you like your family took everything from me."

I try another tactic.

It is obvious that this bastard is ruled by emotions, and maybe I can use them against him. "We are your family." Fuck me. That left a bitter taste in my mouth.

"Oh, no." he laughs, and this time it reaches his eyes. This fuck is demented, and that's saying a lot coming from me. "You're nothing to me. Just like Demetrio was nothing. No one. Not even a memory. You see, Lorenzo, I was voiceless and unseen for half my life. I've lived in the shadows for so long that I don't even know what it feels like to bask in the light. Darkness is all I see. All I feel. I just wanted to see what it felt like."

"What?"

"To be seen, for once."

Oh, please. He did all this shit to be seen. This is definitely Demetrio's son. He was always a whiny little bitch and by the looks of it, the apple didn't fall that far from the tree.

"How does it feel then? I see you."

The smile falls from his face. "But do you really?"

He got me there. I could care less about this asshole, and maybe if he went after Valentino, he would've gotten a better outcome, but he chose the wrong twin. I won't ever feel for him because he severed any hope at a connection when he sent the first threat to my girl, and he made my shit list the second he got his hands on her.

My eyes follow his right hand as he gently caresses Mia's face. I hate the look of disgust she has on her face feeling his hands on her. The anger grows stronger with every second.

"What do you want, Darius?" Why do all he did just to get me here to find out about him if he didn't want anything in return? Then, I think about him messing with Tino's family, and that is the last nail in his coffin. "To be seen? I see you. I see a shitty version of the fucker who hurt innocent women. I see the same sad excuse of a soldier who cried like a little bitch because he lived in my father's shadow. That's all I see when I look at you. Nothing else." I grin, trying to drive the point home.

That does it.

He really does not want money or a position in his father's family. He just wanted to see who he could've been.

Me.

Someone like my brother and me.

We might not be the poster boys for a healthy and happy life, but we have everything most people dream of.

At least our father stuck around and gave us all he was able to at the time.

Demetrio never cared or bothered with his son.

Darius' eyes flair with anger, and a second later, with a sinister smile on his face, he pulls my girl's hair and pushes her into the water.
Good boy.
You're done.
He has to know this was a suicide mission for him.
He looks back at me expectantly, waiting for my next move.
But I wait for her.
For my monster.
In a heartbeat, a shot rings out in the night, and the sick bitch falls on the dock, gripping his left shoulder.
Mia.
Mia grabbed the gun as soon as she rose to the surface and didn't hesitate to shoot.
I told her once to shoot first, and I would handle the rest.
This is it.
I let go of the anger I've been holding back since stepping foot on this dock, and let it control me.
None of his men come out of the shadows to protect him when I tackle him to the ground, both falling hard with a grunt. I don't see his face when I plummet it. I only see and feel red. Red on my skin as my knuckles split his skin.
The only sounds I hear are the bones of his face breaking, the distant sound of sirens, and Mia's shout for me to stop.
I don't.
Darius' laugh breaks through the fog inside my head, and I focus on his face. His nose is broken. There are gashes on every single inch of his face and a busted lip bleeding rapidly, staining his teeth. "Finish it. I threatened her and took her from you." He shouts in my face. "Finish me!"
My throat tightens, and my heart hammers in my chest when I feel small hands gripping my injured shoulder. "There's something broken in him, baby. Don't give him what he wants. Don't end his life."

She caught it, too.

All of this.

All this fucker put her through.

All of it was a ruse to get me to end his miserable life.

Is he too much of a fucking pussy that he couldn't put a gun to his head and end it himself? I'll never know because I don't care to know.

"You really do look like her." Darius' eyes look behind me to where Mia is standing over us. There's so much hatred in his gray eyes. Mia's right. The fucker is not right in the read. He's too damaged. His emotions control him, and it is clear in the way his mood changes from unfeeling to angry to hysterical. He lived in the shadows, he said.

What kind of hell was he put through to make him this way?

"Who do I remind you of?" Mia whispers, and I detect a hint of pity in her voice. That's just like her to feel bad for the fucker who put her life at risk.

"My bitch of a mother." He laughs some more at the same time as he coughs up blood. "The same bloody red hair and doe-blue eyes." His gaze turns to me again, "I should've sliced her up like I did the other whore. They're all good for only one thing, you know. All useless whores." He's no longer talking about his mother but Mia.

The sirens sound closer now, and the fire is closing in.

"Baby, let's go." Mia's tone is urgent, trying to get me to release my demented cousin.

"You come near my family again, and I promise you, I'll fucking end you. The only reason I'm not killing you right now is because that's what you want. You want me to end your fucking misery. And a tip about me, cousin, I'm not a merciful man, so if you sought me out to finish the job for you, you failed miserably."

With that, I knock him the fuck out with one last punch to the face.

Rising from my haunches, I leave him passed out on the ground and turn to face Mia, who's looking down at Darius with tears in her eyes.

"Do not cry for him, Red." I look at her face smeared in blood with remains of ashes from the chaos all around us. Her breath hitches when I wipe away the tears as they fall out of her glossy blue eyes. Those damn tears, how much I hate them. They torment me. One tear falling from her eye has the power to make me go off the deep end and annihilate whatever it was that put tears in those baby blues.

The thing is that I'm not able to control her kind heart.

She cries for a man she doesn't know.

A man who threatened not only her life but the lives of the people she cares about, yet she feels empathy for him. For the cousin I never knew about and a man who has a lot of blood-thirsty demons in his eyes.

"I just—" She takes a deep breath and shakes it off. "I just see the same heartbreaking sadness in his eyes that I once saw in my brother. The tragedy and the pain, it was all there."

Looking down at her, I take her face in my hands, wanting to capture her this way forever. Even with dirt and blood on her face, she still looks like the most beautiful creature I've ever laid my eyes on.

She looks like mine.

"I-I love you." Her sultry— yet innocent at the same time— voice breaks through the comforting rage inside my brain. The gentle sound of her voice breaks through the dark thoughts that fuel me. The dark thoughts that feed the blood-thirsty animal inside of me. I haven't said it.

I know she says she doesn't need the words, but I do. I need her to hear me say it. "I won't ever be like him." I won't. It is not humanly possible for me to be like the man she loves and admires the most.

I don't function that way.

"Not like your little friend or like your saint of a brother."

She sighs, "I don't need someone like them. I just need you." She smiles up at me, and in the middle of all this chaos, with her looking up at me with so much love and trust, I've never felt more at home. How pretty she looks, covered in red and surrounded by flames.

Little monster.

"I'm not a poetic soul, nor do I have a tender heart. My heart is black, and my love is dark, sick, and twisted. There's no other way for me. I'm not built like him. I detest emotions, and nothing in this fucked-up world had the power to invoke them within me until you. I didn't understand the depth of what I feel for you, devil. Not until it was too late."

She gasps as a loud explosion sounds from our right. "Say it." She sounds so vulnerable, yet so strong. My brave girl, with a heart of gold and a mind of fucking steel. My bleeding red heart.

"I think I loved you the first night I saw you, covered in dirt and tears pooling in your beautiful blue eyes. You made me your bitch, and I haven't stopped loving you since. This sickness that is my love for you will always be."

"Good. Because I'm sick with love for you, too." I grab the back of her head and pull her toward me, and as the wind blows ashes around us and the fire spreads toward us, I kiss her senselessly and show her with my kiss how much I love her.

Pulling away, I drop my head to her neck. "Do you trust me, Red?" I groan into her ear, biting along the column of her neck. Peaches. Her scent is as intoxicating as her mouth. Everything about my little red monster is an addiction I can't quit. I promised myself to never fall victim to vices that make even the strongest men fall weak on their knees. But here I am, surrounded by fire, with four holes in my body and a smile on my fucking face just for her.

This moment, right here, just proves that life with her will never have a dull moment.

Danger is written all over my girl, but I've never shied away from it before, and I'm sure as fuck not starting now.

She saw me for me from the very first moment, and I was a fucking idiot to have pushed her away before, thinking she deserved better than me, and maybe she does, but fuck it, she's stuck with me.

I might not be her prince charming, but I'm the beast that will always put her first.

My dark urges have always ruled me. Ever since I was a punk kid, I loved the thrill of falling over the edge, but someone always pulled me back. The dark side has always been my home. The only place I've ever felt like myself. People like me who, were raised in chaos find nothing but emptiness and boredom in peace.

That's why I fell in love with the forbidden fruit. The one woman that could bring a monster like me to a heel and make him her bitch with just one look. With just one addictive taste of her cherry red lips.

Everyone else always underestimated Red. They saw her as this meek princess that needed tender care to flourish. Bullshit.

Cara Mia always enjoyed walking hand in hand with the devil. She even fell in love with a heartless bastard like me before she could comprehend the definitions of love and devotion.

"With my life, king."

I breathe in and rejoice in the whispered words.

Here we fucking go.

As the cops arrive at the scene and more explosions go off, I take Mia's hand in mine, and we jump into the water.

May the whole goddamn world burn down and fall on its knees for her.

Benedetto always said I was just like him.

That I was made in his image.
Cruel and unforgiving.
Selfish and a liar.
I am all those things, yes.
I am everything he could never be.
I am feared.
I am death.
I'm the king.
A king that freely gave his violent heart to his queen.
Fire burns in my chest and purpose thrums through me.
I've never felt this alive.
All because of her.
Red.
My dark queen.

EPILOGUE
NERDS & VOWS

SIX MONTHS LATER

Lorenzo

"I'm hungry! I want simp." My nephew, Vade, has been repeating that same mantra all through the ceremony, and by simp, he means shrimp. When we first arrived at the hotel four hours ago, we were served welcome cocktails with fried shrimp on them. Mia gave him one to try, and he has been hooked ever since, asking for more and getting on my last damn nerve. Poe, on the other hand, made a face of disgust when we offered her one.

It's safe to say she's not sold on shrimps just yet.

I lean down to his level. "Shut it, or I'll make you swim with the fishies." I hiss under my breath at the little brat, trying not to interrupt the C3PO impersonator that's officiating our wedding at this very moment. Vade can't seem to shut his goddamn trap for five minutes, so we can get done with this. I'm sweating my balls off.

Not only am I handing my freedom away to another human being, but also, a creepy-looking gold robot and his short vacuum cleaner sidekick are also marrying us.

May God strike me down and put me out of my misery.

Vade looks up, tilts his small head, and stares me down. Little shit. "Do you pwomise?"

"I swear if you don't shut your f—" I catch myself before I drop an f-bomb. I care for this kid, I swear I do, but sometimes just like his mother, he irritates me to no end. He's too much like me. It's uncanny and at times, disturbing.

Vade looks away from me and turns to his mother, giving her a thumbs up. She's been coaching him since he learned to speak on all the ways to get on my nerves.

Ignoring them both, I focus on the moment. We're currently standing inside the Viva Las Vegas wedding chapel having a Nerd Wars-themed wedding, with my brother and his family in attendance as the witnesses, while my sister and her husband watch us through a FaceTime call.

After the bizarre shit show months ago, where my deranged cousin, Darius, kidnapped her to prove a fucking point that he could take everything from me if he wanted, we jumped into the water together and swam to the other side, where there were no cops and no fire.

We swam to safety.

I got her on the back of the bike and drove the hell out of there before she got caught in a scandal, and we both got our asses thrown in jail.

I haven't heard a word from the lunatic since then, but bad grass does not die, and something tells me the crazy motherfucker is out there somewhere, lurking in the shadows.

I'm vigilant now that there's a face and name to the threat.

And as for Mia and me?

We haven't left each other's side since.

One night after, while I was fucking her brains out, I demanded she became mine forever. Not that she wasn't already, but I wanted it to be official.

She said yes, but her only condition was that the wedding had to be small and quirky.

Whatever the fuck that means to her.

Nothing fancy and no traditions.

So, I flew us all here to a corny little chapel in Vegas.
Couldn't get any more quirky and less traditional if you asked me. She chose the Death Star package that includes three action-themed songs, the two idiots dressed as the movie's characters, and six red rose bouquets.
No more bleeding hearts for her.
"I love you." Mia whispers, holding my hands tighter. I play with the diamond on her ring finger. The 18-carat ring consists of a single flawless emerald-cut red diamond on a platinum solitaire band. I might've gotten carried away with the size, but I wanted it to be seen from Mars.
The diamond marks her as mine.
Looking down at her, I don't know how she manages to steal the air out of my lungs every time I look into those blue eyes. Today, they're shining more than ever. Her beautiful red hair falls down her back in soft waves. She's wearing more makeup than usual, with some sort of black thing on the corner of her eyes, giving her an exotic and mysterious look, while her plump lips are painted a light shade of red, almost orange or peach. Who the fuck knows?!
Her clothes match mine. We both opted out of traditional wedding attire. I'm wearing black pants with a black dress shirt with the two top buttons unbuttoned, my inked chest on full display.
Mia is wearing another dress my sister, Andrea, gifted her. A skintight black satin dress with a slit that runs down to the knee and with the perfect amount of cleavage, giving me a perfect view of her full tits.
She does have a great rack.
"My eyes are up here, baby." Mia laughs. From the corner of my eye, I can see my brother grinning and his wife rolling her eyes, trying hard not to laugh.
"I live for you, Red." I tell her honestly, with my heart on my sleeve. I don't say it often, and she doesn't ask me to

because she knows. When I come home covered in blood, she takes me into her arms and embraces all that I am.

She knows I loved her then, even when I couldn't put into words what I felt.

I make sure to show her how much I love her when I wake her up in the middle of the night with my head between her legs.

She's my heart.

I always knew I didn't have one, and all along, it was out of my chest, running wild and free in the form of a small red-headed monster.

My red queen.

The queen of my kingdom.

Before we know it, golden Tin-Man pronounces us man and wife while the other idiot throws black and white confetti at us. In the background, my sister cries and rambles on about double date while her husband threatens to kill me for the third time today. None of those things will ever be fucking happening.

My twin and his wife clap while their kids cheer and throw rice at us.

It all fades into the background when I take my wife's lips in mine, promising her forever with every gentle stroke of my tongue.

Forever.

It's not long enough.

***

A year later

I'm going to strangle her.

I'm going to wrap my hands around her pretty little neck when she pops out this kid, and the doctor gives her the okay to have sex again.

Five hours.

Five fucking hours she's been in labor, and only a couple of minutes ago did she decide to call me.

Stepping inside the hospital room, I find her lying on the bed with her legs spread while the doctor and the nurses hover over her, preparing her for labor.

The moment she sees me walk in, Mia smiles.

I take a moment to save the image of her smiling through the pain while protectively rubbing her stomach in my mind.

Fuck, she's so goddam beautiful.

I've never met anyone as stunning and brave as my wife.

No one.

Rushing to her side, I put both hands to her round stomach and feel her to make sure that everything is alright.

My kid is in there.

Fuck, soon I'll be responsible for another life.

Mia buries her face against my neck, and I breathe her in, wanting to savor this moment forever. The day she showed me the positive pregnancy test was one of the scariest moments of my life, right up there with the time Mia was almost taken from me.

A father.

Me, a father.

I still can't believe we made a life.

A creature that's half of each of us.

Half her.

We decided to hold off on finding the sex until she gave birth. Now, the moment has arrived, and I'm anxious as fuck.

I want a boy.

A red-haired little boy who I won't need to hide away like I would a little girl. I can't handle a mini-Mia.

I don't pray at all, just once in my entire miserable life, and I have these past nine months, asking whoever the hell is willing to listen to a sinner like me to please give me a boy.

"I'm scared." My wife's voice trembles, snapping me out of my head.

She grimaces when a contraction hits her. Holding her hand, I whisper words of encouragement. She can do this. There's nothing she can't do.

Nothing.

"You got this, baby." I reassure her, kissing the crown of her head.

"That kid is so lucky to have you."

"And you." The love of my life smiles up at me with so much love and trust shining in those blues of hers. "I didn't call you sooner because I was—unnhhh." She grabs my hand tightly to fight off the pain.

God, she's perfection.

Even more so now that she's rounded with my baby.

Feeling her tense up, I grasp the back of her neck in one hand and massage it gently, trying to comfort her and ease a bit of her pain. "Breathe through the pain, baby. If you tighten up and fight the contraction, it will hurt more. Just breathe."

She does as she was told in birth classes, blowing out a slow, noisy breath.

I watch as the nurse places an IV in her hand—just in case—and a monitoring band around her belly.

The sound of my baby's strong heartbeat fills the room. The thrill of anticipation rocks me to my core. Before this night is over, we will be holding our kid in our arms.

"Eight centimeters," the doctor announces after checking Mia's progress. She pats my wife's knee and smiles encouragingly. "Not long now, honey."

She's in so much pain.

Dammit.

Hating seeing her in so much pain, I took a clean washcloth from the stack next to the sink in the labor suite and soak it in cold water, wring it out, and returned to her side. Assuming the same crouched position, I wipe her forehead and tenderly kiss her lips.

"You're a fucking badass. I'm in awe of your strength, Mia."
Turning her face, my wife grips the front of my shirt. "Oh my fuck, Enzo." A tear drops from the corner of her left eye and it kills me to see her this way. "It hurts so bad. I can't do this. I literally can't—unnnhhhh." She squeezes her eyes shut and whimpers pitifully. "Shit. Fuck. Blyad!" Yeah, she's learning Russian now, to my dismay. She loves spending time with her psycho cousins. Creep #1 and Creep #2.

"Yes, you can. You're so close. Hurry up and give birth to my kid."

"Oh, I hate you," she says, almost panicked.

"I love you, too, baby." I brush her damp hair behind her ear and trail my thumb over her lower lip.

"Good." She blinks and then grimaces. I watch as she pushes herself up and lets loose a scream straight out of a horror movie that stunts me. "Oh, God. The baby is coming!"

"Here we go. On this next contraction, bear down and push as hard as you can, Mrs. Nicolasi," the doctor urges. "Your baby is ready to meet you." The baby is coming. This is it.

"Push, baby, push." I hold her hand while she expels a loud cry, and then it happens. A miracle. Our child is gently guided into the world, crying like a banshee.

"Oh, what a beautiful little girl." One of the nurses says as they take my kid and place her on Mia's chest.

A little girl. A girl born on June 6th at 6:06. 666. Fuck me.

What am I supposed to do with a girl?

Feeling a bit woozy, I smile at my wife while she sobs as she gently touches our tiny baby girl.

Reaching forward, I smooth my fingers along the wisps of red hair atop her little head.

A redheaded little monster. My baby girl.

Oblivious to the pain, Mia hugs our girl close and turns tearful eyes toward me. With her voice thick with emotion, she says, "We made her."

"We did." Leaning down, I share a kiss with my wife that nearly takes me out at the knees.

"She's perfect."

"Of course, she is. She's ours."

My wife laughs softly, trying not to scare our newborn baby.

"Oh, look, she has your dimples." Mia swoons over our child.

I swallow hard.

God, whoever is tasked to me up there, for fuck's sake, let this kid be all her mother.

My throat tightens as I gaze down at my daughter. Red hair, milky white skin like her mother and a cherubic, sweet little face. I look down at my inked hand and notice the contrast between my harshness and her innocent and pure face. Feeling vulnerable but brave, I admit for only my wife's ears, "She's the best thing I've ever done."

Mia touches my arm lovingly. "I love you so much. She's so lucky to have you as her protector. As her father, to keep her safe and spoil her like crazy."

Rubbing my baby's head gently, I bend down and capture Mia's mouth in a kiss that I never want to end. "I love you both so much. I live for you both."

"Are you happy, Enzo?"

"So fucking happy, baby." So, fucking happy.

Cara beams at me while I take the baby from her arms and press her closer to my chest. So she can feel my skin and listen to my heart beating for her. For both of them. Fuck, I'm a dad.

I'm a girl dad.

Fuck, I just know this angelic-looking child will drive me mad once she starts talking and her mother and I's personality kicks in.

I just know it.

"Have mommy and daddy decided on a name?" One of the nurses approaches with a soft smile on her face.

Mia grins, "We have."

I look down at my baby girl and smile when she attempts to open her eyes. Soon, my baby. Soon you will see all the world has in store for you.

"Verali." I let the name roll off my tongue proudly. "Verali Natalya Nicolasi." We chose a couple of names for both a boy and a girl, but I know it meant a lot to Mia if the baby was a girl for us to name her after her mother. She didn't want to choose between her two mothers, so I did.

I came up with the name, which is a mixture of the name her biological mother chose for her and my mother's name, Valerie. The same woman I didn't give myself the chance to get to know when I had the chance and now wish I had.

Now, I only have the letters she wrote me to give me closure. To make me feel connected to her in some way. To show my daughter when she grows up and asks to know more.

Her middle name, Natalia, is after her heart mother. The one who loved her unconditionally.

"Verali." Cara whispers as she stares at our sleeping baby girl. "Our truth. Our everything."

"Our everything." I whisper back.

A couple of hours later, they clean and measure the baby and help Mia with breastfeeding. She did it beautifully until she passed out.

Now, I'm holding my baby girl, rocking her side to side, trying to get her to fall asleep. She does for a few minutes and then starts crying up a storm. She'll give me trouble. I just know it.

I walk to the window with her in my arms, overlooking the city. Down below, the city bustles with activity.

Brushing my lips across my daughter's head. "Well, look at that. The city. This is our city, baby."

Verali coos as if she understands what I'm saying.

She doesn't, I know that, but one day she will.

"Someday, this will all be yours. Everything I do is for you and your mother. I live for you both." My girl opens her eyes and blinks slowly as I talk to her. I know she can't see shit yet, but she's not been alive for more than five hours, and she's already opening her eyes.

My baby is advanced.

A genius, yeah.

I laugh when I see her work one of her small arms free from the black swaddling blanket and bump her tiny fist against my pinky finger.

A moment later, she captures it, and my heart nearly bursts in my chest. The love I feel for this tiny little creature overwhelms me, leaving me defenseless.

Just like the feelings her mother stirs in me.

I know, right there, holding my girl in my arms as my wife sleeps. Overlooking my city, I smile triumphantly, knowing I got everything I never knew I needed.

I won.

Like I always said I would.

I have the love of my life.

My heir.

My city.

Yeah, I fucking won.

Looking up at the sky, I hope she's seeing me now. I hope she finds peace in knowing the monster she birthed has a heart.

Two hearts out of his chest.

Mia.

Verali.

I'm one lucky fuck.

Yeah, I am.

My baby lets out a soft whimper, catching my attention.

I kiss her temple and hug her closer to me.

"You're so loved, kid. So fucking loved."

EPILOGUE TWO
GIRL DAD

Three years later

Lorenzo

"Oh fuck, right there…" My wife nearly comes off the bed as I thrust my cock hard into her from behind. I love the way her ass jiggles when I fuck her. I also love the way her creamy-white skin turns red when I slap her round cheeks. Having had enough of that position, Mia leaves my body and moves to a sitting position, riding me. I sit back against the bedframe and watch as she bounces on my dick, taking what she wants from me.

I enjoy being in control while fucking, but from time to time, I let her be in charge. Besides, shoving my face between her full tits while she rides me is a great fucking way to start my day. "You feel so fucking good, Red," I rasp, watching her hair bounce at the same rhythm as her breasts. Her cunt is strangling my dick, and I am seconds away from filling her full of my cum. "Good girl. Take what you want."

"I'm almost there!" she pants. Bouncing up and down. Rotating her hips back and forth. I dig my fingers into her ass, making her ride me harder and faster. "Let go, baby. Give me everything." I grip her hips and set her at a wilder pace. Her jaw goes slack, and she clamps down around me. I come deep inside of her, and she falls onto my chest.

"Are you happy, Red?" I ask her when she relaxes against me.
"I've never been happier, king" Her eyes meet mine.
We both freeze when we hear little feet hitting the floor outside our door.
"Incoming."
We scramble in bed, getting dressed before the door to our room bursts open and a sweet voice sings-songs. "It's ma birphday. Ma birphday is todaaaaaaaaaay!"
I fake a groan as little feet jump up and down on the bed. It is early as fuck, and after the quick fuck we had, all I wanted was to sleep a few more hours, but someone didn't want us to have an extra hour of sleep. Plus, my kid is a damn cockblock.
"Daddy is ma birphday today." My now soon to be three-year-old jumps on our bed hard in excitement. "We see Mickey today!" She claps happily while smiling down at me the same blinding smile as her mother. I grab her around the middle and pull her down into the middle of the bed between us, tickling Verali's tummy and distracting her.
"Whose birthday is it, princess?"
"Me. Me birphday," she says and then giggles.
"Yes, baby. It's your day!" My wife smiles down at our daughter.
"Me birphday," Verali says with a nod while hugging her stuffed bunny close to her chest. The same stuffed animal that was given to my wife by her freak Russian cousin and now has been passed down to my kid.
I watch as Mia pulls Verali close, kissing every inch of her face and my heart stills in my chest, staring at them both in this moment. Fulfilled.
That's how I feel when I look at them.
"Yes, it is, my smart girl." I pull her close, tucking her against my heart as I look across the bed at my wife. "Do we really have to go?"

The happiest place on Earth, my ass.
I want to strangle her just as much as I want to kiss her. She damn well knows I would rather put a bullet in my head than step foot inside that hell again. Children screaming. Stupid as fuck cartoon characters walking down the streets, waving at you. The long lines and the fucking heat.

"We certainly do, don't we, princess Ve?" Mia lifts her head, looking at her mini-me.

"We go to Mickey house!" Verali giggles while pointing her small finger to the ugly ass rat on her pajamas. A present from her aunt Fallon.

The woman is to blame for my daughter's obsession with Mickey Mouse, and she's also the reason why we're going on this trip. She told my girl all about their adventure at the magical theme park, and of course, my baby girl asked to go. Day and night.

For months leading up to her birthday.

I couldn't say no.

"It's me birphday, Daddy." Verali tells me again while kissing my hand softly before grinning up at me. She wants something. She sits up, looking down at me expectantly. "I want present now." Cara laughs and gets out of bed.

"Where are your manners, Ve?"

"I want present now, peaseee." She claps her tiny hands together in excitement.

"Presents come later, baby. We're going to the park first."

"Yay. I see Mickey and Domi." She sighs dreamily.

Never believed in heaven until I met her mother, but now, looking at my kid with her blood-red hair messy from sleep, big, bright blue eyes, and blinding smile, I know for sure there must be a God out there who thought me worthy of this angel. But, at times, I ask myself why I had to get a toddler who's boy crazy already. I have to kill Dreago's little boy now, and I liked the brat enough not to kill him.

Domi was one of the babies that were taken and sold to a sex trafficker. The one that no one claimed and that was badly hurt, it's a mystery how he didn't die.
I know why.
He's a fighter.
Draego, just a kid himself, took the baby in, and now because of Mia, I can't get rid of them.
Both my wife and kid have taken a liking to both Draego and his demon spawn, who uses black markers to draw shit on his skin and make it seem like he has tattoos just like his dad. Fucking trouble, that's what the little shit is.
"Wove you, daddy."
I hold her close, breathing in her baby scent. "Love you more, baby girl."
"Yay." She stands up on the mattress and starts shaking her butt. "We go now, Daddy. Mickey waitin'."
"Mia! What the hell are you teaching her?" I groan as I watch my baby shake her butt to her birthday song.
"Nuuh, don't blame me. Blame your sister." My wife laughs and extends her arms toward our daughter, and a moment later, Verali jumps into her mother's waiting arms. I watch as my daughter grabs her mother's cheeks and lays a big one on her lips. "Mm, the best kisses in the world."
"Wove you, Mommy." My daughter rubs her nose against Mia's. I fall back on the bed and look at my hearts outside my chest, embracing each other. Mia's mother didn't get the chance to raise her, and her heart mother, Natalia, didn't get to see this, but she honors them every day by keeping their memory alive in the stories she tells Verali.
She doesn't have stories she shared with Darya, her biological mother, but she honored her by naming our daughter Verali.
Vera.
Our truth.
"Love you more, princess."

I leave my girls cuddling in bed and head to the bathroom. I take my time in the shower, knowing I have plenty of time. By the time I got downstairs, both Mia and Verali were dressed in their theme park matching onesies, headbands and waiting for me with big smiles on their faces.
Shit.
How could I say no to them?
I'm so damn blessed.

The End

FOR CARA AND LORENZO
Turn the page to read the first teaser of book five…

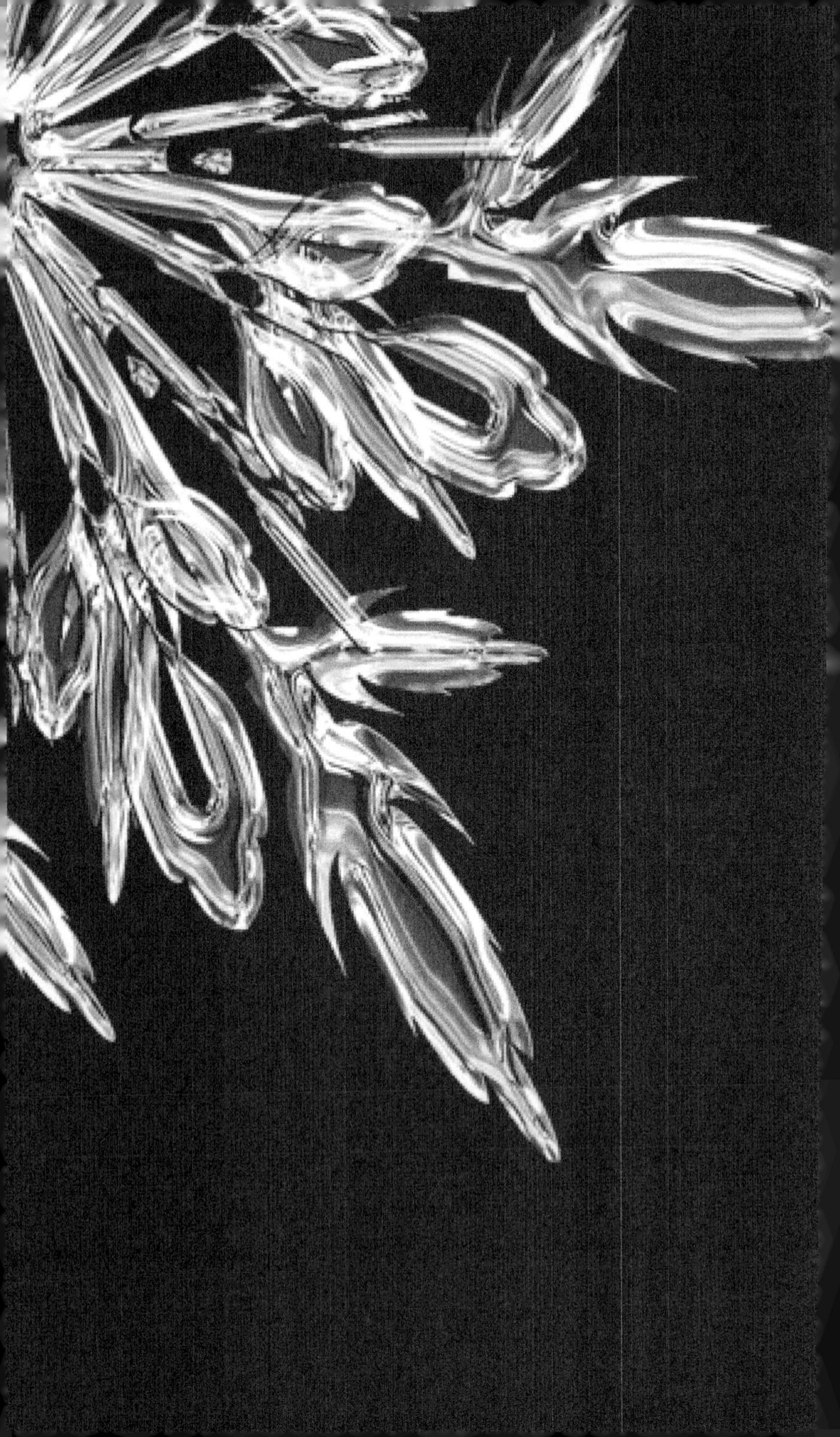

ARIANNA

Prologue
GOLDEN CAGE

> "Even at my ugliest,
> I'm still the best you'll ever have." -A

My mother always told me that my beauty would get me farther in life than my brains and my bloodthirsty need to succeed in a man's world would.

In part, she was right.

My beauty did open many doors, but it also trapped me.

Left me voiceless in a world where it was already difficult enough to be heard as a woman.

Papa used to brag that his name and legacy would open every door for us, but he, too, lied.

Parisi.

A name fit for a king, he said.

A name meant for the boy who one day would carry my father's legacy.

The boy that died.

Then, there was me.

The unwanted firstborn.

So, yes, papa lied.

My name was my golden cage, and my beauty one day will eventually fade. My looks are what got me where I am today. In the hands of a cruel man who believes the world should fall on its knees for him.

My brain is what kept me above water all these years, and it is the only weapon I have against him, in this war he started the day he accepted my family's offer.

Sebastian Kenton thinks of me as a child he will easily manipulate, but what he does not know is that I stopped being a child a long time ago.
I, too, can play the games big boys do, and I never lose.
Not even once.
He is threatening all I ever wanted, and I refuse to lose my life to him.
The man has a God complex, and it will be my pleasure to show him how very wrong he is.
He is a mortal man.
One that chose the wrong bitch for his sick scheme.
I didn't know what I was being thrown into the moment my family handed me over on a silver platter to a faceless man. A man who long ago sold his soul to reach the top of the food chain.
A vicious predator that he is.
He will soon find out, Mafia princess or not, I am no one's prey.
I, too, am a predator.
A ruthless one.
The worst kind.
A survivor.
Arianna Luna Parisi is my name.
A name the world will never forget.

Afterword

If you made it thus far, thank you.
I hope you enjoyed Cara and Lorenzo's story. It was a joy to write.
Please comsider leaving a review. It helps baby authors like me tremendously.

Also by Adriana Brinne

Andrea "The Beginning (Holy Trinity, #1)
Lucan "The End" (Holy Trinity, #2)
Unholy Night (Holy Trinity, #2.5)
Fallon "The Madman" (Unholy Trinity, #3)

Acknoledgments

Mami, I love you. This one is for you. Thank you for listening when I rant about all my ideas and thank you for encouraging me to dream big and never give up.

Elsa and Gisele, I don't know what else to say but thank you. I am so thankful for your help but more than that for your friendship.

My readers, I am forever thankful for your support. Thank you for reading my words and for loving my characters.

Thank you to everyone who read, shared and reviewed Cara. You're the real MVP of the book community.

Thank you.
Till the next one,
Adriana.

About the author

Adriana Brinne is a new author who fell in love with reading from a very young age but never felt brave enough to share her words with the world. She was born and raised in a tropical island surrounded by only beauty and water called Puerto Rico. She is a full-time IT engineer, and, in her downtime, you can find her reading new adult by her favorites, reviewing books, and watching The Big Bang Theory. She has a love for all things dark in romance and almost every trope created except cheating and death trope. I hate them and you won't catch me writing or reading about it. The Holy Trinity characters are screaming to have their stories told and I plan to do so. You can expect from me all the feels, strong girls, and asshole heroes that worship them.

You can connect with her on Facebook www.facebook.com/adrianabrinne or join her reader group Unholy Ground https://www.facebook.com/groups/1105422413262256

Printed in Great Britain
by Amazon

46407486R00274